borrowed Light

a novel

CARLA KELLY

BONNEVILLE BOOKS
SPRINGVILLE, UTAH

The views expressed within this work are the sole responsibility of the author and do not necessarily reflect the position of Cedar Fort, Inc., or any other entity.

This is a work of fiction. The characters, names, incidents, places, and dialogue are products of the author's imagination, and are not to be construed as real.

ISBN 13: 978-1-59955-466-2

Published by Bonneville Books, an imprint of Cedar Fort, Inc.,
2373 W. 700 S., Springville, UT 84663
Distributed by Cedar Fort, Inc., www.cedarfort.com

LIBRARY OF CONGRESS CATALOGING-IN-PUBLICATION DATA

    Kelly, Carla.
    Borrowed light / Carla Kelly.
      p. cm.
    ISBN 978-1-59955-466-2
    1. Single women--Fiction. 2. Women cooks--Fiction. 3. Ranch life--Fiction. 4. Wyoming--Fiction. I. Title.
    PS3561.E3928B67 2010
    813'.54--dc22

                            2010026382

Cover design by Angela Olsen
Cover design © 2011 by Lyle Mortimer
Edited and typeset by Melissa J. Caldwell

Printed in the United States of America

10 9 8 7 6 5 4

To the memory of Doc and Ora Simons,
Torrington, Wyoming,

and to my dear friends Kathryn and Neal Kelly,
Torrington, Wyoming.

The time will come when no man or woman will be able to endure on borrowed light. Each will have to be guided by the light within himself. If you do not have it, how can you stand?

—*Heber C. Kimball, 1856*

One

Julia Darling slid the last little rose onto her sister's wedding cake and then pressed her hand into the small of her back. "I will be sore all night, Iris," she said out loud as she admired her work.

She walked around the cake, decorated with enough flowers to satisfy a Babylonian. Hadn't Papa joked that Nebuchadnezzar would be quite at home with that cake? "Don't tell Iris this," he had whispered to her. "Because she'll get all small-eyed and jittery." He had then looked around cautiously. "But I'm a little relieved to be turning her over to a husband."

It was their private joke in the kitchen that morning, far from the upstairs bedroom where Iris had insisted on tighter lacing, and Mama had insisted that if the laces were any tighter, Iris would faint in the Garden Room.

"I told your mother last week that it would be better to bury Iris and dig her up right before the wedding," Papa had confided.

Julia added more royal icing to one last spot. *When I marry*, she thought, *I intend to be totally serene and in complete control of my faculties.*

The house was empty now. She sat down and pulled up her skirt and petticoat to look at her feet. What a relief they were not puffy from the last two days of moving steadily from cooking stove to sink to counter. There were days at Fannie Farmer's Cooking School when she could scarcely move after hours of working at the granite-topped tables, creating edibles good enough to suit Miss Farmer. She smiled at the memory of Miss Farmer zooming around in her wheelchair, not missing a thing.

It was better in Mama's kitchen, where she could pull up her skirts and fan herself. Only someone besotted with love would ever get married in Salt Lake City in August, and the summer 1909 had proved to be a scorcher. Still, it had been fun to come home in May from Boston, knowing she had kitchen skills her younger sister could put to use.

Julia glanced through the open door into the dining room with its genteel mounds of mints, plates of petit fours, bowls of nuts, and stuffed raisins nestled on Mama's best candy plate. The glacé fruits were cooling in the icebox along with the raspberry ring, which was frozen in the copper mold.

She looked back at the cake, remembering how wonderful the kitchen had smelled last night as she removed the pans from the oven under Iris's anxious eyes. Soon Iris and her new husband would come home from the temple and cut the cake.

The smile left Julia's face. *And then Aunt Carolina will look at Mama and Papa and make some arch remark about "Julia's wedding is this winter, and won't that be a relief?"* she told herself. *The cousins will giggle, and Ezra will say something like "Couldn't be happier," or "Aren't I the lucky fellow?"*

Thinking of Ezra, she looked at his engagement ring on the window ledge over the sink. Funny that she still thought of it as his ring and not hers. She always took it off before she started to cook. *Trouble is*, she thought, *I forget to put it back on.* She went to the sink and pushed the ring onto her finger. He had selected it, vetoing her wish for a ruby. "Diamonds are investments, Julia," he had told her in that patient way that made her want to grit her teeth.

She had given in; it was better than an argument. She couldn't unburden herself to Iris because her sister had a stone so small that Aunt Carolina had to squint to see it.

I am being ungrateful, and that is wicked, she thought as she went in search of old newspapers. *But if Ezra tells me one more time how he argued the jeweler down to a better price or how a diamond is every woman's dream, I swear I will scratch a bad word on the window with it.* She sighed and fingered the pages of Monday's *Deseret News*. *Papa never coerces or gets huffy if I disagree with him*, she thought. *I wonder if Ezra really loves me.*

She knew her fiancé thought she was pretty. Once he had told her that he was engaged to the prettiest girl in the Avenues. But was that enough?

I am being critical today, she thought as she found more newspapers. Julia had heard her father declare more than once that *he* was married to the prettiest girl in the whole universe. Maybe Ezra just wasn't extravagant.

But that was Ezra. Just as surely as he had announced to her that he would never put more than a dime in a beggar's cup, she knew that life with Ezra Quayle would not be like life at home.

It was a dismal reflection. They had been engaged for a year, but he was not generous with his kisses. *And he still asks for permission*, she reminded herself. *I know I want a virtuous man, but he doesn't have to be a stick.*

Julia picked up yesterday's newspaper and tucked it under her arm with the other papers. She had promised Iris that she would pack the rest of her cups and saucers in the crate still open in her bedroom. She glanced at the clock. The wedding party must surely be on the way to the Celestial Room by now, but she had time to do this one last thing for her sister.

Her younger sister. Trust Iris to snare a wide-eyed dairy farmer from Draper before she turned twenty-one! And here Julia was, twenty-seven and a little too cynical for her own good. For three years Ezra Quayle had courted her deliberately—every act, as far as she could tell, planned far in advance as though he followed a schedule. She stopped on the stairs. *I wonder what it feels like to be kissed by a man with nothing more on his mind than kissing me.*

These were not good thoughts to take into a room where a bride's traveling dress was neatly spread across the bed. The hollow feeling in her stomach grew as Julia tore the newspaper into strips and picked up the first cup. *It'd be a shame if I find myself married to someone who knows he needs to be married but isn't quite sure why,* she considered.

"I don't think your engagement is a good idea, Julia," she said aloud.

Aghast with herself, she packed swiftly then, stopping only when she needed more newspaper strips. She picked up another sheet and stared at the page in her hands, distressed as the newsprint grew blurry.

It is stupid to cry when everyone tells me how fortunate I am to have found a man who will provide well for me and never cause me a moment's anxiety, she reminded herself. "This will not do, Julia," she said. She stared at an advertisement outlined in a box, willing herself to focus on those words until she could read them.

It was the classified section. Julia stared down at the words. "'Rancher Desperate,'" she read aloud. "Sir, I doubt you are as desperate as I am."

She lowered the paper, but the two words intrigued her. "'Rancher Desperate,'" she said again, and kept reading. "'A long-time, stable stockman 80 miles northwest of Cheyenne is searching for a chef of mature years to cook for him and four hands and do light housekeeping. Salary includes sixty dollars a month and found. Direct all inquiries to Paul Otto, The Double Tipi, Gun Barrel, Wyoming.' " She looked closer at the ad. "My word," she said. " 'Rancher seeks a graduate of Fannie Farmer's Cooking School.' "

She wrapped a cup in a different page. *How would some old Wyoming rancher have ever heard of the cooking school?* she wondered. She continued packing until all the newspaper was gone, except for the page with that ad. "Bother it," she muttered. Irritated with herself, Julia wrapped the page around the last cup, put it in the crate, and set the lid on top.

She was halfway down the stairs when she knew she could not marry Ezra Quayle. Before reason triumphed, she turned around and marched back into Iris's room. She removed the newspaper from the cup on top and hurried downstairs to the kitchen.

She found a piece of paper and Mama's fountain pen. Washing her hands quickly, she sat down and composed a letter. " 'Mature years,' " she said, as she poised the pen over the paper. "Mr. Otto, I am twenty-seven years old, and if that is not mature, then I do not know what is."

She wrote a quick reply, writing twice over the words "Fannie Farmer's Cooking School graduate," so they would stand out on the page. Room and board and sixty dollars a month? "Mr. Otto, I will cook for you!"

Julia almost ran to the postbox on the corner. She hurried back into the house and was standing on the porch when Papa's new Pierce-Arrow—the pride of his heart, despite the Doctrine and Covenants' injunction not to "covet thine own property"—turned the corner toward the alley behind the house. She dashed inside, pulled the copper mold from the icebox, and plopped the raspberry ice into the punch bowl.

There was just time to remove her apron and touch

up her hair before she had to smile a welcome at Ezra and Mama, who came through the back door together. She stood close to Ezra while Mama exclaimed over the wedding cake. "Kiss me, Ezra," she demanded suddenly, standing on tiptoe to increase his opportunity.

He leaped away as though she were covered with spots. "Right here?" he whispered back. "What will your mother think?"

Better you should worry about what I am thinking, she thought as Iris burst through the door and threw herself into Julia's arms.

"Oh, Jules, I'm so happy!" she wailed.

Julia kissed her sister, admired the gold band, and wished herself in Gun Barrel, Wyoming, cooking for Desperate Rancher.

Two

Julia excused herself for not saying anything right then in the kitchen. Her sister's wedding reception was not the time to squelch an engagement everyone told her was made in heaven.

Nor was the next day a good time either, what with Mama's headache and Papa moving slowly, done in by the petit fours and too many cream mints. Even Friday was too soon, with Mama still mooning about Iris so far away in Draper.

"Mama, it's only an hour away in Papa's auto," Julia reminded her.

Mama wiped her eyes. "Thank goodness Ezra bought the house two blocks over."

Don't remind me, Julia told herself, thinking of all the hours Ezra devoted to the subject, describing every detail of the purchase until she wanted to scream. "Yes, how fortunate," she murmured.

Somehow, Saturday was not the time to make any radical statements, and Sunday was out of the question. A week passed, and she convinced herself she was glad she had said nothing. If she could not extricate herself from her dilemma without help from Desperate Rancher, then she deserved none. *Face it, Julia Darling*, she thought. *You're afraid to say anything.*

She took a good look at Ezra when he came over in the middle of the week, trying to see him through others' eyes. He was nice looking. He would probably never lose his hair like some men, or his teeth either. And nobody ever dresses better than a banker. Her father was proof of that.

His conversation was on the dull side. He had served a mission to the British Isles and taught Sunday School, and Julia knew he attended the temple regularly. He earned a good living. She would never want for anything. She sighed.

"Why the sigh?" Ezra asked.

His comment startled her. "Uh, I was thinking about Iris on a dairy farm," she lied.

"I can't imagine what Iris was thinking to marry such a man. Why, he probably tracks manure into the kitchen on his boots," he said, sounding painfully prissy.

He cleared his throat. She could not help another sigh, knowing that he was about to make a pronouncement of some sort, usually the kindly, improving statement intended for her own good.

"Julia, we really should set a wedding date," he began. "I've bought the house, I'm due a raise, and I'm nearly twenty-nine." She could tell he was choosing his words carefully. "Julia, I've been so patient! I let you go to Boston, and I never complained."

She couldn't help the way her eyes narrowed. *You* let *me?*

He wasn't through. "You'll be twenty-eight in three months and four days, if I'm not mistaken."

You're never mistaken, she told herself miserably. "Yes, I'll be twenty-eight in three months and four days," she said, her voice calm but her heart cracking a little around the edges. "How about right after Thanksgiving?" *Please say no*, she thought.

"That would be unfortunate. I was thinking October 20," he replied. "That's a good time at the bank, so I wouldn't have to take any work along with me if we go to St. George for a week, as we've discussed."

No one but Ezra would think about accounting during his honeymoon. "That's agreeable," she replied, as she writhed inside. "I promise not to bring along my darning egg and needle."

He stared at her for one blank moment and then laughed. "That's a joke, isn't it?" he asked.

She couldn't help herself. "What about January?"

He cleared his throat. She closed her eyes, dreading whatever was to come. "Really, Julia, I would think you would want to be married before you turn twenty-eight. People are starting to talk."

"Ezra, my various parts will work just as well at twenty-eight as they do at twenty-seven!" She knew immediately that she had offended him. She put her hand on his arm, desperate to apologize before he had time to clear his throat again and reprove her in that patient way of his that made her feel like a two-year-old. "I'm sorry, Ezra. That was vulgar."

He agreed promptly. "That is a regrettable tendency that I plan to reform when we are married."

The porch suddenly felt like an escape-proof cell. "October, then," she murmured.

He left precisely a half hour later, as she knew he would. *Two glances at his watch, and then he will pop in a Sen-Sen and kiss me*, she thought, disgusted with herself.

Sleep eluded her that night. Prayer hadn't helped either. She had stayed on her knees longer than usual, but she knew better than to bother the Lord about Ezra Quayle. "I must be the one wanting, Lord," she whispered into her sheet. "I'm sorry to be a bother."

Papa had mentioned that he wanted her special Cecils in Tomato Sauce for breakfast, so Julia dragged herself downstairs at six after an hour's sleep. The thought that by late October she would be cooking in Ezra's kitchen so unnerved her that she had to sit down and rest her forehead on the table.

"My dear, are you well?" And there was Mama, worried.

"I'm a little tired," she replied. "Mama, Ezra wants to get married on October 20."

"Julia, that's so soon!" she exclaimed. "Think of all the arrangements."

"We can do it, Mama," she said quietly. "I've been engaged for a year already, and Ezra is tired of waiting." *Mama, please look at me!* she thought, her mind wild with confusion. *Ask me again if I am well, and maybe I will have the courage to speak!*

Mama only sighed. "I'll miss you. You were a year in Boston, and now this . . . ah, well, you'll just be two streets over."

"That's true," Julia said. Feeling sixty years old, she went to the range to heat the lard for the Cecils.

Mama came to the range and hugged her. "No wonder you're tired! Marriage is the biggest step a woman takes. Shall we take the trolley downtown this morning and look at material?"

"Whatever you want, Mama."

The morning held just that tang of fall that sometimes came to the valley in August. Iris used to tease Julia because she enjoyed riding something as ordinary as the trolley. She sat quietly, grateful for the warmth of the sun, because she felt so chilly inside.

With one wedding to her credit now, Mama wasted not a moment. She marched Julia into ZCMI. "I am partial to watered silk, as you know, Julia," she said as they took the elevator upstairs to fabrics and notions. "What do *you* want?"

"I have no idea, Mama!" She knew she had surprised her mother. "I mean . . . I'll be happy with whatever you suggest."

"Let's look at the silk. Perhaps taffeta."

She led Julia to bolt after bolt of wedding fabric, describing the merits of each with such enthusiasm that Julia only had to nod now and then. She roused herself to smile at Mama's final choice, a watered silk that shimmered as her mother fluffed out the material.

"It's a shade off-white, Julia, but with your dark coloring and green eyes, it should be perfect."

Julia couldn't deny that it was beautiful. Maybe things would be different when she married Ezra. He knew what he wanted, and her own imperfections would give him ample opportunity to mold her into the perfect wife. *I bought all those wonderful molds in Boston*, she thought as the clerk took the fabric to the cutting table. *Too bad I could not find one for myself.*

"Twelve yards," Mama said decisively.

The clerk measured off the yardage until there was a soft pile mounded on the cutting table. Two young matrons walking by caught Julia's eye and smiled at her. *Everyone loves a bride,* she thought in a panic. The clerk picked up her dressmaker's shears, straightened the bolt, positioned the scissors, and looked at her for a final confirmation.

"No!" Julia was shocked by the harshness of her voice. "I'm not totally sure about that fabric, Mama."

Mama quickly regained what Papa called her "public serenity." "Certainly, my dear. You may think about it," she said, with a nod to the clerk.

It was a quiet ride home. Mama, her face thoughtful, stared out the window. Julia felt relief cover her like a shawl. In a strange way that she knew she could never explain, one cut of those shears would have decided the matter for eternity. Julia felt the tears start in her eyes again, and she dug in her purse for a handkerchief. She dabbed at her eyes, thankful that Mama found something to occupy her attention outside the trolley window.

Mama went upstairs to change. Julia hurried into the kitchen, tying on her apron. She had left the scalloped turkey in a low oven with the damper closed. She tasted it, pronounced it successful, and took the tomato jelly salad out of the icebox, along with the cucumbers in vinegar water.

Luncheon was ready almost the moment Papa came home. He smiled to see it on the table. "Julia, you will make a good wife for a banker," he said. He went back to the parlor to pick up the mail that had just fallen through the flap in the door. "Punctuality and precision," he said over his shoulder.

After Papa took the edge off his hunger and told Mama a little bank news, he picked up the mail he had left on the sideboard. It was his daily ritual to parcel it out at the table.

"Julia, who do you know in Wyoming?"

She froze, her fork suspended over the turkey. "No one, really," she managed to say. She held out her hand, hoping that it would not tremble.

Her father handed her the letter. "Someone seems to know you there, my dear. Maude, here's that bill from your milliner that you have been dreading." In silence that almost beat against her eardrums, Julia slit open the envelope with her table knife. She left the money inside, but pulled out a ticket for the Union Pacific and another for the Cheyenne & Northern Railroad. She opened the note. It was written in pencil on lined composition paper. "Miss Darling, I am expecting you Thursday next in Gun Barrel on the noon train. Enclosed are both tickets and a month's advance on your salary. Hire a hack to help you from one depot to the other. Yours sincerely, Paul Otto."

It was firm printing. She read the note again. Silently, she handed it to her father, who read it, frowned, and then handed it to her mother.

"Julia . . ." he began.

She interrupted him. "Papa, I saw an advertisement in the newspaper for a cook on a ranch in Wyoming." The words seemed to tumble out by themselves. "It was the day Iris got married. I supposed I was feeling . . . oh, I don't know, Papa. I never thought that he would reply. He sounded desperate." *So do I*, she thought miserably.

She knew she was making no sense because Papa continued to stare at her. Julia looked at her mother, who gazed back, her expression serene. "Mama," Julia started, but stopped because she had no idea what she was going to say.

To her immense relief, Mama smiled and handed back the letter. "Jed, I'm certain Julia and I will sort this out. Am I right, Julia?"

She nodded as love for her mother showered around her like May rain. "Yes, Mama." She looked at her father. "It's nothing to worry about, Papa."

He looked dubious for a moment. "Just a wild hare? Shall I send this back to," he looked at the signature, "Paul Otto?"

"No," Mama spoke quietly, her voice firm.

Papa opened his mouth to reply, but she could tell he was stopped by the look in Mama's eyes. "Very well, Maude," he said finally, his voice as calm as Mama's.

A slight smile on his face, Papa finished eating, winked at Mama, and left. She heard him whistling as he sauntered down the front steps to the Pierce-Arrow. Julia made a move to rise and clear off the dishes, but Mama stopped her.

"Dearest, you don't want to marry Ezra, do you?"

Julia shook her head. In a moment Mama knelt by her side.

"How long have you known, Mama?" she asked.

"A while," Mama said. "I probably should have noticed sooner, my dear, but with Iris's wedding, I was busy."

"Oh, Mama, I've been trying to get up the nerve to say something for weeks now."

"I knew for certain when we rode the trolley downtown," Mama said. "You were so quiet! And then in ZCMI, I was positive." She leaned forward. "When I took Iris to pick out her fabric, she almost raced me to the cloth bolts! She was so excited." Her eyes misted over then. "When your grandmother and I went to pick out my material—nothing so fine as Iris had—I could hardly contain myself. I could tell you weren't feeling that way."

"No, Mama. Is something the matter with me?"

"Absolutely not. You just don't love Ezra."

Julia hesitated. "Shouldn't I love him? Everyone says what a good idea it is."

"If it isn't your idea, then it would be a huge mistake," Mama replied, "even if he took you to a thousand temples."

"How will I *know*, Mama?"

Her mother laughed, and the sound lifted Julia's heart. "When I fell in love, I fretted when Jed Darling wasn't around. I suppose I still do, even though he sits all day at Zion's Bank and is perfectly ordinary."

Julia squeezed her mother's hand. "But he's not ordinary to you, is he?"

"Not at all."

"I'll find someone like that someday?"

"Without a doubt." Her mother ran her finger over the return address on the letter. "But I'm not certain this is a good idea, Julia."

It probably isn't, Julia thought. "I want to, Mama. I can always come home if it's not a good situation."

"I doubt it's a place to meet unmarried Mormon men," Mama said.

"I'm sure you're right!" Julia said, and laughed. "But just think! I can use all those wonderful skills I learned in Boston." She hesitated. "I want to be on my own."

Mama was silent a long time. "You'll have to write often, or I'll worry."

"I will, Mama."

Mama winked back tears and began gathering the luncheon dishes. "If we hurry up with these, you will have ample time to telephone Ezra and invite him over. It won't be pleasant." She was thinking now, mentally ticking off her own list. "I suggest we make another trip downtown." She handed Julia the plates and stacked the cups on top. "I will visit with your father for a few minutes. He may have been whistling when he left, but I'm certain he'll have bitten his nails off to the knuckles by now. Julia, we'll miss you."

"And I'll miss you," she said quietly. *If I dwell on it,* she thought, *I'll change my mind.* "Why do you need me along?"

"You'll go to Western Union and send a telegram to this Mr. Otto. Do you realize Thursday is barely a week away? Let's meet at ZCMI again and consider winter underwear."

"I'm sorry he wasn't desperate in Arizona, Mama, because underthings would be cheaper," she teased. They laughed together and started for the kitchen.

"Mama, would you have let the clerk cut that fabric?" she asked suddenly.

"I was all ready to stop her, if you didn't."

"Oh, Mama."

Three

Julia wasn't sure at first what woke her from the deepest sleep she had enjoyed in weeks. She closed her eyes, ready to be lulled into slumber again by the rhythmic clacking of Union Pacific wheels on Union Pacific tracks. The clever bed, which the porter had pulled down last night, was comfortable in all the right places.

She heard three soft chimes as the porter walked through the train. "Cheyenne in one hour," he called. "Cheyenne." *That was what woke me*, she thought, remembering she had forgotten to pack her alarm clock.

There hadn't been much time for packing, what with Iris stopping by to lament that she would miss her and Papa making himself at home in her room to offer good advice.

Telephoning Ezra had been difficult, as Mama predicted. He had rushed over from Zion's Bank, hatless and in his shirtsleeves, begging her to think again. They had sat together for a long time on the front porch. She knew she was wounding him, but nothing he said convinced her to change her mind.

He did not want the ring back. "Won't you think about this?" he had pleaded. "I can wait a little while longer."

"It wouldn't be fair to you," she told him as she took off the ring and put it in his shirt pocket.

He didn't say anything, but he sat there with his arm around her for a long while, idly pushing the porch swing with his foot. Even now, lying in the Pullman car, she felt a pang uncomfortably close to regret. His arm around her had felt good and secure, and she wondered why he could not have done that when they were engaged.

With everyone's help, she had finished her packing. The kitchen looked a little bare, in fact, with all of her cookery equipment from Boston now crated and ready for the carter. She used most of the sixty dollars that Mr. Otto had sent with the train ticket to buy gelatin, isinglass, Irish Moss, and maraschino cherries, and "anything else that moved," Mama had teased her. Papa had been properly impressed that Mr. Otto had arranged for a Pullman compartment and not just the open section. "That indicates the measure of his desperation," he had joked.

Papa had helped her stuff in last-minute necessities. "I doubt there is a spice left in all of Salt Lake City," he commented as she rearranged the turmeric and cardamom to make room for the almond paste. "Julia, this is an old, long-time rancher. Don't scare him!"

"I don't know what to expect, so I shall be prepared," she said, standing back so he could tamp down the lid.

"Is that all now, or dare I ask?"

She nodded.

"Here's one more thing." He handed her a copy of the Book of Mormon. "I think it'll fit right here next to the anchovies and sea salt."

"I already packed mine upstairs, Papa," she told him.

"I know. Take an extra one," he said, putting it by the salt. "You never know who you'll run into." He kissed her cheek. "Don't look so dubious! These are easier to give away than you would think."

She nodded to humor him. "I'll even read mine," she teased.

The look he returned was more sober than she expected.

"Do it, honey," he urged. "Maybe you'll find some answers that you need. I always do when I read."

"Maybe I will, Papa." She stood up and watched him as he stopped to close the crate, hammering down the lid. She noticed with a pang that his hair was getting thin on top. "Papa, give me a father's blessing," she asked.

He sat her down, resting his hands on her shoulders for so long that she felt her first real uncertainty. He placed his hands on her head. The only thing that kept her from tears was when he leaned down and whispered in her ear, "Now, what's your full name?"

It was a blessing much like the one that had sent her off to Boston with a light heart. As she sat there with her eyes closed, she knew she would miss the sound of his voice. *I will miss the priesthood too,* she thought. *I wonder when someone will have the power to bless me again. I wonder why I never thought about that when I answered Mr. Otto's letter.*

He paused a long time, and she thought he was through, but then the pressure of his hands increased on her head. "Heavenly Father, protect my child from wind and storm and fire and flood." She could hear him swallow once or twice, and she gripped her hands tighter in her lap. "Help her to discern good from evil, but bless her not to be afraid to look at people different from her with new eyes."

They saw her off on the afternoon train, Mama crying and pressing chicken sandwiches into her free hand, and Iris in tears too. Papa gave her a hug and then held her away from him, looking into her eyes, as green as his own. "Julia, if you see an ad in the Cheyenne paper titled 'Banker Desperate,' will you come home?"

His last official fatherly act was to give her his

handkerchief, after wiping his eyes first. That they parted with laughter was owed entirely to Iris, who blew her nose and announced, "Maybe he won't like your cooking, and he'll fire you!"

"Preposterous!" Mama declared, and blew her nose too.

Julia was standing on the top step and the conductor was about to fold up the lower one when she hesitated. She took a step down and looked into her mother's eyes. *I don't have to do this*, she thought suddenly. *I can return Mr. Otto's ticket and the sixty dollars and tell him that I changed my mind.*

She took another step down, and the conductor stood back, a patient look on his face. "Did you forget something, miss?"

My brains, my heart, my courage, my testimony, she thought, her mind in a jumble. "Mama," she said.

"You said you were coming, and your word has always been good," Mama said simply.

"Do you want me to go, Mama?" she asked. It was the voice of her childhood.

"No. But you gave your word. Good-bye, my dear," she said when she could speak. Her voice was soft, and Julia had to lean out, hand on the rail, to hear her. "Darlings aren't quitters."

Thoughtful, Julia blew her mother a kiss and forced herself to enter the compartment. She sat down and watched her family from the other side of the window as the conductor pulled up the step and signaled to the engineer. *Smile, Julia*, she ordered herself, waving back and blowing kisses. *You can cry from Ogden to Evanston, if you want to.*

And here she was, almost in Cheyenne. She piled her hair into its usual pompadour, wishing the stateroom mirror was larger. Or maybe it showed her too much. The face that gazed back, eyes still anxious, looked too young. "Julia

Darling, you may have prevaricated a bit when you wrote that you were mature," she told her image.

She closed her trunk and waited for the train to stop. There was time enough to indulge in the little fiction that she had created about Paul Otto—that he and his wife had come to Wyoming years ago when it was still a territory and, at great risk to themselves, had scratched a toehold that turned into one of the state's greatest ranches. Now Mrs. Otto was old and needed the help of a good cook who could prepare barley water, arrowroot gruel, and clam frappé for the sickroom.

When that vision paled, she dreamed up a flamboyant Paul Otto, who, with his wife, a famous and slightly scandalous actress, entertained presidents, congressmen, and visiting royalty on their huge ranch, but then wintered in Georgia's Sea Islands.

Mama is probably right; he's just an old rancher who's tired of eating burned steak and greasy hash browns, she thought as the train sounded its warning whistle. She looked out the window, wondering all over again how such a fossil had ever heard of the cooking school.

If I hang onto my hat and my skirt, I will need a third hand, she thought, as it came her turn for the conductor to help her down the steps. She took a firmer grip on her hat brim as she left the train. She glanced toward the depot, and sure enough, there were several cowboys staring at her. She ignored them and stood in the middle of the platform, waiting for her trunk and two crates to follow.

In the efficient manner she liked about the Union Pacific, her trunk and two crates were quickly rolled from the train. She nodded as the porter moved them closer to the depot, where they would not be in the way. He asked, "Are you transferring to the Cheyenne & Northern?"

She nodded. To her chagrin, he announced to the cow-boys that the lady needed a hack. All five of them rushed forward, grabbed her luggage, and hurried toward the front of the depot. Julia only had time to smile her thanks to the porter and hurry after her belongings.

She dreaded the flirtation and sly looks she knew were coming, but there was none of that. The men set her luggage down carefully and held up their hands to ward off her generosity when she dug in her purse for a tip. The bravest one among them secured a hack and blushed brick red when she smiled and thanked him. *I was wrong*, she thought, as she instructed the driver. *Cowboys are shy.*

She didn't notice many automobiles on Cheyenne streets, but she did notice that most women wore last year's hats or even relic sunbonnets. Cowboys walked by in vests and shirtsleeves, with an occasional adventurous linen duster that reached to the ankles. No one was hatless; all wore boots. She peered closer to see if they carried guns.

If the hack driver had slowed down for anything except two nuns crossing the street, she never would have made the transfer connection. As it was, Julia clutched at her hat again and hurried to the train; running was out of the question in her narrow skirt.

There were nothing but day coaches. Soon they were on the prairie, climbing steadily toward mountains and then turning and paralleling a line of bluffs. Her ears popped from the altitude, but her mind was occupied with the view out the soot-coated window. She could not call it beautiful; Utah had more genteel scenery in her cities and towns and spectacular colors and formations in the south. She felt a pull she could not explain as she watched the sparse landscape click by. No compromise of any kind caught her eye.

As the morning passed, she watched people get off at tiny towns with no more to recommend them than a storefront or two and maybe a scraggly tree here and there. Federal. Hat Creek. Chugwater—she smiled at the name—with its impressive cliffs. Dark with trees and deep in shadows, the cliffs seemed to reach down into the valley like giant fingers, ready to claw at the town.

"Gun Barrel," the conductor announced an hour later.

An army officer seated across the aisle took her valise, deposited it on the platform, and then helped her down. There were the usual cowboys; a stockman (she was beginning to tell the difference now) with a drooping mustache and linen duster; two women whispering together; and other men, who focused their attention more on the boxcars. She could hear the bawling of thirsty calves.

"Is someone coming for you, miss?" the conductor asked.

She nodded, and he left her there to pace the platform and wonder who among the crowd was waiting for her. She winced, wondering if she should have been more honest about her age. *One of these men must have a different idea of maturity than I do*, she thought. *I wonder which one is Mr. Otto?*

The breeze had been light when she left the train only minutes ago, but a sudden blast from a different quarter wrenched her hat off her head, yanking out her hatpin. She watched in dismay, one hand to her ruined coiffure, as the hat swooped down the platform. The stockman with the mustache snatched it from the air. She began stuffing in her hairpins again, smoothing down her hair, as he came toward her.

He wore a linen duster that came almost to his boot tops, and she thought it quite romantic, except that his shirt and trousers underneath looked perfectly ordinary, worn out even. His mustache was even more magnificent up close, but he had not shaved in several days, and she noticed that his hair was long at the back of his neck. She tried not to smile as she wondered if any man in the state of Wyoming had completely straight legs.

"Here you are, ma'am." He held out the hat.

"Thank you, sir," she replied as she took the poor thing from him. The wind had torn the netting loose, but the artificial cherries looked worse, all droopy over the brim.

She thought the man's eyes were black at first, but they were just dark brown. He took off his hat and nodded to her. Then he looked at her hat. "If you're staying in the state long, ma'am, you might want to rethink the width of that brim." With another nod, he replaced his own hat and walked back down the platform.

That was impertinent, but honest, she thought. She admired the nice way his slightly turned-in toes made his coat swing as he walked away. *At least I will have something to write to Iris,* she thought. *When I add that he had high cheekbones and looked a bit Indian, she will be in heaven, especially out there on her dairy farm, where there aren't too many exotics.*

The crowd on the platform had thinned. Julia resumed her pacing, glancing down every now and then to look at the watch pinned to her lapel. *I know that telegram said the noon train, and this is Thursday,* she told herself. She wondered for a moment if Mr. Otto's elderly wife had taken a sudden turn for the worse. *I hope not,* she thought. *I have only so many restoratives for an invalid's appetite.*

She continued to pace the platform. The stationmaster shooed away the lounging cowboys and then went inside. The train remained at the depot, and the engineer, stretching and then touching his hand to his back, climbed down from his perch. He handed a clipboard to a waiting engineer and went inside the depot too. Several of the salesmen stood together, talking and laughing, their sample cases clustered around them. She watched as the man in the linen duster approached two older ladies, both of whom turned away when he finished talking to them.

The wind tugged at Julia's hair, teasing out curls here and there. I will make such an impression on Mr. Otto, she thought in dismay. Let us hope he has cataracts.

She noticed that the man in the linen duster kept frowning at her trunk and two crates. *He doesn't look like a thief,* she thought. *But if he pulls up that handkerchief around his neck to cover his nose and mouth, and yanks out a pistol, I'll tell him that he's only getting aprons, winter underwear, and more spices than he will know what to do with. Perhaps he can use the chafing dish and pie crust crimper.* She continued her pacing.

Ten minutes passed, and then the stationmaster called in a loud voice. "Boooaaarding now! Boooaaarding now! Allll Abooard!"

"Oh, dear," she whispered. Within five minutes, the depot was deserted. Even the man in the linen duster had vanished. No, he was inside the depot with the stationmaster, and they were both looking through the pages on the clipboard.

He's having no better luck than I am, she thought as she walked to her trunk and perched herself on it. She gathered the valise onto her lap, grateful that Papa had insisted she take along enough money for the fare home. She could catch the train south tonight.

She glanced over her shoulder. The man in the linen duster was standing in the doorway looking at her, his hands on his hips. She calmly returned his gaze but blanched and glanced away as the horrible realization hit her. Her mouth went dry. *I think I am about to pay for the sin of prevarication. Heavenly Father, I promise to be good! Please don't let him come over here*, she begged.

He did. She winced, afraid to turn around as he stopped beside her crates. *I have made a big mistake*, she thought.

" 'Two crates and a trunk. Stop. Julia Darling. Stop,' " he said.

She took a deep breath, turned around on her trunk, and held out her hand. "Mr. Otto?" she asked in her calmest voice, which came out more like a squeak.

He took her hand in a firm grip. " 'Mature graduate of Fannie Farmer's Cooking School'?" he asked, quoting her reply to his advertisement. She could not overlook the disbelief in his firm voice.

She didn't know what imp made her do it, but the doubt in his eyes stiffened her spine. " 'Long-time stable rancher'?" she quoted.

He released her hand then. She looked over toward the stationmaster, who was standing in the doorway now and stifling what sounded suspiciously like a laugh.

"I've been ranching alone since I was fifteen," he replied, "and that was twenty years ago. I would say that was 'long-time,' especially out here."

He studied her for such a lengthy time that she half expected him to walk around her and then examine her teeth. She felt her toes digging into the soles of her shoes.

"Darling, I suppose the issue remains: can you cook?" he asked finally.

"It's *Miss* Darling, and yes, I can cook," she replied.

"You're too young."

"I'm almost twenty-eight," she replied, trying to sound as firm as he did.

"Twenty-seven, then."

"Well, yes," she said, irritated with herself.

"Always say what you mean, Darling. Second rule for living in Wyoming."

"Did I miss rule number one, Mr. Otto?" she asked.

He pointed to the hat in her hand. "No hats like that. They spook cattle."

"Oh."

He looked around then and indicated the porter with only the smallest flick of his finger. The man started his way instantly. *How does Mr. Otto do that?* she asked herself. One or two words, and the porter turned away to find a dolly and fetch her baggage.

The rancher turned back to her. "You're still too young," he said, more to himself than to her. "I'll have to curb my bunkhouse Romeos."

She blinked. "Will this be a problem?"

"Hardly. People do what I say, Darling."

Outside the depot, the porter had loaded the crates on the dolly. He looked expectantly at Otto, who nodded to him and started to follow. She stood where she was.

"Come if you want, Darling," he said over his shoulder.

"It's *Miss* Darling," she muttered under her breath.

"He calls everyone by their last name, miss," the station agent whispered to her. He laughed, but softly. "In your case, it may be a trial."

"What do *you* call him?" she whispered back as she heard her crates sliding into a wagon.

"Mr. Otto, of course," the man said, surprised.

"But he is younger than you are!" she protested in a louder whisper.

The stationmaster only shrugged his shoulders. "He's

Mr. Otto around here."

Her employer was nowhere in sight. She opened her valise to stare at her purse. *I have train fare home*, she thought. She glanced at her watch. *I could be in Cheyenne by evening.* "Cook desperate. Stop," she murmured.

"If I buy a ticket to Cheyenne, is it valid anytime?" she whispered to the stationmaster.

His grin widened. "You bet, Miss Darling."

Mr. Otto came to the doorway. "Coming?" he asked, in that level way of his.

"In a moment, Mr. Otto," she replied as she took her purse from the valise. She was at the counter then, and the stationmaster quickly sold her a ticket. "Always have an out," she murmured.

Calmly she put the ticket in the valise and turned around to face her employer, who was still silhouetted in the doorway. *Go or don't*, she told herself. "Of course I'm coming, Mr. Otto," she replied. "I came here to cook."

When she was standing in front of him, he stepped aside and took her valise. He held it out, as if indicating the ticket inside. "Insurance, eh?"

Be calm. Be serene like Mama, she thought. She considered everything she could reply and rejected all of it.

"Yes, indeed. *My* rule number one."

Four

"$\mathcal{S}$uit yourself," was his only comment as he walked toward the wagon. "Let me give you a hand up."

Dismayed, she looked at the high wagon seat and then down at her slim skirt, so newly fashionable in Salt Lake City but such a liability right now. "Mr. Otto, I am afraid this is not a practical outfit."

"Rather like the hat, eh?"

Her face grew hot as he walked behind her to survey her predicament. "Can I undo this little button to liberate these pleats?" he asked.

"No! It's just for ornament," she said in a hurry. "It won't come undone."

"Suppose you ever had to run?"

"Mr. Otto, ladies don't run in Salt Lake City," she retorted, aware how stupid she sounded.

"You could hike it up," he said. "I won't look. Put your arms around my neck, Darling."

"I would never!"

He picked her up. She grabbed for his neck as he tossed her onto the wagon seat as neatly as though she weighed nothing. He caught her hat that she dropped and, with a graceful motion, sailed it into the wagon bed, where it came to rest on what looked like a large screw. Her eyes widened as he set the screw on the hat.

"The windmill screw will anchor it," he told her. He climbed up beside her.

"That hat cost five dollars," she said, when she could speak.

He whistled under his breath. "You got taken."

It was on the tip of her tongue to say something about how stylish it was, and even conservative, considering the width of the brims seen at church and on city streets. "I suppose it *is* a little extravagant," she said, gulping down her pride in chunks.

"Sort of like those things that the girls wear over there." He nodded in the direction of the tracks to a house painted an improbable yellow.

She should have known better. She looked and looked away quickly, but not before she glimpsed a woman hanging over the sill of a second-story window, wearing only her shimmy. Her dismay deepened when her employer tipped his hat to the woman.

"Maizie the Mole," he commented. "Fifty, if she's a day." He spoke to his horses, not raising his voice to them any more than he did to people. "C'mon, boys." They moved off with an even stride, ears perked forward.

"I don't care to know how she came by that name," she said but then wanted to bite her tongue. *Why am I making conversation about fancy houses?* she asked herself in total agony.

"I wasn't going to tell you. Need anything in town?"

My head examined, she thought. "An alarm clock, Mr. Otto."

"Waste of money," he said. "I'll knock on your door every morning at five."

"Oh." *I have known this man less than twenty minutes, and I am reduced to monosyllables*, she thought in amazement. *Even Ezra couldn't do that.*

He spoke to his horses and tugged on one rein. In a

moment they had crossed the street and stopped before a general store. "I saw some bananas in here this morning." He jumped down, tied the team, and came around to her side.

She could have cried with relief to be back in her own element again. "Yes, that would be excellent," she said as she leaned over. "I have a wonderful recipe. You mash a banana with flour and lemon juice, and then deep fry it."

He helped her down. "I had in mind just peeling them and eating them."

She laughed. "Miss Farmer would tip over in her wheelchair if she thought I ever let a banana leave my kitchen untouched!"

"Hmm," was all he said.

She didn't know what demon drove her to continue talking. "You'll never know it's a banana, especially with enough powdered sugar."

"H'mm," he said again, in exactly the same tone.

He didn't take his hat off in the store, but none of the other men were bareheaded, either. The clerks were busy, but as soon as he approached the counter, one of them broke free. He had the clerk pull down the banana stalk and slice off a dozen green bananas.

Mr. Otto made a few more purchases, chief among them several bottles of liniment. She must have stared at the size and number of the bottles because he said, "We're heading to the high pastures in a few days," as if that explained it.

As they waited for the clerk to wrap the bottles, she glanced behind the counter. "Maraschino cherries, if you please," she said to the clerk. "All of them." She knew that her employer was staring at her; he seemed to do that more than she liked. "Miss Farmer always said that one cannot have too many maraschino cherries. You would be amazed what they do to an ordinary dish."

"Bananas too?"

She looked behind her. *Is there a short man in this state?* she wondered. Mr. Otto was tall, but this man positively loomed.

Mr. Otto was grinning now, and the tall man seemed to be waiting for an answer. She swallowed. "You can stick maraschino cherries all over a banana with toothpicks," she said.

The tall man whistled. " 'Pon my word, but that would snag your bowels!"

"I think you take them off before you eat the banana, you sorry-eyed simpleton," Mr. Otto said with a perfectly straight face. "Don't get off your place much, do you?"

Julia gasped and looked from one man to the other. She stepped back until she was pressed against the counter.

"Hey, Chief, when was the last time I called you a horse thief and a Captain Sharp?" the tall man asked. Anxiously, Julia looked at him for some sign of humor, but she saw none. *Mr. Otto, don't say another word!* she pleaded silently.

Mr. Otto was not susceptible to thought waves. "The last time?" he asked. "It's only been every roundup since I sold you a horse you couldn't ride."

Julia looked around her, wondering why no one was intervening. The clerk was just calmly wrapping the maraschino cherries.

"No one could ride that Satan spawn, and you know it."

"I can." To her astonishment, Mr. Otto turned away from the tall man.

Someone has to do something, she thought in desperation. Her eyes widened as the tall man pulled back the light coat he wore and exposed his gun. She took a deep breath and tugged on her employer's duster. "Mr. Otto, he has a gun!" she whispered as loudly as she dared.

"He shoots about as well as he plays cards, Darling. Get a total on that, Parsons, unless you have a crate of maraschino cherries out back you haven't mentioned to my cook here."

"You've gone and done it now."

Julia whimpered. She didn't realize she was holding her breath until she felt a sudden breeze on her face. She opened her eyes. Mr. Otto was fanning her with his hat and speaking over his shoulder to the other man.

"I suppose I *have* gone and done it. Told you I was getting a cook, McLemore," Mr. Otto said, his tone as even and conversational as before. "She's a graduate of a Boston cookery school and probably knows more ways to cook eggs than you have fleas. McLemore, this is my new cook, Julia Darling. Are you all right?

She shook her head weakly.

"Darling, this is.'. . . . Oh, what is it?" he asked the other man.

"Charlie," the man said patiently. He stuck out his hand. "Charlie McLemore. Paul can't remember a first name to save his sorry self. Shake, miss. I'll double whatever he's paying you."

"I'm already shaking, Mr. McLemore," she said. "Are you two *friends*?"

"Except when we play cards at roundup," Mr. Otto said. "You didn't think. . . . McLemore, you keep your money right there in your pocket. This is *my* cook."

McLemore released her hand. "Nice to meet you, Miss Darling." He winked at her. "Bet you haven't seen the kitchen at the Double Tipi yet."

"No," Julia said, mystified. She looked at her employer. "Is there a problem with the kitchen, Mr. Otto?"

He shrugged. "Kitchen's a kitchen, Darling."

"Told you the chief was a Captain Sharp," McLemore said cheerfully. "If you change your mind, I'll pay you $80 a month. I'm easy to find. Paul and I share a boundary." He winked again. "I eat his beef, and he eats mine!"

"Is that *legal*?" she asked, and both men laughed.

Mr. Otto turned back to the clerk, who was listening with some interest. "Looking at McLemore just reminded me: I need a twenty-pound bucket of lard. Yes, we eat each other's beef."

McLemore grinned at her and took his own purchase from the clerk. "G'day, Miss Darling. I'm just five miles north and west!"

She watched him go. "Mr. Otto, about your kitchen . . ."

If he heard her, it didn't register. Mr. Otto picked up the lard bucket and handed her the maraschino cherries all neatly done up in brown paper.

"I thought you were going to shoot each other, Mr. Otto," she commented as her employer put the groceries in the wagon bed.

"Then you've been reading too many dime novels," he said, and pulled out his watch. "Anywhere else you need to go?"

"I would like to open an account at a bank."

"Good idea."

"And I *don't* read dime novels!"

He pointed down the block. "I bank at National. It's either that or First Thrift here in Gun Barrel. National okay?"

She nodded.

"What were you going to do if he had pulled out his gun, Darling?" he asked as he strolled along.

She glanced at him. *He does have a sense of humor,* she thought. "At first I was going to leap between you two, but since I'm only getting sixty a month, I thought I would duck, instead."

He laughed. "Prudent."

"Then I checked my watch and realized that if you two killed each other, I still had time to catch the afternoon train to Cheyenne."

"Wise of you." He opened the door, and they walked into the bank. As soon as Mr. Otto crossed the threshold, a bank official started toward them, almost at a trot.

The men shook hands. "This is my cook. She wants to open an account, Baldridge."

She tried not to smile as the bank official led them behind a low gate and indicated two leather chairs. He pulled out an application and handed her a fountain pen.

Mr. Otto crossed his legs in that expansive way of Westerners. Julia took off her gloves and filled out the application while Mr. Baldridge fluttered close by—she could think of no better word to describe his hovering. Since he was there and she was curious, she asked him a few questions about interest and quarterly compounds. She resisted the urge, strong within her, to ask about bonds. She signed the application and handed it back.

The banker handed the form to Mr. Otto. "Sir, since she is a woman, a man needs to countersign for her. It appears that she has no husband, and you're the employer."

Mr. Otto sat up straighter. "I can't imagine what difference that makes," he said. He took the form, but he ignored the banker's fountain pen. He looked at her. "She appears normal enough. She has a hat in the wagon, but it met with an accident." He handed back the form unsigned. "Her gloves are clean."

"Um, I think it's a rule, Mr. Otto," she said.

"Blamed silly one," he replied to Julia's gratification. He made no move to take back the application, which was starting to rustle in the banker's hand.

"Sir, she is a woman!" the banker pleaded.

"I'm aware of that, Baldridge," Mr. Otto replied, his voice crisp as though he were suffering a fool, and not gladly. "I doubt this renders her incapable of reason."

"Of . . . of course not, s-sir," the banker stammered. "I was not implying . . ." Baldridge turned to her, his eyes so desperate that she felt some pity. "Miss Darling, rules are rules. Can you suggest the necessity of this to your employer?"

"Mr. Otto, it's this way: if I suddenly start to foam at the mouth and then grab a gun and rob the Cheyenne & Northern, I think Mr. Baldridge would not like the bank to be held accountable in any way," she said. Not daring to look her employer in the eye, she took the paper and fountain pen from the banker and handed them to him. "Sign, sir, if you will."

He uncapped the pen and rested the application on his leg. "Do you have any plans that way, Darling?" he asked.

"Not at the moment, sir," she replied. *Hurry up!* she thought. *I think I'm going to split my corset wide open when I start to laugh.*

"Very well, if you promise." He signed his name next to hers and handed it back to Baldridge, who sank into his chair behind the desk. "Does First Thrift have such a silly rule?"

"All banks do, sir."

"Then it wouldn't make any difference if I took my

money out of your bank and put it in First Thrift, would it? Or even that Cheyenne bank where I also do business? How about the one in Chicago?"

The banker's face turned an alarming color. Julia took a deep breath. "Mr. Otto, it won't make any difference. It's a banking rule, and I don't mind."

He sat there another long moment and then rose. "I suppose we have no choice," he told her. "G'day, Mr. Baldridge. Nice to see you."

He took her arm this time and steered her toward the door. It looked so far away to her. *I can't make it*, she thought.

She did, though, even when Mr. Otto stopped at the door and turned around, raising his voice to be heard across the bank. "Baldridge, I had a thought. What if the business women at the Ecstasy wanted to open an account here? Who signs for them? Customers?"

She tugged on his arm, astounded at him. "Mr. Otto!"

"I was just curious," he told her as he let her pull him through the door. He stopped again. "Baldridge, next time you're over there, ask'm, will you?"

The bank was totally silent. Mr. Otto shook his head. "Bankers are so unimaginative."

She couldn't help herself. She hurried ahead of him until she was away from the bank windows, collapsed onto a bench in front of the newspaper office, and laughed. She laughed until her sides hurt and tears ran down her cheeks. *How can you keep a straight face*, she thought, as she shook her head when he offered his handkerchief. He was nice enough to sit beside her and not walk away as though he did not know her. Finally, she dabbed at her eyes with her lace handkerchief. "Please excuse me," she said.

"I don't think a man should have to countersign for a

woman," he said simply.

"You really were serious, weren't you, Mr. Otto?" she asked in amazement. "I just take those little annoyances for granted."

"About that matter, yes." He laughed then. "I do have a pranking streak." He rubbed his hands together. "There's just something about Baldridge that brings out the worst in me."

"*Just* Baldridge?" she asked. "Tell me the worst, Mr. Otto."

He looked at his watch. "You've already missed the train back to Cheyenne, so I don't have to." He stood up. "Do we dare attempt a meal before we leave town?"

She dared, promising herself that she would eat and be quiet. He took her to a restaurant on the next block north. She turned her head and bit her lip to keep from laughing when a waiter materialized immediately and showed them to an excellent table. She took off her gloves again and accepted a menu. "Aren't you going to order, Mr. Otto?" she asked, when the waiter did not hand him a menu.

"He knows what I want."

How could I doubt it? she thought. She ordered vegetable soup and handed back the menu. *Now what do I say?*

She cleared her throat, looked up from the tablecloth she had been contemplating, and saw two men approach.

They were dressed much like her employer. They nodded to her and pulled up chairs from a nearby table.

"These fleabags must want me to introduce them to you," he said. "This is Miss Julia Darling, my new cook from Salt Lake City. Darling, this is Hanrahan and this is Clements. They ranch near Saltash, and you can't trust them farther than you can see them."

She shook hands with the ranchers, pleased with herself that her employer's assessment of his friends didn't startle her this time. Clements, the one with the blond hair and beet red forehead, turned his chair around to face her.

"You a Mormon?" he asked.

The question surprised her. In Boston, the other students had all wanted the same information, but they had found it out in more subtle ways.

"Yes, I am, sir."

"Then if I kept whiskey in my house, you won't drink it?"

Puzzled, she looked at him and then at her employer, who had a frown on his face. "No, of course not," she said. Something about his question irritated her. "I don't smoke either," she continued, "or chew tobacco or dip snuff."

Clements threw back his head and laughed. "She'll do, Hanrahan!" He cleared his throat. "Miss Darling, I'll pay you three times whatever this penny-pinching cutthroat is offering you to cook for me and Hanrahan."

"No, thank you," she said quickly, noticing how quiet the room had become.

"It's a good offer, miss," the other man said.

"Not good enough. Good day, boys. See you on the range," Mr. Otto said in a tone so final that Julia almost rose to leave herself.

"You'll change your mind, Miss Darling," Clements said cheerfully as he turned to leave. "The chief here has a hard time keeping women on the Double Tipi."

Julia sucked in her breath and held it when Mr. Otto stood up. The room was so quiet now that she could hear other people breathing.

Clement's face had turned the color of putty, and Julia watched in horrified fascination as his Adam's apple moved up and down. "You know I was funning, Mr. Otto!"

"No, you weren't."

He did nothing but stare at Clement, but it was enough.

Hanrahan tugged his partner by the belt buckle and pushed him toward the door.

Mr. Otto sat down and leaned back in his chair. "Sorry about those two."

She mumbled something in reply and could have kissed the waiter when he appeared with their food.

"You'll hear rumors," he said when the waiter left but added nothing more, which didn't ease her doubts.

They ate in silence. When he was halfway through the steak in front of him, her employer set down his fork. "You sounded pretty knowledgeable in the bank," he said.

She sighed. "I was *awful* in the bank, and I should apologize," she began, grateful right down to her stockings for a safe topic.

He finished the hash browns and then leaned back again. "I don't think I ever heard a lady mention compounded interest, either," he said.

"What about the business women at the Ecstasy?" she asked, before she thought.

"Not from them either," he replied with a smile. "How do you know about interest?"

"I should," she said, putting a stern cap on her urge to babble. "My father is a vice president at Zion's Bank."

He raised his eyebrows. "Then why are you . . . ?" He stopped and turned his attention to the rest of the steak.

That must be another rule, she thought. *Never pry.* She busied herself buttering a roll, even though she knew she didn't want it.

When Mr. Otto finished, the waiter appeared at his elbow to whisk away the dishes and then return with apple pie weighed down with a huge slab of cheese. The rancher indicated the pie with his fork. "Want some?"

Julia shook her head. *He likes steak, hash browns, and*

apple pie, she thought. *And bananas. Thank goodness I have come to the rescue with my cookbooks. Pretty soon he will know what he's been missing. I doubt he has ever eaten potted pigeons or lobster salad. I wonder how many men he has killed. I wonder what I'm doing here.*

When he finished, he took the bill from the waiter, but before he could get up, another man approached the table. Julia tensed.

"Darling, let me introduce you to Cuddy," Mr. Otto said.

"Allen Cuddy," the man said, extending his hand to her. "I have a first name."

I used to, she thought, even as she smiled and shook his hand. "I'm Julia Darling."

"We share some range, Darling. You might see him around sometime."

"Probably more than sometime, ma'am," he replied, and she couldn't help noticing that he had wonderful blue eyes and that his shirt was clean.

"You can't have her, Cuddy," Mr. Otto said with a sigh that sounded weary right down to his bone marrow. "She works for me."

"Wouldn't dream of trying to hire her, Paul," he replied. "What do you take me for?" He grinned. "I had marriage in mind, actually." He tipped his hat and left the restaurant.

Julia gasped.

Mr. Otto swore in irritation. "Darling, you're going to cause me no end of trouble. I hadn't even thought of that complication. Well, I did think you would be older."

He was right, of course. She had not been truthful. "Mr. Otto, you're worrying for nothing," she said. "I don't even know him! And I'm not so sure I . . ."

"Know me?" he asked softly. "You don't. No one does around here. Change your mind already?"

Five

"No, I have not changed my mind," she said quietly, not willing to be overheard by the entire dining room. "I was going to say, 'I don't know him, and I'm not so sure I want to,'" she finished, picking up her gloves from the table. "Mr. Otto, if you don't try to tell me what to do all the time, I will cook for you." She frowned. "Oh, that sounds . . ."

"Honest?" he suggested. He was looking at her hand. "Bad marriage? I've been there."

Surprised, she followed his gaze to her left hand; only the thinnest white line remained where her ring had been. "Bad engagement," she replied as she put on her gloves.

He picked up the check and rose. "Change of scenery then?"

She nodded, too shy to say anything.

"Cook desperate, eh?" he said softly when they stood outside again.

She nodded again, walking beside him back to the wagon. *I should apologize*, she thought. *I did misrepresent myself.* "Mr. Otto, I owe you an apology," she began. "I told a Grandpa Haney."

He lifted her to the wagon seat and unhitched the horses. "What is a Grandpa Haney?" he asked, climbing up beside her. He spoke to the horses, and they started up a side street.

"Grandpa Haney was from England. He came west to Utah Territory when he was fourteen, walking all the way," she said, shading her eyes with her hand and wishing her hat wasn't in ruins in the wagon bed. "He had never driven a team of horses before. When he reached the valley, someone told him that if he could drive a logging team, he could have a job."

"Of course he said he could," Mr. Otto said, amusement in his voice. "I almost hate to ask where this is leading. Are you telling me that you really *can't* cook?"

"Oh, no!" she exclaimed. "I can do things to food that you never dreamed of, Mr. Otto."

"I suppose I'm relieved," he murmured.

She made an effort to overlook the doubt in his voice. "Grandpa Haney said he could drive a team because he needed the job so desperately. The day before he was to start, he went to the mouth of the canyon and watched the teamsters."

"Studying?"

She nodded. "The next morning, he got in the wagon seat and became a teamster. He did it, even though he told a monstrous whopper." She was silent, thinking of her grandfather. "He did it," she repeated softly. She turned to him. "Mr. Otto, I suspect that I'm not precisely what you had in mind when you wrote that ad."

"Far from it."

"That's why it's a Grandpa Haney," she said, and took a deep breath. "I suppose I knew all along that what you meant by mature wouldn't be me."

"That's honest enough. I think I can live with your particular Grandpa Haney," he said as he looked back at the town. "You've certainly noticed by now that I didn't stick you back on the train. I want a cook, Darling. That's all."

He turned his attention to his horses, and they continued in silence. She wanted to ask him if he had employed a cook earlier who hadn't worked out. She also wanted him to tell her about the others she would be cooking for. He seemed inclined to keep his own counsel, and she was not inclined to bother him.

They traveled in silence for what seemed like hours to Julia, but which couldn't have been more than one, when he turned the team west, away from the town and toward the bluffs. The wind blew uncomfortably warm from the west, the dust rising and falling in fitful puffs until she tasted the grit in her mouth.

They traveled on a gradual incline, hardly noticeable. Every now and then, she heard the song of the western meadowlark. All around them, the grass whispered and hissed with every wind change.

"Buffalo grass," Mr. Otto said. "Best thing there is for bison and cattle." He pointed toward a distant windmill that towered over a shack. "And there's the worst thing."

She squinted against the sun. Nothing moved around the house. She looked at her employer, a question in her eyes.

"Homesteaders," he said with a frown. "They busted out. Get away from the irrigation ditches, and you can't homestead enough land in Wyoming to make agriculture pay. I think congressmen should be forced to homestead in a tar paper shanty out here. Sure would spare us some silly laws."

To Julia, this sounded like a favorite topic of his. "What happens to the homesteaders?"

He shrugged. "Sometimes stockmen burn them out and cut the barbed wire. Other nesters just get hungry. I don't know where they go."

"That's hard." She looked back at the shack as they passed. In the middle of a sea of grass, a shredded towel or diaper still clung to the clothesline, the loneliest thing she had ever seen.

"It's a hard land. That's why when I said I was a longtime, veteran rancher, it was no Grandpa Haney." He sighed. "I've ranched a long time, and I've seen a lot of stuff you probably wouldn't approve of." He paused, as if gauging her reaction. "Mostly I feel sorry for them. There's a family of Germans in our pass, and I think they must be living on air. Sometimes I . . ." He stopped, obviously changing his mind. "It's hard on the women and children."

As time passed, the sun became more uncomfortable on the back of her neck. Julia wanted to ask how far it was to the Double Tipi but said nothing. She would only be whining.

Her nose was starting to hurt when Mr. Otto suddenly took off his hat and settled it on the ruin of her coiffure, tipping it back a little so she could see out from under the brim.

"You need your hat," she protested.

"Not as bad as you do," he said. "Malloy has some zinc oxide that he'll share when we get to the Double Tipi. He has ginger-colored hair, and he always burns."

That was all the conversation he offered for another lengthy time. They were definitely climbing now, and there was a pass, narrow to be sure, but well-traveled. The sandstone cliffs they passed between were pockmarked with small caves. She thought at first that she saw bats flying in and out, but they turned out to be swallows. Always there was the fragrance of sage and the sound of grass.

To the relief of her parched and burning skin, the sky darkened. She waited for the air to cool, but the heat became more oppressive. She noticed that Mr. Otto glanced more and more often at the sky.

"Sorry about Clements and Hanrahan," he said finally.

She had been expecting a comment about the weather.

"Who?" she asked, surprised.

"Those lumps of chickensh—those two in the restaurant." He was silent for another long moment, but she was grateful that he was concentrating on her now and not staring at the sky. "Do you often get stupid questions about your religion?" he asked.

"Not often," she replied. "Except for my year in Boston, I've hardly ever been out of Utah."

"I'll bet you were a nine-day wonder in Boston."

"I suppose I was," she said. "When one of the students found out I was from Utah, she asked me if my father had a harem."

"Like the Grand Turk, eh?"

"I think she was almost disappointed when I told her that Mama was his only wife. The rest of the students were quite nice, however."

The air suddenly blew cooler. Relieved, she raised her face to the sky just as the heavens opened up and poured water down.

"Turkeys look at the sky like that when it rains, and they drown," was Mr. Otto's comment.

She laughed.

"Well, that's a relief," Mr. Otto said as he tipped his hat lower on her head. "I was afraid you'd blame me."

"Why would I do that?" she asked, thinking of the ruin of her dress, a companion to the ruin of her hat, which was squashed under the windmill screw in the wagon bed, and the ruin of her hair, which sagged as the poof went out of her pompadour.

"I don't know. General principles?"

Her employer reached behind him for a yellow slicker and handed it to her. She pulled it over her shoulders, thankful for its slight protection against the cold rain.

"It's going to rain all night now," Mr. Otto predicted. "Second thoughts, Darling?"

More like fifth and sixth ones, she thought, tugging the slicker closer. "I'm beyond second thoughts," she told him. "Is . . . is the Double Tipi close?" She could see nothing through the curtain of rain.

"Nope."

That concluded the conversation for another mile or two. Julia told herself it was pointless to worry about whether they would find any shelter for the night. She hunkered down in the slicker and hoped that her crates and trunk were waterproof. *I'm no pioneer*, she thought. *Grandpa Haney would not be impressed.*

"You're replacing Little River," her employer said, startling her. He slowed the team. She looked for a road, but it was raining too hard. The incline in elevation became more pronounced, and she hung onto the wagon seat. *I'm glad he knows where he's going*, she thought.

"Little River?"

He shifted the reins to his other hand. "I don't know how the rumor started, but some wise . . . acres spread it around that Pa won Little River in a poker game. He didn't, of course. She came with my mother. You could call her my aunt."

That explains it, Julia thought as she waited for him to continue. *That explains your high cheekbones and your eyes that look black.*

"What was her name?" she asked finally, when he seemed absorbed in more silence.

"My mother?" He said something soft and guttural.

"What does it mean?" she asked, fascinated now.

He hesitated a moment, and Julia wondered if she had committed another indiscretion. *He's probably tired of my questions*, she thought, *or maybe he's just thinking how to say it in English.*

"Child Walking," he finally said. "That's close and the best I can do."

"What did you call her?"

"Ma," he replied, and she could hear the amusement in his voice. "What do you think?"

Julia laughed. "I'm a dunce," she apologized. "Did she speak English?"

"Some," he said. "Mostly Pa and I learned Shoshone. Ma died when I was ten, and Little River became the cook. That was in 1886." He sighed. "I can't believe I ate her food for twenty-plus more years."

The rain pounded down harder, and his attention was taken up with the horses, which had begun to slip in the mud as they climbed higher into the pass. The sun wasn't all the way gone from the sky yet, but the rain thundered down, obscuring any view or landmarks. She heard her trunk slide in the wagon and wondered for a long moment if Mr. Otto had raised the wagon gate when they left Gun Barrel. "Did you—?"

"I raised it," he said. "You don't think all this rain is going to hurt the bananas, do you?"

She laughed. "Mr. Otto, you're amazing. Bananas are like eggs," she assured him. "They come in neat little packages. And those bananas are so green they won't be ripe until after it frosts, I think!"

The sun set, and still he continued driving the team steadily up into the pass, handing her the reins and getting out once to lead them. "There's a pretty sheer drop on your side," was all he said when he climbed up beside her again and took the reins.

"Mr. Otto, I don't want to know!"

He only laughed.

Julia found herself staring down into the darkness. Every time the horses slipped, she sucked in her breath, closed her eyes, and waited to die.

Nothing happened, except that the rain pelted, and mercy, was Mr. Otto *humming* under his breath? Even though he was nothing more now than an outline, she turned toward him. "See here, Mr. Otto," she demanded. "Am I the *only* one who is scared to death?"

He looked around elaborately. "Unless we picked up a drunk or two or a sporting lady in Gun Barrel, you probably are," he replied, his voice as mild as though they discussed a weekly menu. "It's a waste of time to worry over stuff you can't do anything about. Save it for the really bad times. And by then, it probably still doesn't matter."

It was on the tip of her tongue to ask him to let her know when things were at their worst, but he was tugging back on the reins now. "We'll be at the Marlowes in a few minutes," he said as he turned the team. The horses quickened their pace without any command, and she cautiously allowed herself to relax.

"The Marlowes?"

"My nearest neighbors. The Double Tipi is not quite an hour away, but I think you've had enough."

More than enough, Julia thought. "Are you sure they won't mind?"

"Of course they won't mind. We never turn away strangers or wet people up here. Do you do that in Salt Lake City?"

"Well, Papa doesn't take in drunks or sporting ladies." She tried to think when anyone had ever come begging to the house or needed a ride anywhere, but she couldn't.

My employer must be convinced that I'm an idiot, she

thought as Mr. Otto drove his team with some assurance down a road she couldn't see, toward a house that didn't seem to be there. She tried to peer through the rain and the gloom but saw nothing.

"The Marlowes have been here since aught five," he said. "Marlowe was a sergeant of artillery at Fort Russell. He decided to stay."

"Does he have a first name?" she asked, wondering if Mr. Otto would get the message.

"Max. His wife's name is Alice."

Julia wanted to ask him if he called her Marlowe Number 2, but she refrained. She squinted into the darkness. Nothing. She sighed and pulled the slicker closer about her. *This has been the most miserable day of my life*, she thought.

"Alice will be glad to see you," Mr. Otto said. He was pulling back on the reins now. "Do you smell the oats, boys?" he asked his horses as he set the brake. "Here we are."

She looked around. She smelled barn odors, but there was no sign of anything. "I *thought* I had good eyes," she said out loud, but more to herself than to her employer, who was coming around to her side now. She held out her arms to him, and he helped her down.

He took her arm, and she could tell they were on a path now. "I'll introduce you and then take care of my team," he told her. "I think Marlowe heard us."

Over this downpour? she thought, and then watched as a door swung open. "There *is* a house here," she said, feeling stupid when Mr. Otto looked at her in surprise. "Well, *I* couldn't see it."

The man in the doorway spoke over his shoulder. "Alice, he went and did it! Come on in, miss. Alice! Bring a towel! Bring two!"

Julia needed no urging to come in out of the rain, even

though she knew she had never looked worse in her life. The room was lit with the soft glow of kerosene lamps, but she squinted anyway. When her eyes adjusted, she looked around.

The room was not much larger than her bedroom at home, with a horsehair sofa crammed up under the one window and a Victrola next to it. Mr. Otto was even now brushing against a dining table, which filled much of the remaining space. Through an open door, she could see into a lean-to. Pans hung on the wall, so she knew it must be the kitchen. A shelf with books and a china shepherdess dignified the dining area, and somehow a rocking chair was squeezed between the table and the Victrola. It was tiny and crowded but impeccably clean. She groaned inside. *I am the dirtiest thing in this cabin*, she thought in dismay.

A woman came toward her, holding a towel in both hands. With a smile of welcome, she draped it over Julia's head and began to gently squeeze the water from her hair, all the while scolding Julia's employer. "Paul, shooting is far too good for you! What were you thinking? Why didn't you just get some rooms in Gun Barrel for the night? I'll be surprised if . . ." She paused and looked at Julia, her eyes kind.

"Julia Darling," she said, her voice muffled by the towel that the woman was applying more vigorously now.

". . . if Miss Darling doesn't hop right back on the C&N tomorrow."

"She did buy a return ticket to Cheyenne," Mr. Otto said.

"Then obviously Miss Darling is too smart to cook for you and those bandits you call hands," the woman scolded. "Is that better, my dear?"

Julia nodded, feeling an absurd urge to fling herself into the woman's arms and sob.

"Introduce us properly, Paul, and then you and Max

give us twenty minutes."

"Darling, this is Alice Marlowe. Alice, this is Darling, my new cook."

"My first name is Julia," she said. She stepped back in surprise when Mr. Otto took the towel that Max had handed him and wiped off her face. She wanted to protest when he tipped her head to one side and scraped away the mud from her ear.

"See there? That's why I didn't stay in Gun Barrel, Alice," he said after he peeled several blades of grass from her cheek and stepped back. "She's already had one proposal in town and two offers of employment, but by Jupiter, I aim to have me a cook."

The three of them stared at her—Mr. Marlowe thoughtful, his wife with a frown, and Mr. Otto with what appeared to be resignation. Mr. Marlowe was the first to speak.

"I see why you avoided Gun Barrel," he said. He poked Mr. Otto in the ribs, a liberty she couldn't fathom. "You're a dirty dog, Paul! I didn't know you changed that ad to include 'pretty.' "

My stars, Julia thought in amazement.

Her employer shook his head. " 'Mature.' That was the word I used. M-A-T-U-R-E." To her chagrin, he spelled it out distinctly.

"Paul saw an article about the cooking school in one of my magazines," Alice said.

Tears welled in her eyes. Before Julia could embarrass herself further Alice Marlowe grabbed the towel from Mr. Otto and snapped it at the men. "Out of here! Now!"

They laughed and went out into the rain. Julia sniffed back tears, as Alice started on the buttons of her suit jacket. "What you need is to get out of these clothes. I'm afraid this lovely suit is beyond salvaging. It's starting to shrink. Let me help you wash your hair, Miss Darling. Please, may I call you Julia?"

Julia barely kept her tears to herself. In a moment the dress was off, her shirtwaist was unbuttoned and pulled down, and Mrs. Marlowe was helping her to the lean-to. Julia blew her nose. Alice poured water from the stove's reservoir, tested it with her elbow, and instructed her to lean over. In another moment, her hair was lathered, and Mrs. Marlowe was murmuring something comforting. Julia sniffed back her tears and got suds in her nose for her pains.

She didn't care. Alice poured warm, clean water over her hair. "I know I always feel better when my hair is clean. What lovely hair, Julia."

"Thank you," she said, pleased all out of proportion with the compliment.

Alice helped her skirt past the table and opened a door into the next room. Before she had time to be shy, the woman had stripped the clothes from Julia and pulled a nightgown over her head. "Now you get in bed, and I'll give you my comb."

"I can't take your bed, Mrs. Marlowe," Julia protested, even as she settled back against the feather pillow that the woman spread with a dry towel and propped against her lower back.

"Don't even worry about it," she said. "I'll sleep here with you tonight, and the men can take the floor in the other room." She smiled at Julia. "Actually, we should make Paul Otto sleep in the wagon under the tarp. Maybe that's even too good for him. What was he *thinking*?"

Julia started to comb out the tangles. "It wasn't his fault it started to rain," she said, surprising herself by defending him.

"I suppose not," Mrs. Marlowe said, sitting on the edge of the bed. She leaned close to scrape a crust of mud off Julia's chin that had escaped the warm water. "Welcome to Wyoming, my dear."

Six

Julia had no more than a vague recollection of that evening, spent shivering in bed, trying to get her feet warm. She woke once in the middle of the night to sidle closer to Mrs. Marlowe, warm in a flannel nightgown. She heard a man snoring in the front room, thought of her father, and settled deeper in the bed.

The sun woke her in the morning. She sat up, listening to kitchen sounds instead of rain, and the men talking in low voices in the front room. Her traveling suit was nowhere in sight; Mrs. Marlowe must have put the garment out of its misery.

Someone—she hoped it was Alice Marlowe—had rummaged through her trunk and found her clothes. She had only one hairpin remaining, so she brushed her hair until it crackled and bound it at the back of her neck with a piece of twine lying on the dresser.

"Sleep all right, Miss Darling?" Marlowe asked when she opened the door. He looked at her with some concern. "Allie took your dress to the burn barrel."

"She is kind, indeed," Julia replied.

Mr. Otto stood up and stretched. "There's a rumor that Alice Marlowe is so kind that she warms the water before she drowns baby groundhogs. Isn't that right, Alice?" he called into the kitchen.

One cannot accuse my boss of being overly sentimental, Julia thought, as she edged past Mr. Otto into the kitchen.

Alice Marlowe looked up from the cinnamon rolls she was slicing with a thread. "You were so busy sleeping this morning that I couldn't bear to wake you," she said. She deftly arranged the rolls in the pan, covered them with a cloth, and placed the pan in the warming oven. "Would you please make coffee while I gather the eggs?"

Julia winced. *My sins have truly come home to roost*, she thought, *and much sooner than I thought they would.* Her eyes wide with dismay, she stared at her hostess's back as Mrs. Marlowe took a basket from the shelf. "I . . . I don't know."

Mrs. Marlowe reached for her shawl. "Of course you can! I expect your coffee is far better than mine." She leaned toward Julia. "I can't imagine anything more important to a rancher than good coffee." She opened the door. "It's not every day that I have a graduate of the Boston Cooking School in my kitchen. Think of this as your moment to shine."

Julia sat down at the table and rubbed the bridge of her nose. Coffee would be the one thing she never learned to make. With painful clarity, she saw that first week's schedule tacked to the bulletin board by the practice kitchen. "Coffee" followed "The Making and Care of a Fire," and came right before "Mixing Water Bread."

For one uncharitable moment, she blamed Miss Farmer. When Julia arrived two days after class began, Miss Farmer had wanted her to come early before class to catch up. Julia had assured her teacher that she was adept at laying fire in a cookstove and that she would never, ever have to make coffee at home in Utah. *This finishes it*, she thought. *I have a terrible suspicion that Mr. Otto may not forgive bad coffee.*

It was failure too soon, she decided as she sat at the table again. Had she come so far, lost a lovely suit and hat, and turned her complexion red to give up so quickly? "I won't go home," she said softly, already dreading the smug way Ezra Quayle would look at her.

"I hope not, Darling."

Miserable, she looked over her shoulder. Mr. Otto was leaning against the door frame and regarding her with what, even in her extremity, looked like a kind expression. After Alice's comment, she knew that his expression would change when she confessed that she had no clue how to create coffee. She gazed back, but his expression did not change. She took a deep breath.

"Mr. Otto, I have another confession," she said. "Do sit down."

"I can't take bad news on my feet?" he asked, but again, it was not unkind. "So far I have managed to bear your confessions with some fortitude. I promise not to stagger around and tear at my hair." He sat down anyway and looked at her for a long moment. "I overheard Alice. I suppose you are going to tell me now that you can't make coffee."

She could tell from his expression that he was joking with her. She avoided his eyes to concentrate on the intricacy of the tablecloth's design. She looked up. He was frowning now.

"You can't make coffee," he said in a flat voice.

She shook her head, thinking with what panache she had created bisque of lobster and bombe glacé in that practice kitchen. *Why could you not have that instead?* she thought. *You want something as ordinary as coffee.*

"I can't make coffee," she echoed, fearing that he might say something she really didn't want to hear, and who could blame him?

Mr. Otto was quiet for a long moment. In misery, she listened to him drum on the table with his long fingers.

"Could you try, Darling?"

She looked up, wishing that he were not so inscrutable, or his voice so level. *I wonder if he is angry*, she thought. *How do I tell? Either he is the soul of patience or more desperate for a cook than any man living.* She could have been mistaken, but as she worked up the nerve to look at him, she imagined that he wanted her to succeed.

"I mean, I just make it with a handful or two of coffee beans and water with no tadpoles."

He obviously wanted her to try. She nodded. "I have my cookbook in the crate, and there is a recipe for coffee."

Brave man, he did not waver. "Get on your shoes, and show me which crate. The wagon's by the barn."

When she went outside, Mr. Otto was already standing in the wagon bed. He had removed the extra tarpaulin that Marlowe had pulled over everything last night, shaking off the water. He gave her a hand up into the wagon bed. "Which one?" he asked.

She indicated the smaller crate. As he pried up the lid, she remembered how stiff Ezra Quayle could be when she disappointed him. She relaxed. Mr. Otto seemed perfectly at ease. He almost seemed to be enjoying himself.

When he pried off the lid, she looked at the trunk. She sniffed; the oil of cloves bottle must have broken. She picked up the almond paste, wondering if everything would now smell of cloves. She picked up the extra copy of the Book of Mormon, sniffed it, and set it back.

Mr. Otto picked up the Book of Mormon and ruffled the pages with his thumb. He put the book back into the crate. "While I do expect coffee, I hardly think it's worth too many frowns and certainly no tears."

Relieved, she searched through the straw until she found her cookbook. She turned to the recipe and handed

Mr. Otto the cookbook. She continued to paw through the straw, which eventually produced a wet measure and two dry measures in one-quarter increments. She showed them to her employer. "These are measuring cups," she explained, pointing to the markings on the side. "I have other cups with markings in thirds."

"Fannie Farmer doesn't just toss in a bit of this and that?" he asked after he replaced the lid on the crate and helped her from the wagon bed.

"Heavens, no! She taught us scientific cookery, Mr. Otto. Don't look so dubious," she added.

"I can't help it." They walked back to the kitchen.

Mr. Otto held the measuring cups and looked at them while she took Mrs. Marlowe's coffeepot to the sink and rinsed it out, counting her blessings all the while that it was granite wear, just as Miss Farmer insisted upon in the recipe.

Taking a measuring cup from Mr. Otto, she portioned six cups of hot water from the stove's reservoir into the pot, and set the pot on the cookstove. In a brief time, she heard the hiss of water heating.

Alice had returned with the eggs. Glancing at the recipe, Julia took the biggest one and cracked it into a bowl, shells and all. She added precisely one half cup of cold water, and then the coffee, which Alice, at her instruction, measured from the tin. "Imagine such a thing as cups to measure with," the woman murmured. "We do live in a modern age."

"Level measures, too," Julia said. "I can't tell you how many times Miss Farmer had us run a knife just so across the top of a measuring cup or a teaspoon."

When the water was boiling, Julia added the coffee and egg mixture to the pot and stirred vigorously, as the recipe indicated. To her dismay, the coffee was cloudy. *Please be right, Miss Farmer*, she thought. After another glance at the cookbook, she set the pot on the range and adjusted the damper again for a hotter fire.

"Do you have a pocket watch, Mr. Otto?" she asked.

Her employer drew back in mock alarm. "I cannot believe Fannie wants you to add my watch to the brew," he said, even as he handed it to her.

She sighed and looked at the watch. "The coffee is to boil exactly three minutes, Mr. Otto."

"Egg and all?"

"Certainly," she replied, hoping that she sounded more confident than she felt. *Why on earth would anyone put an egg in coffee?* she asked herself. *And shells, too?*

While they all watched the three minutes pass, Marlowe joined them in the kitchen, draping his arm companionably over his wife's shoulder. He looked from one of them to the other, a grin on his face. "Is absolute silence part of the recipe?" he asked finally. "Paul, I think we had more fun in here the night that Doc splinted my leg on this table."

"And certainly more brandy," his wife commented.

"Doc does appreciate an occasion," Mr. Otto said, not taking his eyes from his watch. "Three minutes, Darling. What happens now? Should we stand back? Duck?"

She ignored him. With her heart pounding just under her apron bib, she carefully removed the calendar page that Mrs. Marlowe had given her to plug up the spout. After another glance at the cookbook, she added the remaining half cup of cold water and held her breath. *Heavenly Father*, she prayed to herself, *please let this coffee be wonderful*. Her petition almost made her gasp. *What am I thinking? More to the point, what on earth is Heavenly Father making of my petition?*

"The colder water carries the grounds to the bottom,"

she said, wishing for an authoritative ring to her voice, which sounded childish to her ears.

"Egg shells, too?" Mr. Otto asked, peering into the pot.

I most earnestly hope so, she thought. "Now we set it on the back of the range for precisely ten more minutes."

"Exactly ten minutes?" he asked.

"Precisely," she said, crossing her fingers.

He shifted in his chair to look at her. "How can you really predict *anything* done on a cookstove?"

"Cooks do it all the time, Mr. Otto. It helps if you lay the fire right and then use good coal or the right wood when it catches," she explained as she sat down beside him. "I looked at Mrs. Marlowe's fire, and it was fine."

"Little River used to just heave in a log or two when the mood was on her," he said. "I've seen her stuff a log through the stove lid and let it burn down."

That does not sound promising, she considered, remembering Charlie McLemore's disparaging remarks about the Double Tipi's kitchen. "Is . . . is Little River still there?" she asked, hopeful of denial.

Her employer handed her four cups. "Funny thing about that, Darling. When I told her that I was getting a cook, she left the next day." He smiled. "Makes me wish I had said something years ago. I got a letter a couple of weeks later from my uncle on the Wind River Rez. Said she showed up one morning and announced that she was cooking for him now."

"Oh, dear," Julia murmured.

"It's worse. He also told me that he had decided not to leave me part of his herd when he dies. Darling, retribution is swift among the Shoshone."

She laughed and looked at the pocket watch. Her smile

vanished. Feeling like the Queen of France in a tumbrel, she lifted the coffee pot from the back burner. Alice, her face red with the heat, was stirring down the lava-like oatmeal. She smiled her thanks when Julia slid a trivet under the pot.

She had hardly moved the pot from the stove to another trivet on the table when Mr. Otto held out a cup. Marlowe covered his face with his hands. "I can't stand the suspense," he declared.

Julia took a deep breath, decided that a last appeal to the Almighty about coffee was quite out of order, and poured the brew into her employer's cup. *If it comes out cloudy, with shells and slimy strings of egg, I will tear up my diploma*, she told herself, *if Mr. Otto doesn't do it for me.*

The rancher sniffed the coffee, and then took a cautious snip. And another. "Heavens," he said, his voice almost reverent. He sipped some more, holding it in his mouth for a lingering moment like the wine taster who lectured one morning in Miss Farmer's fancy cooking class.

Wordlessly he drank slowly, pausing to blow on the coffee but not stopping until he drained the cup and held it out for more. Just as silent, she filled it again. Max Marlowe snatched up two cups from the table. Her heart full, and not knowing whether to thank Miss Farmer or the Almighty, Julia filled the cups. Marlowe handed the other to his wife, and the three of them drank silently, reverently.

When his cup was empty, Mr. Otto raised it to her in a salute. "Level measures, eh?" he asked. "Just so much water? No guessing?"

She shook her head. "It's the scientific way, Mr. Otto."

Her employer looked at the Marlowes and then back at his cup. "This is our little secret," he said. "Marlowe, if word gets out that my cook makes the best coffee on both sides of the Divide, we can just forget the niceties of courtship among my neighbors. I'll be killed and dumped into a borrow pit, and she will be abducted."

Alice laughed and took the oatmeal from the stove. "Your little secret!" she scoffed, and then glanced out the front room window. "Too late, Paul. In fact, I think it was too late when you took her into that dining room in Gun Barrel. You know how news travels. What were you thinking?" She gestured toward the window.

Mystified, Julia joined her employer and Mrs. Marlowe at the window. Alice was shaking her head. "I never imagined Charlie McLemore owned a suit," she mused, her voice full of wonder. "Where do you suppose he got those flowers?" She sucked in her breath. "Paul, do you suppose he has—"

"—come to propose?" Mr. Otto finished sourly. "I don't doubt it." He glared out the window.

"Julia, I'll get out the cinnamon rolls, and you get another cup," Alice said, putting her hand to her mouth to hide her smile. "I hope you are prepared with a lot of small talk, my dear."

"No!" Mr. Otto said, not leaving his spot by the window. "Don't encourage him!"

"This is my house, Paul," Alice reminded him. "He already has sufficient encouragement, anyway. Max, do be quiet or go in the bedroom."

His eyes merry, Marlowe gave Julia a sympathetic look and bolted for the bedroom. Julia looked at her employer. "Mr. Otto, he cannot possibly be coming here to propose to me! Can he?" she added, when he was silent. "I don't even know him."

"Doesn't matter," he muttered.

Mrs. Marlowe was in the kitchen, separating the cinnamon rolls. "He's probably only the man on the fastest horse.

From that direction, it looks like he's come from the Double Tipi. Paul, can you imagine what your hands must be thinking? And James?"

Julia jumped when Mr. Otto banged his hand against the door frame. "If you couldn't be mature, Darling, couldn't you have had the foresight to be more than usually *plain*?"

"Mr. Otto, I have no intention of marrying *anyone* in Wyoming," she told him, her words distinct. "It is the farthest thing from my mind. Please believe me!" she added, opening the door when McLemore knocked.

She stepped back, bumping into Mr. Otto, as Charlie leaped into the room, holding out the flowers. They looked like goldenrod.

"How . . . sweet," she managed, wishing that her employer would back up. He seemed disinclined to budge, however.

"Charles McLemore, we went through all this yesterday. This is my cook," Mr. Otto said in terrible tones. To her amazement, he put his arm around her. "My cook."

He might have been speaking to a post. McLemore flung himself down on one leg. "Miss Darling, I am a man of temperate habits—" Mrs. Marlowe coughed suddenly. "—No diseases that I know of, and I would be honored if you would make me the happiest man in Wyoming and marry me!" he concluded in a rush. "My kitchen is much nicer," he added, pleading with her now.

"No," said Mr. Otto.

"I'm not asking you," McLemore said, getting up off his knee. "Besides, Otto, you had a chance before and—"

Mrs. Marlowe took his arm and tugged him toward the kitchen. "Have a cinnamon roll and some coffee," she said hastily, her eyes on Mr. Otto.

"I'll overlook that because you're my neighbor," Mr.

Otto said in the same voice Julia remembered from the restaurant.

She extricated herself from her employer's grasp and took McLemore's other arm. "Mr. McLemore, you are extremely kind to make me such an offer, but I must decline. Coffee, sir?" She put the cup in his hand and pushed him toward the kitchen. Mrs. Marlowe whisked him around the corner and out of sight.

Julia held her breath, alarmed at the bleak look on her employer's face. In another moment, he shouted into the kitchen. "McLemore, I hope you have no further plans to marry, court, befriend, or in any way harass my cook!"

McLemore was silent. In a moment, Alice Marlowe led him to the table, coffee cup in his right hand and a plate of cinnamon rolls in the left, but a broken man, anyway.

"Take a sip," Alice urged.

His lower lip out like a small child's, McLemore drew it in finally and did as she said. Another sip and another, and the frown left his face, only to return as he must have considered what would never be his if Mr. Otto had breath in his body.

"I'm sorry, Mr. McLemore," Julia said. "I've already promised to cook for Mr. Otto."

"Indeed she has," Mr. Otto said, unable to resist a glance at Julia. "I doubt even Darling knows how good her coffee is."

I deserved that, she thought.

She could tell this was not a good moment in Mr. McLemore's life. *I believe I have broken his heart,* she thought, with some regret. She watched the rancher, slumped in his chair, made more pathetic by the goldenrod pollen all over the suit that must have been new the first time Cleveland was president. *Will I be treading on broken hearts before my tenure is up, cry uncle, and return to Salt Lake? There ought to be some way to prevent all this needless pain in Wyoming,* Julia thought.

She considered the matter and then turned her attention to her employer as a solution came to mind. It was so simple that she almost laughed out loud. Mr. Otto was still watching her over the rim of his cup, the expression in his eyes inscrutable again.

"I have an idea, Mr. Otto. What would you think if I signed a contract stating that I was under legal obligation to remain in your employ for an entire year without marrying?"

"You mean it?"

"Most certainly."

Max had returned to the kitchen for more coffee. "You could print the thing in local newspapers."

Heavens, just don't let it show up in the Deseret News, or Papa will be on the next train east, Julia thought.

"Maybe even the Billings *Gazette*," Marlowe threw in. "Pretty women are scarce, and news does travel."

Mr. Otto turned his attention to her again. "Darling, are you willing?"

"It was my idea, wasn't it?" she countered, glancing at Mrs. Marlowe for support.

"Julia, it's a wonderful idea! Max, get some paper and my pen."

With a sound suspiciously close to a sob, McLemore stood up. "I can't stay here and watch such goings-on!" he declared. He went to the door and flung it open dramatically. "Think what could have been yours, Miss Darling!"

Mr. Otto shook his head in disbelief as the door slammed shut. "Darling, any idea how much trouble you're going to be to me?"

She drew herself up to her full five feet two inches. "Mr. Otto, let us write a contract!"

Seven

$\mathcal{J}$t only took a half hour to create the contract.

Max handed her the page. "Do the honors and read it out loud, Julia."

She studied the page and cleared her throat. " 'Whereas it is already well-known in the County of Platte that Julia Amanda Darling (party of the first part, hereinafter referred to as Darling) is a real dilly . . .' Mr. Marlowe, *why* did you insist upon that?" she exclaimed in exasperation. The Marlowes chuckled; Mr. Otto did not. She continued. "Oh, never mind! '. . . and a bona fide graduate of Miss Fannie Farmer's School of Cookery, Boston, Class of 1909; that Paul . . .' " she squinted at the page, "Hixon . . .' " She put down the document. "Have we spelled that right, Mr. Otto? Should it be H-I-C-K-S-O-N?"

It was his turn to look uncomfortable. "Not sure," he mumbled.

"Your own name?" Max said with a grin.

"It's in the Bible at the ranch. I think it's H-I-X-O-N, Marlowe," he replied. "Keep going, Darling."

" ' . . . Paul Hixon Otto (party of the second part, hereinafter referred to as Mr. Otto) has engaged her services as cook and general housekeeper at the Double Tipi . . .' " She looked up. " 'General housekeeper'?" she asked. "Very well. I will allow that. '. . . and feels the necessity of protecting his investment . . .' "

His investment. I am chattel! Julia thought, chagrined.

She turned over the paper. " 'Whereas it is equally well-known that the population of the aforementioned Platte County, as well as Albany and Laramie counties, are seriously lacking in ladies, both parties do hereby agree to contract the following, to whit . . .' "

" 'To whit,' " Marlowe repeated. "Nice. Sounds like birds."

She frowned at Mr. Marlowe. " ' . . . to whit: that both parties agree by their signatures affixed to this document that Darling will continue her employment with Mr. Otto for the period of not less than twelve months without contracting any engagement of marriage, further explained as a period from September 15, 1909, to September 14, 1910 . . .' "

"Suppose before a whole year is up that you meet some Wyoming gent you just can't resist?" Marlowe asked.

"I most certainly will not," she answered firmly and kept reading. " ' . . . that there are no mitigating circumstances which will allow for this contract to be broken, excepting only death or terminal disease.' Mr. Otto, is that necessary?"

"It's what counties seriously lacking in ladies will understand, Darling," Mr. Otto said. He looked at the Marlowes. "I *know* these men! Besides, I might as well put all those rumors to good use, eh?"

With a glance at her employer, Julia hurried on. " 'That no stockman, surveyor, attorney, military man, or any man—employed or otherwise—will in any way seek to coerce, harass, importune, tempt, intimidate, or plead with Miss Darling to enter into a matrimonial agreement, on threat of painful ejection from the boundaries of the Double Tipi by the party of the second part. . .' " She frowned at her employer. " 'Painful ejection,' Mr. Otto?"

He shrugged. "Don't think I can't."

" ' . . . that the party of the first part will have the

option to renew this contract on September 15, 1910, if she so desires.' " *Pigs will fly first*, she thought. " 'Because this is Darling's choice alone, the party of the second part cannot exercise any franchise in the renewal of said contract without her express permission.' Any changes?" she asked, looking around.

No one could think of any. Max uncapped his fountain pen and handed it to her. "Sign if you want, Miss Darling."

"Oh, don't!"

Julia stopped, the pen suspended over the paper. Mrs. Marlowe put a hand on her shoulder, but she was looking at Mr. Otto. "I believe you should add something like this: 'Darling is entitled to do her work in a kitchen that meets cooking school standards.' "

"I protest!" Mr. Otto said, but his voice was good-humored. "I told my boys before I left the Double Tipi that I expected everything to be clean. They always do what I say." He put his hands on his hips. "Besides that, Alice, I don't believe you have ever even been to the Double Tipi, much less seen the kitchen."

"No, I haven't, have I?" she agreed, her voice as affable as his with just the slightest edge. "All the more reason for an addition, Julia. Agreed?"

"Certainly," Julia said.

"Quite all right with me," Mr. Otto acquiesced. "I haven't known my hands to ever disobey an order of mine." He laughed. "And while you're at it, add something about Darling here cooking what we want to eat."

"That's why you hired a cooking school graduate!" Julia protested. "Very well, if you must have the last word. Certainly you can add that, although it seems a trifle redundant."

She handed back the document, and Max added the

sentences. He passed it around, everyone nodded, and then he handed the document back to her. Julia signed her name and handed the pen to her employer. He stood up, looked over her shoulder, and read the document again. "Always read'um twice, Darling," he said before he signed the contract. "Especially treaties." He handed it to her, and Julia continued reading.

" 'This document is attested to by the following witnesses, Alice Victoria Marlowe and Maximilian Marlowe.' You sign here now," she told Mrs. Marlowe. "And then you."

Mrs. Marlowe seemed to be entertaining more second thoughts. "Are you certain this is a good idea?" she asked Julia, the pen poised over the paper.

"Alice, it will keep me out of your kitchen and alive for an entire year," Mr. Otto said, his impatience evident. "Didn't you think it was a good idea in the first place?"

"Very well," she replied, her voice equally pointed. "Although I don't think it *is* a good idea until Miss Darling sees your kitchen."

"I told you the boys were cleaning it up," Mr. Otto said. He set the document in front of Mr. Marlowe. "Sign, Marlowe."

They left a half hour later, after Julia showed Mrs. Marlowe how to make coffee with an egg. The men left the door open when they went outside to hitch up the team, and Julia watched her employer as he peered under the tarp again, picked up the bunch of bananas, and inspected each one. They were still far too green to eat, but he almost pulled one from the stalk anyway, until he saw her watching him.

"I can make him the most wonderful side dish with those," she said as she sat down and let Mrs. Marlowe twist up her hair and anchor it with her own hairpins. "It's called

Bananas Thorndyke and involves deep frying the entire peel."

"He might prefer them plain," Mrs. Marlowe said, with a note of caution that Julia could not overlook.

Then why on earth did he hire me? Julia asked herself. "Is the kitchen as frightful as Mr. McLemore seems to think it is?"

"Well, if he told the hands to clean it . . .," Mrs. Marlowe began, but seemed unable to complete the thought.

Julia leaned toward Alice Marlowe, keeping her eyes on Mr. Otto, who appeared to be thumbing through the Book of Mormon in the crate again. "Should I worry about Mr. Otto's other employees?" she asked.

"No," said Mrs. Marlowe quietly. "Paul will take very good care of his cook."

Julia was silent in her turn. She watched Mr. Otto put the book away and tap down the lid on the crate again. After another inspection of the bananas, he secured the tarp over her baggage. "I gather from something those men in Gun Barrel said . . . he had a wife?"

Mrs. Marlowe nodded. "It was before anyone else lived around here. His parents were already dead, I believe. But how do we know?" She hesitated.

"Please," Julia said. "I think I should know."

"She ran away, apparently, and then there was a rumor about a man being found dead in a ditch with a knife where it oughtn't to be," she said, her voice low as she watched Mr. Otto, too. "Of course, that was before our time."

"Is everything rumors?" Julia asked.

"I suppose it is." Mrs. Marlowe hugged her. "I'll bring you eggs and chickens, as I promised. It's about time I saw the Double Tipi. You'll be lonely."

I'm lonely right now, she thought after Mr. Otto helped

her into the wagon and spoke to his horses. She waved good-bye to the Marlowes, tried to think of some topic she had in common with her employer, and then resigned herself to more silence. She wanted to ask him about his employees, his kitchen (which was beginning to loom as large in her mind as yesterday's clouds), and the wealth of rumors at his expense, but she knew better. *I have been raised right*, she thought, *and what a pity*.

After a mile of steady climbing, when Julia thought his attention was focused on his team and she had resigned herself to a thorough study of her fingernails, Mr. Otto spoke. She jumped.

"You wouldn't consider marrying a Wyoming man?" he asked. "I'm just curious."

"Never," she said promptly but then amended, "unless he is a Mormon." Mr. Otto frowned, and she knew she had not expressed herself correctly. "Mormons marry Mormons in the temple."

It sounded so sensible right before she spoke, but when the words were out in the open, they almost smacked her with their arrogance. *I know he will ask me why*, she thought in panic made suddenly worse by the painful realization that she had no idea how she would answer him. *Oh, mercy, I either know too much or not enough. Don't, Mr. Otto*, she pleaded silently.

"Why?"

She sighed, knowing that saying, "Because they're supposed to," would be worse than no comment at all. In real dismay, she contemplated her own ignorance.

Mr. Otto glanced at her. "I'm sorry," he murmured. "I suppose your religion is none of my business." He turned his attention to the team again. "Please excuse me."

If there is a worse missionary in the entire church, I don't know who it is, she thought, horrified with herself. *I will keep my mouth shut if I cannot say anything intelligent.* To her mortification, she blurted out, "I only came to cook." She could have willed the earth to swallow her whole when Mr. Otto apologized again and said nothing more.

Papa would have had a good answer, she berated herself as they jolted along in silence so profound that her ears hummed. *What is the matter with me?* She didn't like to think about her shortcomings, so her relief was almost palpable when Charles McLemore came cantering toward them. Mr. Otto stopped his team.

"We signed a contract at the Marlowes," he said, resting his elbows casually on his knees, the reins dangling from his hands.

"Paul, I want to ask you something."

Julia couldn't see Mr. Otto's expression, but from the way the other rancher put up both hands, she knew it wasn't a pleasant sight.

"No, no! This has nothing to do with Miss Darling," he protested. He edged his horse closer. "When I was coming back from the Double Tipi earlier this morning, I noticed that the Rudigers were still on that claim."

"And?"

"The Rudigers aren't gone yet!"

"It appears not," Mr. Otto said as he sat up straight and gathered the reins.

"You wouldn't be feeding them or doing anything to encourage them to stay, now, would you?" McLemore asked.

"I want them gone as much as you do, McLemore."

"Is it going to take some persuasion?" McLemore asked, glancing at Julia.

"They can't survive another winter here," Mr. Otto

said patiently. "Now if you'll excuse us." He started the team again, and McLemore had no choice but to tug his horse back. "Maybe he's tough like we were, when we were his age," Mr. Otto called over his shoulder as McLemore coughed in the wagon's dust.

They continued in silence. Julia didn't expect him to say anything, and he didn't disappoint her. She turned her attention to the view around her and wondered all over again why she couldn't have just told him that Mormons marry in temples so they can live in an eternal family union. *He would only laugh,* she thought, *or give me one of those stares he so far is reserving for everyone else. And maybe it would sound silly when I said it.* She touched her jaw right under her ear, aware that they were climbing. *Maybe I need to know more myself.*

"If you swallow or yawn, you'll feel better," Mr. Otto said, after the quickest glance at her. "It levels out soon."

She nodded and swallowed. When her ears cleared, she heard the river that she could not see, running faster now, with more of a hum than a whisper, like the rustling of taffeta. The fragrance of cedar drenched the air and combined with the hot smell of the September sun on the tree's resin.

Mr. Otto made no comment as they passed a cultivated field of corn, too short for September and blasted almost sideways by the wind that hadn't stopped blowing since she left the train yesterday.

"You can't grow corn here," Mr. Otto said suddenly. "I told him, but I know he thinks I'm just trying to discourage him." He nodded toward the clearing. "Karl Rudiger."

She looked in the direction he indicated and saw a man standing at the far edge of the field, leaning on a hoe.

"Down closer to the Platte, the Pathfinder ditches are almost done. Another year, maybe two, a man could irrigate any crop there. Maybe even get three cuttings of hay."

"Why doesn't he move there?" she asked, her eyes on the distant figure.

"That land's already gone. He's too late." Mr. Otto sighed, and she thought of her father, who always called a sigh like that "owning the problem." "Maybe in Danzig or Hanover he got hold of an old railroad promotion handbill. Trouble was, he believed it. All Rudiger could buy was this spot, and he only got that because I was laid up with a broken leg and couldn't buy it out from under him when the original homesteader bailed out."

She frowned at his matter-of-fact, spare words, even as she marveled at such a flow of language from a man she knew already was reticent. "Why would you . . . ?" She stopped. It was too rude to ask.

"Why would I snatch some paltry acres from an immigrant with a wife and child?" He sighed again. "And another on the way, I think?"

"Well, yes, since you put it that way." They passed the claim shack, the boards scored and wind-blasted from too many blizzards, the tar paper peeling back to expose gaps. She shivered, thinking of winter. A woman stood in the doorway, shading her eyes with one hand, her other hand on a little girl's head. Julia scrutinized her. *Mama would say that she is in an interesting condition,* she thought.

The little girl waved vigorously until her curls bounced. To Julia's surprise, Mr. Otto waved back. He tipped his hat to the woman in the doorway, but she stepped back into the shadow.

"Ursula Rudiger and Danila, who is three," he said, when they were alone on the road again. "I don't think Ursula Rudiger trusts any ranchers. I wouldn't either."

"Are the Rudigers your nearest neighbors?" she asked.

"Not my neighbors," he insisted. "I want them gone, just like all the other ranchers want them gone. This is cattle country, and I own a big hunk of it. Except for Rudiger's spread. No one can make it on a homesteader's allotment, Darling. Do you know how many acres it takes to feed one cow?" He stabbed at the air for emphasis. "No? Congressmen don't either. Don't look at me like that! My father was the first man in this area. He bought and stole and got his hired hands to claim 640 acres each when the Desert Land Act was passed, and then they sold it to him. He left me a big spread, and I know how he did it, right down to the last clump of rabbit brush." He nodded in the direction of the Rudiger's. "That's the last of it. When I own it, I won't have to watch any more immigrants living on air and paper from the government. It turns my stomach."

Chilled to the bone, she thought about what Mr. McLemore had said. "I gather that the ranchers have vowed not to hire Mr. Rudiger for any extra work, so he'll starve out and quit?" She tried to keep her voice level, but it was difficult.

"It's a kindness, Darling. A kindness."

She sat numb with the idea of all that premeditated calculation. *Maybe I shouldn't have signed that contract*, she thought suddenly. She looked back at the claim shanty and sighed.

"I can't think of it as a kindness," she said.

He made no attempt to hide the bleakness in his eyes. "Spend a winter here. You'll understand more by spring."

She knew he would not say anything else, so she turned her attention to the land, happy enough not to think about the Rudigers.

Something about the land pleased her. She swallowed several more times to clear her ears and then yawned, even though it seemed so unladylike. A deep breath brought her the heady resin smell again and the earth itself, the odor of sand and leaves and rocks heating and cooling for millennia. Mingled with that was the slightest fragrance of bay rum and wood smoke from her employer. "Nice," she said out loud. Mr. Otto looked at her and smiled but made no comment. She noticed that he was still smiling when he turned his head to watch the team again.

"Mormons marry in the temple so they can be with their family members forever," she said quietly. "We believe in doing special work in the temple for our kindred dead so we can be united with those who have gone before." *So there,* she thought, and then swallowed. *Please don't make fun of me.* "If we're baptized, live right, and keep covenants, we can live forever with those we love." She was too afraid to look at her employer. "You weren't asking impertinent questions, Mr. Otto. I just get . . . shy about it."

He nodded. "Too many people say too much cruel stuff, like those yahoos in the restaurant?"

"I suppose," she agreed. *And maybe I don't know as much as I should, Mr. Otto,* she thought.

Her explanation must have satisfied him. He nodded to her and relaxed a little more, even though his posture was as dignified as ever. She listened for the river again and realized that it was farther away now; they were climbing again. The road leveled out and then rose slightly once more. She clutched the wagon seat when Mr. Otto suddenly pulled up the team and made a sharp turn to the north on a smaller road she had not noticed.

"I didn't even see that," she murmured in surprise.

"You're not the first to miss it."

As best as she could judge, they continued another quarter mile and then broke into a valley. Mr. Otto had straightened up even more and leaned forward with a look of anticipation on his face. She watched him with delight. He must have seen the place thousands of times, yet it still had the power to command all his attention.

The view before her made Julia pause and draw in her breath, too. The ranch buildings were to the north of the road, across the river, which now flowed in the distance, flanked by cottonwoods. She noticed the corrals, the horses in the meadow directly west of a tumbledown log shed, and the general air of disorderly order that she was familiar with from visits to her brothers, who ranched and taught school in southern Utah.

Mr. Otto edged forward in the wagon seat, his back even straighter. *I wonder what it would be like to have someone look at me like Mr. Otto looks at his ranch*, she thought as she contemplated him. *If Ezra ever had, I would be married by now.*

He stopped the wagon and pointed. "House. Outbuildings. A smokehouse and an icehouse. Milk keeps pretty well there until August." He pointed at what looked like a privy, newly built, to the west of the shed with the leaning lodge poles. "The gents thought you might like your own."

She laughed, more amused than embarrassed. "How kind."

"Corrals, barns, the usual."

She knew it wasn't the usual, not with all that pride in his voice. She looked behind her. "A person could ride right by on the road and not even know this was here," she marveled.

"That was the idea, Darling," he said as he started the team. "You're observant."

He occupied himself with the horses again, which had picked up speed as they came closer to the horse herd.

"That's the bunkhouse. Oh, criminy, they were supposed to haul away those cans." A veritable mountain of cans rose beside the bunkhouse. "It was our only defense against Little River," he said, apology evident in his voice. "Probably not time to move it now, before we bring down the cattle. We'll do it after."

She looked but could not tell which of the buildings was the house. Mr. Otto stopped the team in the middle of the horse herd with no other intention she could see than to admire his animals. He spoke to them in a language unfamiliar to her. To her delight, the horses started slowly toward the wagon.

"Do you ride, Darling?" Mr. Otto asked, reaching out to a buckskin, who whinnied and nosed his hand.

"Sometimes."

"We'll find one of these hay burners that won't give you fits. You'll probably want to visit Alice Marlowe now and then." He frowned and sighed, owning another problem that she was not about to question. "I think I still have a sidesaddle."

There was nothing to say to that artless admission. *I can change the subject*, she thought, *and what a perfect time to do so.* "Mr. Otto, I wish you would tell me something about your ranch hands," she said.

"Didn't I tell you about them?" he asked in surprise.

"No, sir."

He laughed. It was a quiet sound, but one of the horses by the wagon stepped around in a nervous circle. "I have only four right now," he said.

"For so much land?"

"All I need. My land is fenced now. The high country's still free range. We generally just ride fence. We ride to the high range in a week or two to bring down the steers. I'll hire more hands for that and then more for the spring roundup."

But not Mr. Rudiger, she thought.

"Malloy is my general all-around hand. He's from Ireland and usually says what he thinks. I suppose you could call Doc my foreman, although I've never dignified him with a title."

"He's a doctor?" she asked. "Is he the one who set Mr. Marlowe's leg?"

"And mine two years ago, when I thought I was still young enough to break horses. I leave that to Who Counts now."

"What?"

He gestured. "See those lodge poles leaning there?"

She looked where he pointed, mindful that Mr. Otto had not answered her question about Doc. *I will just have to learn what he considers prying and what is not*, she thought. "Lodge poles?" She looked more closely, noticing the thin poles that reached well above the roof.

"My cousin leaves 'em here when he's at Wind River. My cousin Dan Who Counts. He'll be here in a week. Likes his own place when he visits." Mr. Otto gave the reins a slight jiggle. "Let's see. Malloy, Doc . . . oh, Willy Bill, and Kringle. He's from Germany and doesn't say much, but he'll be your worst critic, if the food isn't just so. And . . ." He rose from the wagon seat, looked around, and then nodded toward the bunkhouse. "James, over there."

She couldn't have mistaken James, who was jumping up and down and waving both arms. "He's enthusiastic," she commented. "And he has a first name?" She looked closer. "He's so young!"

"Only has a first name, far as I know." He looked at her. "I suppose you want to know more."

"Of course I do!" she exclaimed.

He winced and then looked at the sky. "All I wanted was a cook. You're going to make me talk, aren't you?"

"That is the silli—" she burst out but then stopped. "Yes, I am, sir."

James had stopped waving now. He started ambling toward them in an awkward gait that reminded Julia of the Clawson's son in her Salt Lake ward. He had that same bright smile that made her smile back. *You're such a hard man, Mr. Otto*, she thought, *and here is this child.* She folded her hands in her lap and looked at her employee for explanation.

He stopped the wagon again, obviously wanting to talk before James arrived. "He wandered onto the place about three years ago. He was eight, as near as Doc could estimate."

"Heavens!" Julia looked at the boy as he came closer, in no hurry, and not afraid of the horses milling about. "Didn't he have—?"

"Parents?" Mr. Otto shrugged. "I don't know. No one ever claimed him, and we advertised. It was February. Doc didn't think his feet would ever heal."

A lump grew in Julia's throat so big that she thought her employer would see it if he were looking at her. He was looking at James, who had stopped to pat a horse. Mr. Otto was even smiling. *So you probably carried him everywhere and took care of his most basic needs, didn't you?* she thought. "What a lot of work for you," she managed finally.

"I suppose. He's a little vague at times, and the only song he knows is 'Sweet Evalina.'"

Julia laughed, remembering the old love song from her glee club days.

"It's the only song I know. Hello, James. Did you behave yourself while I was gone?"

The boy was standing by the wagon now. He held up his arms and Mr. Otto picked him up and sat James between his legs. The boy wiggled until he was comfortable and then leaned back against Mr. Otto.

"I was good," he said, holding onto the reins just behind Mr. Otto's hands. "Matt teased me, and I didn't cry."

"Good. Ranch hands don't cry. James, this is Julia Darling, my cook. You'll be hauling wood and water for her."

"And she'll make stuff we like to eat?" he asked Mr. Otto after the merest glance in her direction.

"What do you like, James?" she asked.

He frowned then. "I don't know, Mr. Darling," he admitted finally. "Mostly we eat out of cans. There's something else?"

I'm going to cry right here, Julia thought. "I . . . think so," she said.

"What would I like?" He asked Mr. Otto, tipping his head back to look at Julia's employer.

"Pie, maybe," Mr. Otto said.

"I can do much better than mere pie, James," she assured him. "Miss Farmer doesn't hold with pie too much."

"We'd settle for pie, Darling." Her employer stopped the wagon.

"Maybe you *would*, if you hadn't hired a graduate of Fannie Farmer's Cookery School," she said, pleased to be on safe ground again. The lump was smaller in her throat now. She leaned toward the boy. "It's Miss Darling, not Mr. Darling."

Mr. Otto spoke in a quiet voice. "I don't think he understands the difference, Darling. That's probably what he'll call you."

"Mr. Darling it is, then," she replied. She took her attention from James and looked around when Mr. Otto nudged her shoulder.

"My house."

He had stopped the team in front of the old building with the lodge poles leaning against it. "This is . . . it?" she asked.

No doubt about it; the house had looked much better from a distance, even picturesque. Julia swallowed and tried not to stare. She peered closer, unable to figure out what it was made of. She thought it was logs, but if it was, they had been smoothed and chewed on and burned in spots. Someone had tacked smashed cans onto the logs. National Biscuit Company boxes hammered up by the door overflowed with tools and shoes and all kinds of ranch detritus.

Dwarfing even Mr. Otto was another mound of cans beside the door. Only a few flies buzzed around now. She put her hand to her nose, not wanting to think how bad it must have smelled during the really hot days of summer. There appeared to be no other entrance. Words failed her completely as she stared at the place where she was to work for the next year. *That's 365 days*, she thought, suppressing a groan. Fifty-two weeks.

Her eyes still on the ranch house, she let Mr. Otto help her from the wagon seat. She knew he was watching her, but she could think of nothing to say.

Julia let Mr. Otto lead her to the door. She stared at the mountain of cans and then shrieked at a scrabbling noise from somewhere in the depths of all those tins and moldy food.

James whooped. "Rats, Mr. Otto! You said they were gone!"

Her employer picked her up and carried her through the doorway. The window was so fly-spattered that most of the light came from the open door. She stood still in the middle of the room where Mr. Otto deposited her.

"Sit down, Darling."

She glanced where her employer pointed to a chair draped with a hide and shook her head. "I'll just stand here," she told him.

Julia stared at the kitchen, at the mound of clothes piled in one corner; at an entire wall full of calendars with women her father would have charitably called "interesting"; at the table that looked an inch thick in grease; and at the sink piled high with crockery. She took a step, crunched something underfoot, and vowed that she would never move again. Bloody ropes dangled from the rafter overhead. Her breath started to come in gasps.

Her employer yanked down the ropes. "It's a handy spot to leave them during calving season," he muttered. "Guess we forgot to take them down." He had the grace to be silent as he tossed them toward the piles of clothes. Something else rustled under the pile. Julia shuddered and pulled her dress tight around her ankles.

"I . . . thought . . . didn't you tell Mrs. Marlowe that your hands cleaned up the kitchen?" she asked at last, but it didn't sound like her voice.

"They did!" he assured her. "Welcome to the Double Tipi. There's the range. What's for dinner?"

Eight

Julia cried then, wailing like a child in front of her startled employer, unable to stop herself. Mr. Otto whipped a frayed handkerchief out of his pocket and pressed it into her palm as her lips trembled and her hand shook.

Someone else came into the kitchen. Humiliated, Julia turned away and sobbed into the handkerchief. Whoever it was backed out the door. In another moment, she had the kitchen all to herself; even the scrabbling under the pile of clothes ceased. With the instinct that men—and mice?—possess, Mr. Otto and James chose discretion over valor.

Not one of the chairs was clean enough to sit on, so she stood in the middle of the kitchen, her skirt still tight against her ankles, and wailed into her employer's handkerchief. She could not recall a bout of weeping as profound as this one, interspersed with pity for herself, followed by so much anger at Mr. Otto that she even found herself looking around for a knife block.

She cried until her eyes burned. The only thing that eventually stopped her tears was the realization that her throat was as dry as alum. She made herself sit in a hide-backed chair, waiting for bugs to march over her in ranks. Nothing happened. "I have even frightened off the vermin," she muttered.

The men had certainly disappeared. Julia felt another wave of embarrassment crash against her. *Julia Darling, even if you wouldn't keep a goat here, this is Mr. Otto's home, and you have frightened him away from it!* she scolded herself.

When she took a moment to think through her emotions, she had to admit only a fool would suppose that single men would keep an orderly kitchen. *There are four or five busy men on this place*, she thought as she looked around, *and no woman to insist on cleanliness.*

She looked around the room, taking in the dust-covered icebox and the range. The range. Her eyes widened. "It can't be," she said, scarcely breathing. "Not here. I'm dreaming."

Julia got to her feet, moving slowly as though she did not wish to startle the object of her sudden interest. *Was I so agitated when I came in here that I overlooked this?* she asked herself in amazement. Keeping her dress tight around her, she squatted decorously in front of the massive cookstove. The afternoon light was going quickly, but she ran her finger over the raised letters on the oven door.

"The Queen Atlantic," she whispered reverently. She stood up, admiring the beautiful lines of the range and thinking of the visit that the plain cooking class had made to the Portland Stove Showroom on Union Street. Miss Farmer had extolled the Queen's virtues right down to the keep-ash pit. "This is the last word in kitchen ranges," Miss Farmer had pronounced. "I doubt we shall ever see a finer one."

The gloss was long since gone from the Queen's surface. One claw foot curled under itself like a deformity with a block of wood to level the range. Julia tried to lift one of the stove lids, but it was anchored shut by a rim of grease, which had solidified and turned to concrete. She peeked in the water reservoir, but there was only a handful of bones. She shuddered and dropped the lid.

The warming oven contained the mummified remains of what might have been a loaf of bread. Someone had stuck a jar of grape jelly next to it. Greasy streaks formed a deckle around the splashboard and matched the solid fat covering the range. She wondered if someone had just cooked on the stove top, without benefit of pans.

Julia walked to the side of the range. Leaning over, she tapped on the stovepipe, listening for the echo found on a healthy specimen. "Your Majesty, that stuffy sound tells me you have far exceeded the Wyoming state creosote limit," she announced, on sure footing now. "One good blaze in the firebox, and you would burn down this wonderful house. Oh, I am tempted."

Could it be that this range has never been cleaned? she asked herself. She pried the knife from the jelly jar, ran the blade around a stove lid until she could lift it, and peered inside. "My stars!" she exclaimed, staring at ashes that were level with the stove hole. She replaced the stove lid slowly, careful not to stir up ashes.

She peeked in the oven instead and coughed. *No one has ever cleaned this range,* she thought. She backed away from the range as the enormity of the work before her became amply clear.

It was a daunting thought, and one best not contemplated for too long on an empty stomach, she decided. She turned around, wishing the problem away. She opened the door next to the stove, into a small room that must be hers. She saw a bed frame with a fairly new mattress, a limp curtain on a string pulled back to reveal a row of clothes pegs next to a bureau with a drawer missing, and a washstand. "Home, sweet home," she murmured and shut the door. "I don't know how I shall bear to part with all this in a year and return to Salt Lake."

She opened the other door off the kitchen, which turned out to be the pantry. Julia sucked in her breath at the sound of scurrying feet and closed it quickly, but not before seeing kegs and barrels and smelling the pungent aroma of dried fish and mouse nests.

She opened the outside door and took a deep breath. There was no one in sight; the men must be hiding. No matter. The sun was going down in a flame of red and gold. Hand on the latch—there wasn't even a doorknob— she stood still and watched the sun set behind the tin can mound that distinguished the bunkhouse from the other nondescript outbuildings. The air was redolent with the fragrance of wood smoke: Mr. Otto's odor minus the bay rum.

Julia remembered where she stood and hurried away from the step beside the house's tower of cans. It was still light enough to read some of the labels. Probably the rest had been chewed off by glue-eating rats. Peaches and pears seemed to be the favorites in the ranch house, plus green beans and bully beef. She wondered if her employer had been eating his meals cold from the cans and surprised herself by feeling sorry for him. The moment passed.

She sniffed the air and salivated at the smell of meat cooking. She started toward the bunkhouse and then stopped, wondering at her effrontery. Her resolution wavered and then strengthened again. *I will not return to that . . . that shack with all those resident rodents*, she told herself. *At least, not alone.*

The setting sun skimmed the mountains and then seemed to steel itself for the descent. Night was coming, and Julia debated her options. She took a deep breath and crossed the yard, with its dirt packed solid by years of feet, horses, and wagons. She looked back at the ranch house, thinking how it cried out for a row or two of zinnias to disguise its worst deficiencies. Really tall zinnias.

She stopped, realizing that it would never do to go

inside without a plan. She thought of Miss Farmer, sitting at her desk and advising her soon-to-graduate students on the importance of confidence in the kitchen. " 'You are in charge,' " Julia remembered, and spoke the words softly. " 'Always have a plan, and remember that cooking in someone else's kitchen is only a business.' "

She thought it through, shivering a little as the sun dipped lower and the valley was cloaked in early darkness. "I will not cry," she reminded herself. "This is a business. I doubt Mr. Otto cries for his cattle buyers when prices are low."

The idea of Mr. Otto prostrated by tears was so ludicrous that she laughed, covering her mouth with her hand so no one in the bunkhouse would hear. She smiled to imagine her father at his desk in the bank, weeping when interest rates plummeted.

She took another deep breath and knocked on the bunkhouse door. *Now let us see what a diplomatist I am.*

A man scarcely taller than she was opened the door and greeted her with a smile that displayed much enthusiasm but few teeth. He nodded and bowed. "Willy Bill, ma'am," he said.

Touched in spite of her shyness, Julia held out her hand. "Mr. Bill, I am pleased to meet you."

The man stared at her hand as though she had disconnected it from her wrist. James laughed from across the room when Willy Bill wiped his own hand on a vest no cleaner than the stove top. "I've never shook a lady's hand before," he temporized.

"I've never been in a bunkhouse, sir," she said. "I suppose there is a first time for everything."

Willy Bill blushed beet red and looked over his shoulder. "Mr. Otto, she's got a hand like little bird bones! If I press too hard, will I break it?"

"I know, Bill," her employer replied, and got up off the table where he was perched. "But Darling appears to be made of sterner stuff. She's still here, isn't she? Have a seat, Darling?"

I won't look before I sit. It's rude, she thought, as she sat on the Nabisco box he offered. "Thank you, Mr. Otto," she said with what she hoped passed for serenity. "Here it is: I am not of stern enough stuff to manage your kitchen in its present state."

That's enough, Julia, she advised herself as she waited for him to speak. *I will not say another word until my employer says something.* She held her hands tight together, so they would not shake. *Key West will freeze before I speak again. The Tower of Pisa will stop leaning.*

Mr. Otto was in no hurry to speak. She thought for a moment that he was going to wait her out, but a glance into his eyes indicated some concern. *Either that or his stomach aches,* she told herself. Julia looked at the table where she sat, noticing all the tin cans. *I think it is the latter.*

"Do you mean you won't stay?"

Something in the way he asked the question and some instinct of her own told her that she could leave, if she chose, despite the silly contract they had both signed. Maybe it was the tight way he held his lips; she couldn't help but think of her sister Iris as a child, when she expected some disappointment.

Whatever the expression meant, she gave her own interpretation. "Of course I will stay," she replied quietly. "I signed a contract. Tomorrow morning you and your hands must move away every can beside the door of your house."

Mr. Otto shook his head. "Can't. We have to stretch some fence in that west pasture right away before we—"

"No, Mr. Otto," she interrupted, speaking no louder

than before and drawing herself up to her full height. "When the cans are gone, and that . . . that pile of clothing is out in the yard, then you can tidy your fence and fetch your cattle."

The redhead with the accent—it had to be Malloy—started to laugh but then clamped his hand over his mouth and turned away, his shoulders shaking. Willy Bill coughed until Julia wondered if she should thump him on the back. She hoped he would recover on his own; the idea of touching his greasy vest was almost more unpalatable than staring down Mr. Otto.

"And you will also find me a mouser," she continued steadily.

"No cats."

"A cat, Mr. Otto," she repeated, wondering where all this courage was coming from. "One with long ears. Mama says they make the best mousers."

Mr. Otto glared back at her, and no one moved in the small room.

Willy Bill had stopped coughing. Without taking her eyes from her employer, she spoke to him. "Mr. Bill, is there rat poison in the barn?"

"Mebbe."

"I want it in the pantry tonight. You can sweep out the carcasses in the morning."

"All them little corpses? That's women's work," he protested.

"Do it," Mr. Otto said abruptly.

"Yessir."

Thank you, Heavenly Father, Julia prayed silently. *I didn't think I could stare at him one more moment.* "The cans and the clothes?" she asked.

"Tomorrow morning."

She couldn't tell if he was angry, but she thought he must be. "The cat?" she pressed.

"No promises." He nodded to her then, and she knew she was dismissed. "Don't let us keep you up, Darling."

I'm not high on your list right now, she thought. She noticed James, who had been watching the whole exchange from the warmth and safety of a stool by the stove. She held out her hand to him. "It's too late for you to be up, James," she said. "Come along with me."

James looked at Mr. Otto, as she knew he would. To her relief, her employer nodded to him, then sat down and was soon in quiet conversation again with the men still seated at the table. She had no reason to remain there; she was being ignored. Her footsteps seemed loud as she crossed the room and let herself out the door, James clutching her hand.

He was silent until they were almost at the ranch house. "Mr. Darling, you shouldn't speak to Mr. Otto like that," he said.

"I know I shouldn't," she agreed and then sighed. "James, it's not healthy to live in the middle of vermin. People get diseases."

James shook his head. "Not here, Mr. Darling. No one ever gets sick."

Of course you don't, she thought in irritation. *Living at the Double Tipi has probably made you immune to all diseases.* "I'm a silly one, James, but I get nervous when mice run over my feet while I'm cooking." James stared at her in amazement. "I told you it was silly," she couldn't help adding.

Whatever dwelled in the can mountain must have gone to sleep, because nothing stirred as they walked inside. She froze when a mouse on the table leaped onto the clothes pile and disappeared within, but she said nothing.

She was pleasantly surprised when James went to the washstand just inside the door and washed his face and hands. His ablutions were too brief to even be called perfunctory, but the effort counted in her eyes. There was no towel on the rack, so he shook himself dry like a dog.

"We'll have hot water tomorrow," she assured him.

"What for?" he asked, with a final shake.

"For your face and hands," she answered. "Don't you . . . ?"

"No, Mr. Darling," he replied, "but it does sound like a nice idea." He shivered. "Will I like it?"

Again there was that lump that wouldn't go down in her throat, the same one that had bothered her when she thought of Mr. Otto eating canned peaches day after dreary day. "You'll love it," she assured him. "Show me where your room is."

James yawned and then indicated a candle high on a cracker box shelf. On tiptoe, she reached into the shelf, praying that nothing would leap out and complicate her life. In a moment she found a matchbox next to the candle, extracted one match, and lit the candle. James took it from her and started toward the arched doorway. Each room connected to the next without doors.

It was her turn to hold his hand and follow him. They walked into a room with shadows so deep she could not see far beyond the candle flame. There appeared to be a chair or two, and possibly several saddles. The smell of leather predominated.

"Is that the parlor?" she asked, whispering for no reason other than that the place was so silent.

"I don't know what a parlor is," he said.

"Where people sit in the evenings, listen to a Victrola, read the paper, and talk," she replied, surprising herself with a sudden longing for Mama's warm parlor. The only carpet here seemed to be a buffalo robe that almost tripped her.

James walked with the sure step of someone who knew the location of every obstacle. "Mostly Mr. Otto just sits at the table in the kitchen," he told her. "He reads sometimes, and then he falls asleep there."

The room led into the next one, which belonged to James. There was no door on the room beyond, but she assumed it belonged to Mr. Otto. The wood on the walls was better milled than the kitchen, with its shabby log walls. Mr. Otto or his father must have added on rooms when the need arose.

James lit a kerosene lamp beside his bed with the candle, and blew out the smaller flame. Carefully he leaned the candle against the base of the lamp, watching it to make sure that the wax did not drip. "Mr. Otto says I am to be careful with fire," he explained as she watched him.

"You are quite careful," she agreed. "I'll tell him how well you did that." *If he ever speaks to me again*, she thought.

The better light of the kerosene lamp revealed walls covered with newspapers and posters from Buffalo Bill Cody's frontier shows. On one poster Annie Oakley, "Little Miss Sure Shot," aimed over her shoulder through a mirror to hit a target, while elderly Indians in feathered bonnets chased a stagecoach in another. Several fliers of wanted men decorated another wall, and a calendar, the picture torn off, graced a spot where the newsprint wallpaper was peeling. She was prepared to disapprove, but as Julia looked around while James removed his trousers, she knew any boy would like a room like this one.

When she looked back, James was sitting up in bed, watching her expectantly. She was pleased to see that the bed had sheets and several blankets. She smiled back at him.

"Do you say a bedtime prayer?" she asked.

He shook his head. "Mr. Otto always reads to me," he said, and pointed to a magazine on the cracker box that served as a bureau.

She picked up the magazine, pleased to see that James' socks and underdrawers were folded neatly in the cracker box. And it was a book, not a magazine, but in tatters and brittle, with the covers torn off and threads dangling to indicate a section of the volume missing. "Goodness," she said as she carefully turned to a page where a simple strand of beads with a feather tied to the end marked a place. "I will have to be careful, won't I?" she asked.

James nodded and lay down. Julia perched on the bed and began to read. The story was unfamiliar to her, a tale of Cavaliers and Roundheads and fleeing into exile with Charles II. The story was old-fashioned, quaint even. The pages ended before the story did, so she looked at James, wondering what to do. His eyes were half shut, so she gently closed the book. *It's a wonder what turns up on a place like this*, she thought, remembering Grandmama's tales about traveling in a wagon train to Deseret and finding books, picture frames, and high chairs jettisoned beside the road when the trail grew steep. She thought that the Double Tipi must straddle some portion of the old trail; maybe that was where the book had come from.

"I just make up an ending each time. That's what my father always did for me."

Julia looked over her shoulder at Mr. Otto, who was leaning against the frame where the door would go, if there had been a door. "Something with more pages would be nice for him."

"I tried that, but for some reason, he likes that half story." Mr. Otto shrugged and straightened up. "He's been here three years, but I still don't understand how James's mind works."

You're probably wondering how mine works too, Julia thought in sudden contrition. "Mr. Otto, I'm sorry I spoke to you like that in front of your men," she whispered. "I was rude."

"You were, but you were right," he said and motioned to her to follow him.

She followed Mr. Otto back to the kitchen, squaring her shoulders for the scold she probably deserved, no matter how much the kitchen had distressed her. She should never have embarrassed him in front of his men.

He seemed in no hurry to reprimand her but stood in the kitchen much as she had earlier, looking it over. He cleared his throat and looked at her over his shoulder. She steeled herself for his rebuke.

"Actually, Darling, they did clean it up. You should have seen it before."

She laughed, relieved that he wasn't angry and also amused by his droll delivery. "No wonder Mrs. Marlowe insisted on adding to the contract," she said. "She must have suspected something."

"She hasn't been here," he protested, but there was humor in his voice now. "I suppose she knows ranchers . . . maybe just men . . . better than you do, Darling."

He looked around some more. "Willy Bill will sprinkle rat poison around the storeroom," he said, gesturing toward the pantry. "I have some mouse traps we can bait and put here and in your room, if you wish."

"That's a good idea."

"If I promise James a nickel apiece for each mouse or rat he disposes of, he'll keep you safe from predators." Her employer chuckled. "And probably break my bank account.

Darling, I'm sorry it's a mess."

"I'm sorry I made such a fuss," she said in turn.

"So we don't need a cat?" he asked, hopeful.

"We need a cat," she repeated.

He made no comment but opened the door when someone kicked it. He stood back while the Irishman and Doc carried in her trunk, with the valise perched on top. "In there, boys," he said, indicating the door to Julia's room. "Darling, this is Matt Malloy, and this is Doc. I forgot my manners in the bunkhouse."

She smiled to the men as they passed her, carrying the trunk, and took the valise off the top. "Rocks in here?" the Irishman gasped as Doc tipped the trunk to get it through the doorway.

"Cookery books," she replied.

Malloy flashed her a wonderful smile. "In that case, m'dear, we'll carry it twice farther, if you wish."

You're charming, she thought as she watched them. *You're just like every other Irishman who whistled and rolled his eyes when I took the trolley to South Boston or Roxbury last year.*

The men left, leaving Julia amused at the glare Mr. Otto fixed on Matt. "Please don't worry about Mr. Malloy," she said, trying not to smile. "I have utter confidence in my ability to resist him. And now, sir, good night."

He stood up then and followed her to the door of her room. "Little River slept on the floor, so the mattress was hardly ever used. It'll do."

She opened her trunk and removed a set of sheets. "I think I will be fine now, Mr. Otto," she hinted, but he wasn't paying her attention. While she watched, the sheets in her arms, he picked up the pillow and frowned.

"I have a better one in my room," he said, starting for the door. "And blankets too."

"But I can't take your . . ." she called after him, but he was gone. "If you insist," she murmured under her breath as she made the bed. "I wonder how much of this year I will ever dare tell Mama."

She was smoothing down the top sheet when her employer returned with an armload of army blankets and a pillow. He set them on the room's one chair and pulled out a blanket, spreading it over the bed. "You'll want at least two now, I think. The nights are pretty cool. I'd leave the rest for winter." He held out the pillow. "I don't use this one on my bed anymore."

She took it from him. *I can't imagine why your wife fled the charms of the Double Tipi*, she thought. He seemed determined to make sure she was warm enough.

"We got two lots of blankets at auction when Fort Laramie closed twenty years ago. Is that lace?" He was fingering the row of crocheting around her top sheet.

"Crocheted lace. Mama insisted that I learn," she said, shy again. "I was sixteen. I crocheted everything in our house with a plain surface. It got so Papa wouldn't bring home his ledgers from the bank."

It was a lame joke, but he grinned and pulled on another blanket, tucking it under the mattress. "When I was sixteen, my Pa had been dead a year, and I was running this place. We'll be up early to move those cans because we still have to check the fence. Stuff some rags under the door at the bottom so the mice don't just run back in here. Good night."

"Good night to you," she said after she heard him going down the hall to his own room. She tucked the pillow under her chin and reached for her pillow slip, unable to overlook the slight fragrance of bay rum.

She put the pillow at the head of her bed and rested her hand on it. An extra pillow, breakfast and dinner from cans, and a beautiful cooking range ruined by ill use—Iris, an inveterate romantic, would deduce that Mr. Otto had endured a difficult time. *I will be a good cook, Mr. Otto*, she promised. *If you cannot be happy, at least you can be well-fed.*

Nine

Julia was closing her eyes when she heard the coyotes howl. The sound had never bothered her, and she would have slept then, except that James began to cry. Julia sat up in bed. It was more than tears; it was a lament that raised the hair on her neck. She thought of what Mr. Otto had said about James just showing up at the ranch during a cold February.

Julia threw back the covers, got out of bed, and opened the door a crack. She heard the faint rustle of another mattress and quiet footsteps, and then James became quiet. There was the murmur of voices, and in another minute Mr. Otto was humming "Sweet Evalina." The tune was faint and delivered in a good baritone at lullaby tempo. Julia leaned her head against the door, her eyes drooping, as though he hummed to her: ". . . the child of the valley, the girl that I love. Dear Evalina, sweet Evalina, my love for thee will never, never die."

The rotten curtain fabric allowed in plenty of moonlight, so she padded to her trunk, opened it, and found her scriptures. She left the Bible there but felt the familiar slimness of her copy of the Book of Mormon. It was just the right size to rest her head on and block the fragrance of bay rum.

Morning came gently, the sky light, the air cool. *Papa would call that the advantage of altitude*, she thought, as she lay on her back with her hands under her head. The ceiling was covered with newspapers of fairly recent origin, as though an attempt had been made to fix the room a little before her arrival. As the room lightened, she reacquainted herself with the news of the world and wondered where the year had gone.

She was about to burrow back under the covers when she heard her employer's firm steps in the kitchen. Her eyes barely open, Julia listened to the familiar sounds of a damper sliding and the stove handle being inserted into a stove lid. Mr. Otto set down the lid with a clatter, swearing with some fluency at the racket he caused. *I suppose he is going to make further amends by lighting the stove for me,* she thought.

Julia gasped and threw back the covers in one motion, looking about for her robe. "No, no, no," she muttered when she heard him crumple newspaper and then strike a match on the range. "Don't!" she yelled, as she tugged down her nightgown and opened the door at the same time.

The newspaper tucked under his arm, Mr. Otto lit the lamp with the match in his hand. "What on earth . . ." he started but then held up his hand to stop her. "Don't take another—"

Julia shrieked as a mousetrap reached out and bit her heel. She stood on one bare foot as tears welled up in her eyes from the sudden pain.

"—step," Mr. Otto concluded in a normal tone of voice.

Before she could object, he pushed her into the nearest chair, pressed her foot against his thigh, and removed the mousetrap. Almost faint with relief, she gingerly crossed her leg and looked at her heel, where the indentation was still white. "I was afraid you were going to light the range," she said, too embarrassed to look at him.

"I wouldn't dare light that range," he said as he sat down

next to her and looked at her heel. "I got the message last night." He touched her heel and she winced. "Hurt?"

"Not much," she admitted. "Mostly it's just my pride." She looked at him. "Mr. Otto, I don't usually hurl myself into rooms barefooted, but I heard you lift that stove lid!"

"Just to look at the damage inside," he explained, releasing her foot. "I had no idea there was so much . . ." He stopped suddenly and stared at the ceiling. "Excuse me, Darling, but watching you throw yourself into the kitchen and step on the mousetrap was the funniest . . ."

He was gone then, carried off by a gust of helpless laughter that rendered him almost boneless as he leaned back in the chair. He tried to stop one or two times but gave up the attempt, laughing until he had to press his hand against his side.

I suppose I deserve that, Julia thought as she watched him. *I must look like a wild woman.*

Mr. Otto stopped laughing and dabbed at his eyes. Suddenly quite mindful that her oldest flannel nightgown was also her thinnest one, Julia stood up and prepared to retreat with whatever remained of her dignity. "I'm sorry I haven't yet been able to put my best foot forward at—"

"Oh, stop!" he said in a weak voice and started to laugh again.

Julia was too humiliated to look at her employer. She went into her room and quietly closed the door, wondering why she had ever answered the ad. She sat on the bed, reminding herself that she came to cook, suddenly aware that she had no idea where to begin. And now her boss was laughing at her.

She sniffed back the tears. *He laughs at me*, she thought, *and I can't even blame him.* She glanced at her Book of Mormon lying on her pillow and touched the leather covering. Mama always knew where to look for answers when suffering life's crises.

"I'm so sorry things are a muddle," she whispered out loud, not sure if she was apologizing to Heavenly Father or Mr. Otto. "I have stepped off a bank into water far too deep for my puny talents, and I have no one to blame but myself."

Nothing she said was calculated to make her feel better, but she did somehow. After another moment spent thinking about Mama, Julia lifted layer after layer of cooking books and clothing from her trunk. Her very oldest dress lay in the bottom; she had almost not packed the thing until Mama insisted.

She decided against a corset because she didn't want to ruin it with soot and ashes that day. She was tucking her camisole into her petticoat when Mr. Otto knocked on her door. She knew it was her employer; everything about him was deliberate, and so was the knock. Well, not everything, she qualified, as she quickly pulled her dress over her head. He had a certain spontaneity when he encountered a good joke at someone else's expense.

"Not now, Mr. Otto," she said. "I will be out in a moment." She touched her bosom, hoping that the camisole was sufficient. *Doesn't matter*, she thought as he knocked again. *I have a whacking big apron somewhere, and I won't leave this room until I find it.*

"I just wanted to apologize," Mr. Otto said from the other side of the door.

She stopped where she was, bent over the trunk. She had to be hearing things. She should be apologizing to him, but she had been apologizing to him for two days now, and it was getting wearisome. She found the apron and cinched it tight around her waist, enjoying the feeling of at least being in control of her figure, if nothing else. He knocked again. She took the cord that bound her braid, picked up her brush, and opened the door.

"Mr. Otto, you needn't apologize for anything," she said, wishing that she had inherited some of Mama's serenity. She yanked the brush through her hair. "You've been kind to tolerate me thus far, and if I provide some small amusement, perhaps that is something."

She hadn't meant to sound so wounded. Mama would have made that observation sound matter-of-fact. Julia knew that she richly deserved whatever he chose to dish out. "I am only stating a fact, Mr. Otto," she added, surprised by the startled expression in his eyes. "I did not say that to churn up your sympathy."

"I . . . well . . ."

"You have a business to run, sir," she pointed out when he still just stood there. She noticed for the first time that he was barefoot, and he had not combed his hair. *I wonder how often he must get up each night to see to James?* she thought with sudden sympathy of her own. "I intend to clean the range, Mr. Otto, and the storage room. I cannot suppose that any of this will be done before you have to leave for . . . where was it?"

"The summer pasture," he filled in. She could almost feel the relief in his voice to have something to talk about that was more in line with his usual communication, she was certain. "Time to bring 'em down, separate them, and send the lucky lads to Chicago. You have a huge task, Darling, and I wish I could help."

He can't mean that, she thought, returning to her room to pocket the hairpins from the floor by the bed. She brushed past him and went into the kitchen again, pulling down the least scurrilous calendar. She plunked the hairpins on the calendar to keep them from sticking to the table, wound her hair onto the back of her head in a smooth roll, and secured it with the pins. "You're kind to offer, Mr. Otto, but you did not take me on to do my work for me," she assured him. "When you return, I will have a meal for you that you will never forget, cooked on that marvelous range, which I fully intend to raise from the dead."

Look him in the eyes now, Julia, she ordered herself, *so he will know you mean it. If you can't be mature, you can at least be sincere.* "That is what you are paying me for, Mr. Otto," she concluded.

"Yes, I am," he said finally, as though she had reminded him. He turned to take more calendars off the wall. "I was afraid you would leave."

"I won't," she told him, less sure of herself than before and feeling like a hypocrite as she thought of Ezra's sorrow when she abandoned their engagement. "After all, sir, we have a contract, don't we? I'm bound to stay for a year."

He said nothing, only removed another calendar and another. "May I wake James, sir?" she asked, when he did not speak. "I brought eggs from the Marlowes, and if you will locate the Arbuckles Coffee from the wagon . . ."

Mr. Otto pointed to the storeroom, but she didn't give him a chance to speak.

"I will *not* go in that storeroom until every mouse is dead beyond resuscitation, Mr. Otto! I will make coffee and fix you breakfast in the bunkhouse. It won't be quite to my usual standards, but I will do my best."

As she swept past him and down to James's room, Julia knew Mr. Otto was regretting he had ever written that ad. She made the mistake of looking back at him and was rewarded with a slow shake of his head and a curious half smile. As she hurried into James's room and bent down to touch him, she wondered if she was less than Mr. Otto had bargained for—or more.

Breakfast went surprisingly well, despite the fact that she yearned to show off her talents with petijohns with sugar and cream, fried smelts and baked sweet potatoes, or cecils, her father's favorite. *This is ghastly and ordinary, and Mr. Otto will wonder why he is paying me $60 a month*, she grumbled to herself as she poked the ham around in the cast iron frying pan.

The bunkhouse cookstove had only two stove lids, but she managed, putting the coffeepot on the farther burner to do its work. Matt Malloy was watching her from his perch on the table. To her amusement, he didn't even flinch when she added the egg and shells to the coffee. He did take mighty exception to the process when she stuffed a handkerchief—her last clean one—into the spout.

"Hold on now, Julia Darling," he said. "You're taking away the one pleasure I've had in months!"

"Mr. Malloy, let me do it my way," she said.

"I agree," Mr. Otto said. "It's safest that way." He reached for the plates in one of the everlasting wooden crates that someone had nailed to the bunkhouse wall. "Malloy, these plates are filthy!"

The men laughed. "It's all the flannel cakes and hash browns you've been cooking for us, boss," Doc said, and held out his hand for the plates. He winked at Julia. "They don't even come off the plates anymore. We just set 'em on the shelf as is and wait for another meal."

I will not rise to the bait, she told herself. She cracked the eggs expertly into the hot grease and stifled laughter when a chorus of "Ahhs" rose around her.

James came closer. "You didn't mess up one of those yolks," he said, his eyes wide with the wonder of it all.

"I wouldn't dare," she told him. "Miss Farmer would flunk me." She surprised herself by kissing the top of his head, which smelled of nothing worse than boy sweat and wood smoke. James smiled and tucked his hand into the waistband of her apron in a proprietary gesture.

She added more eggs. "James, take these pot holders and put the ham on the table," she ordered, turning over the eggs, which to her relief cooperated like good soldiers with not a rip or a crack of the yolks. "Gentlemen, do stand back from James. I fear you are making him nervous."

Mr. Otto found a can opener in the depths of a mound of dirty dishes and opened a tin of pilot bread. He stood staring at the ham on the table until she wanted to laugh. The eggs slid nicely onto a plate, and she set it on the table. With almost one motion, the men sat on the benches.

"We don't have any napkins," she said, returning to the stove to crack in more eggs. No one seemed to hear, so intent were they on the eggs and ham. She could have sworn the Irishman had tears in his eyes when she unstopped the coffee and circled the table, pouring the brew into each tin cup. In a moment, all was silent, except for the chuckle of eggs in the frying pan.

"I wanted it to be something special," she apologized, but stopped when she realized that no one was paying her any attention. Julia shook her head, turning back to the eggs.

She poked the eggs into orderly rows and then looked around the room, pleased that someone had removed the more outrageous pictures from the walls. There had been an attempt to make one of the bunks, and clothes that were strewn everywhere last night were in a pile that came all the way up to the room's one window. She smiled to see a daisy drooping in the narrow neck of a liniment bottle.

The men went through the fried eggs with barely a pause. Doc had even hooked his arm around his plate in a protective gesture. He noticed her watching him. "No sudden moves, Julia," he warned her and grinned when she laughed.

No cook ever had a more appreciative clientele, she told herself as she went around again with the coffee. "I wish it were better, Mr. Otto," she said as she filled his cup.

"Don't ever do a thing different," he told her quickly.

"You can't be serious," she replied. "I have not even begun to provide an adequate breakfast."

"No, I mean it," he said. He looked around the table. "Well, boys, start on those cans." He grabbed James as he started outside with the others. "You have a special task."

James made a face and appealed to Julia. "When he says that, I never have much fun."

"I do not think cans will be much fun, either," Julia replied. "Not unless you enjoy mice."

"That is the whole point, Darling," Mr. Otto said. He knelt beside James. "I will pay you five cents each for every mouse you kill. Today and every day until we return with the herd."

James made no attempt to hide his disappointment. With a quiet dignity that made Julia's heart soften, Mr. Otto took the boy on his lap. "James, I mean for you to stay with Darling this time. I'll take you on the spring round-up."

James was silent. "She needs your help," Mr. Otto cajoled. He set James on the bench. "I would stay if I could, but someone has to keep Malloy, Doc, Willy Boy, and Kringle in line." Mr. Otto looked at her. "There's a lot Darling doesn't know about this place, and she could use your help."

"I really could, James," Julia said, sitting on his other side. "If you aren't there to dispose of all those mice, I will probably run away." She smiled. "For some odd reason, Mr. Otto doesn't want me to do that."

"You don't want to run away," the boy said suddenly. "You might get lost. If you left, I would be alone." He leaped up and grabbed her around the waist.

The chill went right to Julia's bones, and she shivered. Her heart pounding, she glanced at Mr. Otto and saw that his expression was the same as hers. She waited for James to say something else, but he didn't.

"James, I won't leave you alone," she said softly, resting her hand on his head. "I couldn't."

With a sigh, he burrowed in closer, and she put her arm around him. "I'll catch the mice," he said, and looked at Mr. Otto.

"Well done, James," Mr. Otto replied. "You may have just saved me a cook. Tell you what. You pile the dead ones by the tack shed, and I'll count them and pay you tonight." He leaned forward to look at her. "Darling here will find you a quart jar, and you'll put in the tails of all those you kill while I am gone."

Julia shuddered. James grinned at her. "What about the ears instead?"

"And pay you twice as much?" Mr. Otto laughed. "You are too shrewd, James!"

"Like the rest of you?" he asked. Julia could hear the yearning in his voice.

"Like the rest of us," Mr. Otto said gently. "Now go get the garden hoe. Just give'um a whack, but leave the rats to Kringle or Willy Bill."

James hurried out the door, hollering for the men to wait for him. Julia started to rise, but Mr. Otto tugged at her apron and she sat down. "That's more than I have learned from him in all these years," he said, keeping his voice low, as though James could hear. "Did someone *leave* him, I wonder?"

"I have no idea," she whispered back, her head close to his. "Do people *do* such things?"

"I wonder," was all he said.

⁂

Julia spent the day in the kitchen, dismantling the Queen Atlantic. The hands moved the can pile, the yard coming alive with evicted rodents. With steely-eyed determination, James raised the level of terror to new heights as he chased the mice with the hoe. The dirty clothes mound was already in the middle of the yard, with mice darting in and out.

Matt Malloy worked in the storeroom. He swept out a generous helping of mice, which had been done in by Willy Bill's liberal broadcast of rat poison last night.

Matt squatted by the funeral mound. "Look at that, Julia Darling," he said in his rollicking accent. "Little paws on their neck as they breathed their last. It would make even a hard-eyed woman go all trembly-lipped."

She laughed but stayed well away from his collection. "Just get them out of here, Matt," she ordered, "and I will mourn them at a later date, if I think of it."

"I ask you, boss, would you have ever thought your cook to be such an iron-willed colleen?" he joked, addressing his appeal to Mr. Otto, who stood in the doorway, slapping his gloves from one hand to the other.

"Can I help you with anything right now?" Mr. Otto asked.

Julia looked at the Queen Atlantic. *Poor, shabby old girl*, she thought. "You can loosen the bolts on the stovepipe. Don't take them off, or you'll be covered with soot. Better it's just me."

He looked at her dubiously. "Are you going to take the whole thing apart? And get it back together?"

She nodded. "I have to set a fire in the stovepipe and blow out the creosote, just for starters."

He frowned at the cooking range for a long minute. "Sure was a lot of work to get it up here," he murmured, "for all the good . . . Well, let me get some pliers."

He returned with a wrench and a bandanna. "Wrap that around your hair," he told her. "Creosote's pretty greasy." After a few minutes of tugging, aided by some choice words that Julia generously overlooked, Mr. Otto loosened the bolts and some other fastenings at strategic locations that she pointed out. When he finished, his hands were black.

Julia began her frontal assault on the Queen Atlantic. The stovepipe came off with a groan and a shriek of metal that made her skin crawl. Soot floated in the air and settled around her as she blinked her eyes and coughed. She tacked an old sheet to the archway leading to the rest of the house and retied the bandanna over her nose. The bandanna also smelled of bay rum, much more pleasant than the evil smells from the stovepipe.

The pipe was heavy with creosote, but she struggled outside and dropped it in the yard. With no small satisfaction, she went back inside and took several of the more lurid calendars off the wall.

She jumped when Mr. Otto reached over her shoulder and took the matchbox.

"You are entirely too quiet," she scolded.

"Can't help that," he said as he pocketed half the matches and pulled the bandanna down from her nose. "Oh, it's my cook!"

As he said that, a mouse under the influence of poison staggered out of the storeroom and collapsed dead at her feet. She shrieked, and he winced.

"It's just a mouse." He pulled the bandana back over her nose, raised his hands as though she held him at gunpoint, and left the kitchen whistling.

She decided Mr. Otto was a worse trial than her brothers and turned her attention to the stovepipe. She gathered the calendar pages into a bundle and tied them with string. One good bang with a well-placed fire would rid the Queen of creosote.

She took the bundle and matches outside. Mr. Otto sat on his horse by the newer barn, one leg casually draped across the saddle as he spoke to Doc. The men laughed about something but neither glanced her way. She lowered the bandanna and gulped in the fresh air. Mindful of time passing, she went to the stovepipe, which lay on the road between the house and the bunkhouse, and stuffed the bundle of calendars inside the pipe. James, his hoe raised high to flog another mouse, stopped what he was doing and came over to her.

"Mr. Darling, I don't think you will be able to cook with the stovepipe out here," he said solemnly after watching her for a long moment. Matt laughed; James hung his head.

"Don't tease him, Matt," she said. "Stand back, please. I aim to blow out all the creosote. Best cover your ears, James."

Julia struck the match on the stovepipe, knelt, and lit the end. To her satisfaction, the calendars with the racy women burst into flames. Julia ran back to the ranch house steps and covered her ears.

The explosion was even more impressive than the model the students had used for practice in cookery school. Julia lowered her hands cautiously. Even for a demonstration model, she was certain that Miss Farmer would never have allowed them to use a stovepipe with more levels of creosote than a torte had layers. "In extreme cases, the sound will amaze you," Miss Farmer had said, and Julia could not argue.

Before Julia even had time to survey her handiwork up close, James shouted, pointed, and started running. Alarmed, Julia looked where he pointed, and her mouth dropped open.

She had forgotten Mr. Otto and Doc by the barn. Her eyes wide, she stood rooted in horror as her employer's horse, spooked by the blast, reared until she thought it would topple over backward. Unprepared for the explosion, his face set, Mr. Otto hung on to the pommel and tried to bring his leg back over the saddle and into the stirrup, which dangled too far back to reach now. He grabbed at his horse's neck as the animal rose higher and higher.

I can't watch, she thought, and covered her face with her hands. She looked again just when Mr. Otto fell off the horse and landed on his back with a smack that she heard from the kitchen step.

Julia gasped. "I just killed my boss!"

Ten

$\mathcal{M}$r. Otto lay still on the ground. For some reason, Julia thought of the newspapers overhead on her ceiling. "Cook Kills Wyoming Employer," she murmured as she started toward the prone man, who was beginning to move his legs.

Before she could say anything to stop him, James darted toward the plunging horse. She watched in further alarm, and then relief, as he grabbed the flapping reins and quieted the horse. In another moment he had led the horse toward the barn.

Doc knelt beside Mr. Otto, who gasped like a fish hooked and tossed onto the bank. *Oh, Heavenly Father, I thank thee that I have not killed my employer*, she prayed silently as she knelt next to Mr. Otto. *Especially on my first official day as cook on the Double Tipi. Amen.*

Holding her own breath, she waited for Doc to do something. To her astonishment, he looked at Willy Bill, who was calmly rolling a cigarette. "Willy B, I never thought I'd see the day . . ." he began, but stopped to shake his head.

"Boss pulling leather?" Willy Bill licked the cigarette paper shut and turned away as his shoulders shook with silent laughter.

These men are insane, Julia thought in desperation since no one made a move to help her employer. After only a slight hesitation, she grabbed Mr. Otto by the shoulders and sat him up until his head plopped against her bosom. "He can't breathe," she stated to Doc and the other hands, enunciating carefully, as though they spoke another language.

"He *is* gasping a bit," Doc replied, more amused than alarmed. "Julia, just hold him like that, and I'll whack him. Ready?"

She wasn't, but she tightened her arms around Mr. Otto. Doc casually tugged out the rancher's shirt and felt his ribs through his union suit. "Don't you think you should . . . ?" she started.

"Who's the doctor here?" he asked mildly.

"I have no idea," she snapped, not even trying to hide her irritation and worry. When Doc thumped his employer's back, Julia felt the blow right through her body too.

Mr. Otto gasped and started to breathe again. Julia started to breathe along with him, so great was her own relief. Doc knelt beside her and tugged up Mr. Otto until his head rested against her shoulder. "Can't let him think too many naughty thoughts," he said companionably as she blushed fiercely but did not loosen her grip.

She also wished he would take another breath, but he seemed to have forgotten. "Mr. Otto, do breathe again," she pleaded.

"Lord love you, he will, Miss Darling," commented Matt Malloy, coming up to enjoy the show. "He's just embarrassed because every one of us—and the new cook—saw him pulling leather."

"What on earth are you talking about?" she burst out.

"You don't grab the saddle horn," Matt said as he squatted beside her and took a good look at his boss. "That was my first lesson here at the Double Tipi. He's not pinking up much, Doc," he observed. "Looks more like plumber's putty."

"He *doesn't* pink up, Malloy," Doc said wearily. "You

wouldn't either, if you were some part Injun. That's better, boss. In and out."

Julia could have sobbed with relief. Doc sat next to her and reached for Mr. Otto. "Julia, let me have him now. When he regains his senses, he's going to be more irate than you've seen him yet, and I can't vouch for his language."

She did as he said and walked away. Not looking back and stopping only to grasp the culprit stovepipe with the end of her apron, she gave it a good shake. Creosote and the relics of many a failed dinner oozed out into an oily rainbow that puddled on the ground at her feet. She felt Mr. Otto's eyes boring into her back as she crossed the yard. The kitchen step was only a stride away when he spoke to her.

"Darling, I have only one suggestion in the future," he called out.

She turned around but was too afraid to look at him.

Matt Malloy was beside her, having followed her. "You'll probably hear words you've never heard before, miss," he whispered out of the corner of his mouth. She nodded and gritted her teeth. She held her breath as she looked at Mr. Otto and then let it out slowly. There was nothing in his face to frighten her. He didn't glare or even frown.

"Just . . . just warn me next time, Darling," he said, and then let Doc help him up.

That was all, and the effort of so many words left him trying to breathe. She tried not to stare as he accepted his hat from James and mounted his horse again. Julia watched until he and Doc were just specks on the other side of the pasture. "I didn't expect that," she said to Matt. "I certainly didn't deserve it."

She wanted to be by herself then, to clean in peace, to wear herself out with work so she could point to some progress by the time Mr. Otto returned that evening, but the Irishman appointed himself her assistant and stayed with her the whole, long day. James bounced in and out, sticking mouse tails in the mason jar and pointing out each new addition until she felt distinctly queasy. Or her nausea may have been caused by the fumes that came in waves from the cookstove as she doggedly scraped down through the layers of grease and burned food.

The first shock was the worst. She opened the oven door to find a roasting pan inside. Lifting the lid cautiously, she gasped to see the desiccated remains of baby chicks. At her exclamation, Matt left the storeroom where he was working and peered over her shoulder. "So that's where they went," was his only comment.

Hours later, covered with soot, her eyes red-rimmed and sore, Julia shook her head when Matt offered to bring her some dinner from the bunkhouse. "I just can't face it," she told him, and continued scraping soot and ashes from the Queen Atlantic. She flayed herself with her thoughtlessness in blowing out the stovepipe, reliving it again and again until finally she could only kneel before the open oven and rest her forehead on the door. *I could have killed him*, she thought.

She wanted to cry, but Matt was in the storeroom. She sat up to look at all he had accomplished—the room swept out, the stale food tossed into a burlap sack, and the moribund mice transported outside on a shovel and left for James to discover. Matt must have sensed her need for silence because he hardly said a word all afternoon. And here he was now with wet cloths to wipe down the shelves.

"Here, you need this, too," he said as he squatted on his haunches beside the oven door.

Gratefully, Julia wiped her face and arms with the wet

towel he handed her. She sat on the floor then and leaned against the Queen Atlantic.

"Doc made up some boric acid for winter blindness," he said. "I'll get you some and a little cotton wadding."

She nodded her thanks and sat there, wordless with exhaustion and regret until he returned. She dabbed the solution around her eyes and sighed with relief.

"If you stop every now and then and wash your face and do your eyes, you'll feel better," he murmured as he pushed the cork back in the bottle. "No sense in flogging yourself anymore."

"I could have killed him, Matt," she said, fighting back the tears, "but he didn't even raise his voice."

"Don't think he was able, miss," Matt began, "not after a tumble from a horse that tall."

"Don't joke about it," she begged. "That was more forbearance than I deserved."

Matt nodded and leaned against the icebox. "Can I tell you how I met Mr. Otto?"

She nodded, wondering what it had to do with her own private purgatory but too tired to ask.

"It was winter, and I was rooting around in the garbage behind the Trail Café. You know, right there by the U.P. depot in Cheyenne?"

She nodded again, remembering the worn out building. The café had looked none too prosperous, and she could not imagine that a tour through that garbage would yield anything edible.

"I'm Irish, and no one would hire me," he said simply. "I'm sure you've seen those signs too where you come from, right?"

She had, even in Salt Lake City. "I thought the Irish stayed in big cities like Boston or—"

"Not me," he interrupted, as if he wanted to finish his story. "I got to Chicago, found my uncle, took one look at his two-room flat and six little ones . . ." His voice trailed off.

"You couldn't impose," she finished, rubbing the wet cloth around her neck.

"I couldn't. I went to the depot, handed the agent all my money, and asked how far it would get me," Matt said. "Cheyenne or maybe New Orleans, he told me, if I wanted to go south on another line and wasn't too particular. I went west."

She couldn't help smiling. "After Nauvoo, Illinois, my own relatives weren't too particular about where they ended up, either."

"So there I was in Cheyenne, seventeen, more hungry than I had ever been . . . even in Ireland." He shook his head. "It was winter, of course. There were cowhands all over town looking for work. Why should anyone hire me?"

"Why, indeed?" she murmured.

He sat at the table and leaned forward. "I don't know how long he stood there at the alley mouth, watching me—he's kind of quiet when he walks."

"I've noticed."

"The morning train from the East had pulled in. Something he said later told me he must have been in Chicago, but I do not think it was the Chicago I knew. He had on a handsome overcoat and a really nice suit and gent's hat. Shoes too, and they were shiny."

Julia couldn't picture it, but she said nothing. James stood in the doorway, eager to show her his mason jar again, but Matt waved him away.

"He squatted down right by me in that muddy alley and offered me a job," Matt concluded. "He didn't ask if I could rope, or . . . or even sit on a horse." He looked at the floor then. "I told him I was Irish and didn't know anything about stock. All he did was ask if I thought I could learn."

Julia nodded, remembering Mr. Otto's question about the coffee. "You took the job," she said, wanting him to continue.

"Aye, miss, I did." He looked at her then, and she was struck by the amazement in his eyes, as though the incident had happened only last week. "I'm sure I looked like a cadaver, and I know I stunk, but he took me into a really nice restaurant—"

"Not the Trail Café!"

"No! I ate until I was full. Then he bought me clothes and even some leather gloves. He said I would need those for riding." He stopped, looked at her, and then swallowed and continued. "I couldn't help it. I started crying on the train ride to Gun Barrel, but all he did was hand me a handkerchief, tip his hat over his eyes, and go to sleep."

"I've already cried in one of his handkerchiefs," Julia confessed.

He smiled then, his melancholy gone. "I'd be betting that most of us here have, Miss Darling."

"Just Julia." She stood up and began applying the putty knife again to the stove top. "What did you do all winter here?"

Matt went back into the storeroom with the wet cloths, and she heard him wiping down the shelves. "He taught me to read, and we practiced roping in the barn." He stepped into the kitchen to look at her. "When he finished practicing with me each day, I kept going until I had blisters on my blisters, even through the gloves."

She looked at her hands and the spots that already felt tender and then wiped the grease in the lard bucket that

Matt had provided earlier. "You've been here a while then?" she asked.

"Going on eight years now," he said. "Fancy this, Julia. I even get offers from other stockmen at every roundup. Some offer me more kale to work for them, but could I leave here?"

No, you couldn't, she thought, as she directed her attention to the cookstove. "The others?" she asked finally. "No one would hire them either?"

"I suppose." He came out of the storeroom, looked at her, and took the putty knife away. "I'll do that for a minute. You sit down."

She didn't but took the cloth from him and went into the storeroom to continue his task. "Not even Willy Bill? He looks like he has always known what to do."

Matt laughed. "Especially Willy Bill!" He came to the storeroom door. "No one wanted him at all." He came closer and lowered his voice. "He and a partner spent the winter of '86 snowed into a line shack at the Two Bar. When spring came, there was just Willy Bill and the other gent's heels and palms left."

Julia shuddered. "He didn't . . . ?"

"Old Willy claims the man died of starvation." He shrugged. "Maybe he did. Anyway, he didn't waste a morsel. Boss hired him anyway. We made him promise that Willy Bill wouldn't do any of the cooking."

Julia laughed and applied herself with more vigor to the shelves. *What on earth do I dare write my parents about this place?* she thought. She heard the Irishman scraping some more, until even he had to stop. He looked into the storeroom. "Clean enough for you?" he asked.

She nodded, wondering what she would use for shelf paper and what would air out the odor of mice. "Thanks, Matt."

He nodded. "Boss told me to help you, but I was going to anyway." He handed her the broom. "He's probably already told you how James came here."

"Yes. What about the old German who doesn't say anything?"

"Kringle? He can't ride much anymore, but he's a genius with making and repairing harnesses," Matt said as he took the dirty cloths and added them to the lard bucket. "He rides in the wagon at roundup, and everyone uses his services. I don't even know if Boss was aware of that skill when he hired him."

"Then why . . . ?" Julia swept the scraps from the floor onto the piece of shirt cardboard that Matt held down for her and began a mental list of things to look for on her next trip into Gun Barrel—a new stovepipe, dustpan, more resolve.

"I asked Boss once," he said, dumping the contents in the bucket. "I think it embarrassed him. He mumbled something about the fact that we're all beggars, one way or another, and that was all he would say about it."

"Odd," Julia agreed, but she surprised herself by returning to the Queen Atlantic with a little more enthusiasm than she had felt before their conversation. *I am most definitely not a beggar*, she told herself as she scraped away. *I don't need this job like Mr. Otto's other employees.*

He glanced out the open door. "Willy Bill's calling. Are you far enough along here?"

"Yes." She smiled at him. "Thanks, Matt."

Her conversation with Matt Malloy was enough to fuel her through the rest of the afternoon. Standing upright with her hand on the small of her back, Julia stopped only long enough to direct the unloading of the wagon, with her crates and the supplies from Gun Barrel.

Brave words, she chided herself later as the late afternoon sun slanted into the kitchen and she felt herself no farther along on the Queen Atlantic than she was hours ago when she started. After a carefully superintended washing of his hands and the promise never to bring that jar full of mouse tails into the kitchen again, James had done as she directed and replaced the storeroom items that Matt had so carefully cleaned for her. While she watched, unwilling to touch the staples herself in her present state of sootiness, he filled the sugar canister and the flour bin and lined up her purchases on the shelves. She could only shake her head over all those maraschino cherries, which looked remarkably out of place now. Her hands were too dirty to touch her extra copy of the Book of Mormon—smelling sweetly of cloves—so she had James set it on the shelf too. The bananas, still relentlessly green, went on a hook by the window.

It pained her to relegate the crew to another evening of canned food, but there was no way to use the Queen Atlantic yet. She had managed to wrestle the grate out of the clogged firebox, and it leaned outside the door, ready for her to tackle in the morning. She had propped the oven door against the icebox, and the oven shelf was soaking outside in a concoction of Sapolio and ammonia that she mixed in desperation.

Canned food it would be, cooked and eaten in the bunk-house again, which at the moment looked far cleaner than the kitchen. She sent James off to supper and resigned herself to an evening devoted to subduing the Queen Atlantic.

She heard Mr. Otto and Doc ride into the yard when it was full dark. To her relief, and then her guilt, neither man stopped at the house. After they spent time in the barn, she heard the bunkhouse door slam. *I have driven my employer out of his own house*, she thought with chagrin as she struggled to chisel off another layer of grease from the range top.

She ached everywhere from bending over the cooking range for the better part of the day but nowhere worse than her back. Her eyes burned from the soot, and her hair was as dark as Mr. Otto's now and itching her scalp in the worst way. " 'A successful cook is a dainty cook,' " she muttered grimly under her breath, remembering the saying over the blackboard in the fancy cooking lecture hall.

The stove defeated her finally. Both hands pushing against the small of her back and beyond caring about the sticky table top, she perched herself on it and stared at the Queen Atlantic. "You are a monster," she told it, already dreading the days ahead. She sniffed herself and wondered if the smell of old grease would follow her around from now on like an evil perfume. Her hands were cracked and bleeding, her carefully manicured nails chipped and broken.

Maybe the Queen will look better in the morning, she thought, not stirring from the table. *By the end of the week, I can have it positively gleaming.* She shook her head. *If I live that long.*

Someone knocked. With a groan she could not stifle, Julia turned her head to the open door. "Mr. Otto, you needn't knock," she said. "It's your house, although you probably would not recognize it right now, I suppose."

Without a word, he sat next to her on the table and looked at the cookstove. He started to say something but then shook his head and continued to stare at the dismantled oven, still deep in grease. Finally, he handed her the bowl he was carrying. "Pears," he said. "Nothing else in the bunkhouse looked edible. Malloy said you haven't eaten all day."

She took the bowl, contemplated its contents, and then set it aside. "Maybe later," she murmured. "I'm too tired to lift a spoon."

"Maybe now," he replied, reaching for the bowl. "Sit down."

Too tired to argue, she did as he said, getting off the table and seating herself. Mr. Otto sat beside her, watching her until she speared a pear and dragged it to her mouth. She chewed, tasted nothing but grit, swallowed, speared another section, and then another until he looked away.

"We leave at first light for the open range north and west of here," he told her. "Keep eating. Two of my cousins from the Wind River Rez will likely show up tomorrow or the day after. They speak English, so just tell them we're starting at the range beyond McLemore's. I hire them every roundup."

She nodded and pushed away the bowl. Mr. Otto pushed it back, so she picked up her spoon again. "Curtis McLeish and Dan Who Counts. They won't scare you."

She managed a smile. "I might scare them. I look a fright."

He sighed, and she knew the whole kitchen was making him uneasy. "This really is a coolie job, isn't it?"

She nodded. "I'll have it so clean you won't recognize it, provided the roundup lasts about a year or two." She felt more hopeful when he laughed and brave enough to set down the spoon.

"Fourteen days, tops, Darling, and then we expect a fabulous meal." He picked up her hand, looked at the broken nails, and put the spoon back in her grip. "I have a pair of lady's kid riding gloves I'll leave on the table in the morning. They'll be a little big, but they might keep your fingers from dropping off."

She finished the pears as he sat there, gratified that the last few spears tasted more like fruit and less like the Queen Atlantic. A wave of exhaustion swept over her, so she pushed the bowl away and pillowed her head on her arms. "I'm just going to rest my eyes for a few minutes, Mr. Otto," she murmured. "Then I'll get back to it."

The morning sun was making a faint impression on the sooty window when Julia woke, stiff almost beyond pain. Her head was still resting on her arms, but Mr. Otto must have put the quilt around her shoulders. *I wonder if I can straighten up*, she thought. She did finally and turned around slowly, hoping the Queen Atlantic had disappeared during the night.

She stared at the range top. "Oh my stars," she said. "My stars."

The lard bucket was brimful of old grease. Salt lay scattered on the range top, which was almost free of grease now. Just a little more scouring with the salt and some warm water would remove what remained. "My stars," she whispered again, wondering how many hours Mr. Otto had stayed awake and thinking of his own long day, which had begun with him thrown from his horse when she blew out the creosote. *I don't deserve this*, she thought as she got up and ran her hand across the range top. "Maybe you are a beautiful old girl," she told the cookstove. "And maybe I'm a beggar too."

A glance out the door told her much more than the sooty window could. The sun was well up, and even now she could hear James yawning in the back room where he slept. She went to the wash basin to make an attempt on her hands and face. There was a shaving mirror tacked to the wall above the basin, but she was grateful to be too short to see into it. She washed her face and took some solvent to her hands, gritting her teeth when the solution flamed each tiny nick in her skin.

The result did not satisfy her, but she knew there was

not going to be a remedy for it until the Queen Atlantic had been restored to its former charms. She looked back at the cookstove, amazed at Mr. Otto's perseverance and the depths of her own exhaustion, to have remained oblivious as he must have scraped and chipped all night at the stubborn grease.

⁓

She stood in the door and watched Matt Malloy back the horses to the doubletree of the wagon that was loaded now with what looked like bedrolls. As she walked closer, Julia recognized branding irons and cans of food neatly stacked in boxes. "I thought calves were branded in the spring," she asked Matt as he harnessed the team.

"They are. But in the fall we always find a few more that escaped us. If we can brand them before they leave their mothers, then they're still ours. Isn't that right, Boss?"

Mr. Otto must have walked up from the river. His hair was wet, and he smelled of Ivory soap. Suspenders still hung below his waistband, and he wore moccasins. "Yep. Morning, Darling. Walk with me, if you will. It'll just be you and James for two weeks, so I want to tell you what to expect."

She did as he said, keeping her distance because Mr. Otto was so clean. "Something I said?" he asked finally.

"No!" Julia laughed. "I'm so dirty!" She stopped walking. "Mr. Otto, thank you for cleaning that range top. Did you get any sleep at all last night?"

"Oh, not much," he said, and he sounded a little shy. "Doesn't matter. You needed the help." He stopped in front of the ranch house. "I told you about my cousins. Just send 'em on."

She nodded. "Curtis Scots Name and Dan Who Counts. I'll listen for James at night."

"McLeish. Good. Now you might not care for this, but I left a loaded pistol on the shelf above the bureau in my room. If anyone—and I mean anyone—shows up that looks even a little scary, shoot'em."

"I couldn't!" she exclaimed.

"You ought to keep an open mind about that," he suggested. "Alice Marlowe might visit. Don't shoot her!"

She stayed outside while he went inside the house, coming out in a moment wearing socks and carrying his boots. He sat down on the step and pulled them on. "I can't think of anything else, except that we'll probably have several ranchers with us when we return who'll want to check out your cooking." He glared nowhere in particular. "But *not* marry you!"

He was halfway to the wagon when he turned around. "We have a tin tub in the horse barn. But if the weather stays nice like this, I recommend that spot where the cottonwoods overhang the river. It's plenty deep for you. Ivory floats too. See you in two weeks, Darling."

Eleven

She worked hard all afternoon. Mr. Otto had chipped loose the worst of the grease from the Queen Atlantic's interior, and that mere fact of benevolence made her writhe inside with her own ill-use of him, no matter how unintentional. The work was like soap and water applied to her soul. She doggedly chipped away years of culinary disasters, earning a relief from her distress that felt remarkably like restitution.

James was content to help. He was a good worker, not objecting when she gave him orders and set him to tasks of his own. He didn't even complain of hunger throughout the long day. When the sun was low and her stomach started to rumble, she realized that neither of them had eaten anything since breakfast.

"You should have said something, James," she told him, as she finally sat down at the table. He grinned at her, and she knew he was probably not used to the most regular hours for meals. "But you don't complain much, do you? I should take lessons."

James moved his chair closer to her. Touched, she put her hand on his shoulder. "But you don't mind canned food, do you? Or dirty hands? Or even that I don't measure up?"

He shook his head. "I guess I don't mind anything, Mr. Darling," he said.

"I'm just Julia."

"Yes, sir."

"I think you haven't been around ladies too much, have you?" she asked.

"No, sir. You smell nice."

"Not at the moment, James, but you're kind to say so," she replied.

Still she sat. "I like pears, Mr. Darling," James commented in an offhand way.

"So do I," she told him, wincing as she got to her feet. "What about pears, cheese, and crackers?"

Since the can dump was gone, she took the food outside. They sat on the front step, the food between them. James reached for a cracker, but she put her hand on his. "I think I should ask a blessing on the food."

It was obvious from his expression that he hadn't the remotest idea what she was saying, but he put down his hand and waited. She folded her arms. "You can do that too, James," she suggested, and waited until his arms were folded. "Close your eyes too, my dear," she told him. "We're going to thank the Lord for this."

"Why?"

Such a simple question, she thought, and then realized that the question was new to her in a way she wouldn't have credited, only a week ago. "Well, everything we have comes from Heavenly Father," she told him after a moment. "We want to express our appreciation." She bowed her head. "We thank thee, Father, for this food. It is simple, and I promise it will get better. But we're grateful. And please keep the men of the Double Tipi safe from any harm or accident. Oh, dear, and keep Mr. Otto safe from me. In the name of Jesus Christ, amen." She looked up. "You can say amen too, James."

He did, his voice soft. "Amen. Can I eat now?"

"You certainly may, my dear. It's been blessed." She

leaned against the door frame, weary right down to her soul, but feeling a measure of contentment all out of proportion to her situation. *I meant every word of that blessing*, she thought. *I don't believe that except for Thanksgiving I really listen to blessings on the food, even when I say them.*

She smiled as James leaned against her. She thought to wave him off because she was so dirty but decided against it, gathering him close against her. James sighed and closed his eyes.

"You're softer than Mr. Otto," he said.

"Ladies usually are."

"I don't know why we never had a lady here before," he said, and then turned his attention to the pears.

Because no lady in her right mind would ever stay here, or at least stay for long, apparently, she thought. *But I must, and the Double Tipi has to improve.* She leaned back and admired the fiery way the sun began its descent behind the rim of hills. No need to improve the sunset.

"Do you know, James, I believe we can light the Queen Atlantic and heat some water for a bath for you. Mr. Otto said something about a tub in the barn."

"Well, maybe," James replied, his voice wary.

He sounded so uncertain. "It's a luxury you deserve, after catching all those mice," she told him. "*Especially* after catching all those mice! Eat that last slice of cheese and we'll find the tub."

They found it leaning next to the grain bin, cob-webbed and housing a mouse nest. Amazed at her agility, even after a day with a chisel at the cookstove, Julia quickly perched on the grain bin while James chased away the mice and righted the tub. Bottle flies droned in the last patch of sunlight next to a roll of tar paper. She wrinkled her nose at the mingled odors of tar, grain, and manure, even as she decided that barn smells were superior to old grease from a cookstove.

They carried the tub to the kitchen. While James wiped out the tub, Julia arranged wood in the firebox, laying each stick just so. "This moment begs for a little ceremony," she told the boy as she lit the fire. In a minute's time she had reattached the reservoir and began pumping water to fill it.

"What do we do now?" James asked.

Julia hid her smile at the suspicion in his voice. "We wait until the water is hot, dip some into the tub, and add cool water until it's just right. Then you may wash yourself."

James pulled up a stool and sat by the Queen Atlantic. She watched him sitting so still, patient for whatever lay ahead, and his trust touched her heart. She took a jar of maraschino cherries from the storeroom, opened it, and handed James the jar and a fork.

He speared a cherry, and his eyes widened. "I never ate anything this good," he assured her, as he speared another, his attention distracted from the reservoir.

She laughed and added more wood to the firebox. "I can make a cake that has cherries and chocolate."

He stared at her, a cherry poised at his lips. "Does Mr. Otto know you can do that?"

"He doesn't think I can whistle and walk at the same time," she assured him.

James made no objection to the bath. After she declared the water ready, he obediently stripped off his clothes and stepped in the tub. "You can sit down," she said, when he just stood there.

He did as she said, cautious at first. The warmth of the water seemed to mystify him. He sat down, and in another moment was leaning back against the raised lip of the tub, his eyes closed. "I could like this," he said without opening his eyes.

"Then you can make bathing at least a weekly habit," she told him as she reached for the soft soap she had retrieved from her trunk. "I'll wash your hair, but then you're on your own."

Three different applications of soap finally satisfied her, and James offered no complaint. While he finished, she found his nightshirt, a cut-down shirt of Mr. Otto's, she was certain. *I could hem these sleeves*, she thought, as she held it away from her sooty apron. *I could even sew him a regular nightshirt.*

His eyelids drooping, James was asleep before she even finished one page of the tattered book that he handed her before he crawled into bed. She kept reading aloud anyway, not for the story, but for the sound of her own voice. *How quiet it is here*, she thought as she left his room.

In the parlor, she pulled the rocking chair away from the wall and sat down, not bothering to brush the dust from the seat. *Mr. Otto, this is a lady's chair*, she thought as she rocked and rested, gratified to be seated in a chair just the right distance from the floor. The room was not unpleasant, she decided, and the furniture—what she could see of it in the gloom—newer than she had first judged. *If I moved that jumble of harnesses off the settee and took the feed bucket from the wing chair . . .* She stopped rocking. Why would a man put a whole roll of building paper in a parlor and just leave it there?

The parlor was too sad, and she was too dirty. Just enough water remained in the reservoir to wash the grease off her face and arms. She refilled the reservoir. When she was certain that James slept, she found a towel and wash-cloth and picked up the lavender soap she had brought from home. The moon was large and the stars so brilliant. She stood a long time on the front step, picking out constellations and soaking in the serenity around her.

She walked to the river toward the spot Mr. Otto had pointed out to her that morning, where the overhang of cottonwoods was the greatest. She looked back at the house, wondering why Mr. Otto's father built it so far from the river.

She was reluctant to undress, even in the shelter of the trees, and chided herself. "There is no one to see you, Julia," she said as she removed her apron. She stood a moment longer and undressed. She knew she would only be able to do this when the men were off the property.

The water was so cold that she nearly changed her mind about the virtue of cleanliness. "Resolve, Julia," she declared, and then waded in farther, gritting her teeth. She washed quickly while minnows nibbled at her legs. *When I can't feel the minnows, then it is time to get out*, she decided. The gentler fragrance of the lavender was quickly subdued by the odor of sagebrush. She breathed deep and felt the weight of the day wash from her. *I suppose no prospect is so dismal that soap and water will not help*, she considered, and waded in deeper until the water came almost to her chest.

She noticed that watercress grew in the shallower protection of the cut bank, and she waded over to pluck a handful of the peppery green, relishing the taste of something fresh, after crackers and tinny pears. *I wonder if a garden would grow here.*

She thought about a garden again before she slept that night, thinking of the Rudiger cabin with its can-patched siding and skinny row of zinnias, all blasted and leaning almost completely over, scoured by the wind. *I don't honestly know if I would have enough faith to plant anything in this land*, she thought.

The reminder of faith compelled her out of her blankets to kneel beside the bed. She folded her hands together and then rested her head on them, weary with her day. She thought of her father, never at a loss before the Lord, and Mama's serenity when it was her turn to pray. *I can say all the words I usually say*, she thought, *or I can ask the Lord to forgive me when I complain. Do I doubt which He would prefer?* She closed her eyes and stayed on her knees a long minute. "I'm sorry for all the trouble I was today, Heavenly Father," she prayed finally. "I think that maybe I understand repentance and restitution a little better too, even if my lesson came from a Gentile. In Jesus' name, amen."

In the morning, after more cheese and crackers, she set James to carrying the clutter from what she was already calling the parlor into the barn. "It will never be a parlor if we do not start calling it one," she told him. "Expect the best, my father would say."

While James hauled out what looked like years of debris, stopping now and then with cries of delight to ultimately add to his mouse-tail jar, Julia finished the resurrection of the Queen Atlantic. By the middle of the afternoon, she stood back against the far wall to admire the stovetop, blacked and buffed to a state of newness she'd not have believed had she not participated in its exhumation.

She built a proper fire and considered supper. A long moment in the smokehouse contemplating a ham swayed her opinion to ham chowder. "This won't be sufficiently impressive for Mr. Otto's return," she announced, slicing off a chunk of ham and setting it in the graniteware basin James carried. "But it will do for us. You don't mind eating strange for a day or two?" she asked.

While the chowder simmered on the back of the stove, Julia mixed up corn bread in a frying pan and put it in the oven. The corn bread was done slightly beyond her expectations, but it was impressive because it was the first offering of the Queen Atlantic in her recovered state. "Think how we will astound Mr. Otto," she told James, deftly sliding the golden mass to a plate and dividing it into pie wedges.

"He'll like this," James said. He rested his chin on his hands, watching her split the wedges and butter them.

"I'll make something much grander than mere corn bread," she said. She sat down and asked James if he wanted to ask the blessing this time. "Just thank the Lord for the food," she suggested when he frowned.

"Suppose I do it wrong?" he asked. "Will He be angry?"

"No. I think He just gets sad when we don't appreciate what we have."

He carefully laced his fingers together and bowed his head. "It smells so good, Lord," he said, after considerable thought. "Supper is a great idea," he concluded and then picked up his spoon.

It certainly is, she agreed after saying "amen." Ezra Quayle might quibble over that blessing, but she didn't intend to. "Thank you, James," she said.

James ate his chowder in appreciative silence, opening up the corn bread hunk once or twice to watch the progress of more butter as it melted.

After supper, James helped refill the Queen Atlantic's ample reservoir.

"Do I have to take another bath so soon?" he asked.

"Two days in a row?" she teased. "I wouldn't dream of such torture. I want to wash clothes in the morning, not you!"

James smiled at her little joke. He poured in the last bucket of water and set the cover carefully on top of the reservoir. "Mr. Otto will be surprised, I think."

"He doesn't usually wash his clothes?" she asked, looking out the door at the mound of clothing in the yard with renewed suspicion.

"He takes them to a man in Gun Barrel with a pigtail. He bows a lot." James demonstrated with a series of quick bows.

Julia laughed. "There's a Chinese laundry in Gun Barrel?" she asked.

"His name is Mr. Yee," James told her. "I watched him iron once. He spits on the clothes to get out wrinkles. Do you do that when you iron?"

Julia suppressed a shudder. "No! I usually blot them with a little sponge. Dear me." She went into the pantry and came out with a washtub, which she set outside the door near the dirty clothes.

To catch the last of the sun before it dipped behind the mountains, Julia perched herself on the overturned washtub and picked out the loose stitches in the flour sack. "I will wash this too and make curtains for the kitchen," she told James, who was leaning against her now and holding quite still. "James?" No answer. With a smile, she leaned over and kissed the top of his head. "And then maybe I will look around and see if there is some more sacking for a nightshirt for you," she whispered.

There were no protests when she woke him gently and led him to his bed. Wordlessly, he handed her the tattered pages from the book but closed his eyes before she even had time to read. "And they probably all lived happily ever after," she said, and took up the kerosene lamp. "But we'll never know because we don't have the ending."

She stopped in the parlor and sat down in what she was already calling the lady's chair. It was pulled up companionably close to a larger chair, but both were dust covered. With the saddle and bits of harness gone from the settee . . . she stopped her imagining and shook her head. "It will still be very much a sow's ear," she announced to no one. And there was that building paper leaning next to the bookcase full of what must be ranch ledgers. She wished she knew how to tack the paper onto the walls but then reminded herself that Mr. Otto was interested in a Fannie Farmer graduate, not a contractor.

Julia was up long before James. Humming to herself in the clean kitchen, she laid a fire in the Queen Atlantic and soon had a pot of oatmeal on the edge of a well-mannered simmer. She would wake up James soon, and they could have the wash done before mid-morning. But maybe that was James now, she thought, as the floorboard vibrated.

"What'd you do, lady? Kill Paul and throw his old bones behind the smokehouse?"

Julia gasped. She clenched her hand around the wooden spoon and froze. The floorboard vibrated again.

"Aw, Dan! I think you scared her! Here she's come back, and you scared her. Hey, it's okay, Mrs. Otto."

Julia turned around slowly, and stared—eyes wide and mouth open—at two Indians standing just behind her. "I . . . I'm not Mrs. Otto," she managed to squeak. "I'm cooking oatmeal."

As frightened as she was, even Julia had to wince at the silliness of what she just said. One deep breath, and then a second, and she looked again at the two men—Indians obviously, with their long hair in braids, but dressed much like Mr. Otto—both of whom were smiling at her now.

"Naw, I guess you're not Mrs. Otto," said the man who had spoken first. "Don't think she ever cooked."

She looked at him and then remembered what Mr. Otto

had said before he left. "Oh, go ahead and laugh," she said, hoping that her voice still didn't sound shaky. "You must be Dan Who Counts . . ." She looked at the other man. ". . . and Mr. McLeish. Mr. Otto's cousins?"

"Curtis," the other Indian supplied. "I'd like some oatmeal."

She dished up two bowls and set them on the table. "Do you want me to make coffee?"

Dan nodded, his eyes on the oatmeal. "If you have it. Indians like lots of sugar," he hinted.

The water in the reservoir was almost simmering, so it was only a matter of a few minutes to have coffee in the pot and then on the table. Julia sat down with them and ate a small bowl of oatmeal. "Mr. Otto wanted me to tell you that they are working north of McLemore's place," she said when she had finished and wiped her mouth.

McLeish nodded and pushed himself back from the table. Dan spoke, "We'll be going then." He looked at her but glanced away quickly. Julia decided he was either shy or Indians didn't think it polite to stare. "Anything you need doing, before we go?"

Happy for their help, she directed them to fill the cauldron in the yard with hot water. Dan did as she directed while Curtis pumped cool water into the other pot. She put the white clothes into the cauldron and added a generous sprinkling of Ivory soap flakes she had brought with her from Salt Lake.

"Anything else we can do?" Curtis asked.

She found a length of rope in the barn next to the tar paper and had them string her a clothes line between the smoke house and the tack shed. She looked for a broom handle to stir the wash around. "Anything else?" Dan asked when they finished.

She shook her head, suddenly shy. They were both so tall. She looked for some resemblance to Mr. Otto but could see none. "Thanks for your help."

Dan nodded, tugged on his hat brim, and swung himself into the saddle again, gazing around the yard. He leaned forward then and edged his horse toward the bunkhouse. Curtis smiled at her. "Good food, ma'am."

She smiled back and thought of something. "When he came in, your brother called me Mrs. Otto. Do . . . do I look like her?"

Curtis gave her another quick glance but looked away, polite even when scrutiny was allowed. "She was taller and had kind of a grim look." He mounted his horse and tipped his hat to her. "But I only saw her once." He gathered the reins in his hands.

"What happened to her?"

He tugged gently on the reins and his horse backed up slightly. "All kinds of stories. Someone said she killed a man. Someone said Paul killed a man. Someone else told me that he saw her all trussed up in a backward shirt with long arms." He shrugged. "Lots of stories."

"Goodness," she said faintly, backing away a little herself. "Does . . . does anybody know?"

He shrugged again. "Maybe Little River knows, but she doesn't say."

He started out of the yard, but Dan still sat motionless, looking past the bunkhouse. With a small gesture, he motioned to her. "Someone's in your can dump."

"What on earth?"

He motioned again. "Can you see them?"

She came closer to him, shading her hand against the rising sun. After a moment of squinting, she could just make out two figures, one a woman, the other a child. She knew it was the Rudigers and remembered the smashed cans on the side of their shanty. So this was where they got their siding.

"I could shoo them away," Dan offered.

"Oh, no, that's not nec—"

But Curtis had spotted them as well. He kneed his horse in the direction of the can pile and dug in his spurs. The horse leaped forward. The woman shrieked and ran from the can pile, tugging her child after her.

"Oh, wait!" Julia called, dismayed to see them scatter and run. "He didn't mean anything!"

But they were gone, running quickly toward the river. Curtis looked at her and then at the two. When she waved him over, he turned away from the river. She could see the reluctance in his face, but he slowed his horse to a walk and went closer to the dump. He leaned down and picked up a small wagon, the kind a child might own.

Julia sighed in dismay. "They didn't mean any harm!"

Dan called in Shoshone to his cousin, who placed the little wagon across his lap and joined them in the yard again. He dangled the wagon by the rope that served as a handle and lowered it to the ground. "Sorry, ma'am, but you don't need trouble from nesters."

"They aren't trouble," she replied. "I think they smash the cans and use them for siding on their house." The sun was coming up, but it was still low on the horizon. She shivered. "Winter's coming."

Dan tipped his head back, as though he could see something in the sky that she couldn't. "Well, maybe he ought to do a little more than send his women for cans. Come on, Mac. It's a day's ride."

With another nod to her, the Indians left the property, traveling north, away from the clearing and the river. Julia looked down at the wagon, unpainted and with high sides.

She picked up the rope and tugged the sorry little vehicle after her, remembering a red wagon with flowers painted on it that Iris used to tug everywhere with all her dolls inside. The wagon rolled after her, noisy in the quiet morning.

Halfway to the house, she stopped and looked back at the barn, thinking of the roll of tar paper inside, obviously not of use to anyone. *You know Mr. Rudiger will never take charity*, she told herself. She looked at the house then, thinking about pleasant winter evenings ahead in the parlor with gray building paper on the walls, and curtains hanging in the windows. "I wonder, will you barter with me, Mr. Rudiger?" she asked aloud, just to hear her idea. "And you can be certain I'd never dream of stopping by for a visit without bringing something to eat."

Twelve

he first load of wash was on the line before James woke up. She had made another pot of oatmeal too, larger than the first, and set it to warm on the back of the Queen Atlantic, after she dumped out the remaining coffee and opened Miss Farmer's cookbook to her favorite chapter.

I could never visit the Rudigers without bringing along a cake, she thought as she turned the pages. *Besides*, she reasoned, *I have to experiment with this oven a few times before I dare prepare anything for Mr. Otto and his men.* Cornstarch Cake was white beyond belief and amazingly consistent, but it took five eggs. She decided on Snow Cake, which only needed the white of two eggs. It would probably travel the best too in the little wagon because it was a loaf cake.

Practicality triumphed again, and she stirred together a simple confectioner's frosting. White Mountain Cream frosting was her favorite, but she knew from experience that it didn't travel well. Besides that, its soft mounds would probably attract every fly and gnat between here and Cheyenne. She could depend on confectioner's frosting to harden into an effective, but sweet, barrier to bugs. She knew it was child's play, when she thought of all the towering post-dinner delights that she planned to conjure up for Mr. Otto and his crew. Even Iris, a reluctant cook at best, was able to make Snow Cake; it was no challenge.

James wandered into the kitchen a half hour later,

rubbing the sleep from his eyes. He sniffed the air. "I want some of that."

"You'll have to settle for oatmeal with cinnamon in it," she said, ruffling his hair. "What you're smelling is the cake I'm making right now to take to the Rudigers."

"I don't think Mr. Otto takes food to them."

"Nobody does," she said, "but this is different. We're paying a social call and asking a favor, so a cake doesn't count." *Will you buy that?* she thought. *I know Mr. Otto wouldn't, but he isn't here.*

"I suppose you're right," he said finally, but he sounded doubtful.

"I am," she told him firmly. "Good manners say that we should do this."

"Why are we going to see the Rudigers?" he asked as she ladled him some oatmeal.

"Mrs. Rudiger and her daughter were here really early to gather cans, and they were scared away by Mr. Otto's cousins from the reservation. She left behind the wagon, and we're going to return it."

He ate silently, like Mr. Otto and the hired hands. When he finished, she sent him to get dressed while she removed the loaf cake from the oven. She set the cake outside on the front step to hurry its cooling.

James watched the cake intently as she carried it to the table and prepared the frosting. As Julia worked, it struck her that he was not eyeing the frosting bowl with the notion that it was his to lick when she finished. She was sure the thought had never occurred to him because this was probably the first cake he had ever seen in his life.

"There. I'm done," she said. Julia handed James the knife and pushed the frosting bowl closer to him. "You can eat what's left, if you'd like."

His eyes grew wide. He licked the blade tentatively and grinned at her. In another moment, the blade was clean. He dipped it into the bowl, careful not to miss a single swirl of icing.

"Mr. Otto will like this when he comes back," James announced, setting down the knife.

"I'll make him a much grander cake," she told him. "Can you find me a small box? I'll set the cake in it, and we'll be on our way."

He came back with a wooden box with a hinged lid. "Mr. Otto keeps his writing paper in this, but I dumped it on his bed," he said, opening the lid. "He won't know we used it."

"Indeed, no," she agreed as she gently set the frosted loaf cake inside. "We're just borrowing it. Take the can of oatmeal and follow me, James."

She closed the door behind her, set the cake into the wagon by the porch, and showed James where to put the can of oatmeal. The sun was high overhead now.

"I need a hat," she said out loud, wishing she had brought her straw hat from home.

"Mr. Otto has one. I'll get it." He ran back inside.

"No, James!" she called, but he was gone. He came back with a straw hat with a pink ribbon tail and silk rose on the brim. "My goodness," she said as he held it out to her.

"It's in his room," James said. "I think there was a lady here once."

"I believe you're right," she said and took the hat from him. It fit perfectly. She knew she should have put it back, but she didn't want to disappoint James. "This is just right," she announced.

Tugging the wagon behind her, she and James walked to the river, which was so low that they crossed easily on the stones without getting their feet too wet. "Is it always this low?" she asked.

"In the fall. After it snows and spring comes, there's lots of water. Mr. Otto won't let me play here in the spring."

"You always do what he says, don't you?" she asked.

He shrugged. "Mostly."

They crossed the river, steadied the wagon, and continued on the trail worn smooth by years of horses and wagons. James skipped a little ahead of her, whacking at the buffalo grass with a stick he found. She watched him, a smile on her face, and remembered doing just that with Iris when her mother went visiting teaching years ago and took them along.

I suppose this is my visiting teaching itinerary now, she thought but then brushed away the idea with a pang of guilt. *Except that I believe Mr. Otto would be angry if he knew I was taking food to the very people the ranchers want to starve out of this valley.* She stopped, wondering if she should continue. James skipped ahead, oblivious to her guilty conscience. She started walking again, after assuring herself that Mr. Otto would be so pleased with the renovation in the parlor that he wouldn't ask how it had happened. She didn't think it was more than a half mile from the ranch to the turn-off to the main road. The day was warm, but there was just enough nip in the breeze to remind her that it was September.

James joined her on the main road, a little less exuberant as they approached the bend before the Rudiger's shack. "Do we know them, Mr. Darling?" he asked. "Do you think they will be angry?"

"No, I do not," she replied. "We're paying a friendly visit, and we need Mr. Rudiger's help. Besides, we have to return their wagon."

Ursula Rudiger was pumping water beside the house

when they came into the clearing. The wagon made plenty of noise, so she looked up, startled, but then set down the bucket and ran into the house, closing the door behind her.

"Uh-oh," James said under his breath. "Is she afraid of us?"

"I think so," Julia replied, her voice equally low. "She must think we're angry about the cans. Chin up, James. We have a good deed to do."

She didn't feel confident as she crossed the yard, tugging the noisy wagon, and knocked on the door. After a long moment it opened, and Mr. Rudiger stood in the doorway, his arms folded. "Good afternoon, Mr. Rudiger," she said, and held out her hand. "We wanted to return your wagon."

She didn't think he would shake her hand, but eventually he did. He looked at her silently, and in a panic, she wondered if he spoke any English. *Forge on, Julia*, she told herself. *If an idea seemed good two miles away, it ought to still be good.* "Mr. Otto's cousins didn't mean to frighten her this morning. Oh, my name is Julia Darling, and this is James."

Rudiger smiled then, and she felt herself relax. "I told her not to worry, Miss Darling, but she's afraid of men on horses."

"I can understand that," Julia said.

They stood there in the doorway awkwardly until Mrs. Rudiger spoke in German from the shack's dim interior. Mr. Rudiger nodded and motioned her inside. "It's hot in the sun. Come in."

Julia opened Mr. Otto's wooden box. She carefully took out the loaf cake, which she had placed on a piece of heavy cardboard. "James, bring the can, please."

She squinted in the dim light of the single room. There was one window, but it was small and had only two panes of glass. She looked around at the single bed, pallet on the floor—probably for Danila—table and chairs, and steamer trunk against one wall. Everything they owned must be in this room. A pan of water simmered on the pot-bellied heating stove, and she could see no kitchen range. Mrs. Rudiger must cook on that small surface.

She set the cake on the table. "I didn't want to visit without bringing you something. Besides, I just cleaned the kitchen range and must practice cooking on it before the men return."

She stopped, realizing that she was talking too fast. "That's oatmeal. I . . . I made too much this morning, and it won't keep. I . . ."

She stopped again and realized that the Rudigers were staring at the cake. She stared too, hoping that a bug hadn't dived into it. It looked fine. Mrs. Rudiger gave a small sigh and then turned away in tears.

Julia appealed to Mr. Rudiger. "I hope I didn't hurt her feelings! It isn't really too festive, I suppose, and it did get jostled in the wagon."

He raised a hand to stop her. "Miss Darling, the cake is fine." He paused and swallowed, and she looked at him in panic too, wondering what was the matter. "It . . . it's just that we have not seen anything like this in a long time. No one comes here."

"Oh," was all she could think of to say. "I wanted to visit," she said simply.

His face red, Mr. Rudiger indicated one of the three stools in the shack. "We use the cans for siding. That's why my wife was there." Julia saw the humiliation in his face. "We don't have anything else."

Mr. Rudiger spoke to his wife in German. She nodded, skirted around the room, and added a stick of firewood to the heating stove. She looked directly at Julia for the first time and pantomimed drinking tea.

"Oh dear, I don't drink tea," Julia said to Mr. Rudiger.

"You can drink this tea," he told her with that same look of humiliation.

The silence seemed to hum in the small space. Julia indicated the cake. "Do you have some plates and forks?" she asked. "A slice of this would be really good, you know, to go along with tea."

Mr. Rudiger spoke again, and Ursula turned to the cracker box shelf, much like the one in her own kitchen at the Double Tipi. She brought four tin plates to the table and spoke to her husband.

"Ursula said she and Danila can eat from the same plate," Rudiger translated, telling Julia all she needed to know about the state of the crockery in the shack.

"That is excellent," Julia said. "Who wants to wash too many dishes?"

Rudiger smiled and nodded, content to keep up the fiction of normality, if he could. He handed her a knife, and Julia sliced the loaf cake, deeply aware how closely everyone in the room was watching her. She slid each slice onto a plate and two on the plate for Ursula and Danila.

There they sat. Ursula went to the pot-bellied stove, where she added what looked like a bedraggled green twig to the simmering water. As Julia watched, she swirled the stick around a few times and then removed it, placing it back on the cracker box shelf. She ladled the hot water into two tin cups and one small can and brought them to the table, using a corner of her apron in place of a pot holder. She sat down, a slight smile on her face.

"It's . . . it's mint tea," Rudiger explained, his embarrassment painfully obvious.

"Then I will be happy to have some," Julia assured them

both. *Dear God, these people have nothing, and I have only served to remind them,* she thought in horror. She looked at the Rudigers' patient faces and changed her mind. *No, they are offering me the best they have, to complement what I have brought.*

"Please tell your wife that mint tea is the perfect accompaniment to a loaf cake," Julia said as she handed around the slices.

Ursula pushed a tin cup closer to Julia, who picked it up, even as she felt tears well in her eyes. *Don't you dare cry,* she scolded herself. She took a sip and smiled at Ursula. "Exactly right."

The Rudigers ate quickly, not leaving a crumb anywhere. Without a word, Julia sliced off larger pieces for the second helpings, and watched those disappear just as fast. *I wish I had made a layer cake,* Julia thought. *Two layer cakes. Maybe a torte. Where are loaves and fishes when you need them?*

When she finished, Julia held out her tin cup. "A little bit more, if you please?" she asked.

Ursula beamed as she added another ladle of hot water and returned the cup to Julia. Rudiger held out his cup for more too. Julia glanced at James, relieved to see him taking the matter in stride, as though he drank hot water every day. In another moment, he and Danila left the table and went to the red wagon, where he brought in the leftover oatmeal. In another moment, he and the little girl were playing in the dirt beside the shack.

Julia turned her attention to Rudiger. "Mr. Rudiger, I have come to ask a favor."

If the German was surprised, he didn't show it. "Whatever I can do," he told her.

Taking a deep breath, Julia told him about the building paper rolled up in what was Mr. Otto's parlor. "I think there is enough to paper that room and probably the kitchen too. I don't think I can do it myself, but if you could help me, it would look so nice."

Mr. Rudiger was silent for such a long moment that Julia feared she had not made herself clear. "Mr. Otto and the others . . . they don't want us here," he said finally.

Julia writhed inside; nothing could have been more true. She chose honesty. "I know that, but Mr. Otto left me in charge, and I want that place to look better. Here's what I can do." She leaned closer and lowered her voice, as though Mr. Otto stood over her shoulder, glaring his disapproval. "If you will help me, I will give you the tar paper in the barn, so you can side your home." She overrode his skeptical look. "Mr. Rudiger, it's just lying in there, covered with cobwebs and bugs. No one is using it." She was pleading with him now. "It will make your house warmer for Danila."

Rudiger's glance wavered, and he looked out the open door, where his daughter was running a small wheeled cart down a sandy road James was building. "Warmer for Danila," he repeated. He sat back, crossed his arms, and thought a moment.

"We begin this soon, *ja?*" he asked.

"Tomorrow, if you wish," Julia replied, feeling Mr. Otto's eyes boring into her back even though he was miles away by now.

"You will not get in trouble?"

Julia thought about the contract she and Mr. Otto had signed. *The party of the first part expects a decent kitchen to work in,* she reminded herself. "Mr. Rudiger, I signed a contract with Mr. Otto saying I would remain his employee for one year. In exchange, he is contracted to provide me with a decent kitchen to work in. Once the building paper is up in the kitchen, he will fulfill his side of the contract. It's in writing."

Rudiger nodded, his face thoughtful now. "And if we paper your parlor, that is also in the contract?"

"Not precisely," Julia hedged. "Yes, it is! I am to have a comfortable place to sit in the evening. It's all part of the agreement he signed." *Sort of,* she thought. "Everyone is entitled to life, liberty, and the pursuit of happiness, Mr. Rudiger. Thomas Jefferson said so in the Declaration of Independence."

That seemed to clinch the matter for the immigrant. "Thomas Jefferson," he said. "Ah, *ja*. It must be so." He held out his hand. "I will do it, *Fraulein* Darling. Tomorrow is soon enough?"

She held out her hand and they shook while she stashed all her misgivings into that elastic corner of her brain. "Tomorrow is fine. If you want, let Danila and Ursula come, too. She can help me bake bread."

Rudiger gave her a calculating look. "*Fraulein,* anyone who can make a cake this good doesn't need help with bread."

Julia crossed her fingers. "I strained my shoulder, cleaning my cooking stove. I can use her help." *Heavenly Father, that is a useful, all-purpose lie,* Julia thought. *If I must repent of it, then I don't know thee very well, do I?*

"Very well, *Fraulein*, we will see you tomorrow morning," Rudiger said.

I will not worry about Mr. Otto, Julia thought as she and James walked back the way they had come. He was going to be gone for two weeks. Maybe he would develop amnesia and forget that the parlor and kitchen had been bleak and grimy when he left. *Two weeks is two weeks*, Julia decided. She would worry about Mr. Otto later.

She stopped again at the almost-hidden ranch turn-off. It was almost as though the Ottos had never wanted anyone to know where they lived. The Ottos had secrets, she decided. She touched the rim of the lady's straw hat she wore, wondering what had gone so wrong.

James idled along beside her, reminding her how kind her employer was, taking in strays in human form. Surely he could have no serious objection to helping his nearest neighbors.

"The Rudigers don't have much, do they?" James asked.

"No, they don't."

"We have more."

"We do. We're going to share what we have."

James tugged her hand. "Is that important, like saying prayers when we eat oatmeal?"

"I believe it is." *I am Ursula Rudiger's visiting teacher,* Julia thought. *That's the way it is, Mr. Otto.*

Thirteen

$\mathscr{D}$inner was stew and baked apples—simple fare that thrilled James but that made her mindful of what she would really cook when the men returned. James helped her with the dishes and didn't object to dumping ashes. He must have thought it reward enough when she dusted off the Victrola in what was to become the parlor and found one unbroken record.

"Enrico Caruso," she said, looking at the faded label. "There must be other records." She looked into the corner of the room and felt the hairs rise on the back of her neck. Someone had stuck shards of shattered records into one earthenware pot, like little plants. Julia rubbed her arms, suddenly cold. While Caruso sang, she swept up the shards and disposed of the pot, trying not to think about it.

When the Victrola ran down, she wound it again. "Caruso has one of the great voices of the opera world, James," she said. "I heard him in a recital last fall, when I lived in Boston."

"Did he sing 'Sweet Evalina'?" James asked.

Julia laughed, glad to dispel the bleak feeling of the room. "Not that night! Maybe he was saving it for Carnegie Hall."

After James went to bed, Julia stood in the doorway of the parlor, rubbing her arms again. In the morning, she would see if there were more feed sacks in the barn, some for curtains in here, and others to share with the Rudigers.

Almost against her will, she sat in the small rocking chair. She had wiped it clean and rubbed a shine into the arms, wishing she knew something about the lady who had used it nearly a decade ago.

She didn't sleep well; she woke as dawn came. The water in the Queen Atlantic's reservoir was still warm, so she poured herself a basin of water and washed her face, hands, and underarms after pulling down her nightgown and knotting it around her waist. She wouldn't be able to do this when the men returned. Maybe she could ask Mr. Rudiger to build her a washstand for her room.

By the time the Rudigers arrived, she and James had pulled the parlor furniture into the center of the room and moved what they could in the kitchen. She told the Rudigers she had waited so they could eat breakfast together—pancakes bloated with butter and maple syrup, with fresh milk a sleepy-eyed James had coaxed from the Jersey cow now cropping grass by the door.

She expected no complaint from the Rudigers and encouraged them to eat. No one objected when she added sausage links from the smokehouse. Finally, Mr. Rudiger held up his hands, as if to surrender, which warmed Julia's heart.

While Ursula dried the dishes, Rudiger walked around the parlor, nodding to himself. He fingered the building paper and nodded again. "A hammer, nails?" he asked.

She went with him into the barn, where he found what he needed. She pointed out the tar paper, and he nodded again. "It will be enough," he told her. "A knife?" They found that too.

Back in the house, Mr. Rudiger bowed and formally asked James to help. Soon Julia heard tapping as the homesteader tacked the paper to the wall. She turned her attention to bread, pretending a sore shoulder as she carefully dumped level measures of flour into the largest bowl she could find and set cakes of yeast in warm water.

She knew Ursula could not understand her, but Julia kept up a steady conversation, telling the shy woman about her plans for a meal the men of the Double Tipi would never forget, when they returned. They both kneaded bread as Danila greased the few loaf pans Julia could find. When the pans were packed, covered, and rising in the heat of the warming shelf, the women sat at the table and shaped the remaining dough into rolls.

As Julia shaped rolls, Ursula put her hand on Julia's fingers, stopping her. She deftly shaped the dough into another form.

"That's lovely," Julia said. "Show me again, please?"

Ursula did, and Julia copied her, pleased with the effect. "We shall do all the rest that way," she said. "It's much prettier than my way."

How to do this, Julia thought when the rolls were rising. She gestured for Ursula to come with her to her room, where she had folded all the clothes she'd washed yesterday. She sat Ursula down on her bed, held out the smaller clothing that James had outgrown, and then pointed to Danila, who had followed her mother into the bedroom.

Ursula understood, nodding as Julia held out the clothing. She held up a shirt to Danila and nodded again.

"I wish I had clothes for little girls, but perhaps you can use these," Julia told her. "I wish you understood me."

Maybe it didn't matter. With a bob of her head and another smile, Ursula took the clothing. When Mr. Rudiger declared he was done for the day, the clothes were packed into the little wagon, along with most of the bread and rolls. Rudiger just smiled and shook his head when he saw what

Julia had done. In that courtly gesture Julia decided she could like very much, he took her hand and bowed over it.

"You are kind to us, *fraulein*," he said. "Why, if I may ask?"

A week ago, maybe even yesterday, she would have been flustered and embarrassed. Something had happened while she kneaded dough and talked all day to a woman who didn't understand what she was saying.

"I need your help, Mr. Rudiger, if I am to have this place presentable by the time Mr. Otto returns," she told him. "As for the bread . . ." She looked at Ursula. "No one has used this kitchen range properly in many years. I am determined that it will work, and the best way to test it is to use it."

Julia didn't care if he believed her or not. *I dare you to tell me to stop*, she thought. *Please don't. I want to help your family.*

Rudiger must have sensed the futility of arguing over someone else's generosity. He bowed again. "You go in that room tonight and tell me what you think. I will start on the kitchen tomorrow."

After the Rudigers left with James accompanying them to make sure they reached the main road safely, Julia went into the parlor. She stood in the doorway, admiring the way something as pedestrian as gray building paper could bring a touch of comfort to what used to be little more than a glorified tack room with a Victrola. Even Mama would be pleased.

She couldn't help looking in the corner where she had uncovered all those broken records planted weirdly in a pot. Feeling unsettled, she went into the kitchen.

It took Mr. Rudiger three days to finish the work in the kitchen and parlor. Silent for the most part, he skillfully measured and cut the building paper, anchoring it firmly to the worn logs underneath, patching where he needed to around the window, and working around the Queen Atlantic, which bubbled with Connecticut chowder. James and Danila had provided trout from the river, which Julia had cleaned, scaled, and beheaded, dubbing it cod.

Rudiger came back the next day to fetch the tar paper, bringing a skinny horse and a feeble excuse for a wagon. Julia instructed James to make sure the horse was well-fortified with as much feed as it would eat, while the Queen Atlantic produced split pea soup weighed down with ham chunks from the smokehouse. By the end of the day, the kitchen was done, and so was the soup. Julia lugged a bucket of it to the wagon and wedged it next to the tar paper. She added a pound of the butter she had made earlier.

"We can't possibly drink all this milk," she said, settling a well-filled crock into a tight spot by the tar paper. "For a little cow, she really produces."

When she and James said good-bye to the Rudigers that night, Julia felt her misgivings grow. Maybe Mr. Otto had plans for that tar paper. Still, if he had wanted to use it, he wouldn't have stuffed it under feed sacks and machinery. *He won't even know it's gone*, she thought, brushing aside another twinge of conscience that seemed to float around like smoke.

When she woke in the morning, Julia felt a surge of disappointment that the work was done, and there was no reason for the Rudigers to visit. As she stirred a small pot of farina, she glanced at the calendar, surprised to see that it was Sunday. She added a handful of raisins to the pot and set it at the back of the range, missing her family.

Elbows on the table that had been scraped clean of years of detritus, she stared at the Queen Atlantic and wished herself home. Mama would be smelling of talcum powder and getting ready for Sunday School. Papa would already be at an early morning meeting. If the weather was nice in Salt Lake, she and Mama would walk to Sunday School. There would be roast beef and baked beans for dinner, a nap, and then sacrament meeting later: a day of church and talk, letter-writing and visiting. There had been a time when it bored her.

Julia had enjoyed Sundays in Boston, meeting at the small branch and sloughing off a week of cooking classes and other students who politely thought her strange. She enjoyed the fellowship of other displaced Saints a long way from the Rocky Mountains. Here there was nothing: no friends of like mind, no Sunday School, no sacrament meeting. If she was not mindful, Sunday could become as ordinary as Monday.

It was a distressing thought; maybe she was guilty of taking the Church for granted. She looked around the kitchen, with the clean, gray paper; the gleaming Queen Atlantic; the curtains she had strung late last night; and the neatly filled wood box. All was orderly, but she wanted to be in church.

What is it I am missing? she asked herself. Julia frowned and looked at the loaf of bread on the table, thinking of the deacons at the sacrament table with the bread and water. If she took ill in this lonely place, no one could give her a blessing. The good advice from her father could come in letters, as it had in Boston, but these letters would probably sit in a postal box in Gun Barrel for weeks until someone fetched them. With an ache in her heart, Julia knew she was missing the priesthood, a constant in her life that was no longer available.

Lonely, she wandered to the door of James's room, where he slept, his hand over his eyes. The gentle rise and fall of his chest soothed her and reminded her of her duty to him. The boy had been left in her care. If she had been thinking for even one second about leaving the Double Tipi—and how could she, since she had signed that pernicious contract—she made herself think again.

She watched James another moment, went to the front step, and sat down on the rough bench. She stared at the corral, empty of everything except a lame horse and the Jersey cow and her calf. "From now on, Julia Darling, Sundays will be what you make them," she said, "even if they are bare of everything you're used to. It's up to you to fill the day."

Julia began with her mother's Sunday dinner, roast beef and baked beans, ordinary in the extreme. By the time James came into the kitchen, rubbing his eyes, everything was cooking slow in a low oven. Lonely for company, Julia sat with him in the barn while he milked the cow. While Julia strained the milk, she lamented that the cow was drying up, which meant canned milk for the winter. There was cream enough for cream cake. When all was done, Julia took a sheet from her trunk and shook it onto the table, where it billowed and flattened.

James watched her. "What's that for?"

"It's for us," she said as she set out the heavy ranch crockery. "It's a sheet I have renamed a tablecloth. While we're waiting for dinner to cook, we're going to read from the Bible."

"Mr. Otto does that sometimes," James said, surprising her.

"I didn't know he had one. Where is it?"

He turned without answering her, and she followed him to Mr. Otto's room. As she stood in the doorway, too shy to go in, the boy went to the bureau and took the wooden box that he had emptied to use for the loaf cake.

He held it out to her. It contained an old Bible, well-thumbed and divided here and there with pressed flowers, a Jack of Spades—which made her smile—and a paper-thin scrap of paper with faded printing on it.

"My goodness, James. This is indeed a Bible. Do you have a favorite story?"

"Joseph and his coat," he said without hesitation.

"Let's find it," she told him, taking the book carefully in her hands. Out of curiosity, she turned to the front. "'Peter Otto,'" she read. "'Cherry, North Carolina. Born December 8, 1846. Son of Lucy and James Otto.'" She closed the book. "Mr. Otto is a long way from home."

"He's just around Laramie Peak," James reminded her.

She smiled. "True! James, I think we should read about Joseph in our parlor."

"Mr. Otto usually reads to me in here."

"It's not my room, and I wouldn't feel right doing that," Julia explained.

James understood. "You'd probably fall asleep, like Mr. Otto does."

"I probably would," she said with a laugh.

They read in the parlor, sitting close together on the settee that used to hold windmill parts. Luckily, James was an uncritical audience, which soothed Julia's soul, considering how long it took her to find the story of Joseph and his brothers. *I am a scripture slug*, she scolded herself as she searched the pages, hunting for Joseph and his pesky coat through Exodus and Deuteronomy before slapping her forehead and turning to the end of Genesis.

She read the story of Joseph and his brothers, thinking of her own two brothers, who ranched and taught school in Dixie, and Iris, who was just learning to be a wife on a dairy farm. *I'm glad we get along better than Joseph and his brothers,* she thought.

James dozed. She took a deep breath, certain from the kitchen odors that dinner was nearly ready. The potatoes she had cooked and left in the warming oven were ready to mash. She opened the Bible again and carefully ruffled the pages to find a bookmark.

Julia found that scrap of paper and placed it in Genesis. Before she closed the Bible again, she looked at the much-creased piece of paper, squinting to read the one sentence underlined in fading ink. She read it out loud softly: " 'For behold, are we not all beggars? Do we not all depend upon the same Being, even God, for all the substance which we have?' "

That was odd. She read it again. "Well, well, Mr. Otto, I think this is from the Book of Mormon," she said, keeping her voice soft. "I can't remember where, but I think it is."

She closed the Bible thoughtfully, thinking of Matt Malloy and how he came to the ranch. Mr. Otto had told him something about everyone being a beggar.

"Are we not all beggars?" she repeated softly. "How would you know that, Mr. Otto?"

After dinner, Julia and James took a walk down to the river. James needed no coaxing to take off his shoes, roll up his pant legs, and cross the slippery stones to where the bed of watercress grew in the lengthening shadows. "If you can fetch me a big handful, I will make watercress soup," she told him.

He did as she asked, waving the bunch over his head and laughing at himself when the water on the peppery grass sprayed him. "You eat this?" he asked, his voice dubious.

"Try it. Just take a few leaves. There now."

He nodded and ate some more. "What else can we eat around here?" he asked.

"Dandelions in the spring. We'll have to look around. I might just make watercress soup for Mr. Otto."

He came back to her, balancing on the rocks, and handed her the watercress. "I think mostly he likes beef."

"That may be so, but we have to branch out and flex our gastronomic muscles," she told him, remembering a lecture from Miss Farmer on precisely that subject. She glanced at James, who plainly had no idea what she was talking about. "We have to try new things. That's why I am here."

She spent the afternoon writing letters that would never be delivered in anything close to timely fashion. She spent the most time over her letter to Iris, telling her sister about the ranch, the kitchen, and the Rudigers. By the time she had finished, folding the pages and looking around in her trunk for an envelope, the day was over. One Sunday gone, fifty-one to go. In fifty-two more Sundays, she would be home.

James needed no urging to go to bed, especially when she promised to read the rest of Joseph's story. She followed it up with the little half-book. He was still awake, but just barely, by the time she reached the last page, so she made up her own ending, with the children reuniting with their family after weeks and weeks away, sipping watercress soup and toasting cheese.

"I've never toasted cheese," James said after an enormous yawn.

"We'll do it this winter," she assured him, thinking of all the cheese she and Iris had toasted in the parlor fireplace while Mama and Papa read out loud from the *Improvement Era*. Maybe Mama would send her copies of the *Juvenile Instructor*, with its poems and stories with endings.

When James was asleep, Julia took the Bible back into Mr. Otto's room, taking the wooden box from the bureau.

She sat down on his bed, wondering if there were other scraps in the Bible. She looked at the impromptu bookmark she had placed in Genesis. Beggars.

She put the Bible back into the box, but not before she noticed a small double picture frame, folded on its hinges. "Where are your manners, Julia Darling?" she asked aloud. "No one will know." She picked up the little frames and opened them.

She gasped and dropped it back into the box, her heart pounding in her chest. When her breathing slowed to nearly normal, she opened the frame again, holding it at arm's length.

She hadn't been mistaken. It wasn't her imagination. Dressed in wedding clothes, a man and a woman looked out at her from their separate frames. Someone in an obvious fury had taken scissors or a knife to each sepia-toned photograph, breaking the glass, and then dragging the sharp edge across each face. Holding her breath, she bent closer for a better look.

Without question, the man was Mr. Otto.

Unnerved, Julia closed the frames. With shaking fingers, she positioned the Bible back in the box and quickly returned it to the top of the bureau. She couldn't leave the room fast enough.

Fourteen

Julia took a long time getting to sleep. After making sure the latch was fixed on the outside door, she propped a chair against the door in her room and climbed into bed. After a moment of wide-eyed fear, she flung back the covers, disgusted with herself. If her door was closed, she would never hear James if he cried out in a nightmare. Too bad there wasn't someone to comfort her if *she* cried out.

She opened her door, certain she would see the photographs propped on the kitchen table, staring at her from maimed eyes. "You're ridiculous," she said out loud to bolster her courage. The only things on the table were condiment bottles.

Mature chef, she thought, as she got back into bed. *You're the adult here. Act like one.* She toyed with kneeling by her bed for evening prayers but then vetoed it, just this once. No telling what was underneath her bed.

She pulled the covers over her head and lay awake a long time, remembering all the aggravations in her engagement to Ezra Quayle. She knew that some of them were petty and shallow; others were real. None of them even came close to willfully gouging out the eyes of a photograph.

Before she dropped off to sleep, Julia knew that no matter what she thought, there was no way she could ever bring up the subject with her employer. If she said anything, Mr. Otto would know she had been snooping in his belongings. True, she had only been returning the Bible to its receptacle, but bumptious curiosity had compelled her to open the double frame.

As she shivered and resolutely kept the blanket over her head like a child, Julia could not help asking herself: what kind of marriage led to such mutilation? It was nothing she was remotely acquainted with. As much as she did not want to consider it, she also had to wonder which of the partners had done the photograph damage. Was it Mr. Otto or his wife, whoever and wherever she was?

She could solve her problem immediately. A letter to her parents would bring her father to Wyoming to take her home, contract or no contract. Julia considered it for a long moment, but pride kept her in bed and not at the table, writing a letter. *I agreed to come here,* she thought. *I will work this out myself.*

By morning light, the terror diminished. The simple act of stewing some dried apples and liberally sprinkling cinnamon and sugar over the bubbling goodness restored some peace to her mind; cooking did that. She stirred the pot, breathing deep of the soothing, familiar odors. Still, later that day, it was a relief when James came running inside from playing by the river to announce that Mr. Marlowe was coming.

Can't be, she thought, pushing a stray pin into her chignon. *He's with the roundup.* She went to the front step, and shaded her eyes against the sun's glare, and laughed out loud. Poor James. He was destined to never know the difference between Mr. and Mrs.

Dressed in trousers and a flannel shirt, Alice Marlowe brought eggs in a basket. Julia sighed with relief and led her inside.

"Be it ever so humble," she told Alice as they stepped inside. "It's a far cry from what I walked into, a few days ago, if you'll please excuse Miss October! We need a dignified calendar—"

"—which you may never find in Wyoming," Alice finished.

"There were calendars covering all the walls, but that was nothing to the calving ropes in the rafters and the layers of grease on everything," Julia said. "Would you like some treacle loaf? I even made a pot of hot chocolate this morning."

Julia handed Alice a slice of the treacle loaf, chewy and fragrant with nutmeg and cinnamon. "Mr. Otto only believes in tin plates, I think, but the forks are genuine silver." She sat down too. "He's a contradiction."

"Then I would say he is like most men." Alice touched the egg basket. "I'll keep the eggs coming as long as my barnyard girls are laying." The Queen Atlantic caught her eye. "I must say, this is better than anything I imagined you would find! I had visions of you using flint and steel to make a twig fire."

"It's so much better since Mr. Rudiger put up this lovely building paper and—"

Alice sucked in her breath. "Julia, you didn't ask them for help!"

"Well, yes. They're my nearest neighbors. Alice, you should see how poor their shack is. Ursula only had hot water with a swish of mint to serve me."

Alice put her hand on Julia's arm. "I'm sure Paul told you not to have anything to do with them."

"He did, but—"

"The ranchers are trying to starve them out of the valley," Alice said. "It's for their own good."

You can't mean that, Julia thought. *If you only could have seen Ursula's eyes, so deep set, and how they lit up when*

I brought oatmeal and a little loaf cake. "I was being neighborly," she said lamely.

Better spill all the beans. "I made a bargain with Mr. Rudiger. He put up the building paper in here, and in what I can honestly call a parlor now. In exchange, I . . . I gave him a couple rolls of tar paper that were just gathering dust in the barn."

"You did *what*?"

Looking at the dismay on Alice Marlowe's face, all of Julia's misgivings returned. "No one was using it," she said in a small voice. "You've seen how they have tacked tin cans over the walls. It must be freezing in the winter."

Alice glared at her. "That's the whole point, Julia! Those people have to leave. You're just prolonging the agony!"

"No, I'm helping people who need my help. It's what my mother would do," she said quietly after a moment considering it. "It's the way I was raised." Some spark in her made Julia keep going, despite the militant look in Alice's eyes. "It's what I learned in church, too."

Alice said nothing for a long moment. "Maybe that's how Mormons think, but you're not in Utah now, and Paul Otto is going to be really bothered by this." She sipped her hot chocolate in silence while Julia stared straight ahead, embarrassed.

The moment passed. Alice sighed and held out her tin cup for more. "Julia, you're young. Life is so hard here, and the Rudigers are in over their heads. What you did is not a kindness."

"Maybe Mr. Otto will fire me," Julia said as she poured more hot chocolate.

"He might," Alice said, offering her no reassurance. "I know. It's hard to see them starve. I don't know what they are living on now."

A lot of my stew and bread and rolls, Julia thought, *but you don't need to know that.* Alice said nothing else, but she didn't need to. The silence thickened in the kitchen. With an effort, Alice changed the subject. "I guess what you did can't be helped now. I also came to tell you that I am going to Gun Barrel tomorrow. If there is anything you want, I can get it."

"There is," Julia replied, grateful to move on. "I'm planning a most excellent dinner for when Mr. Otto and his men return."

"Make me a list. I'll charge it to Paul's account." Alice's face was thoughtful. "I wouldn't do anything too elaborate. They like their fried steak and hash browns."

"He didn't hire me to do steak and hash browns," Julia said. *I thought Alice would understand,* she told herself. "Alice, he did title that ad 'Desperate Rancher.'"

"I know! He was at my kitchen table when he wrote it. Julia, he had just spent the morning suffering from eating extremely mature canned peaches, following an evening of Little River's Vienna sausages in tomatoey goo." She shuddered. "He just wants a decent, home-cooked meal."

Julia didn't feel like surrendering. "But he specifically asked for a graduate of the Boston Cooking School," she reminded Alice.

Still looking thoughtful, Alice finished her hot chocolate. "I guess you know best."

Julia could hardly overlook her dubious tone of voice. "Alice, I know what to do. I truly do. I'm going to start with cream of watercress soup and follow it with a string bean salad, then beefsteak with an oyster blanket. Which reminds me: I'll add more canned oysters to my list. I have some, but probably not enough."

"An *oyster* blanket?" There was no mistaking Alice's skepticism.

"It's delicious. They'll love it. You'll see."

As the week passed, Julia began to doubt herself. Determined to assuage her fears, she sent James to the river to gather watercress. She chopped it fine and added it to her white sauce, bubbly and thick. She filled a bowl for James.

"Blow on it. It's hot," she admonished.

He did as she said, blowing until half of it flew off his soup spoon. He took a bite, his face giving away nothing.

"Well? How does it taste?" she asked.

He thought a moment, rolling the mouthful over his tongue. "Green."

She took a sip from her bowl. Delicious. "It's nutritious, James, just what men need after a hard time on the range."

He was more enthusiastic the afternoon she experimented with Duchess Potatoes. She took out her pastry bag and tubes, selecting the flower tip and loading the bag with mashed potatoes generously fortified with three eggs. James stared in amazement as she piped a mound of delicate potato flowers on a platter, brushed them with egg white, and then sent them into the Queen Atlantic's oven for a brief sojourn. James cleaned the platter when they were done and looked around for more. *That's a relief,* Julia told herself. *It's hard to go wrong with Duchess Potatoes.*

He wouldn't have anything to do with the string bean salad, beans doused in French dressing and arranged like a bonfire, surrounded by croutons. "I don't think they need that," he told her, pointing to the orange dressing.

"It's one of Miss Farmer's signature salads," Julia assured him. "I've seen members of the Massachusetts state legislature sit in her test dining room and demand more."

James only shook his head.

"Well, they did," she told him feebly.

Not happy with the look on his face, Julia flipped a few

pages in her cookbook. "If string beans won't do, what about warm liver salad with perry vinegar dressing?"

James stared at her with a shocked expression. "Mr. Darling! No!"

It was hard for her to keep a defensive tone out of her voice, but she tried. "James, when it comes to cooking, I really do know best. This recipe never fails to please. That's why Mr. Otto hired me."

"Not for warm liver," James persisted doggedly.

We will have to agree to disagree on this matter, she thought as she sat at the wonderfully clean and stick-free table in the kitchen she was rapidly coming to think of as her own and outlined a menu that would prove to Mr. Otto that she knew what she was doing.

Her doubts returned at the end of the week, when Alice Marlowe returned with three letters—one each from Iris, her mother, and her father—more eggs, and all the canned oysters she could locate in Gun Barrel. She also carried news that the men would be returning from the roundup by Tuesday, trailing the cattle bound for Chicago's stockyards, and hungry.

"There is a note for you from Paul," Alice said, handing her the eggs, cushioned in salt in a small wooden box. "I stuck it in with the eggs."

Julia set the eggs on the table and directed James to put the cans of oysters in the pantry. She shook the salt from the note and sat down to read it.

She didn't mean to frown over the note, but she couldn't help herself. "He says he is sending Matt Malloy on ahead to butcher a yearling. He says he likes his steak medium rare." Julia shook her head. " 'Lots of red, but no moo,' he says." Julia put the note in her lap. "Matt can just as easily carve me off a big roast."

"Julia, I've told you they like their steak. Fried," Alice added more firmly.

It stung her to hear Alice speaking so slow and cautious, but Julia tried not to let it show. *I have to live on this ranch for a year, and I need a few friends,* she reminded herself.

After reading the note again, she took a deep breath. "When they finish the dinner I'll prepare, they won't even think about something as boring as steak and greasy potatoes."

Alice's eyes were kind. "I'm certain Mrs. Farmer could never envision the Double Tipi, but Julia . . ." She stopped. "Well, do your best," she concluded. "I'm certain no one will ever forget this dinner."

"They won't," Julia assured her. "Not in a million years."

⁓⁓

Matt carved off the roast she wanted, hanging it in the meat room to drip and age. He also sliced a huge platter of steaks. To humor him, she fried a well-done steak at his request, cringing inside as the beautiful meat curled and darkened. He seemed pleased with the results, tucking in at the table after slicing off a generous hunk for James. Tentatively, she tried the Duchess Potatoes on him, and he nodded his approval. "Make lots of these," he told her, wolfing down all the delicate rosettes she had prepared for the three of them. "This too," he told her after he inhaled nearly half the dried apple pie she had thrown together at the last minute.

"Actually, I'm making a Queen Cake with opera caramel frosting," she told him. "I'll make it tomorrow."

"Plenty of biscuits too," he suggested, wiping his mouth with the napkin she hastily handed him when he started going for his sleeve.

"I'm making bow-knot rolls," she said, as he stood up

and stretched, patting his stomach. "They're really dainty and pretty."

Matt laughed. "Julia Darling, you're a source of amusement," he told her, exaggerating his brogue. "Big baking powder biscuits. Willy Bill told me two days ago he's been dreaming about that." He winked at her. "Better than eating his bunkie, eh?"

Julia shuddered.

"Probably just a rumor, anyway." Matt put on his hat and looked at James. "Come on, lad. Mr. Otto said specifically that you were to help me check the fence, 'cause a big herd's coming." He tipped his hat to Julia. "That steak was perfection. Come on, James. Mr. Otto is counting on you."

She cooked all day, starting with the bow-knot rolls when the Queen Atlantic was hottest and then moving to the Queen Cake, long and luscious in a loaf pan. When it had cooled, she set it on a slab of wood she had covered with a bit of green oilcloth she had found in the pantry, since Mr. Otto had no serving dishes.

She made ornamental frosting instead of opera caramel, applying it in dainty whorls and then using her frosting tubes to create delicate rosettes all over. She centered a silver candy dot—one of the many treats she had brought from Salt Lake—in each rosette until the whole cake shimmered. The cake went in the pantry, carefully covered with a large pot.

By the time night fell and Matt and James returned, Julia was too tired to cook more than steak and fried potatoes again. Neither man nor boy objected, which delighted her, thinking how much happier everyone would be tomorrow evening when she unveiled the meal of her dreams. Matt left in the morning to return to the roundup crew, assuring her that the men and cattle would be at the Double Tipi by suppertime. Julia sent James to the river for watercress, over-looking his dubious frown. "Watercress is good for you," she told his retreating form.

The oyster blanket for the roast was even better than the one she had made for her Boston final examination. Miss Farmer would frown, but Julia couldn't help peeking in the oven at the roast, all crusty with spices and bubbling. When she took it from the oven, she would cover it with the oyster blanket and then set it aside to harden.

She sniffed the kitchen's aromas, a far cry from the noxious fumes that had made her burst into tears—so unprofessional—on her arrival three weeks ago. The bloody calving ropes overhead were long gone; the Queen Atlantic gleamed; even her feed sack curtains gave the room a certain dignity. Best of all was the soft grey of the building paper Mr. Rudiger had attached so well in exchange for the tar paper.

There wasn't a thing in the kitchen Julia wasn't proud to display. Earlier in the week, she had boiled an extra sheet into submission, turning it white again, like Mr. Otto's shirts. After stitching up some holes, she ironed the sheet and spread it on the table.

"Mr. Otto, now you'll see what I can really do," she murmured, hand shading her eyes as she watched for the men.

She was shaping grated potatoes into miniature birds' nests when James ran in to say he could see the dust from the cattle. She nodded to him, her eyes on the potatoes. A mound of Duchess Potatoes was in the oven now, but after watching Matt demolish the whole pile last night, she had decided to augment the meal with Potatoes en Surprise. The peas in their cream sauce simmered on the back of the Queen, while she deftly rolled the potato nests in flour and eggs and deep fried them.

While the nests cooled on the work table, she removed the roast and covered it with the hardening oyster blanket and set it in the warming oven. After pouring perry vinegar over it, Julia set the warm liver salad, quivering on water-cress, in the middle of the table next to the string bean salad. Quickly she filled the fried potato nests with creamed peas and put them next to the Duchess Potatoes. Careful not to disturb it, she carried the roast in its oyster blanket to the head of the table, where Mr. Otto could carve it.

When she heard the cattle, Julia went to the kitchen door again and stood there as the men of the Double Tipi, plus others she didn't know, rode over the ridge and through the open gate of the corral that Matt and James had strength-ened yesterday. She couldn't help blushing when Mr. Otto, sprouting several days' growth of whiskers, tipped his hat to her. *Oh, Mr. Otto, I have such a meal for you*, she thought, barely able to contain her excitement.

She went into the kitchen and traded her stained apron for a spotless white one. Eager to share what she did so well, Julia went back to the door to watch the men corral the noisy cattle and then stable their horses. Impatient, she silently urged them to speed through the currying and graining.

Mr. Otto came in first. Suddenly shy, Julia put her hands behind her back like a little girl. "Welcome back," she said. "I've fixed quite a dinner for you."

He looked over her shoulder at the laden table. "I brought along a few extra mouths to feed," he told her, his eyes on the food. "McLemore still thinks you'll swoon over him and start cooking in *his* kitchen. Marlowe wasn't about to miss this, and there are two cattle buyers all ready to be impressed."

She watched his face, wondering what he was searching for, and stepped back so he could get closer to the table. He stood there for the longest time. She could hardly keep her delight to herself. "Takes your breath away, doesn't it?" she asked finally, unable to resist.

He turned around and stared at her until she felt a slow blush rise up her chest to her neck. "Darling, where are the steaks and hash browns?"

"Oh, that. I told you I could do much better, Mr. Otto." She gestured to the table, suddenly less sure of herself. "This is what happens when you hire a graduate of the Boston Cooking School."

She stepped aside as the other dusty men came into the kitchen, hats in hand, with their eyes on the table.

"D-do be seated," Julia said after clearing her throat, which suddenly felt dry.

Chairs scraped out, but to her discomfort, no one sat down. The room was quiet as the men looked up and down the table.

Mr. Otto whispered in her ear. "Where's the steak?"

"I cooked a roast," she whispered back.

He looked at the table and frowned. "I don't even see that," he whispered again.

Julia felt her heart begin to sink. "It . . . it's under the oyster blanket. Right there."

"Good grief," he said as he sat down heavily. He looked around. "Sit down, gents."

Julia couldn't overlook the men's reluctance. She went to the stove and returned with the soup tureen she had brought from home. "We're starting with watercress soup, which is followed by string bean salad and warm liver salad."

Ten pairs of eyes looked at her simultaneously, and she felt her heart slide down to her shoes. Doc looked away first, staring down at the tin bowl in front of him as she ladled in the pale green and creamy soup. Matt sighed and stared briefly at the ceiling, as though invoking saints. Charlie McLemore's expression was unreadable. To Julia's horrified eyes, it looked more like relief than anything else—relief that she had not actually accepted his proposal of two weeks ago.

She went around the silent table, doling out the lovely watercress soup that two Congressmen and a Boston alderman had praised when she served them a year ago, at her Fancy Cooking examination dinner. She darted a glance at Mr. Otto, but his expression was unreadable. He dipped a cautious spoon into the smooth goodness that had been rewarded with an A grade in Boston.

"It's cream of watercress soup," she managed. "Very nourishing."

"Very green," McLemore said softly as he set down his spoon.

The silence seemed to hum. "Try some of the warm liver salad," she whispered.

"Not in my lifetime," he said. As she watched, her eyes wide, McLemore got up, put on his Stetson, and walked out the door without another word.

"But it's my best meal," Julia said to no one in particular as Marlowe rose too.

"I'm sure it is, Julia," he said, and his expression was kind. "I just remembered that Alice wanted me to come right home."

"We'll come with you," one of the buyers said hurriedly, his face red. "Miss Darling, we need to get to Cheyenne. You know, lots of paperwork there, to get ready for this shipment."

"I . . ."

She stopped. She was just speaking to their backs. Horrified, she didn't know where to look. As it turned out, it didn't matter, because no one was looking at her except Mr. Otto.

She reached out to pass him the warm liver salad and stopped. *Alice Marlowe warned me, and I didn't listen,* Julia thought, as the acutest humiliation settled around her like the oyster blanket around her beautiful roast. She looked around the table, deeply aware that not one man still seated there wanted what she had prepared. In her confidence— maybe her arrogance—she had gone against every gentle hint lobbed in her direction.

"I'm truly sorry about this," she said. Her voice seemed unnaturally high to her ears, but at least she wasn't in tears. "Matt, you know where those steaks are that you cut yesterday."

He nodded.

"I've left a mess here in the kitchen, so perhaps you could take them to the bunkhouse, and you all can fry your own dinner."

All the chairs scraped back at the same time; they couldn't leave the room fast enough.

She looked at James, who was watching her, his eyes uncertain. "James, you and Matt know how good the Duchess Potatoes are. Carry that platter to the bunkhouse, will you?"

"They *are* good," Matt said.

"Take the cake too," Julia said. She went to the work-table by the Queen Atlantic and picked up the lovely loaf cake, all speckled with silver dots. She had spent hours placing each little medallion.

Willy Bill eyed it with suspicion. "Looks like buck-shot."

"Take it, Bill."

There wasn't any arguing with Mr. Otto's tone of voice.

The old hand picked it up gingerly as though he expected it to explode and held it out far in front of him.

Julia watched the men file out the kitchen door, James bringing up the rear with the Duchess Potatoes, each a little dollop of perfection. He looked back at her, and she gave him the only smile she had left anywhere.

"Have a seat, Darling."

She hadn't heard Mr. Otto rise, and there he was behind her. She gave him only the quickest glance, too ashamed to actually look in his eyes. She did see that he was holding a chair out for her. She sat down, her hands in her lap, her eyes on her plate, so embarrassed that she almost asked the Lord to open up the floor and let her slide away in blessed oblivion.

He sat down again. Her cheeks burned, and she held her lips tight together, determined not to cry. In her ignorance, she had fixed the best meal she knew how. Her return ticket was in the bureau in her room. She could be on her way tomorrow. *Fire me, Mr. Otto,* she thought. *Just fire me, and get it over with.*

Fifteen

She stared down at the table, blinking back tears. When she finally looked up, Mr. Otto was eating the warm liver salad, his eyes on her as he chewed and manfully swallowed. He managed two bites and was about to fork up another when she stopped him.

"You needn't eat that, Mr. Otto," she said, her voice scarcely above a whisper.

"I won't argue," he told her. "I've never been partial to string beans, so I'll let that one go, as well." He tapped the oyster blanket covering the roast in front of him. "What's underneath this?"

"A roast, medium rare," she whispered, not certain if he was trying to humiliate her or if he just was curious. *Julia, you know he's not cruel,* she reminded herself. "You can just peel back the blanket and slice off some roast."

He did as she said without comment, slicing off a healthy slab of meat, pink all the way through. "I usually like my meat a little more done, but I'll give it a try," he told her as he cut himself a piece and popped it in his mouth. He nodded. "Not bad at all."

It wasn't precisely fulsome praise, but she felt some of the heat leave her face. She tried to arrange her expression along neutral lines as she looked at her empty plate again, convinced that she would never eat or cook another morsel at the Double Tipi. Her brief tenure was coming to an end.

"And those little bird nest things over there?"

Julia looked up. He was pointing with his fork at her lovely Potatoes en Surprise, those crisp little baskets holding creamed peas.

"Potatoes en Surprise," she told him calmly, even if she couldn't look him in the eyes. "I fried the shredded potatoes, shaped them into nests, and put creamed peas in the nests."

"That *is* a surprise." He took one, eyed it a moment, and forked into it. "Not sure about that one," he said when he finished one nest. "Still . . ." He took another nest onto his plate.

Why did it take her so long to realize what he was doing? Deserted by his hands, friends, and business associates and all by himself, he was being kind to someone who had come up fearsomely short. She didn't know Mr. Otto well, but she knew he did not suffer fools gladly. He was being more considerate than she had any right to expect.

Julia Darling, he at least deserves the courtesy of your regard, she thought, as she mustered up her courage and looked him in the face. *And it certainly won't hurt you to apologize.*

"I'm sorry, Mr. Otto," she said, grateful to speak the words and thankful for her own calmness, especially when she was churning inside. "I . . . I just thought that when you specified a graduate of the Boston School of Cookery, you wanted what a graduate would do. You're being awfully nice about this, but you can go ahead and fire me. I deserve it and I don't mind."

He was silent for a long moment, idly twirling his fork in the potato nest, agitating the creamed peas. "I can't do that, Darling," he said finally. "Remember that contract we signed? It protects me, but it also protects you. Nope. We have a year to get it right."

He had her there. She wanted to say something; what,

she wasn't sure, when she heard horses in the front yard. She looked out the window to see Charles McLemore again, Mr. Marlowe at his side. Both men looked tight-lipped and grim, and she knew why.

"H'mm. Maybe they changed their feeble minds about dinner," Mr. Otto commented as he sliced off more roast.

"No, Mr. Otto. I've done a worse thing. Let me show you what I did."

The men hadn't dismounted yet. They seemed to be arguing. Julia rose and beckoned Mr. Otto to follow her. She led him into the parlor, warm and inviting now, with the lovely building paper Mr. Rudiger had applied. Mr. Otto looked around, appreciative.

"Maybe you didn't notice it in the kitchen too, what with all of my culinary distractions." She clasped her hands together. "Without your permission, obviously, I gave Mr. Rudiger some tar paper gathering cobwebs and mouse nests in your barn. In exchange, he tacked up these rolls of building paper rolled up in that corner. I think Mr. McLemore and Mr. Marlowe have just been by the Rudiger shack and seen the improvements."

She hurried to confess her felony before the men stormed into the ranch house. As she did, she felt her heart give a little lift. "I haven't been here long, but everyone has made it amply clear that the Rudigers are not to be helped. I helped them. When you left me here with James, you told me I was in charge. I only did what I would have done back in Salt Lake City. I also took them food, because they're hungry. I did everything you told me not to do. I wish I felt worse about it, but I don't."

"That's an honest answer." Mr. Otto regarded her and then looked around the parlor, a half smile on his face. "Jeepers, he did a nice job."

"This isn't covered under any clause in the contract. I went against everything you told me to do," Julia said simply. It was easier than she thought to confess, even as she heard McLemore and Marlowe bang on the door before coming into the kitchen. "Don't defend me, Mr. Otto, if you're so inclined. I was wrong."

"You sure about that?" he asked, and turned to the doorway. "Darling, I think we have company. McLemore and Marlowe, I thought you'd gone. Forget something?"

McLemore hardly glanced at Mr. Otto as he barreled into the parlor, his face red. He shook his finger at Julia, advancing toward her with such a look that she felt her blood run in chunks. Mr. Otto stepped between her and McLemore's rage.

"That's far enough, McLemore," he said, his voice the quiet menace Julia remembered from the restaurant.

McLemore stopped, but he peered around Mr. Otto to glare at Julia. "No one's supposed to help them!" he roared. "You knew that! Guess you obey your employer about as well as you cook!"

That stung. Julia looked away, humiliated.

"There's nothing wrong with her cooking," Mr. Otto said in that same controlled voice.

"I wouldn't have her in my kitchen now," McLemore said, his voice softer, more menacing.

"Then it's a good thing you'll never have that problem." Mr. Otto gestured to the settee. "Have a seat. Tell me what you think of this parlor."

Neither man sat. Julia glanced at Mr. Marlowe, still in the doorway, looking indecisive as his own indignation faded.

"Seriously. Look around. When you barged in here, McLemore, and upset my cook, she had just told me that she traded a roll of tar paper in my barn to Karl Rudiger, if he would put up the building paper that's been gathering cobwebs in this parlor for eight years."

Still keeping himself between Julia and McLemore, Mr. Otto gazed at his parlor. "He did a wonderful job. Darling now has a good place to sit in the winter. Shoot, I could probably even read my paper in here and put my feet up. The kitchen looks better too."

He walked closer to McLemore. Mr. Otto was several inches shorter, but it didn't seem to matter. McLemore backed up toward the doorway. "Did Rudiger do a good job on his shack?"

McLemore swore.

"Not in my house, McLemore," Mr. Otto said, and there was no mistaking the steel in his voice. "Things are different here now. No swearing." He looked at Marlowe. "Did he do a good job?"

"First rate, Paul," Marlowe said. "He's got that shack all buttoned up for winter."

"That's the problem, Paul! What's the matter with you?" McLemore glared at Julia again. "She's probably been *feeding* them too!" He flung the word at her.

"I hope to heaven she has," Mr. Otto replied, his voice even softer now. "They're all too thin because they've been subsisting on *our* charity. That adds up to a mean supper." He turned to look at her. "Thanks for reminding me of something I shouldn't have forgotten. Gentlemen, this conversation is over."

And it was. With another filthy look in her direction, McLemore swore again and stomped out of the parlor. When he slammed the kitchen door, Julia heard a glass break.

"Temper, temper," Marlowe said, as he looked after his companion. He straightened up from the parlor doorway, where he had been leaning. "Paul, you know it's in the Rudiger's best interest to be forced off this land. You said so."

"I know, and shame on me," Mr. Otto replied. "It's more my problem than anyone else's, because his little piece of property abuts mine." He turned around to look at Julia. "Darling, I've been going at this all the wrong way. You've reminded me that there might be a simpler solution." He nodded to Marlowe. "We'll trail the beeves past your doorway tomorrow by mid-day. See you then?"

"You will," Marlowe said, the tension gone from his voice. He tugged at his hat brim. "G'day, ma'am. See ya, Paul."

Mr. Otto didn't move from his stance in front of Julia until she heard horses' hooves receding down the valley. "Well, that could have been worse," he told her, his tone mild again. "Have a seat in this nice parlor."

She sat, mainly because her legs felt unequal to the task of maintaining her upright. "James and I fixed the rest of the room when Mr. Rudiger finished," she said. "He was so helpful. Even Mr. Rudiger said so."

Mr. Otto sat next to her, and she leaned toward him, suddenly alarmed. "I hope Mr. McLemore doesn't cause you any trouble. I'd feel bad about that."

He laughed. "I believe you would! Don't worry about ol' McLemore." He looked around again. "Yep. It's a nice job. Are those feed sack curtains?"

She nodded. "I bleached most of the writing out. If you look really close, you can still see 'Big Chief Flour.' "

"Hardly noticed. What did you do around the edges?"

"Crocheted scallops."

"Mighty fine ones."

Julia couldn't help but smile at that.

Mr. Otto got to his feet. "I'll talk to those prima donnas

in the bunkhouse. No reason why we can't compromise, if you're willing to bend a little, and they are too."

She nodded. He gave her a small salute and left the parlor. When she thought she could stand again, she went into the kitchen and surveyed the ruin of her beautiful dinner. She tried to look at the lovely oyster blanket, the warm liver salad—sagging now—and the wilted string beans through different eyes. *Papa would tell me Rome wasn't built in a day,* Julia reminded herself as she gathered up the mostly unused tin plates and carried them to the sink.

With fewer pangs than she would have thought possible, Julia consigned the oyster blanket to the garbage can, following it with the liver salad. She sat down and ate some of the string bean salad, still happy with it, even if no one else was. Mr. Otto was correct: the roast was done just right. The creamed peas had made the potato nests soggy, but she ate one anyway as she wondered how her Duchess Potatoes had fared in the bunkhouse.

Dusk had come and gone before the kitchen met her standards again. Humming to herself now, she cut into the crusty loaves of bread she had baked yesterday and made enough roast beef sandwiches to fill her largest enamel basin. Propping it on her hip, Julia took a quart jar of dill pickles and carried them to the bunkhouse.

Doc opened the door even before she knocked, and there was no overlooking the penitence in his eyes. "Don't worry," she said quietly. She set the sandwiches on the table, left the pickles, and quietly closed the door after her.

Sandwich in hand, James joined her before she reached the ranch house. She ruffled his hair. "Tired?"

He nodded.

"Wash up, and I'll read to you."

"Me too?"

She turned around and laughed at Mr. Otto. "Only if you can find another book that James will be interested in."

He walked with them to the house, held open the door for her, took a towel from the pile she had folded yesterday, and a bar of soap. "James, you have her all to yourself."

"We can wait," James said.

"No, no. Tell you what though, Darling. When you get James all tucked up, wait for me in the new and greatly improved parlor, and I'll give you a report from the bunkhouse." He looked her right in the eye. "Don't look so wary! I think you can live with it."

In another moment he was out the door. She heard him whistling as he headed into the dark. "I would think it's a little cold for the river now," she murmured.

"He's tough," James said, and yawned.

He was also quick in cold water. Mr. Otto was seated in the parlor, his hair wet and slicked back, when she finished reading to James, making up yet another ending to the scrap of a book, and singing "Sweet Evalina."

"Nice rendition," he told her as she came into the parlor.

Julia rolled her eyes. "I auditioned three or four new songs while you were gone. The only one with any appeal was 'What Do You Do with a Drunken Sailor.'" She sighed. "But here we are again at 'My love for thee will never, never die.'"

"Blame me," he told her cheerfully. "It was the only song my father knew, and he willed it to me, apparently."

She sat where he indicated, across from him in the little rocking chair. "I hope your hands ate the roast beef sandwiches."

"They did. They saved one for me, which I enjoyed after my attempt to clean off two weeks of trail dust." He took the notebook from his shirt pocket. "They added a few more items to their wish list. Let me read it to you." He cleared his throat. "Mind, now, we're not too sophisticated when it comes to grub. Hash browns. They like 'um real thin and crispy, kind of like those little bird nest things. Fried beefsteak." He looked closer at his list and then moved the kerosene lamp toward him. "Doc really likes fried chicken. I know he'll shoot you some grouse and call it good. And he says that's best with white gravy over mashed potatoes." Mr. Otto laughed. "Doc has the sophisticated palate."

Julia smiled at that. "Would I dare throw in some peas?"

Mr. Otto was in the swing of her humor. "That might be a bit too advanced, depending."

"On what?"

"If you need to cover them with creamy stuff. Peas all naked and bare would stick really good to mashed potatoes."

"True." Julia sat back, enjoying the list now. *Remember how Papa told you in his blessing to look at people and things with new eyes?* she reminded herself.

He flipped the page. "Here are a couple of additions. Apple pie. Everyone agreed to more of your bacon and eggs, and they want to know if you make good flapjacks. You know, with butter oozing out and maple syrup in rivers."

"Mr. Otto, you are poetic," she teased.

There was no denying the relief in his eyes. He looked back at the list. "They rounded it off with saleratus biscuits and fried fish. James already volunteered to drown a worm anytime anyone asks."

She smiled again. "What about you, Mr. Otto? Any preferences, beyond those listed?"

He looked at the list again. "I'm pretty much in agreement with my men." He tore out the little sheets and handed them to her. "I know, I know. There's no accounting for some people's tastes."

"That's what you want me to cook?" she asked, looking at his precise printing.

"Yep. Will you do it?"

"Of course I will, since you and I have a year to get it right," she told him. Julia thought a moment. "I'll do this, but you have to do something for me."

"It's only fair. Shoot."

"Once a week, I'll make something from Miss Farmer's cookbook, and you and your hands have to at least try it."

Julia didn't think it was too much to ask, and the way Mr. Otto smiled at her, with the weather lines crinkling around his eyes, assured her he agreed.

"Done, Darling."

She stood up then, ready to go to bed and put the day behind her. Mr. Otto motioned for her to sit down again. He leaned closer in conspiratorial fashion, which made her lean closer too.

"I got an idea about what to do about the Rudigers. Tell me what you think. We'll trail the herd to Cheyenne and get the stock on the train to Chicago. I'll send the hands back to Gun Barrel. I have a friend in Fort Collins. He's a builder, and only last spring he was griping to me how hard it is to find good carpenters."

He looked at her, his eyes bright, and she caught his excitement. "You're going to tell him about Mr. Rudiger."

"Better than that. I'll guarantee Rudiger a job, because my friend will take me at my word."

I don't doubt that for a moment, Julia thought. *You're not a man someone says no to.* "You're persuasive," she told him.

"I know it," he replied, his tone matter-of-fact. "I'll stop at Rudigers' on the way back, give him the good news, and offer to buy his place for far more than it's worth. It'll get him out of here and give him employment he can be proud of. What do you think?"

He was asking her, as though her opinion mattered. "I think it's a wonderful idea, Mr. Otto."

"So you're guilty of feeding hungry people." He leaned back then, regarding her from more of a distance, as though assessing her. "I'd bet my best horse that you told them you were trying out that cooking range and had to do something with all that old food lying around." He laughed—he could read her expression like a book. "That's what I thought!"

He sobered quickly. "Thanks for doing that and reminding me of something I was forgetting."

She looked at him, inquiring with her eyes. He shook his head. "It's a little thing. Maybe a silly thing. Just a scrap I found in my mother's possession. Something about, 'that ye may walk guiltless before God. I would that you should impart of your substance to the poor.' " He paused and shook his head. "I forget. Something about feeding the hungry. Well, I needed to be reminded."

I've heard that before, Julia thought. *Where?*

"I've been reading and rereading the Bible for years, because it certainly sounds like scripture. Haven't found it yet, but I'll keep looking."

He looked at her, embarrassment in his face now. "I'm just rambling." He slapped his knees and stood up. "I need an early start tomorrow. Back to eating dust again."

Julia rose too, and they went in opposite directions. She stopped at the door to the kitchen.

"Will you look in Cheyenne for a cat?" Julia almost smiled at his pained expression. *Someone doesn't like cats,* she thought, amused.

"I suppose." He sighed. "Anything else?"

"One thing." Julia went into the parlor again, shy now but willing to seize the moment. "Could you . . . would you check around and see if there is a Latter-day Saint Sunday School organization in town? My father thinks Cheyenne is probably too small for a full-fledged Mormon ward, or even a branch, but there might be a Sunday School."

"And if I find one?"

"Maybe I could go to Cheyenne once a month, if the weather is good," she said in a rush. "I . . . I didn't think I would miss it, but I do."

Mr. Otto gave her that assessing look again, as if trying to understand her. "Which do you want? Sunday School or a cat?"

"Both," she told him, on firm ground now because his expression was benign.

"You're a lot of trouble," he said, but she could tell he was teasing her.

"That's what my father says," she told him serenely. "Good night, Mr. Otto."

Sixteen

ext morning, the hands approached the table with what looked like stealth, as though expecting an ambush. Relieved, Julia watched them tuck in all the flapjacks she could make. More confident, they took the edge off what remained of their hunger with bacon in thick slabs and eggs, sopping up the yolk with lightly browned and delicate biscuits.

"I trust that will tide everyone over," she commented, as she poured coffee all around.

"Precisely," Mr. Otto said, holding out his cup. "We're joining up with another rancher farther down who brings his chuck wagon and his wife. We'll be in Cheyenne six days, tops."

"And then I suppose you boys will hoorah the town," Julia said, amused.

She got a tableful of innocent stares for her pains. Mr. Otto just smiled benignly. " 'Hoorah,' Darling? Do you read the *Police Gazette* or the more antique, lurid dime novels? This *is* the twentieth century."

Her gaze was just as benign. "Mr. Otto, I have two older brothers. I don't think my parents ever knew, but my sister Iris and I used to read their old raggedy dime novels in the closet under the back stairs."

He got up from the table, reaching for the canvas duster he had slung over the rafter yesterday. "Cheyenne's too civilized now, what with churches and schools. There were days, though . . ." He left the thought unfinished. "Hurry along, gents. Our cows are waiting. Darling, walk with me."

She dried her hands and did as he said, remembering the last time he had made the same request. He shortened his stride as they walked toward the corral. He draped his arms over the top rail and stared at the horses. Julia did the same, wondering briefly what her mother would say if she could see her daughter.

"Mr. Otto, I've already broken all your rules, so there probably isn't much you can tell me this time," she said when he seemed disinclined to talk.

She could tell he was amused because the wrinkles around his eyes deepened. "You're a smug soul, Darling! You're leading me in a merry dance—something I hadn't anticipated. I just wanted to tell you that I went out earlier this morning and rode down to Rudiger's, just for a look at the shack. He did a really good job. No wonder McLemore was so exercised."

"Good for Mr. Rudiger."

"My sentiments precisely," he told her. "And wouldn't you know it? I practically stumbled over a deer on the way home, so I shot it and left it on Rudiger's door."

Julia turned to face him, not shy anymore because something had changed. "You are now as officially guilty as I am," she said.

"Without a doubt," he replied cheerfully, his back to the railing too. "If you want to keep testing the Queen Atlantic, I think that bread you served yesterday was a mite tough. Another ten or twelve loaves should fix any deficiencies."

"Ten or . . . it was nothing of the kind!" she burst out, slapping him on the arm, as though he was one of her older brothers. She looked at his face then and hit him again. "Mr.

Otto, you are a trial! But, yes, I'll work on that deficiency, if you don't think the Rudigers will mind."

"They won't mind a bit," he said, serious again.

"Even if it makes Mr. McLemore angry?"

They started back to the house. "No fears. I'll always stand between you and him."

He said it in such a matter-of-fact way that Julia felt any fear dissolve. "You mean that, don't you?" she asked before she let her own awe of Mr. Otto restrain her.

"Indeed, I do," he replied. "So that's my order: keep feeding the Rudigers with any threadbare excuse that comes to mind. I'll send my hands back, but I'm taking the train to Fort Collins. See you in a couple of weeks, Darling. I know better than to ask you to behave yourself . . ."

"Mr. Otto," she said, "I am the soul of circumspection."

He nudged her shoulder and kept walking. "And I'm Catherine the Great."

A little while later, hat in hand, Mr. Otto came back into the kitchen while she was cleaning up. "Any last rebuttals?"

"Just remember the cat, and see if you can locate me a Sunday School."

He made a face at the word *cat* but nodded and put on his hat. "A Presbyterian Sunday School won't do? A Methodist one? They're as plentiful as fleas."

Julia shook her head.

"Why does it matter?"

Why, indeed, she asked herself. *A few weeks ago, I thought I could manage a year away from the Church. Well, I can't.*

He must have seen something in her expression. "Is that something I'm not supposed to ask about?"

"Not at all," she replied, determined not to drive him off

this time with her stupidity. She dried her hands. "I think I get lonely without Mormons around. We believe different stuff too."

"All those wives."

"No! My father never had more than one wife, and the Church doesn't hold to polygamy anymore." She dried her hands again.

"I think they're dry by now," he teased. "I'll look. I promise." He nodded to her. "Leave me alone now! I'm going to be late!" He winked at her and closed the door behind him. He opened it immediately. "Maybe sometime you'll tell me what those differences are, if it's not a secret."

"It's not," she assured him. "Mr. Otto, go away now!"

He laughed and closed the door. She opened it almost immediately, so he hadn't gone far.

"Mr. Otto, one more thing! If you stop at the Rudiger's on the way back, Ursula will probably serve you hot water. It's all she has, and I know you don't want to look surprised."

"I promise I won't, Darling," he said, his expression kind. "I like hot water. Why muddle it up with tea?"

I wonder why I ever thought he was frightening, Julia told herself as she closed the door quietly.

She opened the door a few minutes later to watch the men leave. James joined her in the door, and her hand went automatically to his head. After a moment, he ducked away from her and went into the yard, his hands deep in his pockets. She could tell how much he wanted to go with Mr. Otto.

Maybe Mr. Otto was one of those people susceptible to scrutiny, just like Iris. As she watched his back, he turned around to look at her again from halfway across the yard, as if he knew she was watching him.

"I promise to feed the Rudigers," she said softly. She knew he couldn't hear her, but something must have satisfied him because he turned around and occupied himself with the business at hand: getting cows to Chicago. His attention to duties left her ample time to admire the effortless way he mounted his horse and his ramrod straight posture in the saddle. "Longtime rancher looks good on horseback," she murmured. "Mature cook had better find some way to cook what she wants and make sure everyone thinks they are getting what they want. So there, longtime rancher."

Julia was less lonely during the week before the hands returned from Cheyenne. Taking Mr. Otto at his word, she baked more bread for the Rudigers. She made no pretense any more of trying to pass off her cooking as an attempt to improve her skills. She fixed the best she knew how, considering the contents of the pantry, and the side of beef still hanging mostly undisturbed in the smoke house.

While James and Danila played near the little stream that fed into the river farther below, Julia brought along her knitting needles and knitted soakers for the baby to come, sharing her yarn cache with Ursula. Karl Rudiger expertly turned Mr. Otto's venison into sausage, giving James a large link to take back to the Double Tipi for their own supper.

Mr. Otto had given her permission to look through the clothes piles in his room for something Karl Rudiger could wear. She took James with her, so he could chase out the mice that had made nests in the lower layers. Three boiled white shirts seemed worthy of saving, but most ended up as rags, minus their buttons. She looked a long time at a cheerful calico shirt she could never imagine Mr. Otto wearing, crisscrossed as it was with ribbons, some sewed down, and others flowing free.

"Have you ever seen this before?" she asked James, holding it up as they sat on the floor, now that the mice were gone.

He shook his head.

She traced her finger across the ribbon, noting the tiny stitches that held it in place. She decided it was something his mother must have made and brought from her home on the Fort Washakie Reservation. "I'll wash this and save it," she said.

When the hands returned a week later, accompanied this time by Mr. Otto's two Indian relatives from the Fort Washakie Reservation, Julia had a meal waiting for them that she knew no one would question: beefsteak broiled, not fried; mashed potatoes so fluffy that Matt Malloy put down his fork and sighed; apples stewed with cinnamon and butter; biscuits so light that Willy Bill cupped his hands over the four on his plate ("So they won't fly away"); and deviled eggs that made Doc sit back with an entirely satisfied expression and murmur something about "home in Indiana." Even Kringle smiled, which astonished the other hands.

Julia enjoyed every moment. When she whisked out the apple pie from the warming oven and topped it with whipped cream, the chorus of sighs that rose from the table soothed her heart. She held up her hand when Matt finished and scraped back his chair, ready to rise.

"Just a moment, gentlemen," she said, coloring a bit when everyone looked at her. "I told Mr. Otto that I would happily fix what you want, but that I had to be allowed to try new things once a week."

The wary looks returned; she ignored them. "Tomorrow for breakfast, I'll cook you buckwheat pancakes, with plenty of maple syrup."

The men nodded, still wary.

"I'm also going to serve you cecils, which you will eat, because that is the deal we made. Remember?"

Doc spoke up finally, amused. "We did, didn't we, boys? Come on now." He looked at her intently. "What's in a cecil?"

"Your favorite things—beef, only it's minced really small. I roll it in a mix of breadcrumbs, eggs, and flour; then I fry it."

"Aahh." It was a collective sigh. "And you can dip them in ketchup," she concluded, wisely changing the tomato sauce in the recipe without a qualm.

"And if we don't like them?" Willy Bill asked, his expression pugnacious.

"Then I won't serve them again. Mr. Bill, all I ask is that you try everything I cook." She worked her dimple magic on him. "My mother used to insist that my sister Iris and I at least take two fairy bites."

Matt Malloy chortled. "Just two fairy bites, Willy Bill!"

"Come now, Mr. Bill, I have to earn a living, same as you," she coaxed.

"He'll eat them," Doc said, getting up from the table now. "Willy B, you remind me of a four-year-old."

"And how many four-year-olds do you know, Doc?" the old German asked.

The others were laughing, but Julia watched Doc's face and sucked in her breath at the pain etched there. There was no mistaking the bleakness.

Does everyone here have a story? Julia asked herself as she took her time over the dishes. She had never minded doing dishes. There was something soothing about warm water and a task so simple that she could do it blindfolded and still have time to think.

"Need some help?"

Surprised, Julia looked up from her contemplation of greasy bubbles at Doc, who was taking a dishcloth from its hook by the warmth of the Queen Atlantic.

"I can always use help," she told him.

He dried the plates in silence. "I had a four-year-old," he said finally. "I saw the look in your eyes." He reached for another plate.

"I'd . . . I'd never pry," she stammered. "It's just that, well, everyone here seems to be a work in progress, as my father would say."

"Your father would be right."

Julia started on the tin cups. "How did Mr. Otto come to hire you?"

"I suppose it's not as dramatic as Matt Malloy's story. I wasn't starving and checking out garbage bins in Cheyenne." He shook his head. "I probably shouldn't even tell you, Julia, because it probably won't reflect well on me or our employer."

"That bad?"

"Nearly so." He appraised her. "You're an adult."

"I'm supposed to be."

Doc perched himself on the table, one leg dangling. "Hard part first—my only child died of diphtheria when he was four. My wife was certain I could have saved him, if I hadn't been tending other children. I disagree with her, but the point was, I wasn't there."

Quietly, Julia sat down at the table, the dishes forgotten. "I'm so sorry."

"She cut me loose, and I ended up in Denver, deep in a bottle. It's not a pretty place."

Doc sat down, too. "I kept practicing medicine, but it

was a shady kind of medicine." He colored and looked down at the table. "I was the physician of choice in the tenderloin district. I performed a few surgeries I wasn't proud of, but I mostly patched up the girls who got in fights with each other or came up against the wrong side of a . . . of a client." He shrugged. "I could work a few days a week and have plenty of time to drink."

He was silent. Julia asked, "So, how did . . . ?"

"How did Paul Otto find me? He was in town for the Denver stock show. By then, I was working a rougher level of medicine around the sale barns." He frowned and looked away. "Maybe I shouldn't tell you this."

"You've already started," Julia said. "Were you taking care of four-legged patients then?"

"Yeah, I was, and some of the more . . . uh . . . some of the coarser women of the profession. They, uh, worked out of the stalls."

Julia shuddered. "And Mr. Otto?" *I'm not sure I want to know,* she couldn't help thinking.

Her expression must have registered with Doc. He held up his hands. "Oh, no, wait! I think Paul frequented the . . . um . . . upscale part of the tenderloin district, you know, around Market Street." He chuckled. "Oh, my goodness, Jennie Rogers' and her House of Mirrors, just a short walk from where the state legislature used to meet. Or Mattie Daw's place."

I shouldn't be surprised, Julia thought, more amused than disgusted. *After all, Mr. Otto is on a first-name basis with the business girls in Gun Barrel.*

Doc smiled and then remembered his audience. "Oh, Julia, I'm a bounder for even mentioning this! Paul had a prize steer that needed some coddling, and I helped him. One thing led to another, and I told him my whole story."

He scratched his head. "I'm not sure how he does it—just a question here and there—but I started talking. He finally asked me if I really liked the life I was leading." Doc looked at her, his gaze intense. "Julia, in a handful of years, no one had cared enough to ask me that." He tipped back in the chair to contemplate the ceiling. "He didn't judge me. I thought about his question and decided I didn't much like anything about the life. Then he offered me a job." Doc set his chair down and looked her in the eyes again. "Right there on the spot. Said he wanted me to keep an eye on his livestock, and maybe patch up a human now and then, if the occasion arose."

"You said yes?" Julia asked.

"I turned him down flat."

"But—"

"I'm here, eh? Paul just nodded. He shook my hand, told me to think about it—you know how he is: he doesn't ask, he just tells—then he said the strangest thing."

I'm not sure anything would surprise me, Julia thought.

The expression on Doc's face reminded her of Matt Malloy's face when he told her how he came to the Double Tipi: incredulity mixed with something close to humility. "Julia, he looked me in the eye, just like I'm looking at you, and said in the nicest voice, 'Doctor McKeel, does a boy decide one day, "When I grow up, I'm going to be a physician for fancy women and ailing cattle and make just enough money to drink myself sick?" I don't think so.' That's what he said."

Red-faced with the memory, Doc looked at her. "John McKeel. That's my name. I guess he saw it on my black bag. It's the only thing I could never bring myself to pawn."

"Doc, that's hard," she whispered.

"It was, but kindly meant. Paul told me he'd be at the

depot at six in the morning, if I changed my mind. Then he shook my hand and strolled away." He interrupted himself. "No. There was one other thing. Something about all of us being beggars. I don't know what he meant."

Neither did Matt Malloy, Julia thought, racking her brain again for the quotation. Nothing came to mind. "I guess you saw it his way."

"Took me all night. I doctored some more cattle, then spent the rest of the night trying to save the life of a young girl—I doubt she was fifteen. I'm sorry, Julia, I shouldn't be telling you this. I held her hand until she died, covered her face, picked up my black bag, and walked to the depot. I didn't even go back to my rooming house. Nothing there I wanted. I always carried my son's photograph in my bag."

Julia closed her eyes. When she opened them, Doc had a handkerchief for her. She wiped her eyes. "You were living a harsh life, Doc," she said.

"Not now," he replied softly. "You know what's funny? I don't think Paul was surprised to see me at the depot. He's a man of firm convictions." He regarded her. "Why are you here, Julia? I mean, are you the only winner Paul ever picked?"

"Not if we can believe everyone's reaction to my roast beef in an oyster blanket! Or maybe it was the warm liver salad." Funny, it felt good to laugh about her disasters now.

"The liver, Julia. Trust me on that one."

Her smile faded as she thought of Ezra Quayle. "I gave back an engagement ring to an excellent man that everyone considered the perfect husband for me."

"Oof."

"I just didn't love him. I could have tried, but it seems to me that if you have to try, then it isn't a very good idea."

"And nobody understood."

She considered Doc's comment. "My mother did. My father came around to the idea when he saw how Mama felt. He trusts her judgment." She looked at the man shyly. "I think that's what I want to find: someone who trusts my judgment."

Doc laughed and stood up. "And you think you'll find someone at the Double Tipi?"

She laughed too. "No! I'm calling this my retrenching year."

I do need to retrench, she thought, after Doc left. *There's no one here to help me, and no one who believes what I believe. Maybe it's time I figured out just what it is I do believe.*

Mr. Otto's Indian relatives left after the noon meal, setting off at a brisk pace. No wonder; the air turned colder and the wind was louder than usual in the cottonwoods. She looked up. A flock of geese honked overhead, flying in a V formation. She watched them as they seemed to take autumn along for the ride. The wind picked up all afternoon. By suppertime, everyone seemed happy to troop indoors and warm up by the Queen Atlantic.

Doc came to her, rubbing his hands. "You need to know there's another mouth to feed."

"Who might that be?"

"An old Indian," Matt said. "He lives in the extra tack room by the stable."

She blinked. "Does Mr. Otto know about him?"

"Sure he does. The old boy shows up like clockwork," Doc said. "He likes lots of sugar in his coffee. Maybe that's why he doesn't have many teeth."

Julia shooed the men away from the Queen Atlantic so

she could open the oven door. She smiled to herself at the great exhalation all around her.

"Boston baked beans, gentlemen."

They sat down to eat. After two bites, Doc nodded. "Superior." He reached for the bread. "There's one thing else you should know about the Indian. It always snows the day after he shows up. Winter's here, Julia."

Seventeen

$\mathcal{D}$oc was right, or maybe the Indian was. Snow covered the ground the next morning. "Well, what do you know?" Julia murmured as she knelt on her bed and peered out of the little window.

She felt the usual lift she always felt at the turn of the seasons, but it was followed by a sudden longing to see that annual change from her own bedroom, and not this small, newspaper-covered room. She dressed quickly, thinking of Iris, who, when they were children, would pester her for rides on the sled once the hill by their school was snow-covered. Over and over they would clutch each other and scream all the way to the bottom. In a few years, Iris would be hauling her own children up and down hills they would see as mountains.

A glance at the calendar in the kitchen reminded her that it was Sunday. James wasn't up yet, and no one had come in from the bunkhouse, so she sat at the table. Maybe she could pretend she was home and getting ready for Sunday School. She clasped her hands in front of her, nearly overwhelmed by a powerful yearning to walk beside Iris and her mother on the way to the meetinghouse; to listen to two and a half minute talks by terrified youngsters; to try not to laugh when Sister Flowers led—or maybe dragged— the congregation in a practice hymn dug up from what her father called "the sealed portion of the hymn book."

Maybe I didn't think I would miss church, Julia thought

as she sat so still. With snow outside and the seasons shifting, suddenly church mattered very much. Before she left for Boston, her father had made inquiries at the Church headquarters, arming her with the exact location of Boston's one branch. He had also asked around and sent letters to Church members living in Boston, asking them to keep an eye on her. And they had. She had never missed a Sunday in the Boston Branch.

This was different. He had made no such inquiries to pave her way in Wyoming. She had wondered about that on her train ride to Cheyenne, why her father had not made things easy for her this time.

The answer was obvious to her now. Papa expected her to make her own inquiries now, if she chose. It was her decision.

She shivered a little and lit the Queen Atlantic. By the time the men straggled in from the bunkhouse and James had set the table, the bacon and eggs were ready to eat and she was just ladling the Cream of Wheat into a serving bowl.

In addition to eggs, she prepared a generous bowl of Cream of Wheat—well-sugared—for the Indian in the tack room. Doc volunteered to accompany her, taking the breakfast in its pail as she carried the bowl and spoon.

"You don't need to do this," he told her, as they crossed the snow-covered yard.

"I want to," she assured him. "If he's on the Double Tipi and he eats, then he's my responsibility."

Doc laughed and opened the door to the tack room for her. She stood a moment in the entrance as her eyes became used to the gloom. The room smelled of leather and old saddles. Welcome heat came from the pot-bellied stove in the corner, opposite a rustic bed where the old man sat, a buffalo robe around his shoulders.

"Does he speak English?" Julia asked Doc.

"Don't think so," Doc told her. "Mostly he just smacks his lips if he's satisfied."

Julia carefully ladled Cream of Wheat into the bowl, added more sugar, which elicited a murmur of approval, and handed him the bowl with the spoon in it.

He accepted it with both hands and a nod. Julia watched with interest as he ate the bowl's contents and held it out for more. He smacked his lips and then spoke to them. When neither of them answered, he repeated himself, shrugged, and accepted the fried eggs.

"Any idea what he said?" Julia asked.

"Not a clue. We'll have to wait for Paul to return."

As the next week passed, Julia found herself looking for Mr. Otto. The weather turned warm again, but the nip of autumn was in the air, especially in the evenings when she and James sat in the parlor. She spent most evenings at the small parlor table with James, showing him how to write his ABCs. He wasn't quick, but he was interested and dogged in his persistence.

When James slept, she stayed in the parlor, adding on to the lengthening letters to her parents and Iris. She wondered at first if there was enough to write about, but there was always something, even if it was as simple as the Indian's huge, toothless smile after she served him baked beans. There was more to write about when Doc and Matt took her riding.

She didn't tell her parents about the riding skirt she acquired. Doc had taken her to the newer tack room, where Kringle generally sat, muttering in German and repairing the ranch's harnesses. Doc had pulled down a small trunk from the shelf.

"There's something here for you," he had said. "It . . . uh . . . belonged to his wife."

"I shouldn't."

"I don't know why not," Doc countered. "Paul wanted you to learn to ride one of his ranch horses so you could visit the Rudigers. It was his idea." He opened the trunk. "You think about it. I'll go saddle my horse."

She thought about it and looked inside, her eyes opening wide at the exquisite lace night gown and robe on top. Carefully, she worked her way through the trunk, stopping halfway down at a serviceable pair of divided-skirt breeches that didn't even look used. She took them out and held them up to her waist. So far, so good. The leather jacket that accompanied the skirt was a little loose but fit well enough when she put on a flannel shirt from deeper down in Mr. Otto's clothing pile, back in the ranch house. She didn't have any boots, and there weren't any in the trunk, but her father had insisted she bring along some sturdy lace-up brogans.

Doc or Matt took her out riding every day. By the end of the week, Julia—accompanied by James, mounted on his small horse—felt brave enough to pack a tin of stew and a walnut quick bread with brown sugar glaze to the Rudigers' shack. They drank hot water and finished up the lady fingers she had brought over earlier.

Two days later, Doc told her to address her letters because he was taking Mr. Otto's horse down to meet the Cheyenne & Northern at Gun Barrel.

"I'll mail them for you before they get so heavy they need a crate," he teased.

"Mr. Otto's coming back?"

"Yep. At least, he told me when he left to be there at the depot on the twenty-eighth. If he's not there, I'm to leave his horse at the livery stable. Want to come along?"

Julia shook her head, suddenly shy at the idea and not so sure Mr. Otto would appreciate seeing her in his former wife's clothing. "Maybe you could explain to him how I got my riding gear," she said as she addressed the letters.

"He won't mind, Julia. Before he left, he mentioned the trunk. The boss is not a sentimental man."

Doc was back on the Double Tipi that evening, without the boss. Two more days passed, and then Mr. Otto returned. She and James were in the parlor at the time. The boy heard him first, leaping up from the game of pickup sticks that Willy Bill had whittled. Julia followed, opening the kitchen door to see Mr. Otto coming across the yard. Matt was leading his horse into the barn.

He smiled to see them standing in the doorway and then laughed out loud when James ran to him and put his arms around his waist.

"I wasn't gone that long!" he exclaimed as they walked together into the kitchen.

"Yes, you were. Mr. Darling is teaching me my letters."

Mr. Otto looked at Julia, appreciation in his eyes. "Well, I expect Mr. Darling is a fine teacher, James."

Julia smiled and held the door open wider. "I hope you're hungry, Mr. Otto. Main course is chicken and dumplings. Alice Marlowe has been ruthless among her flock, weeding out the slackers."

He set his Stetson on James's head and took his long duster off, draping it carefully over the chair at the head of the table. "Darling, take a look in the left pocket."

Julia did as he said. "Oh, my," she breathed. "You found one." She gently lifted out a tiny kitten, its eyes barely open. "A mighty small one." She sat down and put it in her lap so James could touch the little creature. "James, give this kitten a few months, and you'll be out of the mousing business."

The boy lightly petted the kitten's head. "I don't mind."

Mr. Otto went to the Queen Atlantic and ladled out his own bowl of chicken and dumplings. He sat beside Julia. "I wanted a larger one, but blamed if they aren't going for five dollars in Fort Collins, and I have my tightwad moments." He tugged on a velvety ear. "Got this little guy in a bar in Cheyenne for two bits. Seems the mother ran afoul of a beer wagon and left a few orphans." He grinned, and she was delighted to see how boyish he looked. "I've been calling him Two Bits. You can name him what you want."

"Two Bits will do," Julia said. "Unless we like Gulliver, because he's had some travels. You're sure it's a boy?"

"No, but I'm optimistic." Mr. Otto reached in his shirt pocket. "I've been feeding Two Bits with an eyedropper every two hours. My word, he's a lot of trouble."

Julia lifted up the kitten, which fit comfortably in the palm of her hand. "I'll take over the menu, Mr. Otto." She smiled at him. "Thanks for doing this."

"Anything to keep the cook happy."

She looked closely at Two Bits, who had already settled down in her palm, his eyes drooping. "How will I know when he's hungry?"

"He'll set up a real racket and start nosing around." He touched James's head. "James, there's a small tin of milk in my saddlebag. You can get that for Mr. Darling. I fed him last at the Rudigers, so he has an hour to go." He grinned at Julia, and she was struck all over again how much younger he looked. "He'll start up just about the time you want to go to bed. Good luck there."

Julia set the kitten in her lap again. "You stopped at the Rudigers? And?"

His grin widened. "He's got a job in Fort Collins, and I'm now the owner—well, after we sign some papers—of

160 acres I don't really need."

Julia touched his sleeve. "Mr. Otto, you're a good man."

He shrugged, but she could tell he was pleased with her praise. "Nothing to it, really. Told you my friend in Fort Collins needs a reliable carpenter. We'll get the Rudigers to the depot in Gun Barrel by Friday. Bledsoe has a little house waiting for them. After that, it's up to Rudiger."

"All he needs is a chance."

"You're right." He was sitting close, so he nudged her shoulder. "Mrs. Rudiger gave me hot water, like you said, but she served it with someone's walnut bread. Good stuff, Julia."

Good heavens, he called me Julia, she thought, pleased. *I'm sure that will pass.* "I'll serve you some too."

She sent James to find a small box and some clean rags for Two Bits. While Mr. Otto ate, she set her own loaf of walnut bread to bask in the warming oven. By the time he finished his second bowl of chicken and dumplings, James was back with a well-lined box. Julia set the sleeping kitten in his new home, close to the Queen Atlantic. James sat cross-legged by the box, watching Two Bits.

Mr. Otto had no trouble demolishing a generous slice of the walnut bread. "Get yourself a slice," he told her. "No need to leap up and start doing whatever it is you do. You're pretty good company, Darling."

She knew that "Julia" couldn't last. She got herself some dessert too, and they ate in companionable silence. Finally Mr. Otto put down his fork and leaned back in his chair with a satisfied air.

"I found you a church, too."

She didn't know why the tears welled in her eyes just then, but they did. Mr. Otto dropped his chair down and flicked at her face before she even realized.

"A simple thank you will suffice, Darling," he told her, his voice kind.

"Thank you," she whispered, barely able to get the words out, surprised at her own reaction. It was just church, after all. "Was it hard to find?"

"Not really, once I got a little smarter," he said, tipping back again. "I asked around the saloons first—I mean, if you're in one, why not ask?—but that got me nowhere."

She couldn't help smiling at his honesty.

"Then I got to thinking—if you want a church, ask a minister. Well, the ministers were less than helpful. Mostly I got an earful about Mormons." He tipped his chair down again. "Do Mormons really have horns?"

Julia just rolled her eyes at him. He chuckled and tipped his chair back again. "My next tactic was to hit the professionals, and I got lucky there."

"We do believe that the glory of God is intelligence," Julia said.

"Smart of you. I had to talk to my lawyer about a land deal with Rudiger, so I asked him what he knew. Jackpot! He told me about an attorney in town who belonged to some farfetched little group. I figured that was your bunch."

Julia laughed. "And?"

"I was right. I stopped in on Heber Gillespie, except his wife called him *Brother* Gillespie when they invited me to dinner. He's a lawyer and superintendent of Cheyenne's Deseret Sunday School Union. Says they're too small to be a branch yet, which he told me was what you call a really small congregation. They meet on Sundays in the Odd Fellows Hall, once they sweep out the cigar butts and empty the cuspidors." He set his chair down. "I suppose you'll want to go, now and then."

"I'd like to," she told him. "Would it be possible?"

"Don't know why not. Doc tells me you can ride. You can catch the train at Gun Barrel and leave your horse in the livery there. Mrs. Gillespie—she told me to call her Sister Gillespie, but I'm not so sure about that—anyway, she said you could spend Saturday night with them and then catch the Sunday train. If the weather's good, you can be home by dark. It's doable, Darling, if you don't mind some Gullivering yourself."

"I don't mind."

He nodded and then yawned. "Plan on it. I'll go with you the first time, just to make sure you're the rider Doc swears you are. Besides, the weather can turn up here. If it works, and the winter isn't too harsh, why not?" He got up. "It might be onerous more than once a month, but that's better than nothing. G'night."

She turned her attention to the kitten and James, but still Mr. Otto stood in the doorway, watching them, a smile on his face. He wagged a finger at her. "Just remember, you two: I got the kitten, but he's your responsibility. I'm not much for night feedings." He thought a moment. "Which reminds me. Did Blue Corn ever show up?"

"So that's his name. He came, and it snowed the next day."

"Don't know how he does that," Mr. Otto told her. "He like your cooking?"

"Seems to. He smacked his lips. He has a lot to say to me, but I don't know what he's saying. Doc said maybe you might understand him."

"I don't speak much Cheyenne, but I sign, and so does he. I'll come with you for breakfast tomorrow. He'll sign to me."

He still didn't leave. "What does he like for breakfast?"

"Cream of Wheat, mainly." Julia laughed. "Oh, he likes my cecils, and so does your crew."

"I haven't had those yet, have I?" he asked.

Julia laughed inside at the wariness in his voice. "You will, Mr. Otto."

Julia was up twice in the night to feed Two Bits, cuddling with him on the floor, her back against the still-warm Queen Atlantic. The eyedropper worked well enough, but she found Two Bits also enjoyed sucking her little finger, after she dipped it in the milk.

"I think you might relish some Cream of Wheat for breakfast tomorrow," she whispered. When he finished, Julia wiped his fur with a clean rag dipped in the Queen's reservoir. Gently she rubbed Two Bits' fur and was rewarded with purring so loud that it shook the kitten's small body. "Back to bed now," she said. "I'm tired."

She fed Two Bits again early in the morning before the men came to breakfast, adding just enough Cream of Wheat to thicken the evaporated milk and still get through the eye dropper. She turned the chore over to James, who made himself comfortable a short distance away from the Queen, now that the stove was warming. Julia smiled to hear him whispering to the kitten.

Breakfast was oatmeal and flapjacks, tempered with ham. The men ate silently, as usual. She caught Mr. Otto glancing at her now and then, a satisfied look on his face. He nodded to her once, and she felt pleased beyond all bounds at such a slight gesture of approval. *Just keeping the hands happy, Mr. Otto,* she thought. *You too.*

Mr. Otto gave his orders for the day as she set the dishes to soak and ladled oatmeal into the pail for Blue Corn. Two flapjacks subdued with maple syrup went onto a tin plate. Mr. Otto carried the pail and bowl for her across the yard, the spoon sticking out of his pocket.

"I'll be going to the Rudigers later in the afternoon to see what kind of help they need to move," he told her as they came to the tack room. "If you want to prepare any food, I'll take that too."

"I was thinking about dried apple pie for dessert tonight. One more is no trouble."

Blue Corn ate the oatmeal first, smacking his lips and beaming at her. He exclaimed over the sweetness of the maple syrup and made short work of the flapjacks. Julia stood by the door, her arms folded in front of her, while Mr. Otto squatted on his haunches by Blue Corn's sleeping platform. They exchanged signs that made the rancher laugh.

"What's he saying?" Julia asked.

"He approves of your cooking," Mr. Otto said. "See where he gestures with his hand to his heart and then extended to the side? And then see how he cups his fingers to his lips? That means 'good food.' "

"How can I tell him thank you?"

Mr. Otto showed her, and she repeated the gesture. Blue Corn nodded his approval and made several more signs in rapid succession.

"What's he saying now?"

"Darling, he wants to know if you're my wife."

"My goodness, why would he think that?"

"Beats me. I just told him that you're here to cook." He watched Blue Corn through another series of signs and then grinned at Julia. "He tells me, 'Too bad for you.' "

The room began to feel too warm and small. Julia gathered up the empty plate and bowl, picked up the pail, and then opened the door, saying something about kitchen work. Apparently unperturbed by Blue Corn's questions, Mr. Otto nodded to her and returned his attention to the Indian.

She didn't see Mr. Otto again until hours later, when she sent James to call the men to the noon meal, a substantial roast with small potatoes clustered around, soaking in the meat juices, canned green beans liberally seasoned with bacon left over from breakfast, and sour milk biscuits. Dessert was prune whip, served cold with custard sauce. Mr. Otto looked around the table as his hands ate it without a quibble and sampled his portion gingerly before digging in. She laughed when he made the sign for "good food" at her.

He decided to take James with him for afternoon chores as she sat down with Two Bits on her lap, nosing about for his dinner.

"If you have something for the Rudigers, I'll leave in two hours or so."

She nodded, her eyes on the kitten, who had latched onto her finger, wet with milk.

"Persistent little beggar, isn't he?" Mr. Otto commented, coming back to sit beside her.

"Everyone has to eat," she said, dipping her finger in the milk again. She looked at her employer. *Mr. Otto takes in strays,* she thought. "How did the Indian come here?"

Mr. Otto rubbed Two Bits between his ears. "He just showed up one day. He hung around the house. Pa tried to shoo him away, but he wouldn't go. Pa opened up a can of peaches and gave him a loaf of bread. Don't know how he ended up in the tack room, but he did."

"Where did he come from?"

"Hard to say. I think he was one of the old Fort Laramie coffee coolers. That's what the soldiers called the old Indians who hung around the fort doing odd jobs and begging." He shrugged. "When they closed the fort and sold the buildings at auction, the elders mostly wandered away."

"Does he do anything useful for you?" she asked, curious.

Mr. Otto laughed under his breath. "Well, he lets me know when the first snowfall is coming. And just wait, when the weather is cold and the snow never seems to leave, he'll just vanish. A Chinook wind will blow through that night, and spring will come the next day."

Two Bits was asleep now, still gumming her little finger. Gently she removed her finger from his mouth. "Mr. Otto, I've noticed that people do what you say, and you don't have to do anything to exert your influence," she said candidly. "Do they have any idea how kind you are?"

She knew she had embarrassed him because he didn't look at her. "That's our little secret, Darling," he told her and then changed the subject. "Any surprises for supper?"

"No. Apple pie and roast beef sandwiches with lots of onion in them tonight. Maybe hot chocolate, if I'm in the mood."

"I hope you are," he replied as he took his Stetson from its peg and left her in the kitchen with the slumbering Two Bits.

She sent him and Matt Malloy off to the Rudigers with a tin of food, which Mr. Otto balanced in front of him in the saddle. The day was warm, and Julia was content to finish her chores inside and then sit under a cottonwood tree in a canvas-backed chair. The only sound on the place was the stirring of the leaves, an occasional whinny from the horse corral, and geese high overhead, heading south now.

It was a far cry from the noise and hustle of Boston or Salt Lake. As she sat there, a smile on her face, she slowly became aware of a new sensation, one she had not felt in months.

She was content.

Eighteen

The Rudigers were packed and gone in two days, thanks to the efficiency of the men of the Double Tipi. Julia accompanied the wagon on horseback as far as the Marlowe Ranch, where she spent the afternoon, enjoying their company and telling Alice of her disastrous dinner.

"You were right, Alice. I was an idiot," she admitted.

"I'm hearing nothing but good reports now, so I think you weathered it," Alice said as she sorted eggs into a salt-filled carton. "Need any more?"

"As many as you can spare," Julia said. "I'm thinking an angel food cake with cream maple sugar frosting drizzled on it will maintain my job security." She laughed. "These are trying times, after all!"

Mr. Otto was right. The ride back to the Double Tipi was just enough time on horseback to create a twinge. *I should ride every day, if I intend to actually make it all the way to Gun Barrel to catch a train for Cheyenne and church,* Julia told herself.

She shivered and looked at the sky—sharp blue, with geese in excellent formation now. Matt was carrying her letter home to the post office in Gun Barrel, the one to her parents asking for a warmer coat and a divided skirt for riding. No sense in using the former Mrs. Otto's clothing one moment longer than necessary. Hopefully, Iris would catch the vision from her comments and write a little more. She smiled to think of talkative Iris on the dairy farm, out in the middle of nowhere.

Since Matt and Mr. Otto were still in Gun Barrel with the Rudigers, she invited Doc into the parlor.

"What happens around here in the winter?" she asked, picking up a half-completed dishcloth and her crochet hook.

"Not much. We take turns riding the fence line to make sure it's tight. There's a lineman's shack about ten miles from here, and we use that."

"That's you, Matt, and Willy Bill?"

He shook his head. "Paul. Willy Bill is probably too old for it, anyway."

"Mr. Otto doesn't turn him off for the winter?" Julia asked. "Alice Marlowe said they let go of most of their hands until the spring roundup."

"Mr. Otto wouldn't do that to ol' Willy Bill. Who on earth would hire him in town? Nah, he sets Willy Bill to odd jobs here. And Kringle fixes harnesses." He sat back, comfortable. "It's kinda slow here, Julia. I hope you don't bore easily."

"When I have all of you sweethearts with delicate stomachs to cook for? Not a chance."

After Mr. Otto and Matt came back from Gun Barrel the next afternoon, an itinerant preacher accompanied them. He changed everything.

His name was Reverend Levi Pierson. From the look on Matt Malloy's face, Julia could tell that the trip from Gun Barrel to the Double Tipi, with Pierson riding along beside the wagon, was about six hours too long.

"I tried to convince him to stay at the Marlowes' ranch, but he likes to give us the benefit of his wisdom," Matt whispered to her as she put the finishing touches on dinner.

"He's been here before? Is he a friend of Mr. Otto's?" she whispered back.

"Probably not. We see him every year, about this time." He sighed. "Mr. Otto is too polite to turn down someone who looks like he could use a meal."

There was no denying that Levi Pierson had the look— tall and thin, with sharp features and squinting eyes. He was dressed in rusty black, and his hat had seen better days. The only thing that kept him from looking like a derelict was the Bible he clutched to his chest and a certain purposeful air.

His own expression inscrutable, Mr. Otto introduced the preacher to Julia. "Pierson, this is my cook."

Pierson reached for her hands, holding them in his bony ones. "You're a serious improvement to the Double Tipi," he said, blasting her with bad breath that came from rotten teeth. "She the wife of one of your hands?"

"No. She just answered an ad in the paper, and I hired her," Mr. Otto said, indicating a chair for the reverend.

Pierson looked closer at her before he sat down. Julia felt her skin crawl. He shook his finger at her. "Being a weak vessel, you wouldn't do anything to tempt these men now, would you?"

Julia stared at him.

"She's my cook," Mr. Otto said firmly. "Not your concern, Pierson."

The preacher gave her an arch look. "If you say so."

"I most emphatically do," Mr. Otto replied, clipping off his words. The ranch hands looked at each other, but any warning was lost on the reverend, who picked up his spoon and blew on it, rubbing at an imaginary spot.

Her lips tight together, Julia brought the fried chicken to the table, setting it in front of Mr. Otto. The mashed potatoes followed, and then the cream gravy, along with stewed tomatoes with toasty hunks of bread in it, and creamed peas. She started to pour coffee when the minister held up his hand.

"Stop right there," he ordered. "It is time to return thanks."

Julia set down the coffeepot and folded her arms. The hands looked at each other and then at the reverend, who glowered back.

"I can see I ought to visit here more often," he said, glaring at each man in turn. "Bow your heads, you heathens."

He began to pray, one hand upraised like an Old Testament prophet, droning on and on. He asked the Lord to bless the food and then went into a tangent, calling down warning on sinners, some of whom might be seated around that very table. Julia opened one eye and looked at Mr. Otto. A nerve seemed to be twitching in his jaw.

The food was getting cold, and still Pierson held them captive to his diatribe, as far as Julia could tell, against nearly everything. He seemed to wind himself tighter and tighter, somehow working in plagues and pestilence and the evils of drink and evil women and disease.

"Amen."

Julia opened her eyes in surprise. Mr. Otto had spoken firmly. There was no mistaking the relief on the faces of his men as they settled back. Matt reached for the rolls, and Doc passed the mashed potatoes. Julia let out a tiny sigh and spread her napkin on her lap.

Pierson wasn't about to surrender without a protest. "I wasn't quite finished," he said.

"I was," Mr. Otto said. "We've had a long day, Pierson, and I've been looking forward to this meal for at least half of it."

Maybe Pierson realized he had gone too far. Or maybe he was hungry too. He forked out several pieces of chicken and passed on the platter. He ate with loud smacking noises that made even Willy Bill look sideways at him and slide his chair away.

Chewing with his mouth open, the preacher kept up a running commentary on the general state of affairs in Wyoming, which he referred to as the "Devil's playground." His comments earned only noncommittal grunts from his fellow diners as they tried to eat and ignore him.

Julia couldn't decide if it was worse to hear him going on and on about the evil around him or to hear him complimenting her for the excellent dinner, which was turning to ashes in her mouth just having to sit at the same table with him.

"Miss, uh, Darling, is it? Where did you learn to cook?"

She had to answer. He had asked her a direct question. "At Miss Fannie Farmer's School of Cookery in Boston," she said, wiping her mouth delicately, in the hopes that he might take the hint.

"All the way from Boston? Mr. Otto, you cast a wide net."

"Not so wide. Darling's from Salt Lake City."

She could have told Mr. Otto that was the wrong thing to say. Maybe it was an inborn caution that warned her when he started to pray, that this preacher would have no truck with Mormons. Julia thought of little slights and barbs that had come her way in Boston and kept her eyes on her plate as she heard Pierson gasp.

"Mr. Otto, you are harboring a spawn of the devil in your employ!"

Mr. Otto looked up, startled. "I beg your pardon, Pierson?"

"This is worse than I thought," the preacher said primly.

"You aren't aware of the danger you're in."

Julia kept her eyes on her plate, humiliated and wishing the floor would open. The room was silent.

She had to give Mr. Otto credit. After all, the Reverend Pierson was a guest at his table and apparently worth the benefit of the doubt. He executed a masterful change of subject, talking about the recent cattle drive to Cheyenne. Julia ventured a glance at the other men around the table, all of them as transfixed as she was to hear their boss talking during dinner.

Pierson wouldn't be denied. "Mr. Otto, you'd be wise to send her packing. There's no telling what evil she has already engineered. I pity you all."

Julia felt her stomach begin to hurt. The room was hot, and she wanted to run away. She looked at the others, and they were looking at Mr. Otto, waiting to take their cue from him. He gazed calmly at the preacher, but still that muscle in his jaw twitched.

"Darling, we could use some more of your gravy, if there's any left. And then you might want to see if Blue Corn is ready for dessert."

Eyes down, Julia mumbled something and reached for the gravy boat he held out to her, wishing he would defend her. With shaking hands, she filled it, remembering the time in Boston when one of the class members had refused to partner with her on a project. Miss Farmer had not been pleased, but she had done nothing about it. "Let it roll off," Papa had always told her. "They pay in the end."

She had her back to the minister. He was like a dog with a bone; he had a good subject now and he was determined to gnaw it clean.

"Ask her about Golden Plates, and venal polygamists, and missionaries who steal innocent young women, and—"

"That's enough, Pierson," she heard Mr. Otto say over the roaring in her ears. "She's my cook, and we have no quarrel with her. I'll remind you that you are a guest at my table, but that doesn't give you a license to wound." He had snapped out the words, and the air became electric.

"You need to be warned," the man replied almost prissily this time, oblivious to the tension. "Miss Darling, how about your father? How many wives does he service?"

Julia gasped and felt the anger rise from deep inside her. It was one thing to attack her, but her father and mother—the best people in her universe—that was different.

She heard Mr. Otto's chair scrape back at the same time she turned around and poured the gravy on Pierson's head. Mr. Otto stared at her. "That's my limit," she said quietly. "Mr. Otto, I'll leave in the morning. I know he's a guest at your table."

Pierson just sat there, gravy over his greasy hair and running in smooth rivulets down his face, parting like lava around his nose and rejoining under his chin, to drip into his lap. It was a good gravy too; what a shame to waste it on a bigot.

Pierson tried to rise, but Kringle and Willy Bill, her mostly unlikely champions, slapped meaty hands on his shoulder and forced him to remain in his gravy puddle. She turned on her heel, snatched up her shawl from its peg by the door, and left the house, closing the kitchen door behind her.

She stood in the yard, transfixed by what she had done. Thoughts of "I just embarrassed my employer" chased the defiance of "Reverend Pierson deserved that" around in her brain until all she could do was put her hands to her ears to block out her own misdeed. She could never go into that kitchen again, not in this lifetime.

Julia ran across the yard, her eyes blurred with tears,

and into the horse barn, finding an empty stall and crouching there, her shawl tight around her. Her humiliation at Pierson's attacks; her fierce, hot anger toward the man; and her shame at her reaction made her shake as though she had the palsy. Miserable, she hugged herself. *I have been nothing but trouble and too immature to work for anyone. I can't even swallow an insult from a fool. I should have known better.*

Julia pulled the shawl even tighter. Cold, she made herself as small as she could, with her feet tucked under her. She would wait everyone out, and when all the lights were extinguished in the ranch house, she would go back inside. Contract or no contract, she knew she would be gone in the morning. Mr. Otto would never tolerate such rudeness from one of his employees.

Time passed; how much, she had no idea. Julia listened to the horses and tried not to hear the little rustlings in the hay that made her yearn for Two Bits to hurry up and grow into a mouser. She tensed when she heard the men heading to the bunkhouse, but to her relief, no one came into the horse barn.

"I brought you a blanket."

Julia gasped, her heart racing. *If I don't turn around, maybe he will go away,* she told herself. *If facing Heavenly Father on Judgment Day is anything like facing Mr. Otto, I am in deep trouble.*

"Darling, it's cold out here. Lean forward a bit."

Without looking at him, Julia did as he said, mainly because there was still that compelling way he spoke—a man not to be argued with. He draped a quilt around her, resting his hand for a moment on her shoulder. He sat down beside her in the hay. She glanced at him out of the corner of her eye. He looked calm as he leaned back against the stall.

He's not going to leave me alone, Julia told herself

drearily. She cleared her throat. "I don't know what to say," she admitted finally.

Mr. Otto sat close to her but not touching her. "I think we all discovered you needn't say much to create an impact," he said finally.

"Mr. Otto, I'm so sorry," she said in a rush, looking at him and then looking away because she couldn't bear his strange serenity. "I promise to be off the place tomorrow morning. In a few weeks—days, maybe minutes—you'll forget I was ever here!"

He put up his hand to stop her torrent of words. "Hey, let me complete my thought! You can sure be talkative."

She closed her mouth in a firm line and looked away.

He must have noticed her struggle because he did the one thing she never expected. He put his arm around her shoulders and pulled her close to his chest.

It was too much. She discovered she had tears, after all. As she sobbed into his shirt, his grip tightened. She could not imagine why he was tolerating this, but she cried and let him take some of the pain too.

"I'll wash your shirt and handkerchief before I leave tomorrow," she said.

"You're not going anywhere, Darling." There was nothing in his quiet reply that hinted of anger or condescension or any of the reprisals she knew she deserved.

She couldn't think of a thing to say, but he had more on his mind. "I think if you hadn't done that, I would have."

"Mr. Otto?"

He loosened his hold on her. "Let me explain. I tried to be polite to a guest. That's what we do out here in the range, where ranches are so widely scattered. I never turn down anyone in need of a meal. But after you ran out, I told Pierson that he could spend the night in the bunkhouse, if the boys would have him. I told him to be on his way in the morning at sunrise. I owe *you* the apology for not stepping in sooner."

She could barely believe her ears. "Oh, Mr. Otto, that's kinder than my actions deserve. Papa tells me I should just let words like that run off my back."

Mr. Otto turned slightly so he could see her better in the low light from the lantern he had set near the stall's opening. "Why do people think Mormons are fair game?"

Julia pursed her lips and thought a long moment. "I think we all ask ourselves that. Maybe people don't know too much about us."

He took just as long in replying, and she heard the tentative nature of his comment in his tone of voice. "Maybe you're not so willing to share."

Julia couldn't deny the fairness of his thought. "You asked some questions when we met, and I was vague, wasn't I?"

He nodded. Again he picked his words with care. "I got the feeling—correct me if I'm wrong—that maybe you don't know as much as you wish you did. Or as you should know, perhaps."

That should have stung, but it didn't, considering her current wealth of remorse. "You could be right. It's just that I've always been a Mormon and . . ." She couldn't go on because it was almost more introspection than she wanted to bear at the moment.

". . . and maybe you take it for granted? I can understand that."

Put that way, she could too. "Maybe I do," she replied, her voice soft.

Julia decided that Mr. Otto was entirely too comfortable. She sat up straighter and brushed at her dress. "I have hay everywhere," she murmured.

"It's a barn, Darling."

Mr. Otto stood up and held out his hand to her. She took it and let him pull her to her feet. She kept the quilt around her shoulders. "Is that . . . that man still in the house?"

"No. The boys, uh, escorted him to the bunkhouse. I think the plan was to offer him a bucket of cold water to rinse the gravy out of his hair."

"Oh, goodness! He needs hot water for that," Julia said, waiting while Mr. Otto picked up the lantern.

He held it high and gave her a searching look. "Julia Darling, that's far nicer than I would be."

"Hot water," she said. "Just because that man is a—I shouldn't say what I'm thinking—he still needs hot water to get out the grease." She managed a smile. "I can forgive."

"I believe you can," Mr. Otto replied. "You realize, of course, that is more than Pierson is capable of."

"I know. It's okay."

They walked to the ranch house together. Julia dipped out the water from the Queen Atlantic's reservoir, and Mr. Otto gave James the bucket to take to the bunkhouse. She turned her attention to the stack of dishes someone had placed by the sink.

"Need some help?"

She shook her head. "Thank you, but no. Washing dishes clears my head."

"That's a relief," Mr. Otto said. "I never cared much for dishwashing."

He just looked at her then, making no comment. She knew her employer's expressions well enough by now to know that he was mulling over something.

"I'll get James to bed while you do kitchen patrol. When you're done, go in the parlor and take a seat. I have something you will find interesting."

"Your company ledgers?" she asked, getting more hot water from the Queen. "I did promise to help with those."

"They can wait. This is an entirely different matter."

"Is it legal?" she teased.

"That's not the issue," he assured her. "I think I can trust you with something."

Nineteen

$\mathcal{M}$r. Otto was sitting in the parlor when she finished the dishes. He was looking down at what looked like a page from the Bible, his lips in a tight line, lost in thought. Julia watched him from the doorway for a moment, curious.

"Darling, I have something to show you," he said when he saw her.

She dried her hands on her apron and took the parchment-thin scrap from him. "Looks like someone tore a page from a novel."

"Read it."

She did, pulling the lamp on the end table closer to the scrap. "My goodness, this is scripture, isn't it?"

"It seems so to me, even though the sentences run straight across the page and there aren't any numbers of chapters or verses. Does it sound familiar to you?"

Julia turned over the scrap, running her eyes down the page, which seemed to have been wrinkled from water damage, at the very least. And there it was, underlined: the same sentence someone had scribbled on the scrap of paper she had found in Mr. Otto's Bible: "For behold, are we not all beggars? Do we not all depend upon the same being, even God, for all the substance which we have?" She looked up, a question in her eyes.

"I've read the Bible cover to cover any number of times, trying to find where this page fits, and it doesn't.

It's not from the Bible, is it?"

"No, it isn't. Mr. Otto, it's from the Book of Mormon. I don't remember where, though."

He seemed startled. "You've read the Book of Mormon, haven't you?"

He had her there. "No, I haven't." Julia didn't want to look at the surprise on Mr. Otto's face. "I mean, I know it must be true. I'm a member of the Church." She looked down at her hands, embarrassed. "That sounds awfully lame, doesn't it?"

Apparently Mr. Otto was inclined to charity. "Maybe a little, but I think I can understand. You've grown up around Mormons and it's just something you must have accepted."

He was right. But listening to him try to explain away her misdemeanor made it an even bigger error. *Why haven't I ever read the Book of Mormon?* Julia asked herself. She managed a rueful smile. "Mr. Otto, you don't need to make me look better. I should have read the Book of Mormon before now."

"Winters are long here, Darling. Maybe you'll take the time," he suggested generously, which only made her squirm even more inside.

"Maybe it's neither here nor there," he continued, taking the page from her and smoothing it with his thumb and forefinger, almost as a museum curator would treat a rare treasure. "Call me an idiot, but I've based my life's conduct on that sentence. If that one sentence is so good, think what else there must be inside that book."

He was just warming to his subject; Julia could tell he had been thinking about it for a long time. He turned over the page and pointed to another place. "I mean, look at this!"

He read it to her, but his eyes were on her more than the page, and she knew he had memorized it. "'Believe in

God; believe that he is, and that he created all things, both in heaven and'—I can't read the words here. They've been rubbed away or something. But here, something I can't read, then, 'of your sins and forsake them.'" He put the page in his lap. "I just wish I knew more." He brightened. "Now I know it isn't in the Bible."

She nodded, dismayed at her own ignorance. She was no more use to Mr. Otto than the itinerant preacher. How pleasant it would have been to yawn, excuse herself, and go to bed, leaving him with his mystery. *I daren't do that,* she thought, and then realized she wanted to know more too, even if it meant exposing even more of her appalling density.

"Mr. Otto, where did you get this?"

"From my mother. It was one of those things she brought along when she married my father and they left the reservation to homestead here."

"Your mother?" Julia asked, puzzled. "How did an Indian woman come by this?"

Startled, Mr. Otto looked at her. "Darling, you've been laboring under a misconception." He shrugged. "Not that I ever really said anything." He put the page on the end table. "My mother was not an Indian."

"But you look—" She stopped, embarrassed.

"Like an Indian? I certainly do, but the Indian was my father."

Julia stared at him. "I don't understand. You said your mother came from the Wind River area. And those two Indians who came on the roundup with you? I know you called them your cousins."

"They *are* my cousins, at least, in the Indian way." Mr. Otto propped his boots on the low table in front of the settee. "Better get comfortable, Darling. I have quite a story for you."

She made herself comfortable on the settee next to Mr. Otto, tucking her legs under her.

"Where to begin?" he asked the ceiling, gazing overhead with his hands behind his head. "My father was Peter Otto, a Cherokee from North Carolina. In 1838, the Cherokee got the edict from Washington to move west to what became Indian Territory—you know, Oklahoma. Some of the families, my father's among them, hid out in the Carolina mountains instead. They avoided that Trail of Tears."

"I've heard of that trail," Julia said softly, not wanting to disturb his story. "In 1838, the Mormons were evicted from their homes in Missouri. Not their choice, either."

"Life's not so fair, is it?" he asked. "Gradually, the people in the mountains returned to their holdings in North Carolina, and the government left them alone. During the War Between the States, Pa joined the Confederate Army." His expression was distant. "We know how that ended. After Appomattox, Pa went home to burned-out ruins and then headed West for a new life."

"Goodness. That had to be difficult," Julia said.

"Thousands were doing exactly that. Pa ended up working for the Union Pacific Railroad. Somewhere around Washakie, he met my mother. She and her mother and sisters were washing dishes for the rail crews. She was awfully shy and would barely ever raise her eyes to look at anyone." He stopped, lost in thought for a moment.

"Her mother and sisters?"

Mr. Otto spoke several Indian words. "Those were their names."

"Keep going," Julia urged.

"Well, one day as Pa was leaving the cooking car—the railroad hauled it along—he made sure he was the last man out. He put his hand under her chin and made her look at him. Darling, she had blue eyes."

"My stars," Julia breathed. "Her mother and sisters were—"

"Shoshone. They had brown eyes like mine." He took a deep breath. "I've never told anyone this before. Pa specifically kept it quiet." He put his hand on her arm again. "You'll understand why."

He put his hands behind his head again. "Pa was full of questions. All he could figure was that she had been kidnapped by the Indians and raised as one of them. It happened occasionally."

"I've heard stories."

"Pa didn't have a chance to say or do anything because that was the last he saw of her. The railroad crew moved on, and he stayed with the UP until Promontory Summit."

"Golden Spike, 1869," Julia said. "We studied that in school."

Mr. Otto laughed, ruffled her hair with his hand and just as quickly put it behind his head again. "He was at loose ends and not so enamored of Mormon society—he called them rather standoffish."

"Ouch."

"Railroad crews were rough, Darling. I don't blame your bunch. He wanted to find that Indian girl who probably wasn't an Indian, so he headed into the Wind River Country. By then, the army had established Camp Brown at what was the first Indian agency for the Shoshone, I suppose. Pa was good with horses. He had gone from laying track to wrangling horses for the UP. Anyway, the army hired him to do the same thing at Camp Brown."

"And he found your mother?"

"Obviously. I'm here. Ma's parents were highly protective, at least, until it became easy to see that Ma and Pa were falling in love. Then they told him one night how Ma came to be with the Shoshone."

"Kidnapped from a wagon train!" Julia said, her eyes wide. "This is so romantic."

"I still say you've been reading too many dime novels," he teased. "Remember how I told you her name was Child Walking?"

Julia nodded.

"Her father and a small party of Shoshone found her all alone, just walking. The snows had come early that year, and there she was. There wasn't anyone else around. They did what any sensible people would do and took her with them. Saved her life, I don't doubt."

It was Julia's turn to prop her feet on the table and lean back, lost in thought for a moment. "Oh, it just can't be," she said finally. "Do you have any idea when this was? Does your . . . did your mother remember anything?"

"Ma remembered her name—Mary Anne Hixon."

"Oh! That's your middle name, isn't it? I remember it from that silly contract."

"You're right. She didn't know how to spell it, though. When Mama spoke English—we usually spoke Shoshone when I was growing up here—she had a slight accent. Not an American one, either. I never could place it."

"Surely she remembered something else!" Julia exclaimed. "How old was she?"

"I think she was somewhere around eight years old. She remembered traveling with little wagons with no horses, but she never wanted to talk about it. She said it pained her to remember that hard journey. She remembered days without food, and then some of her brothers and sisters and her mother died."

"Wagons with no horses . . . oh my, Mr. Otto."

He sat up, alert, his eyes on her. "When the Shoshone

got her back to their lodges and took her shoes off, that little page of scripture was stuffed under her foot, as though to keep the cold out. She said there used to be more pages, but gradually they disappeared." He picked up the page almost tenderly. "Darling, she was a Mormon, wasn't she?

Julia nodded, unable to speak for a moment. She looked at the page in his hand. "Mr. Otto, I think she must have been with one of the handcart companies that tried to get to the valley in 1856."

He handed her the scrap of scripture, and Julia held it: a tiny link between a child lost in a storm to the people of the Salt Lake Valley she knew so well. "Mr. Otto, there were two companies who left too late from Iowa and got trapped in the snow, probably not too far from that central part of Wyoming. They suffered terribly through early snows, but the remnants made it to Salt Lake." She looked at him, feeling sudden compassion for a lost child she would never meet. "Mr. Otto, you belong to a Mormon family somewhere."

He shook his head and took back the page. "Mama did, not me. That was a lot of years ago. But you really think that was how she came to be there?"

"I'd be willing to wager my princely salary," she said, silent again as the greater implication took over and left her quiet, thinking. "But did your father and mother never try to find out?"

"They were both afraid that if they really found out where she belonged, someone would demand her back." He stood up then, as though the anxiety of such a tragedy was fresh in his heart, and paced the room, finally stopping in front of her. "It happened. Mama had seen it. Someone traces a white child to an Indian village, and the child is taken away, whether she wants to go or not. Mama didn't want that to happen. She loved her Shoshone family. And remember what my father knew about the army uprooting a peaceful people in the Carolinas and sending them west to die on a Trail of Tears."

"They weren't about to take that chance, were they?" Julia asked softly.

"Not if they could help it. After I was born, they really didn't want anyone to know Mama's possible origins." He sat down again. "You remarked when you came to the Double Tipi how hard it was to see the turn-off."

"I understand now. You three made yourselves pretty small here."

"We did."

They were both silent then, Julia absorbing what she had just learned. She glanced at Mr. Otto. He was leaning forward now, resting his elbows on his knees, looking at the floor. Impulsively, she put her hand on his back. He stiffened and then sighed.

"I wanted to tell you this earlier, maybe just as soon as I hired you from Salt Lake, but you can understand my hesitation, I hope. I wanted to see if I could find my relatives somewhere in the world. I belong to the Shoshone. Our ties of kinship aren't blood ties always. I want to know who *all* my people are."

She patted his back but remembered herself and removed her hand. "It's safe to find out now."

"Who's to say what would have happened, though, if my parents had gone searching? Neither of them had any reason to trust soldiers or settlers."

Just then the clock on the whatnot shelf chimed twelve. It roused Mr. Otto from his contemplation of the floor. "Morning comes early around here."

Julia was amazed at the power of one sentence. "That one page governs your life?"

"I nearly forgot, until you reminded me with the tar paper." He smiled. "You know by now that I've taken in a lot of beggars and strays. Been one too."

You took me in too and kept me when any other boss would have turned me off after warm liver salad or gravy on a guest, she thought. "Mr. Otto, let me write to my father and tell him your story. It's quite possible he can find your Utah family. Maybe some of the Hixons survived the handcart tragedy."

He frowned. "I'll need to think about that." He looked at her then, his shyness back. "Would you loan me your extra copy of the Book of Mormon? That one good verse can't be the only useful one."

"You were interested earlier, and I brushed you off. I'm sorry I did that."

"We didn't know each other too well, did we?" His expression turned serious. "And after your treatment tonight by that son of a . . . that preacher . . . I can understand a bit of caution on your part. I don't have a lot of time to read, but I can begin."

I can too, Julia thought. "I'll give you the book, if you'll think about what I suggested. Your Hixon relatives might not be as hard to find as you think. My father likes a challenge."

"I'll think about it. How about this? Let's go to Cheyenne this Saturday, and you can find that church of yours on Sunday."

She took a deep breath. "I will, if you'll come to church with me."

He drew himself up. "Of course! You don't think I'd let my cook wander around Cheyenne without an escort! Darling, I wasn't born yesterday."

"Mr. Otto, I have to ask: why did you decide to tell me this now?"

"Simple, Darling. After you dumped that gravy on the preacher, I got an inkling about what your church means to you. My story is safe with you."

Twenty

$\mathcal{M}$r. Otto was as good as his word. On Saturday, he made her saddle her own horse while he watched, just to assure himself that she could, and they rode to Gun Barrel. Julia would never admit that the journey taxed her rump to the outer limits, but he must have suspected because he helped her down carefully once they reached the livery stable.

He checked his pocket watch at the depot. "I have time to send a telegram to Heber Gillespie—the Sunday School superintendent—and let him know we'll be arriving this afternoon in Cheyenne," he told Julia. "He wanted you to stay with his family tonight when we talked earlier."

"Not much warning, is it?" she commented.

"He's expecting you," he replied, setting down her valise by the ticket window. "Two for Cheyenne," he told the agent.

"Mr. Otto, I can pay my own way. I mean, you're doing *me* the favor."

"I think this is covered in one of those clauses in the contract," he joked. "Gotta keep the cook happy."

She already knew how futile it was to argue with Mr. Otto, so she waited inside the warm depot while he went a few doors down to send the telegram. He came back with a few minutes to spare and a sheaf of letters, most of which he stuffed in his valise. The rest he handed to her.

"You have a substantial literary following, Darling," he

said as he helped her up. "Sore?"

She winced. "That's the farthest I've ridden before."

"You did well."

Funny about receiving a compliment from Mr. Otto—she beamed almost from ear to ear like James, or for that matter, like Matt Malloy. *I don't think I seek your approval*, she told herself as they settled in the train. *I like it, though, because I generally know I've earned it.*

With a final call from the conductor and a lurch, they started for Cheyenne. Julia itched to opened her letters—one from her parents, one from Iris, and one from her Sunday School teacher—but it wouldn't be polite to do so in front of Mr. Otto.

"Read 'em, Darling," he said after the locomotive built up a head of steam and the train settled into its rhythmic clatter. "I don't mind."

Mr. Otto stretched out his legs and settled into his well-worn seat, turning his attention to the view outside the soot-covered window. She looked as well. There was even less snow on this side of the pass, even though the wind bent the sagebrush and rabbitbrush.

"Dry winter," Mr. Otto commented, a frown on his face. "Means a dry summer coming up, and nobody likes those."

She barely heard him, deep in her letter from Iris, written the same way she wrote letters now: a page here, the interruptions, then another page, usually dated a day or two later. She finished one page, a description of hog butchering—"I threw up," Iris wrote—and started on the next.

It took whatever dignity she possessed not to let out a whoop with the news that followed.

"You're kicking my foot," Mr. Otto commented.

"Sorry! I couldn't help myself," she said, putting down

the letter and then picking it up again to read the same paragraph over. "Mr. Otto, my little sister is in the family way!"

"I'd say that's worth a kick in the boot. Congratulations to . . ."

"Iris Davison," Julia said, reading the paragraph again. "She married a dairy farmer out in the wilds of Draper. It had to be true love, because Iris doesn't much care for animals bigger than cats."

"I doubt he makes her do the milking."

"Well, no." Julia put down the letter. "Mr. Otto, I'm going to be an aunt!"

"Or maybe an uncle, if it's a boy," he teased.

She kicked his boot on purpose. "You're the limit, sir." She looked at the letter. "She must have just found out. By the time I finish my contract here, my niece—or nephew, thank you very much—will be about a month old."

"You mean you're not going to stay here and sign another contract?" he joked, his hand to his heart in mock surprise.

"I don't anticipate falling in love with Mr. McLemore," she teased back. "Besides, you saw the look on his face when I served him warm liver salad. My heart is safe, sir, and I already can't wait to be an aunt."

Mr. Otto just smiled, amused by her enthusiasm, and pulled his hat lower on his forehead. In a minute, he was breathing regularly. She returned to her letters. Mama's letter was written later than Iris's and in much the same vein; Mama was looking for flannel for diapers.

The rest of Mama's letter was more prosaic: Christmas preparations coming up, the ward choir sounding no better than usual, troubles with mice deciding they needed a warmer venue for the winter than the woodshed. *Oh, Mama, if you could see* my *mouse problem,* she thought, turning the letter over for Mama's postscript.

It didn't surprise her, not really. "Guess what? Ezra Quayle is engaged. She's a quiet little thing from Murray," Mama had written. "Probably won't give him a speck of trouble."

Julia put the letter in her lap, surprised at her feelings—part of her grateful she had given him back the engagement ring, and the other part thinking of Iris's good news as she wondered about her own future. She picked up the letter again. "This will make you laugh, Jules—everyone says they are perfectly suited to each other, just as they used to say about you!"

She finished the postscript, smiling at Mama's last comment. "Jules, I'll probably have to repent of this, but I took a look at her engagement ring. It's the same one you gave him back!"

Of course it is, Mama, Julia told herself. *Ezra is practical.*

"The expression on your face doesn't look quite like good news."

Surprised, she glanced up to see Mt. Otto watching her. She returned his gaze, thinking again how nice he looked. He had spent some time in the bunkhouse after dinner last night and she wondered if Doc or Matt had trimmed his hair and mustache.

"What?" he asked, aiming for that frosty tone that used to make her jump.

"Mama tells me that my former fiancé is engaged again."

"That boy didn't let any grass grow under his feet," Mr. Otto said. "I suppose there are enough ladies here and there in Salt Lake to present opportunity. We're short on opportunity in this state, if you hadn't already noticed."

"Don't remind me," she said, rolling her eyes. "Here's the droll part: Mama says his new fiancée is wearing the very ring—setting and all—that I gave back." She looked Mr. Otto square in the eyes. "Would you do that, or would you take a returned ring back to the jewelers and at least get a different setting?"

"Me?" His face flushed again. "The matter never came up."

Julia sighed. "Mr. Otto, I'm sorry! I shouldn't be reminding you of, well . . . you know."

"I know, and don't fret," he told her, a half smile on his face. "Doesn't hurt to talk about it. My former wife only got a wedding ring from me. Come to think of it, I never got it back." He shrugged. "Water under the bridge, Darling." He hesitated. "Would you . . . did you insist on an engagement ring?"

"No, I never did. Ezra just showed up with a ring one day, after we'd agreed to marry. I didn't even have the fun of picking out my own."

"That bothered you?"

She nodded, hoping she didn't sound silly and wistful; she was talking to Mr. Otto, after all. "I guess I just wanted a choice. That's not a lot to ask."

"Nope," he replied and tipped his Stetson down again. "Any regrets?" he asked from under the brim when she thought he was asleep again.

"Not one," she said softly.

He tipped up the hat and gave her a long look, and then put it down again. Julia smiled to herself as he started to snore gently after a few minutes.

The Gillespies had received Mr. Otto's telegram only an hour or two before they showed up on the family doorstep, but Sister Gillespie's welcoming smile was heartfelt. She pulled Julia inside the house while her husband shook Mr. Otto's hand and ushered him in with a little more dignity.

Julia couldn't help but notice how even the Gillespies gave her employer that same formal deference that she had noticed from other people. *I will have to ask Sister Gillespie what it is about Mr. Otto that seems to inspire what looks suspiciously like awe,* she thought as the superintendent's wife sat her down and handed her valise to one of several children nearby with orders to take it upstairs.

"After Mr. Otto contacted my husband, we were hoping you'd be able to come," Sister Gillespie said as she took her baby from an older daughter. "It's not easy to make church meetings in Wyoming, we've discovered." She shrugged. "Brother Gillespie just tells his far-flung congregation to do the best they can. The nearest branch west from here is Laramie or Fort Collins, if you're going south to Colorado. And Denver, of course."

Brother Gillespie and Mr. Otto remained in the vestibule, talking. Gillespie gestured into the parlor, but Mr. Otto just shook his head. He did step in a few minutes later to tell Julia he'd be back tomorrow morning to escort her to church.

"You're welcome to stay with us, Mr. Otto," Sister Gillespie said.

"That's been the subject of my remarks too," Brother Gillespie added. "Mr. Otto says a hotel will suit him fine. I don't think he wants an argument."

I can assure you he doesn't, Julia thought, amused. She stood up and went to the vestibule. "You're coming to church, though?" she asked, trying to strike a balance between the eagerness she felt and the proprieties of urging the man who paid her salary.

"Said I would. Mr. Gillespie said he'd pick me up at the

hotel at 8:00 a.m. so I could help him sweep out the Odd Fellows Hall first. That'll be a new experience, looking at the hall from the perspective of Sunday, rather than Saturday night." He tipped his hat to Sister Gillespie. "See you tomorrow, ma'am. Darling, you might prevail on the Gillespies to turn you loose in the kitchen."

"Good heavens, he calls you Darling?" Sister Gillespie asked after he left.

Julia felt her face turn rosy. "Darling is my cross to bear."

"He calls everyone by their last name," Brother Gillespie said to his wife after he closed the front door. He had a smile on his face as he sat down across from Julia. "Except for me, apparently. Imagine. Mr. Otto, the very Mr. Otto, called me *Brother* Gillespie! I would tell someone, but I'm sure they wouldn't believe me!"

Sister Gillespie gasped and hugged her baby to her breast, earning a squeal from the little one. "That's *the* Mr. Otto?" she asked. "Your *employer*?"

"Well, yes," Julia said, confused. She looked from one Gillespie to the other. "Does everyone in Wyoming know everyone else?"

"Just about," Brother Gillespie said. "His father was one of the first ranchers in the territory. The first Mr. Otto had an Indian wife, apparently, and they kept to themselves. And there were rumors of the current Mr. Otto wounding a man, or maybe killing him, who took too great an interest in his wife." His expression turned dubious. "Sister Darling, do you feel *safe* at the Double Tipi?"

"Completely," Julia assured them, aware that Brother Gillespie had no more idea about who was the Indian in the Otto family than most of Wyoming, apparently. "I fear stories about Mr. Otto have been greatly exaggerated. He's a good employer and a fair one." She had to laugh. "At least, as long as I fry steaks and cook flapjacks and avoid most of what I was taught at cookery school!"

Brother Gillespie beamed at Julia. "You've probably had to learn how to make coffee."

"I have," she replied, laughing. "I hear it's good!"

Julia spent most of the evening in the kitchen, visiting with Sister Gillespie and furnishing cooking tips. She was glad she had brought along an extra set of measuring spoons as a gift, touched that the lawyer's wife would be so appreciative.

"Do you really use them?" the woman asked, fingering the little tin spoons.

"All the time," Julia said. "Accurate measures make foolproof food, or so Miss Farmer taught. Of course, recipe books will have to catch up with modern domestic science. Just think how many of your recipes probably call for a measure the size of a hen's egg, or a thimble of this or that."

"Most of them," Sister Gillespie said, "and don't forget the ever popular half a handful!"

"You'll want this, too," Julia said, handing her a piece of cardboard. "Mr. Otto gave me the cardboard from one of his new shirts. I've translated those hen's eggs, thimbles, and handfuls into tablespoons and teaspoons. You can prop this on your kitchen counter."

"We do live in a modern age," Sister Gillespie said.

There were enough Gillespie children for Julia to take over bedtime story detail and give Emma Gillespie more time with her older daughter, Amanda, who was preparing a two-and-a-half minute talk for Sunday School. She read short stories to an appreciative audience of two boys, sitting in their bed and both of them leaning against her. She thought of James, and his one tattered book, and how he leaned against her that same way. Remembering, she put her arms around the Gillespie sons and wondered what James would do with more than one book.

Before she finished, Sister Gillespie was sitting at the foot of their bed. Julia told the brothers and their mother about James, who had no last name and had just showed up one awful winter at the Double Tipi.

"We read the same book over and over," she said. "The last pages are gone, so we make up new endings all the time." She looked at Sister Gillespie. "And then we sing 'Sweet Evalina,' because that's the only song Mr. Otto says he ever learned. I guess he taught it to James and it stuck."

"Mr. Otto *sings* to a little boy?" Sister Gillespie asked, her eyes wide. "We've heard stories that make that sound impossible. Not that I doubt you," she added hastily.

"No worries. His reputation must be more fierce than the reality I see every day." She yearned to tell Sister Gillespie about the one verse of scripture that her employer used to govern his life. *If only you knew him,* she thought.

She had to sing "Sweet Evalina" for the boys, then. One song led to another, ending with "The Handcart Song," which made her think of Mr. Otto's mother, lost, starving, and cold, wandering in snowdrifts, to be rescued by kindly people who took her in and cherished her as their own. She struggled with tears while the others sang, "As merrily on our way we go, until we reach the valley-o." The hopeful words became a terrible mockery of the reality that Mary Anne Hixon had faced, a child no older than these children singing in their warm bed. No wonder Mr. Otto took in James, kept him, and never questioned his benevolence. He was only doing what the Shoshone he loved had done. *Are we not all beggars?* Julia thought as she wiped her eyes on the sheet.

"That song has memories for you, Sister Darling," the

boys' mother said when they finished. "Do you come from handcart stock?"

Julia was scarcely able to speak. "No, but I know some who came that way." *Or tried to,* she added in her heart.

Sister Gillespie invited Julia to join them downstairs for family prayers, and she joined the family circle, grateful to the bottom of her heart to be in family communication with Heavenly Father again. *Why did I ever take this for granted?* she asked herself, eyes closed, as she listened to each child pray in turn, and then Brother and Sister Gillespie, their arms entwined, pray for each of their children, the missionaries, and the little congregation in Cheyenne and its environs.

Julia took her turn, barely able to talk because of the love she felt for this family she had only met that afternoon but who shared an exquisite bond with her that made them close. She prayed as she always did, for her parents, her brothers in St. George, and Iris and Spencer on their dairy farm. She was too shy to say anything about the expected child, but she surprised herself by asking the Lord to bless Mr. Otto. *He would be so embarrassed if he knew I prayed for him*, Julia thought as she shepherded the boys back upstairs and tucked them in for Sister Gillespie.

She shared a bed with Amanda, who chatted for a few minutes about school and Christmas coming fast. When Amanda slept, warm at her side, Julia listened to Brother and Sister Gillespie walk down the hall to their own room, talking quietly, one of them laughing softly, the other shushing, as the baby went into her crib in their room. And then the door closed.

Lying there, she thought of the little Otto family, so desperate to stay together that they kept themselves a veritable secret from a world they dreaded might separate them. *I want to love like that someday,* she told herself as she closed her eyes.

When Sunday School began next morning, Julia thought at first how amused her family would be to hear of the Odd Fellows Hall, still smelly with lingering cigar smoke and with spittoons lined up neatly against the wall. By the time the meeting ended, she had no desire to make fun of what she had been part of.

The day started with a telephone call from Mr. Otto, humorous enough because she knew he must not have had much opportunity to use such a device. Her hand over the receiver, her eyes merry, Sister Gillespie called her to the phone.

"It's Mr. Otto. He doesn't seem to have much patience with this contraption," she said. "Here you are, Julia."

"This is a blasted nuisance," he told her. "Darling, can you possibly hear me?"

"Loud and clear, sir," she said, doing everything she could not to catch Sister Gillespie's eye because she knew she would not be able to smother her mirth.

"Don't ever ask me to string a line to the Double Tipi," he growled.

"Sir! I would never," she protested. "I'm only going to be there until September 15."

"Hmm," was all he said for a long time, although she could hear him breathing into the speaker.

"Mr. Otto?"

"We'll have to make a dash to the station when Sunday School is over." He stopped talking then, and she could faintly hear Brother Gillespie in the background.

"And Gill . . . Brother Gillespie has promised that Brother Baker—whoever he is—won't give the closing prayer because he takes forever."

"So you want me to have my valise packed and brought to the meeting, so we don't have to return to the Gillespies' house?"

"That's it. You are wise beyond your years."

Julia laughed. "Of course I am. Good-bye, Mr. Otto."

"I just hang up this hand thing?"

"Yes. See you in a while."

She hurried to pack, sorry to have to leave so fast, but grateful Mr. Otto had been kind enough to escort her to Cheyenne this first time. She was certain she could manage by herself from now on, now that she knew how kind the Gillespies were.

She was ready to turn the clasp on her valise when Sister Gillespie, her hair still in rags, came into the room with some books.

"Here you are, my dear. Maybe—James, was it?— would like a book or two with real endings." She popped them into the valise when Julia opened it. "My boys won't even miss them."

"He'll be delighted," Julia said. "You've been so kind to us."

"Nothing easier. Now you'll have to convince Mr. Otto that he can stay here too the next time you come."

"Maybe so," Julia replied, wondering why her face felt a little warm. "He did tell me that this trip was mostly to make sure I could manage by myself."

Sister Gillespie began to untwist the rags from her hair. "You might just have to pretend that you're not so capable, Sister Darling."

"I might," Julia replied.

A half hour later, Brother Gillespie roared up in his Studebaker. "I left Mr. Otto at the hall," he told Julia as he put her valise on his oldest daughter's lap and told them to crowd together. "There were a few happy sprites who wanted to continue making merry, and Mr. Otto was showing them out." He grinned at her. "He's better than a bouncer. One look at him, and they couldn't back down the stairs fast enough."

"His reputation does precede him," Julia said as Sister Gillespie handed her the baby.

By the time she walked upstairs to the Odd Fellows Hall, located over a pawn shop, the cowboys Brother Gillespie spoke of were long gone. Mr. Otto stood in a group of men who looked about like him—tall, lean, dressed in obviously little-worn suits—talking with them.

"Looks like Mr. Otto has found some friends," Sister Gillespie whispered to her.

"Do you think they all know each other?" Julia asked, surprised to see her employer so completely at ease. *Obviously I don't need to ever worry about Mr. Otto in any social situation,* she told herself.

"I think everyone in Wyoming knows everyone else," Sister Gillespie said. "This state amazes me."

Julia sniffed the air. She saw the spittoons lined up neatly against the back wall and the rough benches just as neat facing forward to a large picture of Custer's Last Stand. But there was the sacrament table, and there was Brother Gillespie, talking to members of his flock. She glanced at the Gillespies' oldest daughter, her face serious, looking down at her notes and then at her mother for reassurance. Someone had hauled in a small organ. A serene-looking woman handed her baby to another lady and began the prelude music. It was church and nothing but church, despite the setting. Custer was no stained glass window, but Julia could see it didn't matter.

I could look and criticize, but I don't want to, Julia thought as she sat on the bench next to Sister Gillespie. *Papa would remind me these are my people too, except I don't need reminding. It's so good to be here.*

And it was. With a nod to the other men, Mr. Otto sat down beside her. He had even patted on some bay rum this morning, and she sniffed the air appreciatively. Mr. Otto leaned closer.

"You like that better than *eau de corral*?" he whispered, his breath just tickling her ear.

"Almost as good as *eau de sage*," she whispered back. "Mr. Otto, you look fine in that suit. Maybe you should wear it more often."

"Darling, I can't think of a single steer it would impress."

She looked at him sideways, pleased at this side of him. He listened to the prelude music with a half smile. He moved closer to her to accommodate two latecomers.

He leaned toward her again. "What do I do?"

"When the service starts?"

He nodded. "Darling, I've never been to church in my life. Well, except when I got married."

"You can sing along—I have this hymnbook—and take the bread and water when it's passed, if you want to," she whispered back.

"They don't mind?"

"About the sacrament? No. Everyone's welcome."

She knew he wouldn't know the opening hymn, but by the third verse, he was humming along with the same enthusiasm she recognized from "Sweet Evalina."

After the opening prayer and a few announcements, Brother Gillespie invited a young man to the front to bless his baby. As other men gathered around, Mr. Otto whispered, "What now?"

"There's a baby to bless," she whispered back. "It usually happens when they're really small."

"I'll say. That's a little one."

They were sitting so close she felt him chuckle. Julia looked at him, inquiry in her eyes.

"The baby's father runs the livery stable on First Street," Mr. Otto whispered. "The man in the circle next to him is a physician and the man next to him is an undertaker. I never knew they were Mormons."

Then maybe we haven't been doing our job, Julia thought, struck by his words. *Or maybe discretion is the better part of valor, considering the pastor who was on the receiving end of my gravy boat. I wonder which it is.*

She decided it didn't matter. Mr. Otto might know them better than she did, but these were her people, even if the room reeked of cigars and Custer was being ushered into a better world, courtesy of Sioux Indians. Someday there might even be a ward in Cheyenne, although the possibility seemed remote.

The short talks were the usual she had heard from childhood. Face solemn, eyes riveted on the back wall with its row of spittoons, Amanda Gillespie spoke on the Holy Ghost. She was followed by a missionary, who expounded on Section 89 and the Word of Wisdom. They were the same talks she heard every Sunday of her life, but as she glanced at Mr. Otto, she could see how attentive he was, how alert. *Maybe I should look at this through his eyes,* she told herself. *I would probably hear things I hadn't thought of in years.*

Before the sacrament, Brother Gillespie chose to have

a practice hymn. The lady with the baby went back to the organ, and the chorister opened her hymnbook.

"Redeemer of Israel," she said, calling out the page number.

Julia knew it by heart, but she turned to the page for Mr. Otto's benefit. As the organist played through the hymn, the hymnbook she shared with Mr. Otto began to shake. Julia looked at him in alarm. His face had drained of color. Gently she took the book from his grasp as the congregation began to sing. He closed his eyes and bowed his head. She leaned against his shoulder.

"Mr. Otto, what's wrong?" she whispered, alarmed.

He grasped her hand and held it as though it was a lifeline. He had a strong grip. His lips were close to her ear as the congregation sang. "Darling . . . my mother used to hum that tune. I guess she didn't remember the words. Maybe she never knew them. My mother."

He didn't release her hand through all the verses. Julia hesitated a moment but then put her other hand over his wrist as she listened to the words. She saw in her mind's eye a mother humming to her son what she remembered from her own childhood, changed by tragedy. Julia had to swallow hard against her own tears.

She looked up to see Brother Gillespie eyeing her with some concern. She managed a smile in his direction, with a small shake of her head. By the time the congregation finished the final verse, Mr. Otto was in control of his emotions again. He released her hand. "Sorry," he whispered.

When the congregation began the sacrament hymn, Mr. Otto tensed again. He relaxed when he didn't know the tune and took the bread when it came his way, after an inquiring look at Julia. She nodded and took her turn, her eyes on Custer, but her heart on Mr. Otto and his curious connection with the people in the Odd Fellows Hall. None of them had an inkling of him beyond his being Mr. Paul Otto, an enigmatic figure and someone to be careful around. *If you only knew him,* she thought as she picked up the small cup of water. She considered the matter. Maybe that statement was true of most people. She looked toward the sacrament table; maybe she needed to know the Savior better.

Children and adults separated for classes, each heading to the opposite corner of the room. It was a far cry from her ward in the Avenues, with lace table coverings and a general air of prosperity, but the subject was familiar, taken from *The Instructor,* which Papa always read cover to cover. *And I could never be bothered,* Julia thought. *It was always something I was going to do.*

She listened to the lesson and the discussion that developed, more interested in its effect on Mr. Otto, who sat so still and paid attention with far more conscientious effort than she could ever remember putting forth. He leaned forward on the bench, his back as straight as though he rode his horse, every line of his body alert, as though no one else was in the hall except the instructor. Julia asked herself if there had ever been a time in her life when she had paid that much attention to a Sunday School teacher and felt herself sadly wanting.

True to his word, Brother Gillespie chose a most taciturn member of the congregation to give the closing prayer. After a hug from Sister Gillespie and her children and the promise to return as soon as she could, Julia hurried to the curb. She looked around for Mr. Otto, who stood beside Brother Gillespie, hands in his pockets, head to one side, as relaxed as she had ever seen him. Brother Gillespie motioned for them to get in the automobile.

"It's but a short walk," Mr. Otto protested. "I don't want to take you away from your congregation."

"No trouble," Brother Gillespie insisted. "Would you deny me a chance to puff up my pretensions and show off my Studebaker?"

"Not for the world, sir," Mr. Otto said as he got in the car. He looked around. "You ready, Darling?"

"Heber, remember the shoebox," Sister Gillespie said from the sidewalk. "Julia, it's just sandwiches. You know you don't want to eat that greasy train food."

She nodded, hand on her hat. They made the north-bound train with minutes to spare, Mr. Otto handing her up and then spending another few minutes in conversation with the Sunday School superintendent as the conductor tried to hurry him aboard. A brief, down-the-nose glare ended that, but Mr. Otto got the message. A few moments later, he sat down beside her, tossing his Stetson on the seat opposite them.

"I just promised him I'd bring you back in two weeks for the Christmas party," he told her, selecting a sandwich when she opened the shoebox. "If the weather's good."

"I don't mean to put you to trouble, Mr. Otto," she said, choosing a pimento and black olive sandwich.

"No trouble. I'm riding line this coming week. It's Matt's turn the week after, so there's nothing to stop us, unless it's the weather, which I do respect. Do you think they'd mind if we brought James along?"

"They wouldn't mind," she said softly. "Mr. Otto, what did you think?"

He shook his head and took a bite of his sandwich. He looked at it and frowned. "Darling, she's a fine woman, but you're a better cook."

"You know I meant Sunday School," she scolded.

He grinned at her. "I know." His expression turned serious. "I know," he said again more slowly. "Hard to say, really. Everyone seems earnest enough." He turned slightly in the seat to look at her directly. "How do you feel about what everyone was saying?"

"I believe it," she replied.

"Why?"

She had no answer right away. All her life she had heard the same scriptures and lessons over and over, and no one had ever asked her why. As she looked at Mr. Otto, seeing again the man so near tears when he heard the tune to "Redeemer of Israel," Julia didn't think a glib answer would satisfy him. Even more, she didn't think it would satisfy herself, either. Not now. She couldn't put her finger on it, but something had changed in the Odd Fellows Hall.

"I'm not sure," she said finally. "I just believe it because I've always believed it. And so does everyone around me."

Mr. Otto looked at her until she felt like squirming. He started to speak once, stopped and then started again. "I'm not sure that's a good enough reason."

He was right; she couldn't dispute him. Funny, it had never occurred to her before.

Twenty-two

They reached the Double Tipi just after dark, after the snow began falling in earnest. Julia wondered why Mr. Otto didn't just stop at the Marlowe ranch, but he seemed intent on reaching his own place. Even in their leather gloves, her hands were cold. She gave up any pretense at form and hung onto the saddle horn.

Mr. Otto rode close to her. She caught him looking at her several times, and more than once he steadied her. He seemed not to mind the weather.

"If we stop at the Marlowes', it might be hard to get out in the morning, the way this snow is," he said. "Chin up, Darling. We're about to the Rudigers' cabin, and then it's only a half mile until we turn off."

It wasn't totally dark yet; she knew where the Rudigers' cabin should be, except it wasn't there. Mr. Otto reined in, and she also stopped, her horse stepping in delicate circles. He leaned forward and peered into the gloom, sniffing the air. As her eyes accustomed themselves, she saw only a pile of burned logs and smelled the tar paper. No wonder the horses were uneasy.

"Care to bet that Charlie McLemore just couldn't stand the sight of the place? I may have to remind him who owns that property."

He said it mildly enough, but Julia knew him better now and had to wonder how Mr. McLemore would appreciate the visit probably coming his way.

Mr. Otto sat there a moment more, contemplating the still-smoldering ruin and then spoke to his horse, which had the effect of getting hers moving too. "At least he waited until they left," was his only comment. He turned in his saddle. "Was this the way Mormons used to be treated? Brother Gillespie said something about the wrongs of Missouri during Sunday School."

"Yes, it was," she replied, patting her horse to settle him. "The mobs didn't usually wait until the families were out, though."

"And what did you Mormons do?"

"Moved on, mostly," Julia said. "Papa tells a story about his mother leaving Far West, Missouri. Apparently Grandma Darling calmly swept out her house while the mob brandished torches and watched her. She took the house key, went up to the biggest, meanest mobber, and handed it to him."

"You have tough relatives," Mr. Otto said. There was no mistaking the admiration in his voice.

"I do, indeed. Mr. Otto, I'm cold. I suggest we move on too."

"Remind me not to get on your grumpy side," he said. "Are you suggesting that I not say anything to McLemore?"

"I'd never presume to tell you what to do, Mr. Otto," she replied, grateful when he took her reins and led her horse so she could hang onto the saddle horn in peace.

"Presume away, Darling."

"I wouldn't say anything. You don't know for sure, anyway. Kill him with kindness, if you must. It'll aggravate him to no end." She laughed. "I might even make a gooey butter cake for you to take him."

"Only if you make two and leave one at home," Mr. Otto said. "I've discovered a serious weakness for your cakes."

"Then my job is secure for nine months more?" she teased, even as her teeth chattered.

"At the very least," he told her, his voice so soft that she might have imagined it.

Nothing in the world looked better to Julia than the Double Tipi that night. Mr. Otto helped her down from her horse and whistled. The bunkhouse door opened and Matt Malloy came out, putting on his coat. He shook his head to see Julia.

"Julia, ye look like an icicle. Can ye even move?"

"Not sure," she replied, irritated that she had difficulty forming words.

"Malloy, will you give her horse a rubdown and grain him? Take Chief while you're at it, but I'll be out to curry him. Up you go, Darling."

With less effort than she thought possible—she knew how much she weighed—Mr. Otto picked her up and carried her into the house. James must have heard the whistle because he opened the door, Doc right behind him.

"We thought you might have stayed with the Marlowes," Doc said a few minutes later after Mr. Otto went to the horse barn. Julia was seated at the kitchen table with a mug of warm canned milk with just that touch of nutmeg she insisted on, even if it meant a painful hobble to the spice shelf.

"Mr. Otto wanted to get home," she said, her arm around James, who had crowded in close to her. "Did you take good care of Two Bits?"

James nodded and pointed to the rag-lined box by the Queen Atlantic, where the kitten slept. "Sure did. He likes to curl up on Mr. Otto's pillow. I found him in there twice."

Julia looked at the slumbering kitten. "He's a tenacious little beast. That's a long walk down the hall for something so small."

"How does he get on the bed?" James asked.

"Take a look at those little claws of his," Julia suggested.

"We missed you, Julia, even if it was only a day or so," Doc said.

"You missed my cooking," she teased.

"That too." He took her empty mug and put it in the sink. "Paul said something the other day about how you've improved the ambiance here."

"He couldn't possibly have used that word!" Julia said, pleased.

"Not quite. He said you had decreased the 'rapscallion quotient' of the place. He also pointed out that even Kringle doesn't swear in German anymore, perhaps on the off chance that you speak Deutsch."

Julia's cheeks felt rosy and warm and not from the Queen Atlantic. "I just came to cook."

Doc put his fingers on her cheek, the physician in him coming out. "Touch of cold there, Julia. I've got a little salve for that."

The salve was soothing, smelling faintly of vanilla. "I mixed up my winter batch while you were gone and took some liberties in your spice cabinet," Doc said, dabbing at her cheek. "Always nice to have the men of the Double Tipi smelling sweet."

Doc handed the salve to Mr. Otto when he came inside. "You could use a dab."

"Want some coffee?" Julia asked, wincing as she stood up. "I'm not sure who made it."

Mr. Otto shook his head. He yawned. "Nah. I don't even trust yours after dark anymore. I'm getting old. What did you drink?"

"Some warm milk with just a touch of nutmeg."

"I'll go for that."

"I'll add a bit of cinnamon too."

"You have to tinker, don't you?" he asked with a faint smile.

"That's my job. I do it well."

She brought him the milk, along with the extra copy of the Book of Mormon that had lain on the shelf in the pantry since September.

"You mentioned this once or twice, and I've been slow," she said, shy about giving him the book. "If you still want it, that is."

He took it from her and fanned the pages. "I do. Brother Gillespie wanted to give me a copy, but I knew you had an extra. So somewhere in here is that 'beggars' passage."

"I'm certain." Julia sat down gingerly, wondering if that salve would help in other areas.

"I know it isn't in the Bible, because I've been through that more times than I can count."

Julia nodded. "So that's how it is when you don't have too many other books around to read?"

He looked her square in the eye. "No, Darling, that's how it is when you want to find out something."

She blushed, thinking how her father would say she was coming up short. "I know you've read the scriptures more than I have."

"I have," he agreed. "I'm looking for something, and you think you've already found it." He looked at her again, but his expression was softer. "Have you?"

She stayed on her knees beside her bed longer that night, praying for the Gillespies, who were fighting the good fight in the odorous Odd Fellows Hall, and the Rudigers, who had been directed to a better place by Mr. Otto. She prayed for James, the men of the Double Tipi, and especially for

Mr. Otto. She rounded off her prayers with the usual for her mother and father, her brothers in St. George, and Iris and Spencer and the expected baby.

She prayed for herself too, something she seldom did. "Lord, please help me to be a better example," she asked quietly. "I'm not exactly shining these days."

By the soft glow of the kerosene lamp, she reached for the Book of Mormon. *I think I know so much—I even get proud about it—but maybe I know so little.*

Julia woke up in the middle of the night, listening to a sound in the kitchen. She lay in bed, disinclined to move because she ached and it was cold in her room. Maybe Two Bits was noising about, hungry for a meal. She got up, wincing at the pain in her legs, and put on her robe.

Mr. Otto sat on the floor, his back against the cooling but still-warm Queen Atlantic. She peered closer. Two Bits was in his lap, and he was sucking canned milk from her boss's little finger.

"Mr. Otto, I can do that," she whispered. "I should have gotten up sooner."

"No problem," he whispered back. "Why are we whispering?" he asked in a normal voice. "James sleeps like the dead." He held up the kitten in his palm. "This little devil has apparently decided that I need his company at night."

With a groan, Julia sat down on a chair by the Queen, tucking her bare feet close together. "I should have warned you. James said Two Bits seems to have claimed your pillow."

"He has, indeed." Mr. Otto gently thumbed a spot under the kitten's chin, which brought out a roaring purr all out of proportion to the size of its owner. "I don't even like cats."

"You could have fooled me."

When Two Bits began to exhibit vast disinterest to the milk, Mr. Otto handed the kitten to her. It settled in her lap, eyes closed.

"You could leave your door open and Two Bits might purr in your ear instead of mine," Mr. Otto suggested.

Julia shook her head. "Face it, Mr. Otto. He's your kitten because you picked him up just after his eyes were open and stuck him in your pocket. My mother had a goose that followed her around forever. She said it became a real trial when she started school."

He didn't say anything for a while but just sat there, his eyes closed, obviously enjoying the remaining warmth from the Queen Atlantic. Julia was ready to return Two Bits to his box—even though the kitten apparently felt disinclined to stay in it—but she didn't want to wake Mr. Otto.

"Darling, could you sing that song that my mother used to hum to me?"

Julia sat up as Two Bits stretched and dug his needle-sharp claws into her leg. She winced and handed him back to Mr. Otto, who put the kitten in the box. "Now stay there, you little beggar." He looked up. "Do you know the words?"

"Of course," Julia said. "I'm not a great singer, though."

He shrugged. "I didn't ask for an opera. Just that song."

"I'll sing it for you, Mr. Otto," she told him, glad it was still dark and he couldn't see how rosy her cheeks were. She sang the first three verses, touched when her boss began to hum along.

"That's all I remember. I think there are a few more verses," she said.

"If you have a minute this morning, could you write

them down? I'm riding line this week, and I'd like to learn the words. Could you sing them again?"

She did as he asked, thinking how hungry he was for any connection to his mother. *What could it have been like for you, Mr. Otto, to have heard that song from a woman who, for all intents, was an Indian?* she asked herself. *And what was it like for Mary Anne, who only remembered bits and pieces of another life?*

"How old were you when she died?" Julia asked, hoping she was not intruding on his privacy.

"She died in 1884, when I was almost eleven. I suppose I was about James' age."

"Except you had a father."

"I did," he replied. "Pa and I just kept on doing what we always did. By then, I was his best hand. Little River cooked for me for twenty-five years until I put that ad in the newspapers." He yawned. "Twenty-five years of bad food." He chuckled, and it sounded self-conscious. "Hard to imagine such a stupid man, eh, Darling?" His voice turned wistful then. "I don't know. Maybe I wanted to keep Little River around because she was a link to Mama's Shoshone side, which was really all we knew, at least, until you came."

Julia leaned forward. "Mr. Otto, I'd really like to write my father and tell him everything you've told me about your mother. If any of your people survived that handcart journey—and I know many did make it to the valley—think how delighted they would be to know what happened to your mother? They probably have been mourning her for years."

"I hadn't thought of it like that," Mr. Otto said after a lengthy pause. "There might be brothers or sisters left." He reached out then and touched her hand, his fingers warm. "Let me think about it. You think your father could help?"

"He knows so many people in the Church offices," she told him, impulsively turning her hand over and clasping his before she even realized what she was doing. It seemed to be almost second nature. "My dad's a clever man. He'll find a way."

"Kind of like you, eh?" he said. He let go of her hand then. "He doesn't even know me."

"Doesn't matter. He'll help. I know he will."

"Let me kick the idea around. Meanwhile, in the morning, would you go over those figures in my ledger that we looked at last week? I have a pile of receipts, and I know they need reconciling."

He was all business again; so was she. There was nothing to do then but go to bed. Mr. Otto started down the hall. Before he had reached the archway leading into the parlor, Two Bits was out of his box and on his trail. Julia smothered her laugh and closed her door quietly.

She was up again before sunrise, preparing cinnamon rolls and frying ham. Matt Malloy brought in the cold air with a bundle of kindling. The sudden clatter in the wood box woke up Two Bits, who must have found his way back to his blanket-lined box, or else Mr. Otto had deposited him there earlier. Hands on her knees, she bent over the box and scrutinized its occupant.

"Honestly, Two Bits, you'd better start remembering your place here," she said, bending lower to scratch between the kitten's ears. She felt another gust of wind and cold.

"Are you starting to talk to animals?" Mr. Otto asked, unwinding his muffler and tossing it over the rafter. He must have interpreted her gaze well because he changed his mind and put it on the same peg with his coat. "Most of us don't start talking to the critters until at least February."

"I was simply advising Two Bits to let you sleep in peace," she replied.

"That'll do oceans of good, Darling. Cats don't come when you call them either."

Mr. Otto sat at the table, reading some back issues of the Cheyenne newspaper Sister Gillespie had given him and sipping his mug of coffee while Julia finished preparing breakfast. While the oatmeal baked in the oven, Julia sat beside him and copied all the verses of "Redeemer of Israel" that she could remember and handed it to him.

He looked over the words, smiled his thanks, and pocketed the paper. "It's high time James learned something besides 'Sweet Evalina,' " he told her.

She wasn't going to bother him, but he put down the paper as though he wanted to talk. "Have you decided to let me share your story with my father?" she asked.

"Still thinking."

"Mr. Otto, nothing bad can come of this," she reminded him. "Here I am, telling you what to do again. I'm sorry."

He was close enough to nudge her shoulder, which made her feel supremely better. "No need to apologize. It's just that I—we—spent so many years not sharing our story with anyone. We were pretty isolated here."

"No harm will come."

"I guess I know that." He nudged her again. "As for telling me what to do, didn't I give you permission to do that yesterday?"

"I figured that was a one-time opportunity," she said, curious about his mood. *We sound remarkably like my parents at the breakfast table,* she thought, intrigued with the idea and comfortable with how natural it felt.

"Give me good advice whenever you want," Mr. Otto said as he went to the washstand and lathered up. "I might not take it, but I'll listen."

"Mr. Otto, I'll give you these rolls to take . . ."

She stopped. Two Bits stood between her and the wood box, hissing so loud he could barely maintain his balance. She laughed, glancing at the box just as a rattlesnake slid out from behind it. Two Bits hissed louder, the fur standing up on his back.

As she stared, too frightened to scream, Two Bits leaped sideways, flopped on his stomach, righted himself, and planted himself astride the rattler, just behind his head.

"Paul! Do something!" she yelled.

Startled, he turned around, wiping soap from his face. With no hesitation, he yanked her cleaver from the knife block. Picking up the hissing, struggling kitten by the scruff of his neck, he slammed the cleaver just behind the snake's head. Leaving the viper to writhe in its death struggle, he turned Two Bits around to look the kitten in the face.

"I just thought you needed some help, Two Bits. Calm down, little guy. Julia?"

In another moment, he had one arm around her, holding the spitting kitten at arm's length with his other hand. "Just a minute, little buddy. I'm not setting you down until that snake realizes it is dead. Darling, you're not much in a snake crisis."

She shuddered, disengaged herself from his grasp, and sat on the table. Mr. Otto put Two Bits in her lap and used the ash shovel by the Queen Atlantic to scoop up the snake's head and toss it into the range. He grasped the snake by the tail and tossed it outside but not before holding it up.

"Just a youngster. Are you all right?"

Julia nodded. "How on earth . . . ?"

"Did it get in here?" Mr. Otto gestured to the wood box. "This happened once before. A snake, frozen solid, gets carried inside with the kindling. It warms up and decides to look around for a meal."

She must have looked every bit as alarmed as she felt. "I'll tell the men to look carefully at any wood they bring inside," he said in his most soothing voice. He couldn't help a grin. "Two Bits was all set to fight to the death. Imagine what he'll do when he's two months old! Could be he'll get tired of this boring place and bail out."

Mr. Otto left after taking food to Blue Corn. He picked up the burlap sack of food Julia had readied for him. "I'll be back in a week, and then it'll be Matt's turn to ride fence." Mr. Otto peered closer. "You still look a bit shocked. Just keep Two Bits between you and the wood box."

He tightened his grip on the sack. "Hum that tune for me one more time, Darling."

She did. He thanked her and patted his pocket. "I'm taking along the Book of Mormon. Should get some reading done." He opened the door. "What about you?"

"I'm reading it too, Mr. Otto."

"If I find that passage first, you might owe me an extra six months here."

"And if I find it first, you'd better promise me . . ." She stopped. He looked serious and hopeful at the same time. ". . . no more snakes in the wood box."

"Done, madam," he said, closing the door quietly behind him.

Twenty-three

Julia made popcorn that night, shaking it in a wire basket on top of the Queen, with one of the stove lids removed. The wind roared outside, but no more snow fell. She couldn't help but think of Mr. Otto, all by himself in a shack somewhere on the fence line.

Doc must have read her thoughts. "He's used to it, Julia," he said, reaching for another handful of popcorn. "We all are. It's a good time to think and solve most of the world's problems."

The popcorn was finished popping, so she deftly removed it and poured it into the large bowl on the table. Matt added melted butter, and Doc salted it.

"Any more?" she asked. "No?"

"Sit down, Julia," Doc said. "No need to pace the room. He's fine."

You're seeing right through me, Julia thought, embarrassed. *I have no business worrying about someone who is so capable.* She sighed. "Why does he do it? It's hard to live here."

Doc filled a bowl and handed it to her. "Maybe because he doesn't know easy."

"But you know," she persisted. "Why do you stay?"

Doc thought a moment. "I feel safe from myself here. What about you, Matt?"

"Who else would have me?" the Irishman said with a half smile.

And who else would have me? Julia asked herself, when sitting in bed later. She brushed her hair until it crackled, frowning to think that her relatives back home must be humoring her, working in someone's kitchen for hire. They probably wondered when she would come to her senses and settle down.

"Mama, thank goodness for Iris, eh?" she said, and managed a wry smile. "Iris can be counted on to do the right thing."

Julia reached for the Book of Mormon. She tried to concentrate on First Nephi, really she did. Not until chapter four did she begin to pay attention. *And I was led by the Spirit, not knowing beforehand the things which I should do,* she read. She read it again, and then said it out loud, not thinking of Nephi, but of herself. She put her finger in the book to mark the page, knowing she had never asked the Lord if coming to Wyoming was a good idea. The bishop had suggested she pray about the matter, but she hadn't. *Maybe I was afraid Heavenly Father would say no,* she thought.

She had never asked the Lord and had let the matter gnaw at her on the train ride to Cheyenne. She rested her head against the book and allowed herself the luxury of thinking with her heart. Maybe she had never questioned the matter because it had always felt right. Maybe she had been flogging herself for nothing.

She put the book on the end table, content now to stare at the ceiling, covered with old newspapers. She thought about the preacher with cream gravy on his head, and her smile widened. She thought about the Gillespies and the Cheyenne Sunday School with its row of spittoons and Custer dying every Sunday behind the portable podium. She thought about Mr. Otto clutching her hand as they sang "Redeemer of Israel." She closed her eyes, grateful to be precisely where she was, even if she was far from home and doing something unheard of—earning her living.

"I'm supposed to be here, aren't I, Lord?" she asked quietly. She let out her breath as a warm feeling seemed to settle softly on her, like the spun sugar on Iris's wedding cake. "Is it for my own good or someone else's? Could it even be both?"

Sunday night's snow didn't stay long, mainly because the wind swept it away and deep cold settled in. She left her bedroom door open now to take advantage of whatever heat the Queen Atlantic radiated even after she banked the fire each evening. Not one to turn down an invitation, Two Bits kept her company, curling tight into the warm hollow of her shoulder and neck and putting her to sleep with his extravagant purr.

Initially, James was suspicious of a book with an actual ending. "I like things to stay the same," he told her one night.

"You and most people," Julia said as she turned the pages. "How about this? I'll read your own book and give you a good ending, but then you have to listen to another story from this book."

He grudgingly agreed. By the end of the week, he left his tattered pages in the apple crate where he kept his clothes and asked for two stories from the book Sister Gillespie had so kindly given him.

"And do you know, I think when Mr. Otto returns, he will have a new song to teach you," Julia said as she closed his new book.

"Mr. Darling, that is too much at once!" he declared to her amusement.

"It's called progress, James," she reminded him.

"Jee-rusalem crickets," he sighed, in perfect imitation of Mr. Otto.

There was nothing funny about James in the middle of the night when he started to cry. She sat up in bed, her heart hammering, remembering that Mr. Otto usually comforted the little boy. Now it was her turn.

Julia went quietly on bare feet to James and knelt beside his bed. The cold seemed to come up, even through the rag rug.

"James?" she asked, keeping her voice quiet, because she wasn't even sure he was awake.

He reached for her, sobbing, so she pulled back the covers and got in bed with him, probably the same as Mr. Otto had done. She held the little boy close until his breathing became regular again. His face was pressed into her shoulder, and she felt the gentle flutter of his eyelashes.

"James, what is it that scares you?" she whispered.

After a long silence, punctuated with a sob, he whispered in her ear. "The wind. It was windy like this."

That was all. *Windy like this when?* She wanted to ask, *When you lost your parents? When they turned you out? Will we ever know?* She cradled him close and kissed his head. *Does it even matter?* She couldn't help but think of Mary Anne Hixon, lost in the early snows, searching in vain for a handcart company to find her. Did she cry out at night in the Shoshone lodges? *And what about you, Mr. Otto, after she died, and you no older than James? Is that why you seem to find it easy to comfort this small boy? I can do no less.*

❧

On Thursday, the wind blew from the south and warmed the land and then turned with a vengeance and struck from the northwest again, driving the last of the leaves off the trees, the ones that had clung tenaciously through last weekend's snow. She took an extra blanket to the tack shed for Blue Corn when she brought the noon meal.

She was pulling a raisin pie out of the Queen Atlantic when someone banged on the door. Startled, she hurried to open it. His hat bound tight with a muffler, Charles McLemore came inside and leaned against the door to hold it shut.

"Mr. McLemore! I know you haven't come for my warm liver salad," she said as he unwound the muffler and took off his hat. He kept his coat on but came closer to the Queen to rub his hands together.

"Nope."

"You'll stay for dinner?" she asked, perfectly aware of his wary expression. "It's fried chicken and cream gravy, with canned corn, and this particular raisin pie."

"Maybe," he said, sounding no less wary than he looked. "Is Mr. Otto about?"

"No. He's at the line shack," she said, filling a mug with coffee and setting it before him at the table. He warmed his hands around the cup, took a sip, and then another. The wary look went away.

He reached in his pocket, pulling out cigarette papers, a pouch of tobacco, and lint before he came to a dull yellow envelope. "I was in Gun Barrel this morning, and the operator at the Western Union collared me. He received this telegram for Mr. Otto a few days ago." McLemore held it out to her. "He thought it might be urgent since no one sends a telegram unless there's trouble."

How well Julia knew, thinking of the telegram Papa had received from his brother four years ago, announcing the death of their father's second wife. She put the telegram on the table.

"He'll be home on Sunday, I think," Julia said.

"The line shack?"

Julia nodded. "Should we deliver it to him?"

"I would. Have Matt ride it up."

She wrapped a shawl around her shoulders and walked onto the stoop to ring the triangle. Matt and Doc were there in minutes, James tagging along.

Charlie nodded to them. "This here's a telegram for Mr. Otto. It's been in the Western Union office for two days, and the operator saw me."

"Did he tell you what was in it?" Doc asked.

McLemore shook his head. "You know he can't do that." He put his hat back on and picked up the muffler again. "It's your worry now. I've got to go."

"Can't you stay for supper?" Julia asked.

McLemore held up both hands. "Oh, no! I remember the last time."

"McLemore, you're a fool," Matt said without any rancor. "That meal was a fluke. This is the real deal. Tell him what it is, Julia."

"I already did," she said, "but if Mr. McLemore has something better waiting at home . . ."

"Canned beans and them little Vienna sausages, I'll wager," Matt said.

With her tongs, Julia reached in the warming oven and took out a leg and a thigh, which she wrapped in waxed paper and popped into a bag, along with two biscuits running with butter and honey, and a slab of the raisin pie, all fragrant and moist. She handed him the bag. "Take this with you, Mr. McLemore. It won't poison you."

He grinned at her and left, bag in hand. Doc looked at Matt. "Since you're up next to ride the line, I think you should saddle up and take that telegram. Be prepared to stay, if Mr. Otto has to leave." He picked it up, looked at the envelope, and then turned it over. "Someone wrote Chicago in pencil," he said. He shrugged. "Could be cattle business, but why would that rate a telegram? Nope. Matt, get ready to ride. Julia will fix you a dinner to take along."

She did as Doc said, praying it wasn't bad news as she wrapped up another meal in waxed paper and threw in enough for two men.

"Leave us enough for dinner!" Doc teased. "Hey, don't look so worried! Mr. Otto's a big man. Whatever it is, he can take it."

"I know. I know. Longtime rancher," Julia grumbled.

"But that's what women do, isn't it?" he asked. "Worry, I mean."

Matt rode away in less than thirty minutes, telegram in his pocket and his burlap sack of food slung across the front of his saddle.

"The sun's going down," Julia fretted.

"It always does," Doc replied. "Is your hobby worrying? It's a clear night and the moon is out. Mr. Otto will probably show up tomorrow morning, and we'll wonder what all the fuss was all about."

It was more than that. Julia had just managed to get to sleep near midnight, when she heard the kitchen door open. Two Bits barely moved when she set him to one side and pulled on her robe.

"Matt?" she asked. "Did you find him?"

"It's me."

Mr. Otto stood by the Queen Atlantic, trying to warm his hands. She sighed with relief, grateful that Matt had delivered the message and that Mr. Otto had found his way home in the dark.

"Let me build up a fire," she said, reaching into the

wood box for kindling and paper.

He didn't say anything but sat down at the table and slowly unwound his muffler while she started a fire. When it was crackling to her satisfaction, Julia sat down at the table, wishing he would look up. He kept his eyes on the table.

"I hope it isn't bad news," she ventured.

"It is. Darling, I'm leaving at first light." He passed his hand in front of his eyes, keeping his head lowered.

He gave her no opportunity for conversation, and she knew him well enough by now not to offer any. She sliced off a slab of raisin pie and set it before him.

"Wou—would you like anything else?"

He shook his head and picked up his fork. She stood there, indecisive. That he was in some sort of pain was unquestionable. That he had not asked for any help from her was also obvious. She stood by the table another moment, wanting to touch him and numbering all the reasons why she should not.

As she stood there, she thought of Nephi and chapter four. *And I was led by the Spirit.* It was enough. She put her hand on his shoulder, just a brief touch. He still wore his overcoat, and she doubted he could feel it.

As she started to raise her hand, Mr. Otto put his hand over hers, squeezed it gently, and released it. He looked up at her. Even in the dim light of the kitchen, she could tell he had been crying.

"Mr. Otto," she breathed.

Just as quickly, he shook his head and turned his attention to the pie. She stood there another moment and quietly returned to her room. When he started to sob, she put the blanket over her head to drown out the terrible sound.

Julia surprised herself by eventually falling asleep, and she nearly missed Mr. Otto. The sun hadn't yet clawed its way over the hills rimming the ranch, and the wind had not abated, but his valise was packed and waiting beside the kitchen door. When the door opened, he came inside with Doc, dressed as he had been last midnight. Julia doubted he had even changed clothes.

"Do you have time for breakfast, Mr. Otto?" she asked, her hand on the oatmeal pot.

He shook his head. "Can you butter me some of those biscuits and put some ham or something between them?"

"Certainly. Take the rest of the pie too."

Deeply mindful of him sitting at the table, Julia prepared the food as he talked to Doc.

"I should be back in two weeks at the latest. Matt's set for a week on the line, but I told him to come back anytime if the wind gets on his nerves. The fences are sound. Just do what you do, Doc. I don't anticipate anything out of the ordinary here. Everything's in order." He was brusque, terse, and organized.

No, everything isn't, Julia thought. *I can't bear to see you so sad. But no one asked me.* She prepared what he wanted, adding a handful of dill pickles because she knew how much he liked them. She packed it in the cloth bag he had left on the table from the night before.

She went back into her room, dressing quickly and tying her hair back with a strip of ribbon. She looked at her Book of Mormon on the table beside the bed and just touched it. That wasn't enough. She knelt beside her bed. It was an incoherent prayer, consisting of nothing more than "Please, Heavenly Father, bless Mr. Otto. Nothing is so bad that it can't be cured, but how will we know?"

He was finishing up his coffee when she came into the room again, tying an apron around her waist. Doc must have returned to the bunkhouse or the horse barn. Mr. Otto stood there, looking at her, chewing on his mustache.

"I'm sorry I won't be able to take you and James to Cheyenne for the Christmas party," he said finally. "Doc said he could."

"Don't worry about us."

"I don't, really," he said with a slight smile that didn't even approach his eyes. "You're, uh, a good deal more sensible than I would have thought last September."

"Well, I like that," she replied, trying to inject a little humor into the unknown sorrow that seemed to fill the kitchen.

"You should," he said. "I mean it."

"I'll pray for you, Mr. Otto," she whispered.

"I thought you would," he told her. "I hope I'm not a waste of God's time."

"No one's a waste of God's time, Mr. Otto."

Suddenly, it was too much. Without a word, he put his arms around her, pulled her close, and clung to her for a brief moment. Her arms went around him, and she pressed him close and released him when he stepped back and picked up his valise again. With a look she was completely unable to interpret, he left without a word.

Twenty-four

*D*oc was as mystified as Julia. "He didn't tell me any-thing, but I don't think it has to do with cattle or the ranch." He ran his hand through his hair. "Julia, that's just business. This is something personal."

"I don't know anything except that he's divorced," Julia said.

"You're so sure he's divorced?"

"I have no idea. I guess he made it pretty clear it wasn't our business, didn't he?"

"He did to me, anyway." Doc didn't try to hide the con-cern in his eyes. "I thought maybe he might tell you. No? He's a private man, Julia. We won't know anything unless he chooses to tell us."

I'm too impatient, and it's none of my business, she told herself over and over during the week. She tried to distract herself with Christmas, saddling up with James and riding toward the Rudigers' burned-out cabin to locate a modest pine she had noticed several times during the fall when they were taking food to their neighbors. She marked it and left it to Doc to cut and haul back to the ranch and set up in the parlor.

She put James to work stringing cranberries and then popcorn into long ropes, which twined around the little tree, hiding its more obvious defects. She was at a loss for ornaments, but, to her surprise, Willy Bill used his tin cut-ters and fashioned hearts and stars from soup cans. When she tried to thank him, he just grimaced and backed away.

"Julia Darling, *that* was a smile, sure as God made green apples," Doc said.

Two Bits decided the tree was his to climb. He was still too small to knock it over as he moved from branch to branch up the scrawny pine, and more than once his meowing from a high branch meant James had to retrieve him.

The glory of it all was James. He had never seen a Christmas tree before, but he knew the story of Christmas. When she read the second chapter of Luke to him that night before bed, he had her read it again and then each night after she finished reading from the book Sister Gillespie had given her.

The simple story nestled into her heart too. She had heard it every year as long as she could remember—once, she was even lucky enough to be the stand-in for Mary in the Primary pageant—but she had a glimmer of what shepherds watching their flocks looked like. Maybe they looked like Mr. Otto, and now Matt, riding the line in wind and cold, doing the same thing: watching their herds and seeing that all was well.

Staying up late, Julia finished the sweater she had been knitting for James. She wrapped it in brown paper, made a yarn bow, and called it good. Doc had already promised to take them to Cheyenne next weekend for the Sunday School Christmas party. When she rode to the Marlowes' for eggs, she took along a brief letter addressed to Sister Gillespie, asking her to buy some Christmas candy and a few more items to put under the tree, promising payment when she came for the party. She hoped that the Marlowes were going to Gun Barrel and could mail it.

As it turned out, they were. "You're learning how we do

things here," Alice told her as she walked Julia back to the corral with a basket of eggs packed securely in sawdust. "Up you go, now, and I'll hand you the eggs."

Julia did as she said, holding the reins loosely. Alice watched her. "Charlie McLemore told us about delivering that telegram from Chicago. Any idea what the problem is?"

Julia shook her head. "Mr. Otto was so sad, Alice! I wish we knew how to help."

Absently, Alice fingered the horse's mane. "Paul's used to being self-sufficient." She seemed to give herself a mental shake. "Well, all we know is he had a bad marriage, and we only know that because of rumors. That was before any of us lived around here, so it's his secret to keep."

"Doc thinks he's still married."

Alice shrugged and pulled her shawl tighter. "I haven't a clue." She gave Julia such a measuring look that Julia felt her cheeks redden. "Don't put too many eggs in that basket, my dear."

Julia shook her head. "I'm safe," she said softly. "I'm sure you remember the contract."

"Who could forget it? Still, best not to get too attached to . . . to the Double Tipi."

"I couldn't possibly," Julia told her.

Maybe he will send us a telegram, and let us know how he is doing, she thought, as she rode away. *Or maybe we'll never know anything.*

Matt returned from the line shack the next day, assuring Doc all was well on the range. They were sitting down to the noon meal when Mr. Marlowe knocked on the door and waved a telegram at her when she opened it.

"Something from Mr. Otto," she said, feeling more relief than she ever would have admitted. "You're just in time for steak, Mr. Marlowe. And look, an empty chair."

Marlowe took off his overcoat and sat down as Doc passed the steak platter. Willy Bill sent along the mashed potatoes.

What happened next, happened like a bad dream. Marlowe put the telegram on her plate. She looked down at it, surprised to see it addressed to her, and not to Doc.

"I wonder why he sent it to me," she mused.

"It's not from Paul," Mr. Marlowe said as he poured gravy on his potatoes. "The operator penciled 'SLC' on the back."

Filled with sudden fear, she put it down. Nothing good ever came from telegrams.

"Julia?" Doc asked.

It's Aunt Mary, she told herself. *She has been hanging on for months. But Papa wouldn't send a telegram about Aunt Mary. She's old, and we've been expecting this. He would just write me a letter.*

She knew the color had drained from her face because Doc was looking at her intently, half out of his chair, his eyes full of concern.

"I don't want to open it," she heard herself say, as though from a long distance. "Doc, you open it."

She must have held it out to him because he suddenly took it from her hand. He opened it and read silently, his eyes going to her face. He was pale now.

"Julia, let's go in the parlor," he said, his voice gentle.

"No."

"Julia, just come with me," Doc said. He held out his hand to her.

After a longer moment than any she had ever lived, she put her hand in his and let him help her to her feet, which felt strangely uncooperative.

"No," she repeated. "It's Papa."

He shook his head.

"Mama?" she asked, when he had seated her on the sofa. "Not Mama!"

When he shook his head again, she knew, as surely as if she could see through the yellow envelope and read every terse word. "Iris. Please, no."

He didn't say anything but took the telegram from his pocket, removed it from the envelope, and put it in her hand. After only one glance at the telegram, she knew its words were burned on her brain forever. She would never forget them.

Dearest STOP Iris died of complications STOP Funeral 20 Dec STOP Please come home STOP We need you STOP Papa

She gasped and dropped the telegram as though it were a hot coal. "I can't be there in time, can I?" she said, leaning on Doc, who put his arm around her and held her tight.

"No, honey, you can't. The telegram must have been in the Western Union office for several days before Marlowe got it."

She closed her eyes. Maybe the telegram was wrong. Maybe there was another Iris, another Julia Darling somewhere in Wyoming, another Salt Lake City. "This can't be true," she said.

He made no comment but strengthened his grip on her.

"I mean, think of it: Iris is—was—is—only twenty-two! She's healthy. She's going to have a baby in August. This is a mistake, a bad joke!" She turned to look at Doc as the full horror settled on her like concrete. "I can't be there for the funeral! I hate this place!"

She cried then, her arms tight around Doc as he held

her, until she saw James, the distress on his face unmistakable. Doc handed her a handkerchief, and she wiped her eyes.

"James, sit beside me," she said. "It's all right, Doc. If I don't understand what has happened, I'm certain he doesn't. Please, James."

In another moment his head was resting in her lap. She stroked his hair, grateful for the distraction.

"I didn't do anything wrong, did I?" he asked, near to tears.

"No, never," she told him, her voice stronger now. "It's some sad news I received."

"Mr. Otto left. Maybe that was my fault," he said.

"No, no, nothing like that," she said, giving him all her attention because he obviously had not understood anything that had happened this week, from Mr. Otto's tight-lipped departure to her own anguish. *Why didn't I notice that?* she thought. "You've done nothing this week to cause any of this, James."

She rested her head against Doc's shoulder again. "I have to go home," she whispered.

"I know you do," he answered. "I'll get you to Gun Barrel tomorrow morning. That train comes at noon, and I think the UP leaves from Cheyenne in the evening, doesn't it?"

She nodded. James took her hand. Julia could hardly bear the anguish in his eyes. "You'll come back, Mr. Darling?"

She gathered him close. "James, I can't leave you for long."

"It scares me when people leave me," he whispered into her shoulder.

She looked at Doc over James's head. He put a gentle

hand on the boy's head. "James, I'll stay here in the house with you until Mr. Otto returns. Christmas will still come."

James brightened at this news. "You know about Christmas?"

"I know about Christmas," Doc assured him. A shadow passed over his face. "I had a little boy like you once, and we knew Christmas." He took James on his lap. "Julia has to leave tomorrow morning, and I'll ride with her to Gun Barrel and come right back. Matt is here, and he'll stay in the house. Maybe if Julia has time, she can finish those Christmas cookies she mixed this morning."

"I can do that," she said, grateful to Doc for giving her something else to do, something else to hold off the awful moment when she would be on the train with nothing to think about except Iris. She leaned against Doc again, relieved that he was there. "I need my mother. I have to be home."

⌘

Bless his heart, Doc sat in the kitchen with her and James as she made cookies, the buttery kind she made with a cookie press. He sat there, ready to take her hand and just hold it, when she faltered. Matt distracted James with work in the stable. At some point, they switched places as the sky grew dark and Doc had chores. No one left her alone as she baked cookies, bread, and then fixed dinner—silent, for the most part—her heart and mind on her family.

She thought of Mr. Otto too, knowing that he had been alone when he left the Double Tipi, alone to buy a train ticket in Cheyenne for Chicago, alone to sit on the train as she would be tomorrow. Alone when dark came and there was no comfort.

She packed a valise after she read to James and sang

"Redeemer of Israel" to him. The tune kept revolving in her tired brain as she packed. Finally, she sat on her bed and closed her eyes in sorrow.

" 'Redeemer of Israel, our only delight, on whom for a blessing we call, Our shadow by day, and our pillar by night, our king, our deliverer, our all,' " she said, the words coming out strangled and weary. Mr. Otto shouldn't think she knew nothing about the Bible. She remembered quite clearly the children of Israel, as contrary as they were on so many occasions, being led by a shadow and comforted by that pillar of fire by night. *I need that, too, Father,* she thought. *Comfort me. Comfort Mr. Otto. Oh, please, if you're not too busy.*

Maybe it wasn't even a prayer. Maybe it was just a desperate plea from someone of little consequence, in the greater scheme of things, wishing she were in Salt Lake City right now and not separated from her parents by a whole state. Maybe they were at the meetinghouse now, greeting mournful friends and family in a viewing. Iris's husband was surely there too.

She felt her throat tighten, remembering the huge smile on her brother-in-law's face when he returned with his young bride to the house last fall—was it only last fall?—after their wedding in the Salt Lake Temple. She thought of Mr. Otto's red-rimmed eyes and how he had not wanted to look at her. At least she was going toward people who loved her and needed her. She had no idea what her boss was facing alone. If the grim look on his face had been any indication, it was nothing remotely pleasant.

As she sat on her bed, trying to stifle her tears, Julia suddenly remembered another verse of "Redeemer of Israel." The words seemed to scroll, unbidden, through her brain. She said them aloud, her voice soft.

" 'Restore, my dear Savior, the light of thy face; thy

soul-cheering comfort impart; and let the sweet longing for thy holy place bring hope to my desolate heart.' "

" 'Hope to my desolate heart,' " she whispered again.

She felt anything but hopeful, but as she sat there, hardly breathing, she felt a curious calm replace the misery that had been hers ever since Doc had asked her so quietly to come into the parlor.

Nothing happened, not at first, not until she felt her eyes grow heavy. She fought it, thinking of everything she had to do before they left tomorrow morning at first light: notes to leave, food to organize. Maybe she could send a telegram to her parents and maybe one to the Gillespies. At least she had finished the sweater she had been knitting for James. She had too much to do to sleep.

And then none of it seemed to matter. She sighed and closed her eyes. She opened them long enough to look at the Book of Mormon by her pillow. She had read every night since Mr. Otto had left, but she was too full of sorrow now. Still dressed, she pulled back the covers and put the book on her pillow, resting her cheek against the familiar leather grain, willing morning to come quickly.

Twenty-five

The trip to Salt Lake City was a merciful blur: the silent ride with Doc to Gun Barrel; the train to Cheyenne, where the overcast sky fit her mood; the relief of seeing the Gillespies at the depot.

Brother and Sister Gillespie were waiting at the depot when the Cheyenne & Northern hissed to a stop, steam pouring out and hanging there in the cold air. She reached for Sister Gillespie, sobbing out what had happened. Brother Gillespie's arms went around her too as they stood on the platform, people all around them, curious but intent on their own business.

Sister Gillespie sat with her in the back seat as her husband drove the few blocks to the Union Pacific Depot. She stopped him before he got to the ticket window. "I . . . I bought this last fall, kind of as insurance, in case I hated the Double Tipi," she said, holding out the ticket that she had tucked in the valise and forgotten about in the last few months.

"I'd feel better if you had a sleeping car," he said, reaching for his wallet.

"I don't think I'll sleep," she said, holding tighter to Sister Gillespie's hand.

"You might surprise yourself," he told her as he handed over her old ticket and replaced it with a Pullman sleeper ticket.

"I didn't have time to stop at the bank in Gun Barrel, but I—"

"Pay me when you return," he said. "And don't argue with your Sunday School superintendent."

For the first time in her life, she wasn't shy about asking for a blessing. The weight of Brother Gillespie's hands on her head reminded her acutely how sorely she missed the priesthood at the Double Tipi. His words were a balm to her soul.

They walked her to the train afterwards, but before she climbed aboard, Brother Gillespie put his hands on her shoulders and stooped a little to look in her eyes. "Sister Darling, I know how much you need comfort from your parents."

"I long for it," she said.

He shook his head. "My dear, this time you will need to comfort them."

"But—"

"No matter how much you hurt, and I know you do, please think of them first."

〜◈〜

She was halfway across Wyoming and tossing and turning in a sleeping compartment before the weight of what Brother Gillespie said started to penetrate her sorrow. She rejected it at first, wanting only to crawl into her mother's lap as she had done when she was a child and had sustained some hurt, real or imaginary. And there would be Papa, ready to console her over the loss of her only sister.

She stared at the ceiling, not comforted by the train's rhythmic sound and movement. It did not soothe her this time. Wearily, she picked up the Book of Mormon, wondering where those special verses were that Mama always found, to make everything right.

She found herself going back to earlier chapters in

Second Nephi, reading and rereading that chapter her father called "Nephi's Psalm." Funny how she used to think Nephi was such an annoying prude, driving his older brothers to distraction with his moralizing and his preaching. But here he was, admitting to faults, pouring out his heart to a God he knew cared about him and was listening as he unburdened his soul.

Oh, God, I don't know how it's going to be not to have Iris around to write to, to visit, to talk to whenever I pick up the telephone, she thought. The reality was exquisite anguish, and the pain so great that she was helpless against it until she read Nephi's psalm again, looking again and again at the same verse because it took away the sharp edge of her grief: "Nevertheless, I know in whom I have trusted."

I don't know all I should, but I hope that's true, Julia thought, reading the little phrase over and over until the raw pain seemed to subside. The ache was there but not overwhelming her now.

She read on, reading, backing up, reading more, until she came to verse 33, which she knew, no matter how strange and selfish it made her, that Nephi had put there just for her: "Wilt thou make my path straight before me!" She read no further because everything she needed was there.

The porter woke her in time to dress and get off in Ogden to catch the Short Line to Salt Lake. The winter sun wasn't over the mountains yet, but the car was lamp-lit as she looked again at Nephi's Psalm, glad he understood that God would give liberally to him, if he asked not amiss. *If he did that for Nephi, he will do it for me,* she decided as the train pulled into the depot.

Tears welled in her eyes as she saw her father standing on the platform, scanning each window until he saw her face. She swallowed her own tears because he began to cry when he saw her. She had never seen her father cry before, and it was a terrible sight, almost as awful as the sound of Mr. Otto crying in the kitchen after she went to bed that night. Was it only a week ago? It seemed more like an eternity.

She willed herself to stay calm, thinking of Nephi and the many days he must have done exactly the same thing because people on whom he probably wanted to depend on were depending on him. It was a reality as stark as a seismic shift, and she understood what she had to do as surely as Nephi must have.

As the train came to a halt, Julia ran her hand over the Book of Mormon and put it in the valise. When she began her trip in Gun Barrel, the only thing on her mind was throwing herself into her parents' arms and sobbing her heart out. Something had happened between Gun Barrel and Salt Lake. She wasn't totally sure how she felt about it, but she knew when she stepped off the train, things would be different. For a fleeting moment, she wished with all her heart that Mr. Otto was there to help her. He was so sure of himself, so unflappable.

But he wasn't there, and her last glimpse of him had told her worlds about his own anguish.

It was her turn to comfort.

⌘

They stood close together on the train platform, Papa unable to lift his face from her shoulder until most of the disembarking travelers had moved on. She held him close, much as she had comforted James before she left the Double Tipi. He was dressed in black, and he wore a black armband.

"I'm glad you got my telegram," she said finally as he

stepped slightly away and pulled out a handkerchief. "I would have given the earth to have been here in . . . in time, but we're so remote at the Double Tipi. I guess your telegram was several days in the office."

Papa looked old to her for the first time, his wrinkles more pronounced, his shoulders more stooped, his eyes as red-rimmed as hers had been yesterday. "Oh, Papa," was all she could say then because her voice faltered.

He looked at her and managed a slight smile. "You are a welcome sight, Julia." He picked up her valise. "This is all?"

She nodded. "Papa, I'll have to go back. You know that, don't you?"

As well as she knew him, she couldn't interpret his expression. It almost seemed to her a curious mixture of sorrow and pride.

"I know that," he said as they walked through the depot.

When he summoned a taxi, Julia couldn't help asking why he had not driven his beloved Pierce-Arrow. He didn't answer until they were settled in the cab and he had given the driver the address.

"I backed it out this morning, but Julia, my eyes hurt so bad from crying that I can barely see."

He said it quietly, but the words made her wince. She leaned against his shoulder. "I'm here now, Papa."

A childish part of her heart wanted him to tell her everything would be all right because he was there to soothe her sorrow. What struck her, instead, was the relief in his eyes at her words, as though he had been hanging on until she could arrive to comfort him.

He didn't say anything for several blocks, just put his arm around her and held her close. When they started the climb to the Avenues, he closed his eyes and slept, vividly showing her the extent of his exhaustion. She doubted he had slept in days. *What do I say to my parents?* Julia asked herself. *How do I help them through the unimaginable?*

The answer to her question became clearer as the cab stopped in front of her home, a lovely place with its wide veranda. She looked at the swing where she and Ezra used to sit and felt a momentary pang that dissolved the moment she saw the black wreath on the front door.

"I hate that thing," Papa muttered. "Can't help but think Iris would have hated it too."

He paid the cab driver. As they approached the front door, the wreath seemed to grow larger and larger until it filled the door, like an unsightly blemish.

"I don't like it either, Papa," she said. "I'm taking it down."

He watched, his expression numb, as she did just that. "I'll take it around back to the dust bin after I see Mama," Julia said. "Have either of you had breakfast?"

Papa looked at her as though she spoke a foreign language and then shook his head. "I think we ate something last night, before your brothers left for St. George."

"Gone already? I was hoping to see them."

Papa sat down in the straight-backed chair in the foyer, as if his feet would no longer support him. "Call me a coward, Jules, but I wanted to go with them," he told her, running a hand over his face. "I don't want to go to the office next week and try to act like I'm normal again. I don't even want to go to church and see one more sympathetic face."

This wasn't her father. She knelt beside the chair. "But you will," she said softly with all the confidence she could muster. *Please, please Lord, let him remember in whom he trusts,* she prayed silently. "But first I'm going to make some Cream of Wheat. I remember one class when Miss Farmer looked me in the eye—she looked at all of us—and said there was no crisis that couldn't be made better by Cream of Wheat."

It was the right thing to say. Papa raised his head from his hands and looked at her. "You're serious?" he asked, and she heard the humor lurking somewhere in his voice.

"Completely. Let's see if she was right. Come into the kitchen and keep me company."

He did, first stopping in the doorway and looking at all the cakes, pies, and other funeral food on every surface. "I'm tired of all this," he told her.

"Then I'll get rid of it. I'm here to cook." She took Mama's apron from its customary nail and rolled up her sleeves.

He looked better after a bowl of Cream of Wheat, eaten at the kitchen table she had cleared of funeral food.

She sat with him as he ate. "We haven't had cecils since you left. That's a hint, Julia," he told her. He smiled at her. "This is where you say, 'I honor all requests.' "

Julia leaned over and kissed his cheek. "You know I do."

She left him seated in the parlor with his shoes off, staring at the *Deseret News* but not reading it, and carried a tray upstairs for Mama. She closed her eyes when she passed the room that used to be Iris's, not wanting to remind herself how empty it was—and always would be, from now on.

"Mama?"

She opened the door to her parents' room, dark now with shades drawn. Mama lay on her side, staring into the gloom as Julia came closer. She set the food on the bedside table and felt her heart turn over as Mama reached for her hand. In another moment, she was in her arms as Mama cried.

"I'm here, Mama. We'll be all right," she said.

"To stay?"

"For now."

Mama needed no coaxing to eat. She lay back with a contented sigh when she finished. "Julia, I don't know how you do it, but that was the best thing I've had in days."

"I'd hate to think you sent me to Boston for nothing, Mama," Julia teased gently. "Oh, Mama." Julia took her mother's hand in hers and rubbed it against her cheek.

Mama slid over in bed and patted the sheet. Julia took off her shoes and lay down beside her without a word, cradling Mama in her arms as Mama had done when she and Iris were small.

"It's hard."

"I wanted to be here. I didn't get the telegram soon enough." She raised up on one elbow. "Mama, what happened? Can you tell me?"

"I can, Jules. Most of the people who came to the funeral didn't want to ask or didn't know what to say, so they mostly said nothing. They don't understand how much I want to talk about my baby."

She cried then, and Julia held her, making soft sounds that weren't even words. Nothing she could say was adequate to the occasion, not in the face of Mama's enormous loss.

"What happened?"

Mama sat up again, Julia's arm around her. "She had what is called an ectopic pregnancy. The egg doesn't make its way to the womb, but no one knows until it grows large enough to break out of the fallopian tube." She put her hands to her face. "It's all so clinical and not something anyone wants to talk about."

"That makes it harder," Julia said. "She was alone when this happened?"

Mama nodded, her lips trembling. "Spencer had gone to an auction in Lehi." She sighed, a sob catching in her throat. "When he returned home, she was lying on the kitchen floor."

Julia closed her eyes, praying her sister hadn't suffered. "Oh, Mama," she managed.

Her mother's voice was more firm now. "Her doctor wasn't sure, so he performed an autopsy." She burrowed her face against Julia's breast. "That was it. He said it could have happened anywhere, and there probably wasn't anything anyone could have done." Her voice grew far away then. "I have all this pale yellow yarn. I was going to make an afghan . . ." Her voice trailed off. In another moment, she was lying down again, curled up close to Julia.

She stayed with her mother until she slept and then tip-toed to her own room, standing in the door and reminding herself all over again how lovely it was compared to her little room off the kitchen at the Double Tipi—no newspaper on the walls and ceiling, a wicker rocking chair that creaked in all the right places, and a bed that smelled of lavender. She thought of James's small bed with its pallet on twined rope, the two apple crates that held his possessions, and her wonderful parlor with gray building paper and the leather sofa that sagged in all the best places.

"Julia Darling, you're crazy to miss any of that," she said before she closed the door and went downstairs again.

She cooked all afternoon, filling the house with aromas her parents were familiar with and not the funeral food so kindly given but so painful to look at. She sat at the table for a long moment, wondering if it was wise to ask Mama to help, but then deciding good ideas shouldn't just be allowed to float away. Papa was asleep in the parlor. Julia went upstairs.

"Mama? I'm going to make chicken noodle soup. Someone left a stewing hen, but you know I don't make noodles as good as yours."

Although she did. She had an A plus to prove it from Boston, but Mama didn't know that. Julia went back downstairs, crossing her fingers, and sighed with relief when she heard Mama on the stairs and then in the kitchen, reaching for another apron.

"Sometimes those fancy measuring cups and spoons of yours just aren't necessary," she said as she scooped flour out of the bin with her hand.

"Yes, Mama. I knew I needed your help."

So it went. She was in charge as her parents regained their composure and their optimism. Friends and neighbors came calling, and Julia served them her best cakes. It only took a small nudge for Papa to go downtown for a Christmas tree, one that filled the back of the Pierce-Arrow. Neither he nor Mama could bring themselves to decorate it, but Julia did that by herself after they were asleep on Christmas Eve. She hung the ornaments of her and Iris's childhood—two little girls in a house where their older brothers were getting ready to leave home. It had always seemed like just the two of them. She felt it keenly as she gently placed the glass ornaments and the homemade ones from earlier, more frugal Christmases, on the fragrant branches.

She thought of James, pained that she couldn't be there to celebrate with him. *I can make it up to him next year,* she thought, but remembered that by this time next year, she would be home in Salt Lake to stay.

When she finished, Julia sat in front of the tree, breathing deeply of the pine scent, relishing the calm. The bishop had invited them to Christmas dinner the next day, and she had promised the mince pies and pumpkin pies. She could get up early and make them. There were just a few presents under the tree. Papa had mailed hers to Wyoming a week ago, and in her desperate hurry to leave, Julia had not brought along her presents for her parents, not that they were anything more special than knitted mufflers and mittens.

Papa and Mama had gifts for each other, and she put them under the tree. She held the closet door open a long time, looking at the little cache of gifts they had planned to take to Iris and Spencer in Draper. When she finally closed the door, she leaned against it, her head down, until the tears passed.

On Christmas morning, Julia was up well before sunrise, starting the fire in the cookstove, comparing it yet again to the Queen Atlantic, which easily outranked something called merely "Majestic." The mincemeat was still cooling in the icebox, and she had prepared the pumpkin yesterday between visits from Mama's visiting teachers and block teachers. Everyone asked her to let them know what they could do, but no one stayed long.

Just listen to my folks, Julia thought, as she rolled out the dough. *Don't try to remind us that we'll see Iris again someday. We will, but it's hard slogging right now, even with what we know.*

After a day of being cheerful, she had been relieved each evening to take refuge in her room to read the Book of Mormon. If someone had told her only a month ago that she would find scriptures essential to her heart, she might not have believed them. *I know so little,* she thought, *but I am learning. Maybe Mr. Otto knows what he's talking about.*

Last night's reading had been balm to her soul. She had found that beggar's passage Mr. Otto had been searching for. When she came to it, she had put the book on her chest and closed her eyes in utter satisfaction. Now she knew. She read it over and over, savoring each word, thinking of King Benjamin, near death and wanting to serve his people to the very end by sharing his wisdom.

Have you found it yet? she asked herself. *Are you in Chicago? Are you home at the Double Tipi? Are you doubting I'll return?* Maybe she could write a letter tomorrow, just to reassure him, or maybe, if she was honest, to reassure herself.

The pumpkin pies went in the Majestic at 8:00 a.m., and still her parents slept. Julia sat down at the kitchen table and rested her elbows on it, aware of the pain between her shoulder blades that rolling pie dough always produced. If only she could have cooked Christmas for the men of the Double Tipi before she left. They were probably eating out of cans right now.

Next year, she thought. *No, there won't be a next year at the Double Tipi.* Some things couldn't be helped, she decided as she closed her eyes and rested her head on her arms.

Someone was knocking on the door to the back porch. Julia opened her eyes, startled awake. She sniffed the air; the pies weren't done yet. She stood up and stretched, wondering who would be at the back door on Christmas morning, when none of the tradesmen were delivering.

Maybe she imagined it. No, someone was definitely knocking. She opened the door to the back porch, which was steamy with heat from the cookstove. She could see an outline, even though the sun wasn't quite over the mountains. She opened the door, and her heart turned over.

"Merry Christmas, Mr. Otto," she said. "I knew you would come."

Twenty-six

She stared at his face and absorbed it, seeing only concern there. He hesitated for a small moment and then opened his arms. With a sob, she walked right into them. He seemed to flinch ever so slightly, but he held her so close that she could feel the buttons of his overcoat practically through to her backbone. Her relief was enormous.

"I found that scripture, Darling," he said into her ear, as though they had just finished an earlier conversation a minute ago and not several unhappy weeks in the past. "And I found one even better that got me here."

She didn't want to cry, but something about his presence allowed her to for the first time since leaving Cheyenne. She sobbed into his overcoat, knowing how wrong it was to burden him with her problems but unable to help herself.

He didn't object. He didn't step back or try to distance himself from her anguish. She was barely aware when he picked her up and sat with her in one of the kitchen chairs. He didn't speak, but above her tears, she heard him humming "Sweet Evalina," which only made her cry harder because she thought of James missing Christmas.

"Dear Evalina, sweet Evalina, my love for thee will never, never die," he sang softly.

"I wish you wouldn't sing that," she managed to say as he handed her a handkerchief.

"Oh, harsh. Would you prefer 'Redeemer of Israel?' " he asked. "Thanks to you, I've doubled my repertory."

She leaned against his chest again. "Evalina just reminds me how I failed James. It was going to be such a nice Christmas," she told him, unable to keep the wistful tone from her voice.

"Let me bring you good news from home," he assured her, somehow assuming that his home was her home too. He took her hand. "Darling, remember that James doesn't precisely understand dates and calendars. Before I left the Double Tipi, I assured James that Christmas wasn't coming until two days after you returned."

She started to cry again. He tightened his grip. "Hey now," he murmured. "It's a serviceable lie."

She nodded, relieved again to breathe his particular fragrance of bay rum. "I can do that. Sister Gillespie was going to send me some Christmas candy."

"She did. It's at the Double Tipi, along with more books for James, something for you, and a pamphlet for me."

"Did you read it?"

"Sure I did." He sounded doubtful. "I don't know. That's a lot to swallow."

Maybe it was too much to hope he'd find it fascinating. Julia wiped her eyes and sniffed the air. She was off Mr. Otto's lap in a moment, reaching for her pot holders. The pumpkin pies were perfect, with just a hint of over-brown on the crust that probably only Miss Farmer would notice.

"We've been invited to the bishop's house for Christmas dinner," she told her guest.

"I can leave."

"Oh, no. You'll be coming too."

"They won't mind?"

"Of course not." She couldn't overlook his dubious expression. "Mr. Otto, you need to learn a few more things about Mormons. There's always room for another potato in the pot."

He took off his overcoat and looked around for a peg to hang it on. Julia took it from him and hung it in the back hall closet. She stood in the closet a moment, taking several deep breaths, trying to compose herself. She had been a strength to her parents all week. Mr. Otto's unexpected arrival had released emotions she had stifled because her parents' needs were greater. How did Mr. Otto know?

And there he was, standing by the closet now, that same look of concern on his face.

"Darling, how about you slice me off some of that bread and find me some milk? I'm gut foundered and missing the Fannie Farmer touch, I suppose."

She did as he asked. "It's cinnamon raisin bread," she told him, placing two generous slices on a plate along with butter and honey.

"Jerusalem crickets, that's good!" he said as he ate quickly. She handed him a glass of milk. "Thanks."

She sat down to watch him eat, and he grinned at her a moment later. "You know you do that."

"Do what?"

"Watch people eat. I think it gives you abnormal pleasure."

She knew he was teasing her, trying to coax another smile, and she had no trouble satisfying him because she was genuinely amused by his comment. "I guess I do," she admitted. "It's not abnormal pleasure to a chef!"

"I stand corrected." He held out the now-empty plate. "Any more of that, or are you saving it for a snowy day?"

She glanced out the window to see the snow falling and refilled the plate.

"You eat one too."

She shook her head. He raised an eyebrow. She took a piece, remembering her experience with Mr. Otto and the canned pears. Was that only last fall?

"Did you just get here, Mr. Otto?" she asked after dividing the next piece between the two of them. She knew it was time to build up the fire again before baking the mincemeat pie, so she did that. Mr. Otto poured himself more milk as she worked.

"I got here yesterday."

"Why didn't you—"

"—come here right away?" he scratched his head, looking sheepish. "Didn't have your address. It occurred to me at about Rock Springs that I was missing a key ingredient in this mission of mercy. Didn't know Salt Lake was this big."

She nodded and sat at the table again. She didn't ask, but Mr. Otto poured more milk into her glass. She drank. "How did you find me?"

He ran his finger around his collar and looked at her. "D'you mind?"

She shook her head, and he undid his collar button. "Collars drive me nuts after awhile. I checked into a downtown hotel and remembered that your father worked for Zion's Bank."

"Yes, I told you that, didn't I? Probably back when I was trying to impress you," Julia said as she wondered when talking to Mr. Otto had gotten so much easier.

"Probably. Anyway, the bank manager, or whoever he was, wasn't about to 'divulge sensitive information,' as he said. What a pompous . . . windbag. Maybe he doesn't like stockmen." Mr. Otto shrugged.

"Um, you could have looked in a telephone directory," she said.

He just raised his eyebrows. "Never occurred to me.

Darling, you know very well my limited access to new-fangled contraptions. I went back to the hotel, had a very fine lunch—though not as good as your chicken fried steak and Duchess potatoes—a bath, and sent my suit to be pressed. I've been on the road with it for way too many days."

"And no closer to my address?"

"That's when I got smart." He went to the closet and retrieved a small package from his overcoat. He pointed to the label. "This present from your folks was waiting for you at the Double Tipi when I got there. There was a mighty fine return address. I am brilliant, although it takes awhile."

Julia laughed and took the gift from him. "My father said they had sent my gift." She shook her head and couldn't help the tears. "I forgot to bring theirs along, when I left so fast."

"Hey now," he said again softly. He took the napkin and dabbed at her eyes. "You're the best gift they could have." He held her hand and leaned closer. "Julia, what happened?"

"It was an unfortunate complication of pregnancy. There wasn't anything the doctor could have done," she said when he had both of her hands clasped in his. "Luckily this condition is rare. Poor, poor Iris."

"How are *you* dealing with this? Honestly, please."

"By wearing myself out each day and going to bed so tired that I couldn't stay awake if I tried," she told him, well aware how futile it was to dissemble around Mr. Otto. "I remind myself that I'll see Iris again, and we'll be together forever, but I'd rather see her right now." She felt her cheeks turn rosy. "That doesn't make me much of a Mormon, but that's the truth."

He didn't release her hands as he thought about what she had said. "It makes you a sister grieving for a sister. No harm there, no matter what you're supposed to believe."

She nodded and moved her hands slightly, making him

release his hold on her. She took a deep breath. "This is hard to say."

"Say it anyway, Darling."

"My parents . . ." She leaned forward, unable to speak. He kissed her forehead. "They needed me even more than I needed them."

He didn't say anything but gazed at her thoughtfully. She allowed the silence, which calmed her and let her think clearly as she breathed in and out. As her mind cleared, she wondered what Mr. Otto was doing in her kitchen in Salt Lake City.

"Mr. Otto, why—?"

"—am I here?"

"Were you afraid I wouldn't remember the contract?" she asked.

"I had no doubts. It was far more than that." He leaned back in the chair, making himself comfortable, just as he always did in the Double Tipi kitchen. "I told you I had found that scripture."

She nodded. "I found it too. Mosiah, chapter three."

"Mo-sigh-ah. So *that's* how you pronounce it. Mosiah. I found it on the way to Chicago." He hesitated, looking unsure of himself then. "Things got . . . complicated in Chicago, but on the way home, I started reading again and came to Chapter 18 in Mosiah."

"I haven't got that far yet."

"You will," he told her, his confidence back. "It's really good. Someone named Alma is hiding out from King Noah—he's a piece of work—and Alma's baptizing folks right and left." He reached inside his suit. "It was so good I wrote it down. Here." He handed her a piece of paper. "A nice lady on the train took a page from her little girl's Big Chief tablet."

She didn't think anyone had ever taught Mr. Otto cursive, but she was used to his careful printing. "Chapter 18, part of verse eight and some of nine: '. . . and are willing to bear one another's burdens, that they may be light; yea, and are willing to mourn with those that mourn, yea, and comfort those that stand in need of comfort. . .'" She looked up. "Mr. Otto, you knew I needed you."

She had embarrassed him. He barely glanced at her as he put the paper away again. "Along about Rock Springs—what is it about that awful town?—I had a few more second thoughts. I mean, it takes a lot to upset you, and granted, Mormons seem to have a handle on stuff." He looked decidedly uncomfortable, but his resolve seemed to strengthen. "Then I thought, 'She doesn't need to ride back to Cheyenne alone.'"

"How true," she said softly, remembering her sorrow on the way to Salt Lake. "You were right." She smiled at him. "You must be awfully tired."

"I am," he admitted. "Doc had left me a note at the livery stable, telling what happened. I rode to the Double Tipi, made sure everything was in order there, told my little lie to James, retrieved your package, and rode back to Gun Barrel the next day." He sighed. "Yeah, I'm tired." He managed a smile, "Or maybe, 'yea, behold, I am tired.'"

"I favor 'yea, behold, verily' myself."

Julia looked around Mr. Otto at her father standing in the door, a question in his eyes. He came into the kitchen holding out his hand as Mr. Otto got to his feet.

"You must be Mr. Otto. You're precisely as she described you. I'm the father of this little cook." The men shook hands. "I was going to plunk her on a train in a few days, whether she wanted to go or not," Papa said, putting his arm around Julia. "I couldn't help overhearing you. Mosiah eighteen?"

He passed his free hand across his face, and Julia saw all his bleakness even as he tried for a light tone. "As a family, we're on the receiving end of that one right now. Honestly, it's more fun to give."

"I know, sir," Mr. Otto said. "I figure you've had a walloping handful of commiseration, and that can be tough. I'm sorry for what happened to Iris. It shouldn't have."

Papa nodded, unable to speak.

"It's true I didn't want Darling here to—"

Surprised out of his mood, Papa chuckled. "You really do that, don't you?"

"What?" Mr. Otto asked, mystified.

"Call her Darling. She mentioned that in one or two letters. Maybe all her letters, come to think of it."

It was Mr. Otto's turn to lack for words. "Guilty as charged," he said finally, with a certain amount of deference in his voice that Julia had never heard before. "I call everyone by their last name, with a few exceptions. My pa did. Maybe that's why I do it."

"Not here," Papa told him.

"No?"

"No. There are three Darlings in the house; imagine the confusion. You may call her Miss Darling while you're here." Papa didn't say it with any force but exchanged a long look with Mr. Otto.

"Miss Darling it is, Mr. Darling," he said promptly, not looking at Julia. "If I forget, maybe I can call her Supreme Ruler of the Queen Atlantic or She Who Insisted on a Cat."

"Nah," Papa said. "How about Julia Almighty? That was Iris's favorite."

"You two!" Julia exclaimed, the teasing mention of Iris's name a soothing balm rather than something to avoid out of fear of the pain it would cause. *We can get through this,* she thought. "You say you came for another reason?"

Mr. Otto turned serious. "I did. Miss Darling, I need to talk to your father . . ."

He hesitated, and Julia felt her stomach tighten as the strangest thought came into her head. Surely he wasn't going to propose. She glanced at her father and saw the wariness come into his eyes. *He's thinking the same thing,* she thought in alarm. *Mr. Otto can't possibly be—not that. Papa would never approve of a nonmember. Not ever.*

Would I? Julia asked herself suddenly. She didn't know where to look except down at her hands as she held her breath.

But Mr. Otto was speaking again. "It's hard, sir, and maybe this isn't the right time." He took a deep breath. "I'd better just come out with it. I need a favor. I want . . . I need your help to find my mother's people."

Twenty-seven

The whole story came out over cinnamon raisin French toast and maple syrup because Papa wanted Mama to hear it too after Mr. Otto had begun.

"Do you mind waiting?" Papa asked. "I'll get my wife."

Mr. Darling went upstairs, taking them two at a time, which brought tears to Julia's eyes again, thinking how slowly, hand over hand on the banister, he had tread them last night. She couldn't help herself. She reached out and touched Mr. Otto's wrist. "You're going to give him something to do. Bless your heart."

"I have to," he said simply. "After what happened in Chicago—trust me, that can wait—I kept thinking of your comment that maybe people here are still missing Mary Anne, wondering what happened to her. Maybe they're still wondering if there was something more they could have done. Anything! I know that feeling."

He stopped, his face bleak, haunted even. Julia cupped both hands around his face, knowing how improper this was but thinking of the words on that Big Chief tablet paper. *Can I comfort you?* she asked herself. "Mr. Otto, what happened?" she asked, hoping if she kept her voice low and even, he would answer her.

He did, but only to reply, "It can wait," again, in a more stubborn tone.

She took her hands away. "All right then, but please don't keep it all inside."

"Maybe that's why I came to fetch you, Darling. It's a long, solitary ride."

"How well I know now."

Julia gave herself a mental shake and sliced the rest of the cinnamon raisin bread.

Mr. Otto watched her, happy to change the subject. "Maybe I shouldn't have eaten all that bread."

Julia opened the breadbox and pulled out another loaf. "You know I never make one of anything," she reminded him and sliced the new loaf.

Coated with beaten egg, cream, and a dab of sugar to brown it, the first slices of French toast were ready to be plated when Papa and Mama came downstairs, looking more interested than Julia had seen in a week.

"So you are *the* Mr. Otto," she said, taking his hand gently.

"The one, the only," he said. He looked at Julia. "I'd have known this was your mother in a roomful of mothers, Da . . . Miss Darling. You two look alike." Apparently he couldn't help himself then. "Mrs. Darling, did *you* ever dump gravy on a preacher's head?"

Mama gasped but then burst into laughter. "Oh, tell me Julia didn't," she said, when she could talk.

"She did. He deserved it." He winked at Julia, which made her cheeks go rosy. "You mean you never wrote your mother about that?"

"Mr. Otto, even from a distance, I like them to think I am mature and well-mannered," she scolded but couldn't think of anything else to say, not with Mama still laughing and Papa trying not to. *Bless your heart. I'll forgive you this time,* she thought, grateful for the mood he had set, whether it was deliberate or not. "Breakfast is ready!"

Papa asked the blessing on the food, and her parents sat

CARLA KELLY

down with Mr. Otto, who looked at her. "Keep'um coming, Miss D," he advised. "Just like you do at home."

She kept them coming, pleased to hear Mr. Otto describing, in his colorful way, the events leading up to the gravy episode and why he decided to trust her with the Otto family secret. She glanced at her mother, who was listening and eating. Julia sighed with relief. Mama had shaken her head at nearly everything she had tried to cook, and here was Mr. Otto, making her laugh. He glanced at Julia once to indicate her mother's empty plate with a slight nod. Julia quickly slid another piece of French toast onto her plate, and Papa passed the syrup just as quickly.

We are all of us conspirators, Julia told herself as she prepared two more egg-soaked slices for the griddle. When everyone was full, she joined them at the table as Mr. Otto—hesitant at first, looking at her for encouragement, even—told her parents about his mother. Mama even took his hand during part of the narrative when he faltered. Julia's heart was full.

"That's where I am," he concluded. "Your daughter wanted to write you about this weeks ago, but I wasn't so sure and asked her not to."

"Why?" Mama asked.

He told Mama of their fears his mother would be discovered and forcefully returned to her Mormon family at the expense of the Shoshone, who loved her too. Mama and Papa were silent then, thinking. He turned to Julia's father. "Mr. Darling, could I impose on you to help me? I know you're a busy man and—"

"I have time for this," Papa interrupted. He started to say something else, but the clock in the dining room chimed. "My goodness, we forgot to say Merry Christmas!"

Mama looked startled for a moment, as if wondering

how Christmas could still come when Iris was only a few days in her coffin. *Please, God, don't let her think of it,* Julia begged silently. Mama took Mr. Otto's hand again. "Merry Christmas to you," she said, with no hesitation.

"And to you, dear lady," he replied simply.

"Have you ever celebrated Christmas before?" Julia asked him when her parents had left the room and she had cleared off the table.

"Not recently. Sometimes, if the weather wasn't too bad, we'd go to the Fort Washakie Agency and visit my mother's relatives." He put his hands on her waist, moved her from the sink, and stood in her place. "I'll wash because you know where everything goes. Missionaries were usually there— I can't remember from what church—and they opened up barrels their congregations back East had shipped to the poor, ignorant Indians. That was us." Mr. Otto smiled. "Got my first pair of suspenders from a missionary barrel."

"We've really had different Christmases," Julia said.

"That's almost minor, compared to how different we are," Mr. Otto replied, handing her another plate to dry. "I look around your house, I walk your city streets, I hear a telephone ring—do we have *anything* in common?"

"I guess I never thought about it," Julia replied.

"That plate's dry now," he reminded her, and she blushed. "Well, that was never in the contract, was it?"

"Our differences?"

"That, or maybe our similarities."

She put down the dishcloth and just looked at him. "My stars, do we *have* any?"

His hands deep in dishwater, he thought a moment. She could see his complexion going a bit ruddier than usual, so she knew she had put him on the spot. "Yeah, we do," he said finally. "We both love James. And I think we both love the wide open spaces."

"I do love James," she said, swallowing to keep back the tears that seemed so close to the surface since Iris's death. "Wide open spaces?"

He took the dishcloth from her and dried his hands. "I think so. Were you even aware, after that weekend in Cheyenne, when we were on horseback again, that you gave a really loud sigh after we left Gun Barrel? I do that all the time when I leave Gun Barrel, and it's not because I'm missing the saloons and stupid bankers there. I'm just glad to be where there aren't too many people."

She had to smile. "Maybe you're right." She draped the dishcloth over the back of a chair. "You know, when you and the men were gone on the fall roundup, I'd wait until James was asleep and then go down to the river, just to listen to the water. Maybe I do like the solitude there."

"See? We have a few things in common. Are you coming back to the Double Tipi because of James?"

She knew the answer to that one. "Not really. I made you a promise when I signed that contract."

"Miss Darling, that whole contract was a joke, and you know it," he said firmly, with a touch of that steel in his voice that commanded respect from most people in Wyoming.

"Was it?" she asked. "I don't take promises lightly. You have my allegiance until September of next year."

"What then?" he asked softly.

I go home, where the people I am really like live, she thought. *Is that it?* "I'm not sure what happens next." She sat down at the table and Mr. Otto sat too. *I really can't lie to my boss. Not this one, anyway. He'd see right through me.*

"Mr. Otto, do you realize you have read more of the

Book of Mormon than I have? I've dabbled at it through the years, but you've invested yourself in one verse."

"Two or three now. I came here because of chapter eighteen," he reminded her.

"I need to find out for myself what this church I have belonged to for years and years is all about. You're reading and putting me to shame."

"It's not a contest, Darling," he told her.

"I know that! But doesn't it strike you as strange that I'm the one who should know more, considering my advantages, but you're the one who actually *lives* it? You read a scripture—heavens, the scrap of a scripture—and you govern your actions by it."

He sat back and went into what she had come to recognize as his Indian mode: looking impassive and thoughtful and completely the keeper of his personal views.

"I'm no paragon, Darling," he said finally, when she thought he would not speak. "That matter of the Rudigers—your kindness to them reminded me how much I had forgotten that I was a beggar too, and we all needed to help each other." His expression turned wry. "I haven't been a paragon at all. Let's leave it at that."

Mr. Otto watched her face. There was so much she wanted to tell this good man, who probably had no inkling just how good he was. "You impress me, sir," she said finally. "Maybe I want to be more like you. It's time I quit dabbling in the Church and figure things out for myself."

"Can you do that at the Double Tipi?" he asked finally.

"Between now and September? We'll see."

She heard a slight noise at the doorway between the kitchen and the dining room and glanced over to see her father standing there. His expression was thoughtful, and she wondered how much he had heard of their conversation.

Papa, I'm so imperfect. You thought you were raising a good Mormon daughter, and I know so little, she yearned to tell him.

"Papa?" she asked.

"I wanted to remind you that we're going to the bishop's house for dinner," he said. He held up his hand when Mr. Otto opened his mouth. "I've already called him, and he said of course there's room for one more."

"I don't want to impose," Mr. Otto said. "You had no idea I'd be showing up."

"You're so sure of that?" Papa asked. "Where are you staying?"

"Downtown."

"Not anymore. You'll stay here."

"I really can't . . ."

"Don't argue," her father said. "You and I will drop off the ladies at home after dinner. Then you and I will drive to the hotel, check you out, and retrieve your luggage. You're our guest, and I won't have an argument."

Julia glanced at Mr. Otto and then at her father. She had never heard anyone talk to Mr. Otto that way before, especially someone like her father, who was the mildest-mannered person she knew.

"Yes, sir," Mr. Otto said promptly. "Maybe when we get back from that errand, we can sit down at the table here and strategize how to find my relatives."

"You took the words out of my mouth," Papa replied. "I have some ideas. When are you planning to take my charming daughter back to the wilds of Wyoming?"

Mr. Otto laughed at that. "Pretty soon. I've been away too long. And you'd not have thought her so charming if you'd watched her dump gravy on the preacher. She's pretty much a top sergeant at getting us to clean up our language and wash occasionally. She even banished all my calendars and back issues of the *Police Gazette*. She's a fearsome entity."

Julia put her head down on the table and groaned.

"And I thought her mother and I were raising a lady," Papa murmured. "She never tells us these things in her letters."

"I'm about to declare the two of you certifiable," Julia announced.

The men laughed, apparently in total agreement with each other. Julia tried to glare at them both, but all she could really see was a kind man bringing her shattered father back to life. *You have a deft touch, Mr. Otto,* she thought.

After dinner at the bishop's house, where Mr. Otto shared his stories of ranch life and kept everyone diverted, especially her mother, Papa drove them home and then took Mr. Otto to his hotel.

"Mama, I have to tell you, I never knew Mr. Otto to be such good company," she said as they sat together in the parlor, looking at the Christmas tree. "He doesn't usually have so much to say."

Her mother took her arm and leaned against Julia's shoulder. "I think he's making a wonderful effort to take our minds and hearts off Iris's death," she said as matter-of-fact as if she spoke of the weather. "You are too, dear. Between the two of you, we don't have a chance, do we?"

Julia couldn't help her own sharp intake of breath. "Mama, I'm sure we didn't know we were so transparent."

"Transparent, perhaps. Welcome? Completely." She sighed, and the sound was ragged. "You're putting the heart back into me, Julia. So is Mr. Otto. I'm glad he came." She patted Julia's arm. "I thought he might."

Julia turned slightly sideways to see her mother better. "Really? Why would you think that?"

Her mother gave her a long look, as if wondering to continue. "Are you not aware that for the past few days, you go to the window each night, then turn slightly until you're facing approximately northeast? You miss him. Maybe he missed you."

"Oh, Mama, I think I miss the Double Tipi, but that's all," Julia said when she got over her amazement. "I had no idea you were watching me so closely! I thought, I thought—"

"I'm thinking of Iris to the exclusion of all else?" Mama shook her head. "No, dear. I'm mindful of all my children. Your being here has reminded me of that, and I'm grateful."

"Mama," was all Julia could say. They sat together, arms around each other, until they heard Papa's auto.

"Mr. Otto is so kindly giving my dear husband something to do," she confided to Julia.

"Mama, remind me never to underestimate you again," Julia said frankly.

"I need something too, Jules," Mama whispered. "This is so difficult."

Help me, Father, Julia prayed. *Just a little help.*

The answer came so fast that she held her breath, nearly overwhelmed. It was so simple. "Mama, I have an idea about that yellow yarn you were going to use for a baby afghan. Do you remember the Rudigers that I wrote to you about?"

Mama nodded. "Quite well. The lady who served you hot water and a mint twig?"

"Ursula Rudiger. I wrote you that Mr. Otto found work for her husband in Colorado. Would you . . . could you make that afghan for the Rudigers' baby?"

Mama's lips trembled, but she nodded slowly. "When is she due to be confined?"

"I think in a month or two. Mama, you'll have to start right away, even if it's hard."

The front door opened. Papa was talking to Mr. Otto. After looking in the parlor and blowing a kiss to Mama, he took their guest upstairs to show him his room. At the top of the landing, Papa leaned over the banister.

"Julia, I have a supper request. Welsh rarebit."

They listened to the men continue upstairs. Mama nodded. "I've never been able to cook that as well as you do." She took Julia's arm. "You know, I bought a lot of diaper flannel. I could get some of the Relief Society sisters to help me sew."

"Mama, that would be so kind. The Rudigers have nothing."

"It's time that ended," Mama said, sounding more like the woman who had marched Julia to ZCMI last fall to buy long underwear and aprons for Wyoming. "I probably have enough scraps to outfit a baby. And didn't you say there was another child? A little girl?"

"I did."

Mama tugged her arm. "Don't just sit there! Papa wants Welsh rarebit, and I have to find that flannel. Can you recall the little girl's dimensions too? Isn't her name Danila? I have patterns. Lots of them."

Twenty-eight

<p>elsh rarebit, everyone? Mr. Otto, this one will ruin you forever for boring old fried steak."

"I doubt it, but go ahead."

A half-hour later, he cried uncle after four helpings.

"What? Only four?" Julia teased. "Do you think your little sweethearts at the Double Tipi would scorn this?"

"I hope they do, then I can eat it all, Miss Darling," he said. "I need a nap now."

"Nothing doing! You need to think of as many variations of your mother's name as you can," Papa said, putting aside the empty plates.

"Her name was Mary Anne."

"Two words, or Marian?" Papa asked.

Mr. Otto thought a moment. "I'm not sure. And her last name, as near as we could figure out, was Hixon."

"Could it have been Dixon? Hickham? Hickman?"

"Possibly." Mr. Otto frowned. "I'm not much help."

"It won't be as hard as you think," Papa said. "Church offices are closed this week between Christmas and New Year's, but when they're open, I'll ask the Church historian to help me. We're friends. I do know this: the Willie and Martin handcart companies were caught in the snows not too far from present-day Casper."

"That's the outer edge for the Shoshone range, but it would have been a bad winter for them too." Mr. Otto said. "They'd have been searching for food." He looked at Julia.

"And they found my mother instead. Another mouth to feed."

"It's simple," Mama said. "They came to love her."

Mr. Otto nodded. "And she them, I know." He leaned back in his chair. "It's not so hard to imagine. She was a little girl and helpless. You get to know people, and you love them." He set his chair down, hastily, his face ruddy again. "I mean, I'm sure that's what happened. They didn't want to lose her, so they stayed away from whites." He looked at Julia. "That's what we did, at the Double Tipi, as long as she was alive."

The story seemed too big for him to discuss sitting down. He stood up and walked back and forth, stopping by the Majestic, warming his hands over the hot water reservoir.

"Did she ever mention the Book of Mormon?" Papa asked.

"Not to me. Her family—her Indian family, understand—found scraps of paper in her shoes. Someone in her other family must have put them there to keep the cold out," Mr. Otto said. "Talk about harsh times. It wasn't until later that she realized the scraps had scriptures on them."

They were all silent. Mr. Otto looked away and ran his fingers across his eyes. "She was a good mother, Darling," he said, his eyes on Julia. "The best."

"I don't doubt that for a minute," Mama said quietly. "She raised a fine son."

"I wish I were as fine as you think I am," he said, his voice unsure. "Good night all." He turned and left the kitchen.

Papa spoke first, after they heard Mr. Otto's steps on the stairs. "Deep waters there, Julia. Be careful."

She nodded, knowing exactly what he meant, but too shy to say anything.

Elbows on the table, poring over an old newspaper, Mr. Otto was sitting at the kitchen table when Julia came downstairs in the morning. She knew he was an early riser, so he did not surprise her. She finished twining her hair into a knot and stuck a skewer through it.

"Don't gussy up on my account," he teased her.

"I can look however I want when I lay the fire," she retorted. "I don't usually have company."

"No. I'm usually out in the horse barn by now, stirring up trouble there." He folded the paper and looked at her. "When can we leave, Darling?"

Too many people here? Did we press you too hard last night? All sorts of questions came to her mind. "How about tomorrow morning? I'd like another day at home."

"Fair enough. I could go ahead and you could come later, if you've a mind to stay longer. I'm not your jailer."

She shook her head. "Then I'd still be going back alone." She looked him in the eyes. "And so would you."

He looked away. "You're going to make me tell you what happened in Chicago, aren't you?"

"You don't have to tell me anything, Mr. Otto," she said frankly, "but you might feel better."

"And you might feel worse," he countered.

She laid the fire for breakfast silently, efficiently, and then sat down beside him. "Mr. Otto, nothing you can tell me will ever change what Mama said about you last night. Your mother did raise you well. I'm not someone to intimidate, like the other ranchers around you, because you want people to stay away or just leave you alone on all those acres. I like to think I'm your friend."

Maybe it was more than she should have said. Heaven knows she had tossed and turned enough last night, wondering what else she could possibly learn about her employer that would ever make her like him less. No one else had seen his heart as she had seen it in his dealings with the Rudigers, with James and the all-too-human men of the Double Tipi, and then with her own parents, firm in their own principles and faith, but needing to borrow another's strength until they could stand upright again.

"My friend?" he asked softly. "Then you'd better call me Paul."

"And you'd better call me Julia," she answered, her voice gentle.

"I can do that." He smiled then, and she could have sighed with relief to see the bleakness leave his eyes. "Of course, Darling might slip out now and then. Old habits. You know how they are."

⁓⁓⁓

Paul went for a long walk after breakfast. "He's not used to being cooped up in a house," Julia said to her parents. "On a typical day, he'd be out right after sunrise, tending to cattle or fences. He's hardly ever inside, even in winter."

"Hard life," Papa said. "I prefer banker's hours." He hesitated, almost as if he didn't want to ask. "When are you leaving, Jules?"

"Tomorrow. He said this morning he's been away too long."

Mama dabbed at her eyes but offered no objection. Julia took her hand. "I'll be back in September to stay. You can count on that."

Mama nodded. She handed a skein of yarn to Julia. "You wind this. I think I'll—I'll make my bed." She left the room quietly.

"Papa, it's all so hard," Julia said as she began to twine the yarn.

"I couldn't bear it if I didn't know Iris would be waiting for me when I die," he said finally.

"I'd rather she were here."

"So would I, Jules. So would I. I don't pretend to understand what's happened." Papa took the yarn from her, covering her hands with his. "Julia, when I interrupted you and Mr. Otto last night, you were expressing a lot of doubts."

Here it was. She swallowed and looked at him. "I have a lot of doubts, Papa."

"I realized as I stood there that I've done you a great disservice, daughter. I've assumed you always knew the Church was true."

"Oh, Papa . . ." she began, tears in her eyes.

"Hear me out, my dear. I wonder how many parents assume that very thing? Iris . . . Iris always seemed to know, and maybe I figured you did too."

"Papa, Mr. Otto has read more of the Book of Mormon than I have," she admitted. "I don't know why I never read it before. I've been busy in church and Mutual, and I always go to my meetings."

The room was suddenly too small. She had to stand up and move about as Mr. Otto had done last night. "Papa, I think if I had married Ezra, I'd have gone on as I have, just living on someone else's light. I need to know for myself!"

He stood up and held her gently by the shoulders. "So you do, Julia. Can you do that in the middle of nowhere in Wyoming?"

"I have to try." She let him gather her close. "Papa, can I borrow your light a little longer?"

"As long as you need it, dear."

She was in tears now, thinking of Iris, thinking of lonely

days ahead for her parents and her so far away in Wyoming. "I miss her, Papa," she said through her tears. "There's this huge hole in my heart."

"Mine too, Jules. You were the best big sister to Iris." Papa took the corner of her apron and dabbed her eyes. "Always watching out for her. Maybe now it's Iris's turn to watch out for you."

She blew her nose. "Papa, remember when I wrote you about that silly contract? Mr. Otto asked me if I'd ever marry a Wyoming cowboy, and I told him no, that Mormons marry in temples. He asked me why, and I was evasive. He didn't ask me anything else about the Church until he told me about his mother."

Papa nodded. "Are you getting a glimpse why we marry in temples?"

"I want to see Iris again," she whispered. "I must be part of the family . . . later on. But I have to know why."

He hugged her, his eyes so serious. His expression turned gentle then. "When you find out just how true all this is, you'll understand. You need to find out for yourself, honey. No one can do it for you."

They left at dawn from the Salt Lake depot. Unequal to the task of seeing her off at the depot, Mama had said good-bye at home. She had hugged Mr. Otto for good measure too and had him write down the Rudigers' address in Fort Collins.

"Just Karl Rudiger, General Delivery," Mr. Otto said, handing her the scrap of paper. "You're doing a kind thing, Mrs. Darling, even though I think it must be hard."

Leaving from the depot was no easier, not with Papa trying so hard not to cry. He shook hands with Mr. Otto.

"Take good care of the cook," he said.

"I promise," Mr. Otto assured him. His arm went around Papa then. "Anything you can find out about my mother's family will mean a lot to me."

"Family matters, son," Papa said. He looked at Julia. "Now, and in the eternities."

When they got on the Union Pacific in Ogden, Mr. Otto got a sleeping car in the open section. Maybe it was more for him than her, Julia decided. Mr. Otto looked so tired. It was as though his few days of bolstering her parents had worn him out. They sat together, silent. In a few minutes, he was breathing evenly, asleep.

She watched his face. His mustache needed trimming, and he hadn't shaved as closely as he usually did, for all that he had been hugely impressed with her home's indoor lavatory and hot water almost on demand. *We are different,* she thought, and closed her eyes too.

When she woke, they were on the high plains of Wyoming. She glanced at Mr. Otto, who was awake and looking out the window.

Mr. Otto was silent for several miles. Out of the corner of her eye, she saw him open and close his mouth several times, wanting to talk. She had a feeling again, and this one was different. It was time, and she acted on it without question.

"Paul, please talk to me," she said, trying out his name. "Tell me what happened in Chicago."

"It's awfully personal."

"And you think my visit home wasn't? What happened, Mr. Otto?" she repeated.

"I went to a funeral too." He paused. "My wife's."

She hadn't expected that.

"Maybe I shouldn't—no, I want you to know. Maybe

I'm the one who needs to talk about it. Maybe that's why I came to escort you home."

She didn't hesitate. "Tell me what happened," she said quietly. The conductor walked through the car, checking his roster, chatting with the salesman slapping down solitaire cards on the sample case on his lap, and then leaving out the far end.

"Darling, after years of trying, she finally succeeded in killing herself."

Julia couldn't help the gasp that escaped her. The woman across the aisle glanced at her and moved slightly closer to her own window.

"Your wife? Mr. Otto, I'm so sorry," she said, thinking of the photographs with the gouged eyes. A chill ran down her arms, and she rubbed them.

"Well, my former wife, to be correct," he amended. "After the annulment—it's been eight years, Julia, and there was no divorce—I asked her family to keep me informed. They didn't, at first, and I never pressed the issue."

He sighed and waited for a long time to speak. She knew better than to rush him. The conversation was obviously painful. "Lately, though, her parents had both been writing me, urging me to visit her. Julia, I just couldn't. Call me a coward."

"You're no coward," she assured him. He sat on the seat across from her. She moved to his side, sitting close to him. "This is a private conversation. The whole train doesn't need to hear it."

He nodded, his face deadly serious as he put his arm around her to pull her closer to him. "Apparently she had become more and more withdrawn." He closed his eyes. "This is hard."

"You can wait, if it pains you," she assured him. "I think I understand grief now."

"It's more than that."

His arm was tight around her shoulders, as though he couldn't speak without holding on to something. "I met my wife—my former wife—when I took a trainload of beeves to Chicago in '96. I was twenty, and it was my first time without Pa."

"I thought he died when you were fifteen."

"He did. Another old rancher—Charlie McLemore's dad, actually—saw our cattle to the yards until I felt confident enough to do it myself." He glanced at her, reading her expression perfectly. "Darling, I wasn't always a longtime rancher."

Julia smiled. "And we know I am not mature."

Mr. Otto took her hand and stretched her free arm across his chest. He sighed. "That's better. Call me a cad some other time."

"You're no cad, either."

"I was as green as a spring willow. As I think about it, that was part of the problem." He shook his head again. "Where was I? Oh, yes. She was the daughter of my new cattle buyer, Frank Moss."

"What was her name?"

"Katherine." He stood up suddenly, as if even the name caused him great unease. "I'll be back."

He was gone almost an hour. All she could do was pray for him and look out the window at the bleakness that was peculiarly Wyoming in the winter. When he returned, he had a pillow for her, which she tucked against the window to keep out the draft. His arm went around her again.

"I made the trip every fall for three years. She started writing to me. I thought it was a bit forward of her, but everyone likes to get mail." Mr. Otto took off his overcoat and tossed it on the empty seat facing them. "Mr. Moss brought Katherine along on several buying trips." He managed a rueful smile. "When she wasn't there, he talked about her all the time. He paraded her good qualities. You'd have thought Katherine was a show pony and not his daughter. She was pretty."

"Did . . . did you fall in love with her?" Julia asked when he seemed disinclined to continue.

"I thought I did, especially when Mr. Moss told me she liked me a lot. But . . ."

". . . you didn't see her very much," Julia offered.

"Not enough to know her well." He made a sound of disgust. "I found out later she hadn't written those letters." Mr. Otto touched her head with his briefly, as if to reassure himself that he wasn't alone. "I don't even know how I proposed, but I must have." He seemed to drag out his words. "It was a June wedding. I was twenty-three, and I was dumb."

Julia felt her face grow warm, wondering how her mother would react to such an intimate conversation. *Listen to him,* she thought. *He needs to talk. You might be the first person he has ever shared this awful burden with.*

"I shouldn't say any more," he told her finally. "It's too personal."

"Tell me," was all she said.

Her permission unleashed a flood. "We went to the family's vacation cabin on a lake for our honeymoon. If there was a worse honeymoon in the history of the universe, I can't imagine it. Darling, Katherine had no idea what was expected of her. It was torment."

"Oh, Mr. Otto," she whispered, responding to the pain in his voice. "And . . . and when you took her to the Double Tipi?"

"Worse. She cried when I even looked at her."

Julia winced at his flat tone and the disgust he aimed at himself. "What did you do?"

"I left her alone and continued my former wild ways in Gun Barrel." He didn't look at her. "When her father came on his cattle buying trip that summer, I pretended that everything was fine." He made another snort of disgust, but he didn't seem to direct it at himself this time. "Mr. Moss was quite happy to play along, I later learned."

Julia began to sense the enormity of the lie foisted on her employer. "They knew all along something was wrong with her! Mr. Otto, did they *trick* you?"

He leaned back as though the marrow had leached out of his spine. "You're a lot quicker than I was." He grasped her hand gently. "We suffered through another winter, but then Katherine started wandering off just before spring, nine years ago."

"Dear God," Julia breathed.

"I'd bring her back, and she'd be all remorseful, and then she'd wander off again." He turned bleak eyes on her. "God forgive me, but I had to tie her down when I left the ranch for any appreciable time. I . . . I suppose that's how rumors started."

Julia thought about Iris and Spencer, how much in love they had been, and how they were cheated of a long marriage. She dug around in her purse for a handkerchief, but he beat her to it with his own.

"You poor man," she said when she could talk.

"Poor, stupid man," he amended. "She'd have wild episodes, and then she would be calm, almost normal. She liked the parlor. Or I thought she did, except when I went in there once after she was asleep, I saw she had smashed the Victrola records and stuck them in pots, after she had uprooted the plants. It was grotesque. Sick."

Julia remembered that bizarre sight. "I noticed one pot, when I fixed up the parlor."

"I'm sorry you had to see that. I thought I had found all of them."

He stared straight ahead for a long time. "I thought I could turn her loose. It lasted for several days, until she stabbed me under my armpit one night with one of those record shards. Just scraped it down my ribs like a razor on a washboard." He grimaced at the memory. "I've never seen so much blood."

"Wha-what on earth did you do?" Julia asked, voice hushed.

"I'd be dead, if it weren't for Blue Corn. It was a week-end, and the trail was good, so I'd let my hired hands go into Gun Barrel for a little hoorah. Little River was away too, visiting on the reservation." Mr. Otto shook his head, as if trying to dislodge the memory. "I staggered to the tack shed, and Blue Corn stopped the bleeding. He stitched me together and then went into the house and watched Katherine."

He focused his attention out the window again.

"I think I understand why you're so good to Blue Corn," Julia said.

"I owe him my life."

Mr. Otto leaned forward then and stared at the floor. Julia listened to the rhythmic clack of the wheels on the track, unable to speak.

"She was insane," he said finally, his voice low. "I put a flannel shirt backwards on her and wrapped the arms tight so she couldn't touch anyone. When I was able, I sent a long letter to Mr. Moss." He looked at her. "Julia, it was terrible. When—when I could travel, I took her back to Chicago and I got myself a good lawyer. We had her committed, and I was granted an annulment, since it was pretty obvious she had been married to me under false pretenses."

"Why did the Mosses do that to you? And to her?" Julia asked.

"I asked them that, when my lawyer was arranging Katherine's commitment. Frank just shrugged. Mrs. Moss cried and carried on until a doctor had to sedate her." He chuckled humorlessly. "I guess the apple didn't fall too far from that particular tree."

He was silent then, and Julia had nothing to say that wouldn't sound stupid in the face of such horror. She wanted to take his hand but paused, thinking of the time she had put her hand on his shoulder and how he had flinched, as though another's touch—even a light touch meant only in friendship—had the capacity to startle him. Now that *was* understandable.

"Paul, may I hold your hand?" she asked suddenly.

He glanced at her and then looked away. "You're sure you want to?"

She took his hand in hers, noticing the split-second flinch. Not sure if what she was doing would bring him some measure of comfort, she gently increased the pressure of her hand in his. To her relief, he turned his hand until their fingers were twined together. He closed his eyes. In a moment, his hand opened as he relaxed and slept, exhausted.

Twenty-nine

To Julia's relief, Paul slept most of the afternoon, unburdened for what she suspected was probably the first time in years. She doubted he had ever told his story to anyone, not a reticent man like him, one with a certain reputation to maintain in the hard society he lived in.

That he had trusted her enough to tell her touched Julia's heart. Mothers and fathers. Husbands and wives. Brothers and sisters. She couldn't fathom a relationship as toxic as his had been. Paul Otto was probably more resilient than even he knew. She thought again about the scripture in Mosiah, the one on the other side of that passage about beggars. "Believe in God, believe that he is," she murmured as Paul Otto slept, his head on her shoulder.

Without waking him, she managed to get her Book of Mormon from her valise. For the first time in a public place, she didn't look around to see if anyone was watching her read "Joe Smith's Gold Bible," as a fellow streetcar rider in Boston had called her Book of Mormon to Julia's humiliation. She didn't care who saw her now. She needed to see the rest of that scripture.

There it was. She almost sighed with relief. " 'Believe that man doth not comprehend all the things which the Lord can comprehend,' " she whispered out loud. She prayed then, asking Heavenly Father to somehow ease this good man's heart. *Right now, Father, not sometime in the future.*

Right now, she thought fiercely. *Your Son went through all this and more. Touch Mr. Otto, somehow.*

Me too, she added, *if you have the time. I hurt so much. I miss my sister.*

Paul woke up when the porter went through the car to announce dinner. He sat up and blinked his eyes, uncertain where he was. He looked Julia square in the eye. "I said a lot, didn't I?"

"You needed to," she replied, looking up from Alma. "It goes no farther than me."

"It shouldn't have gone that far."

She marked her place with her finger and returned his penetrating gaze. "After all you've done for me? Paul, just let it alone now." She returned to her reading. *This is it, Lord. Relieve his pain,* she prayed.

"Thank you," he said after a long few miles, his voice normal again, his innate confidence back. He amazed her by picking up her hand and kissing it. "I'm hungry. Let's eat."

❦

"Your potatoes are better than these flabby, lardy things," Paul announced over dinner. He put down his fork and eyed them with suspicion, as though daring them to rise off the plate and defend themselves.

"I thought so too, but Papa says I'm not humble enough."

He picked up his fork again and frowned at the potatoes. "You've ruined me forever for bad food, Miss Julia."

"What I've done, apparently, is turn you into a food snob," she joked, grateful down to her toes at his familiar, teasing tone. "Shame on me."

"It's your fault."

"Then you should never have advertised for a cook."

"You're going to be heartless and leave me in September, Miss Julia?"

"Sooner, if you don't quit complaining."

Silently, Julia thanked the Lord. Sitting across from Paul Otto in the dining car was almost as easy as sitting with him in the kitchen of the Double Tipi, where no one was on their best behavior, and they were used to teasing each other.

"Look, you're obviously more comfortable calling me by my last name," Julia said. "If I hear Miss Julia again, I'll . . . I'll make potatoes like these back home."

"What a threat. Darling, it is," he said promptly. "I do like to hear my name, though, 'cause that Mr. Otto fellow is really old. Still, you could call me Boss, like Doc does, if you'd rather."

"No," she said firmly. "I will call you Paul."

"My choice too." He finished his coffee, making a face. "I'm about to give up coffee too."

"Even mine?"

"Probably. It's nothing personal. I didn't miss it a bit at your parents' house. Getting old, Darling. Me, not you."

When they returned to the Pullman car's open section, the porters were preparing the beds for sleep, pulling out the bottom seats and then pulling down the bed overhead. They pulled discreet curtains around each newly created bed.

Around them, other passengers made ready for the night. Julia watched a frazzled mother march her two little ones down the aisle to the washroom at the end, coming back with her cherubs, somehow subdued in flannel nightgowns.

"I hope someone's been reading to James," Julia whispered. "Doc promised me he would."

"He promised me too, on my one night there after

Chicago," Paul assured her. "You miss James, don't you?"

She nodded, her eyes on another child being boosted into the overhead sleeping compartment across the aisle by his father. "I bought him Crayola crayons and paper for Christmas. Lots of paper."

"I didn't get you anything, Darling." He stood up when the porter moved to their side of the aisle, waiting to arrange the beds. He indicated an open seat farther down where they could wait.

"I didn't expect anything," Julia said. "I have a present for you, and my father sent along something else for you, but it can keep until we celebrate Christmas with James."

Paul watched the porter's deft motions. "The Mosses wanted me to stay in Chicago for Christmas with them. I couldn't leave fast enough." He shook his head. "I don't know, Darling. It was strange, like they were trying to make up for all the pain they caused. They even tried to give me a portion of an inheritance that would have gone to Katherine. I just wanted to leave, but every time I mentioned that, Mrs. Moss cried, which always escalated into hysterics."

"How did you manage to escape?"

Paul gave her a wry smile. "How apt! That's exactly what I did. I crept barefoot downstairs in the wee hours, before anyone was up. I never have to go back there again."

"Upper or lower?" Paul asked later, when the porter finished and moved on down the car. "Better say upper, because I don't much care for heights."

Julia laughed, which made Paul beam at her. "That's the first time you've laughed in days."

"I suppose it is."

When she came back later from the washroom, her hair in pigtails and robe carefully buttoned over her nightgown, she got barely a glance from Paul, who was sprawled in the lower bed, reading the Book of Mormon now. Funny that she should feel shy; for months now they had been sharing the ranch house, which meant enough nights like this one.

"Need a leg up?" was all he said, turning a page.

"Nope. I am sufficiently agile."

The bed was soft, even if it did smell faintly of cigar smoke. She opened the front curtain enough to read a few pages in the Book of Mormon and then composed herself for sleep, which came quickly. She was only vaguely aware when Paul retired to the bed below hers.

For all that she dropped to sleep soon after, her dreams were not peaceful. She dreamed of Iris and a train trip to the Chicago Exposition years ago, when she was ten and Iris a precocious four. Except Iris wasn't four, but twenty-two, and lying on the floor in her farmhouse kitchen in Draper. Julia, still ten, was banging on the door, trying to get in. And then they were in a cemetery, but it must have been a cemetery in Chicago, because there was the Great Wheel from the Exposition, and now she was trying to stop the wheel, because Mr. Otto, dressed in black like her father, was kneeling by an open grave, in tears, and she couldn't reach him.

But it wasn't Mr. Otto in tears; it was her. Mr. Otto had opened the curtain to her upper berth, and he was shaking her gently. "Darling? Darling?"

She clutched his hand, and he clasped hers. "It was the worst dream."

"Thought so."

Julia looked past his shoulder and into the Pullman car, now dimly lit and quiet, except for someone snoring a few curtains over. "I hope I didn't wake anyone."

"Not over that racket," Paul said, amused. "Bad dreams or just sad ones? Scoot closer to the edge, will you?"

She did as he said, dragging her pillow with her. She rested her head on it, Paul's face close to hers as he rested his arms now on the fold-down bunk. He had on his blue and white night shirt, which was faded, the stripes nearly gone.

"It started out fun," she said. "Iris and I were on our way to the Chicago Exposition. We went when I was ten, and she was almost five."

Julia closed her eyes as the tears came. Paul rested his hand on her head. "There now, Darling. There now."

His hand was warm and soothing. Julia felt her eyelids grow heavy as her heart resumed its normal rhythm. "Strange. I can't quite remember what woke me up."

"Good. I'm here. Go to sleep. If you wake up again, I'll still be here. It's hard to leave a moving train."

The train was slow into Cheyenne, and they barely made the connection to Gun Barrel. There was only time to scribble a note to the Gillespies, telling of Julia's safe arrival. She handed a coin to the conductor, along with the note and the address. Losing scarcely a beat in his "Aboard! All aboard!" he gave it to one of the boys standing on the platform, who tipped his ragged cap to Julia and took off running.

"I wish you had a telephone," she told Paul as they sat down.

"You just won't rest until you ruin my place, will you?" he teased. He gazed at her, and she smiled back serenely. "Sometimes I wish we had one too," he said. "Would make life a little simpler, eh?"

Yes and no, she decided, after they changed into riding gear at Gun Barrel's livery stable, mounted up, and started the now-familiar ride to the Double Tipi. During her stay in Salt Lake, Mama's seamstress had made her a divided skirt that fit. Papa had dragged out the riding boots she used to wear on occasional trips to St. George and her brothers' property. "This is better," she announced to no one in particular as they rode. "Now if only I were a better rider."

"Patience, Darling, and practice."

There wasn't much to say. Maybe Paul was right. Maybe she did like the open spaces. The air was bracing, but there wasn't any wind for a change, and no snow anywhere.

"No snow. That's convenient," she said as they rode side by side.

"I'd prefer snow. Could be we're headed for a dry spring and summer: no haying, sunburned pastures, thirsty cattle, range fires."

"Is that common?"

"Common enough." He touched spurs to his horse. "Let's go home."

James was still awake when she came into the kitchen. Eyes bright, face lively, he looked up from the kitchen table, where he sat next to Doc, who was reading an outdated newspaper. James was in her arms in a moment, nearly bowling her over.

"I thought you weren't coming!"

"Told you I was," she said, fighting back tears again and ruffling his hair. She ruffled it again. "It's too late tonight, but in honor of Christmas Eve," she looked at Paul, who winked, "tomorrow, you're headed to the tin tub for a good shampoo."

"That's what happens when the lady arrives," Doc said, getting up from the table, a smile on his face. "Glad you're back, Julia. You too, Boss."

"Everything all right?"

"As rain. Matt will be in from the line shack tomorrow, and I guess we'll be getting ready for Christmas?"

James clapped his hands. "Is it time for Christmas now?"

"I told you it would be, two days after Mr. Darling came back," Paul reminded the boy. "And here she is."

⟡

Christmas was only one week late. James didn't know, and no one else cared. After James finally went to sleep, Doc walked Julia into the parlor and pointed out the tree.

"You did a marvelous job keeping that alive," Julia said.

"That's the second tree," Doc pointed out. "Along about the real Christmas, the first tree—we will call it exhibit A—started shedding its needles. I swear it looked like a dog with mange. After James was asleep, Matt snuck in another tree that he had cut down earlier that day. We took the popcorn and cranberry ropes off really careful and adorned our new, improved tree. It was the grand switcheroo."

Paul laughed and stretched out on the sofa. "Did you really fool him?"

Doc shook his head. "Sort of." He turned to Julia, his eyes bright. "You will observe that Exhibit B is taller and more robust than that puny thing you selected."

"Exhibit A?"

"The very one. James took one look at it, and his eyes got bigger and bigger. Matt and I wanted to crawl into a hole for trying to put one over on him, but he just hugged me and said how wonderful it was that the tree had finally decided to grow."

"Good for James," Julia exclaimed.

When Doc and Paul walked to the horse barn, Julia went through the parlor and into James's room to watch him sleep. "I missed you," she whispered. "I promise you this will be a wonderful Christmas because I missed Christmas too."

She was in bed before she heard Paul in the kitchen again. To her surprise, he knocked on her door.

Julia put down her scriptures. "Come in."

He didn't, but he stood in the doorway a moment. "You going to be all right tonight?" he asked.

"I suppose I'd better be," she replied, shy now, even though they had been so much closer last night in the Pullman car, when she had felt nothing but relief at his presence, calming her fears and coaxing her back to sleep.

"Leave your door open, and you'll probably have Two Bits for company."

Chin on her knees, she listened to his footsteps recede through the connecting rooms in the dark. She smiled when he tiptoed through James's room. She sighed and settled herself to rest as he slapped the lintel on the archway to his room, something he always did. The sound was familiar and reminded her she was home.

The men kept James busy in the horse barn and corral the next day while she cooked and baked to get ready for Christmas the day after. She wrapped her few presents and put them under Exhibit B, which, she had to agree, was flourishing. Everyone was happy with flapjacks for supper, plus sausage and hash browns, which told her worlds about what they had been eating for the past week.

She was even able to coax Willy Bill and Kringle into the parlor that night, serving iced cookies and applesauce pound cake with hot chocolate—surprisingly good, even if it was made with canned milk, something Miss Farmer never approved of.

Paul brought his Bible into the parlor and read Luke 2. By then, James's head was resting in Julia's lap. She stroked his hair, washed and shampooed twice with her best lavender fragrance. Her eyes were heavy too, and she was pleasantly tired after her day of preparation. It would have been better at home, with Mama to help and Papa offering generally useless advice, and Iris. No, not Iris ever again. She closed her eyes, wondering how Spencer could possibly cope in his empty farmhouse.

But Paul was reading. " 'And suddenly there was with the angels a mighty host, praising God and saying . . .' "

Glory to God in the highest, she thought. She listened, taking heart from the story she had heard every year of her life, realizing that she never tired of it. How far away she was from everyone dear to her, how distant from town was the Double Tipi. It was a ranch in the middle of Wyoming, which most people only thought about when they were crossing the state on the Overland Express. But the parlor was comfortable and Paul's voice soothing. Hard to believe now that he had ever terrified her. Even harder to believe that for the moment, she didn't wish to be anywhere else.

Thirty

They opened presents in the parlor after breakfast, when James couldn't wait another minute. Paul accepted her gift of a Gillette safety razor with raised eyebrows and then disappeared into the kitchen. She heard him getting warm water from the Queen Atlantic's reservoir. Fifteen minutes later he returned to the parlor, running his hand over his jaw.

"Superior," he said. "With a little bay rum, I will be the sweet-smelling envy of nations."

Willy Bill put on the vest she had purchased for him in Salt Lake, when she had dragged Mama to ZCMI just to get her out of the house. He took his old one and threw it out the door. Matt looked especially fine with his new belt from ZCMI's exclusive Gentlemen's Collection. She had to hold back tears when Kringle just held his six pairs of new wool socks to his chest, speechless.

She had bought Doc a copy of *Gray's Anatomy*, which he had unwrapped and accepted with no hesitation, turning the big book over and over in his hands.

"I sold my copy in Denver for booze," he said.

"I thought you might have," Julia said. *In for a penny, in for a pound,* she thought, as Paul watched her, a half smile on his face. "In fact, I'm of the opinion that you should be practicing medicine again, Doc."

"I'm not going back to Denver," Doc said, his eyes wary. Still, he cradled the book in his arms.

"Who said anything about Denver? Gun Barrel could use someone besides that old fellow who masquerades as a doctor," Julia said, keeping her voice neutral. "It's just a thought."

James had been nearly overwhelmed with more books from the Gillespies and her gift of Crayola crayons and drawing tablets. He lined them up in a neat row and chanted, "Black, brown, blue, red, purple, orange, yellow, and green." Julia thought of years of largesse from her parents and reminded herself not to whine.

Paul had been pleased by her father's personal copy of the *Autobiography of Parley P. Pratt*. "It's his favorite book, and he thought you might like it," she said.

"I'll take it to the line shack, Darling."

"Maybe when you're done, I can borrow the book?"

"It's a promise."

<hr>

After the dinner dishes were washed and put away, she took the list Paul had written and went through the pantry, pulling items for the line shack and wishing he wouldn't leave so soon. *Tell him how to run his ranch now,* she scolded herself, *like you told Doc to start a medical practice in Gun Barrel. Honestly, Julia, what is happening to you?*

"Walk with me, Darling."

Every time he left the Double Tipi, he said that, just like every time he went to bed, he slapped the lintel. *People's habits*, she thought. *Walk with me, Darling.*

Smiling to herself, she took her coat from its peg and wrapped her muffler around her head. Paul took her arm on the stoop. "Icy," he commented. "I guess that's all we get this winter for moisture."

He had a new blanket over his arm, and they walked

to Blue Corn's winter home. The Indian smiled his nearly toothless grin to see her and went through an elaborate sign pattern, which made Paul laugh and shake his head.

Julia put more wood in the stove while the two men signed, Paul squatting on his haunches, the Indian warm with an extra pillow—embroidered, a gift from Mama— behind his head and now the new blanket.

The air was cool, but not windy, so she didn't mind walking with Paul to the horse corral, where he whistled and Chief's ears perked up. A few words in Shoshone from Paul, and Chief stood at the rail, nosing Paul's chest for carrots.

"Old bandit," Paul said, reaching inside his overcoat for carrots. "Darling, I'll be at the line shack for most of the week, then I'm going to the stock show in Denver. That'll be two more weeks, at least."

"Oh." She didn't mean to sound disappointed. His time was his own. "I guess winter is about your best opportunity to leave the Double Tipi."

"Always has been. I was thinking you and James might want to come with me as far as Cheyenne. I'd leave for Denver after church and you two would be all right to get home from there. Would you?"

"Of course. I'd like James to meet the Gillespie boys."

"That's what I thought too. Thing is, I want us to leave for Cheyenne a day earlier. I'm going to transfer my legal business to Brother Gillespie. Up to now, I've had a Chicago lawyer, but I'm not going back there ever again. An agent can ship my cattle, and I like Brother Gillespie."

"You would be a welcome addition to his practice, I'm sure," she said.

"Here's how it concerns you, if you're amenable." He turned around and rested his elbows on the rail, which made Chief nose at his head. "Pesky horse. I bank in Cheyenne, mostly, and I want to list you as a cosignatory on my account there."

"Oh, no, Mr. Otto!" Julia exclaimed.

"Mr. Otto again? I thought we had seen the last of him. Hear me out. I want you to be able to tap into funds for the kitchen when you're in Cheyenne. You've indicated that the grocery selection in Gun Barrel is poor . . ."

"You're being kind to Gun Barrel," she said dryly.

"True," he agreed. "Point being, there are emporiums in Cheyenne that will crate up your purchases and ship them to Gun Barrel. I—or you—can send Matt or Doc down to the Cheyenne & Northern depot with a wagon to fetch whatever you buy. This way you have free rein, in case I'm not around." He looked into the distance. "I . . . uh . . . I'm not going to be around much this spring."

"You trust me *that* much?"

He stared at her as though she had sprouted another head. "Darling, I trust you completely." He could tell it wasn't going well by her expression. "Uh, is there something I should know?"

She laughed as she knew he wanted her to. "Of course not! Mr. Otto—Paul—is this a good idea?"

He shrugged. "If you here at the Double Tipi are interested in eating regularly—or at least in the style to which even Willy Bill has become accustomed—it probably is."

"Well, if you put it that way," Julia countered, unable to keep the dubious tone from her voice. "I'll think about it."

"That's all I ask. And if you and James want to leave for Cheyenne on Friday, think about that too." He nudged her shoulder, which made Chief whinny. "Don't know about you, but I've been missing that painting of Custer behind whoever's at the podium trying to make the Odd Fellows Hall a more righteous place."

"That's a bit flip," she retorted.

He shrugged again. "Your church, Darling, not mine."

She thought about that through the week, even going into Paul's room one night to see if he had taken the Book of Mormon and her father's gift with him to the line shack. Neither book was in sight, and she wasn't about to pry further. She reminded herself it wasn't his religion as she cooked and cleaned and made the Double Tipi a better place after her absence. Custer probably would look funny to anyone not used to Mormon meetings in strange places. *Be honest, Julia,* she told herself. *It also startled you, at first.*

She decided she had made a mountain out of a molehill after Paul returned from the line cabin, smiling and obviously more at peace with himself since before his trip to Chicago.

"He likes his solitude," Doc told her from the dinner table when he saw her looking out the window after hearing his horse. "It's nothing personal, Julia."

She sat down. Matt and Willy Bill hadn't come inside yet, and James was busy drawing. "Have I been that obvious?" she asked quietly.

"Call me an observer of human nature. I wondered if you two had quarreled."

"Not really." Julia thought a moment, unwilling to mention the Church and knowing that wasn't her only concern. Doc didn't need to know everything. "He wants to put my name on his bank account in Cheyenne! Something about making it easier for me to obtain funds for food purchases, if he's not around. I told him I didn't think it was a good idea."

"Calm your heart, Julia." Doc said. "That's a sound idea. Know this about Boss, because I'm not sure you're aware of it: he's one of the most successful ranchers in Wyoming. He didn't get that way by having poor business instincts. If he trusts you, you're trustworthy. He has a sixth sense about this, I do believe."

"That's it?" she asked in relief. "So I should agree?"

"I would." He grinned at the expression she knew was on her face. "You look like you ate a sour pickle! Maybe you should trust *him*." He looked closer. "He ever given you reason not to?"

Far from it, she thought. "Never. All right. You've convinced me."

He put his hand to his heart in mock relief. She was swatting him with a dish towel when Paul came in.

"Jerusalem crickets, I go away for a few days, and my cook gets violent."

She swatted him next, which made James look up from his artwork and grin. Paul grabbed the dish towel and swatted back. Doc rolled his eyes and turned back to another outdated newspaper while James continued his drawing, a smile on his face. When Julia tried to retrieve the dish towel, Paul slung it over the rafter like he used to sling the calving ropes and grinned at her.

Matt Malloy opened the door about then, watching them. He removed his coat and sat down beside Doc, addressing him specifically. "I disremember, Doc. When did this place turn into bedlam?"

"When Julia showed up," Doc said.

"To think I just hired her to cook," Paul replied as he reached for the dish towel. "Little did we know."

⚭

Little did I know how enjoyable the Double Tipi would become, Julia told herself later when the men were in the bunkhouse and Paul was reading to James in bed. He was in a good mood now, maybe because she had agreed to become a signatory on his Cheyenne account or more likely because the entrée was pork chops. She had bartered for them with Alice Marlowe, tempting her husband with a magnificent mound of hand-dipped, chocolate covered maraschino cherries.

She left enough behind for the Double Tipi men and another cache she was taking to the Gillespies tomorrow, hidden in a tin labeled dried lima beans, a trick Mama had passed on to her after her older brothers moved out.

"Julia, do you have a minute?"

She looked up from a plate rubbed dry. Paul stood there, more serious than she had seen him since Salt Lake City. He held a tablet of James's drawings. "Is something wrong?"

"I'm not sure. Come in the parlor. James is asleep, and we can talk."

Julia put down the plate and removed her apron, following her boss into the next room. He patted the sofa next to him and put the tablet in her lap when she sat down.

Puzzled, she shuffled through them, smiling at yesterday's illustrations of horses in the corral. "I think he has some talent," she said.

"Keep looking."

She turned page after page in the drawing book, amused to see herself, hair twisted in her impromptu topknot, kneading bread. Her mouth was open. "I'm singing. I really tried to teach him 'Silent Night' before you got back today, but he seems to think 'Sweet Evalina' and 'Redeemer of Israel' will do."

"That's about my favorite drawing," Paul said. "The only thing he missed was the flour that's usually on the end of your nose. Keep turning."

She stopped two pages later. She held her breath as she stared down at a midnight sky and a cabin on fire. "Paul," she whispered, as she took in what appeared to be people on fire inside the cabin. The skin on her back seemed to prickle as she saw horses with riders around the burning cabin and a smaller figure in the snow, partly in shadow. "Please tell me this isn't what I think."

He put his arm around her, pulling her close. "Three years ago, that winter when he just wandered onto the Double Tipi, there was a nasty range war going on north of us." He tightened his grip. "It was the usual problem: nesters moving onto what used to be open range and stockmen taking exception to it. They burned a couple of claim shanties and drove off the settlers."

"But . . ."

"Let your mind wander. Think more ill of people than you usually do."

It wasn't a great leap; maybe she just hadn't wanted to think like that. "One of the shanties wasn't empty," she said slowly.

"I know those ranchers."

"Would they . . . ?"

"They would. Apparently they did, though I doubt a judge or jury in this state would ever convict them, provided they even knew they had left a witness alive." He sighed. "Julia, I asked James, just casual like, if he knew who that little boy was. He nodded. Told me his name was Tad, or Thad. I couldn't tell."

"Tad is James?" she asked, horrified.

"I think so." Paul made an effort to speak calmly. "I asked him if Tad had a last name. It sounded like he said Pulaski or Polatki." He put his hand to his eyes. "Darling, this could almost be my mother's story: someone small left to wander."

Julia leaned her head against Paul's shoulder. He was

running his thumb down her arm now, probably an absent-minded gesture.

"I do remember that the homesteaders they ran off were from Eastern Europe," he said, speaking softly, as if the arsonists were in the room with them, watching the claim shanty burn. "No one knows where they went, and I assure you no one made any effort to find them. They were gone, and that's all that mattered."

"Should . . . should we call James Tad now?"

"I asked him that, but he shook his head. He looked afraid, as though they might still come after him." He made an inarticulate sound. "Darling, he told me, 'That was Tad. You named me James.'"

She took a deep breath. "Dear God. Can we do anything?"

"Don't think I'm craven if I tell you no. You know as well as I do that tempers run high on what used to be the open range and what's left of the range. When I think— Julia, I'm so glad the Rudigers are safe. If we hadn't done what we did—if you hadn't pricked my conscience about it—I hate to think . . . And someone burned their house anyway." She watched a muscle work in his jaw.

When Paul spoke again, his words were tentative. "Darling, I've been thinking. We know James is slow, but he learns."

"He does. He might be a little behind, but—"

"When Tad—when James found us here, he didn't speak for at least six months. When he started to talk, it was in short sentences, sort of the way *I* learned English. He's more and more fluent each year. I think his first language was Polish, and he was learning from us."

Julia put her hands to her mouth. "Thaddeus Pulaski, maybe?"

"Maybe James Otto now. It's a safe name."

Both his arms were around her then. They clung together, Julia unable to stop shivering, and Paul taking deep breaths until he seemed to calm down. He still didn't release her, and she was grateful for that.

He spoke into her hair. "I doubt we'll ever know more. Mama never told us much about the time she wandered. Maybe God mercifully lets us forget."

He kissed the top of her head and then her lips next, just a gentle kiss, as if he doubted the wisdom of his action. She kissed him back just as gently. They sat together until the clock pronounced the hour.

"I shouldn't have done that, Darling, but I needed the comfort," he said finally.

"So did I," she whispered.

She was almost sorry when he released his grip on her and stood up.

"We'll leave early so we can catch the noon train to Cheyenne. Good night, Darling. Thanks for . . ." He paused and looked everywhere but at her. ". . . what you shared so kindly."

She thought about his odd statement long after her light was out.

Thirty-one

*I*t was a quiet ride to Gun Barrel, James sitting in front of Paul on his saddle and Julia riding beside them. She glanced at them, gratified to see Paul resting his chin on James's head and letting James hold the reins, or at least letting him think he held them. *You'd be a good father,* she thought. *Too bad Katherine never knew. You call me kind, but you are kinder than you know—or let on.*

Case in point. He had found her that morning, standing by the window in the kitchen that faced the wagon road and horse corral. Since he went away to the line shack, she had taken to standing there at the window, thinking mostly about Iris and occasionally about how cold and hard life was in a line shack.

There she was, dressed, her hair still in braids, twisting the end of one around her finger and thinking of her dear sister and the enormity of her loss. She noticed her grief was changing from a raw pain to a dull ache, one she could almost ignore as she got used to it. She knew enough about herself and her beliefs to comprehend that Iris was safe from trouble. *I wish my knowledge was more comforting,* Julia thought. *I think it will be. I hope it will be, but right now—*

She didn't even hear him come into the kitchen, but that was nothing new. Maybe Indians, even the mixed-blood kind, were just naturally quieter because trouble through the centuries had conditioned them. She should have been more startled when Paul put his hands on her shoulders, but she wasn't. She wanted to lean back, but she didn't. If she noticed anything that startled her, it was that he wasn't so hesitant, not as he had been earlier, the few times he touched her. After his unburdening on the train ride from Salt Lake, he seemed less fearful of her reactions. She smiled to herself. And after last night, when they kissed, well, maybe things had changed.

"You're thinking about Iris," he said. She could feel his breath on her neck.

She nodded. "I like this quiet moment to do that."

"I hope I'm not interrupting."

"Oh, no. I usually reach a point where my thoughts get tangled, and all I want to do is run home and crawl in my mother's lap."

"You about there?"

She nodded again. "Except this time, I'm thinking about James and Tad and . . . and maybe even Katherine."

His hands tightened on her shoulders. "I've been mulling them around too."

He was silent then, looking out the window with her. The horses across the road were close to the fence rail, their breath coming out in big puffs. And there was Matt, moving among them, patting them and then breaking the ice off the water trough.

"I have to tell you something. Please don't think I'm being flippant." He chuckled. "I'm reading Ether now. You know, it occurred to me last night that nowhere in Ether— or anywhere else in the Book of Mormon or the Bible, either—is it written, 'And it came to stay.' Nowhere." He kissed the top of her head. "It came to pass. This'll pass, Julia. It really will."

Before she could say anything, he reached across her shoulder with his forearm against her breastbone and gave a quick hug, like her brothers used to do to her and Iris. Then he ruffled her hair and opened the door without even looking at her. He was whistling before he reached the corral and Matt.

Surprised, she stood there a moment longer. "It doesn't come to stay," she murmured. "It can't be that simple, Mr. Otto, but maybe it is."

❧

James enjoyed the ride on the Cheyenne & Northern, going from window to window until Paul firmly advised him to choose the window next to him, or he would pin his ears back with a tent peg. That succinct phrase earned Paul a stare from the lady across the aisle, but James only smiled and did as he was bid. Julia wasn't sure where to look as she tried not to smile.

"You know, your face'll stick like that if you try to hold back a smile," Paul whispered to her when James was leaning on his other side and staring out the window at pretty much a Wyoming winter nothing.

"You're a trial unlike any I have ever encountered before, Mr. Otto," she whispered back.

He winced. "Mr. Otto again? My word, that man is persistent."

When they arrived at the Gillespies, even Sister Gillespie—who knew something about little boys—was astonished at the speed with which James vanished into the pack. The brothers and James thundered upstairs and slammed the door behind them. "My stars," she said.

"Should we worry?" Paul asked, eyeing the ceiling overhead dubiously.

"No," Sister Gillespie said. "Heber gave our boys a Meccano set for Christmas. I think they are constructing the

Brooklyn Bridge as we speak. Fresh meat and new ideas are always welcome upstairs." She turned to Julia, taking her face in her hands and touching forehead to forehead. "My dear child. Words fail me, but a hug never does."

Paul was kind enough to leave them there, closing the front door quietly behind him and starting for the city center, beat-up attaché case in hand. When he returned hours later in Brother Gillespie's car, Julia had made a gooey butter cake and was squeezing out potato florettes using the pastry bag she brought with her. The roast was already in the oven.

After dinner and far too much butter cake, Brother Gillespie and Paul spread out legal documents on the dining room table. Paul pointed to a chair and Julia sat. He held up two documents.

"Just sign these and you can access a special ranch fund." He grinned at Brother Gillespie. "Heber says I should have set this up years ago. He doesn't understand that I never wanted to encourage Little River to cook even worse than she already did."

"This covers more than food," the lawyer pointed out, "and includes any kind of house and yard maintenance. I thought it best to keep your name separate from actual ranch business for tax purposes."

"Thank you," Julia said sincerely.

"When Paul's gone on business elsewhere, and you're down here, this is *carte blanche* for expenses." Brother Gillespie looked over his shoulder at his wife. "Emma, you'd about kill for a deal like this."

Sister Gillespie just laughed. "At least I don't have to cook for armies! But you specialize in that, don't you, Julia?"

"I like to think I do," Julia said, "as long as it's not warm liver salad."

So it went all evening, Paul and Brother Gillespie talking and laughing in the dining room, taking time out for more butter cake, and Julia and Emma enjoying each other's company in the parlor. Julia remembered the chocolate covered cherries in the lima bean can she had brought from the Double Tipi, which reduced Brother Gillespie to tongue-tied ecstasy.

"I don't know, Julia," Paul said, dipping into the can too. "Maybe he's not the silver-tongued orator I need as an attorney to rescue me from felonious misdeeds."

Emma nursed her youngest daughter while Julia helped Amanda finish her homework before the weekend. The boys were still constructing the Brooklyn Bridge upstairs, James coming downstairs frequently to look around and make sure she and Paul were still there. Not until she told him gently, "James, we'd never go anywhere without you," did he stay upstairs and play.

Julia felt the gradual pull of the Gillespie orbit, never more welcome than now as she struggled with her sister's death. Emma Gillespie's serene expression as her baby sucked was balm to her soul. Julia felt herself savoring the family around her. She glanced into the dining room to see Paul watching her. He smiled and mouthed something she understood perfectly. "It came to pass."

Maybe it would.

James enjoyed Sunday School almost as much as the train ride, especially when the children separated into their own classroom, located in the Odd Fellows Hall cloakroom, once the coats and wraps were shoved to one side. Packed and ready to leave, Paul joined them for dinner. He spent nearly an hour with her in Brother Gillespie's study at home—also known as the laundry room—talking about James and their suspicions.

"I don't doubt you for a minute," Gillespie said, his face as serious as theirs. "Who will ever know how he made his way to your ranch?" He sighed. "For all that I work with stockmen every day of my career, I do not understand this greed for land and what it does to people who otherwise might be sensible and God-fearing. Present company excepted," he added hastily.

"Don't apologize on my account," Paul assured him. "I've had those moments I could chafe about, if I chose to. I think I owe any success I've had to Mosiah chapter four."

As Brother Gillespie listened, practically open-mouthed, Paul gave him a shortened version of his mother's experience, keeping his eye on the clock. "Darl—uh, Julia can fill you in on the rest," he concluded, rising. "I have a train to catch."

He went upstairs to say good-bye to James and came down smiling. "That's an impressive structure," he told Sister Gillespie as she handed him a packet of sandwiches to hold off starvation between Cheyenne and Denver. "Don't you ever worry that you will wake up some morning, encased in a homemade Meccano banker's vault?"

"Now you're worrying me, Brother Otto," Emma said. She looked over her shoulder into the parlor. "Heber, let's go upstairs and make an official visit!"

They did, leaving Julia in the parlor with the baby sleeping on her shoulder. She rose carefully and walked Paul to the front door. "This is so you don't have to say, 'Walk with me, Darling,' and wake up the baby," she explained, her voice soft. "Any instructions?"

"Do I do that? I suppose I do. I can't think of any advice for you this time. I'm glad you're staying another night here. I'd feel bad if you and James ended up on a slow train north and were stuck in Gun Barrel overnight. Better to be stuck at the Gillespies'." He looked toward the stairs. "Good people."

He shrugged into his overcoat and reached for his Stetson. "It's just the stock show. I'll be back in a couple of weeks." He picked up his valise and patted it. "I should be able to knock off the Book of Mormon—what is it Parley P. Pratt called it? 'That Book of Books'?—and then I'll get back into his *Autobiography*." He touched her nose. "You keep reading."

Julia nodded. She stood by the front window, her hand gentle on the baby's back, her eyes on Paul's retreating figure, until the Gillespies came downstairs again. She smiled at his jaunty, swinging walk, the product of many years in the saddle, and wished him well in Denver.

Paul came back two weeks later, as promised, bringing with him elaborate and expensive booklets extolling the virtues of any number of prize bulls, a present for James from Denver, and one for Julia too.

"I looked all over Denver, and sure enough, found a Meccano set," he explained as James ripped through the wrapping and then clapped his hands in delight. "Now you can build me a footbridge over the river."

"That's too big," James said seriously.

"When it continues not to rain this spring, you'll probably be able to jump over it."

"You look tired, Boss," Doc said. "I'll take care of Chief."

"I'll let you. I *am* tired."

"Too much hoorahing in Denver?" Matt asked, his voice solicitous but his eyes merry.

Paul glanced at Julia and his face reddened.

"That's what I thought," Matt said innocently.

"Matt, you're irritating me," Doc said. "How about we both take care of Chief? Julia? Do you want this basket to go to Blue Corn?"

She nodded, keeping a straight face. The door closed.

"Sorry about that," Paul muttered.

"Mr. Otto . . ."

He groaned.

"Mr. Otto, you can do whatever you want with your free time," she assured him, "as long as you're not contagious."

He made himself comfortable at the table. "I think I'll change the subject," he said, laughing and shaking his head.

"A sandwich? French apple pie?" she asked, amused.

"How about both? I mean it. I missed your cooking." He reached in his overcoat pocket and held out a small package. "Here. Maybe this'll make up for my forgetfulness at Christmas."

"Paul, you're my employer," she reminded him. "I don't need presents."

He took it back, and she slapped his arm. He offered it to her again, his eyes bright. "I missed you so much that I went into a slick emporium with ladies in wide hats and found this in the housewares department."

She opened the box and held out a two-cup glass measuring cup. "This is so fine," she said. "Two cups?"

"Why not? You cook for a herd here. Sit down. Keep me company." He reached into his vest pocket this time. "Just promise not to tell Charlie McLemore or any of the other ranchers that I ever set foot in a housewares department. Here's this too."

He held out a smaller package. "Once I got over the shock of housewares, I wandered into the book section."

She opened the little package and took out a slim, leather-bound edition of Shakespeare's sonnets. "Thank you, Paul," she said, turning the pages with their gilt edges.

"I read a few on the way home. Not bad." He took another bite of the pie in front of him. "Finished the Book of Mormon too." He chewed through another bite. "Brother Gillespie said I should pray about it when I finished."

"Did you?" she asked, impatient for once with his silence.

"Didn't have to," he told her. He shook his head. "Why would I?"

"Oh," was all she could think to say.

"You finish it yet?" he asked after the silence seemed to rise up from the floorboards.

"Almost. I'll . . . I'll more than likely pray about it," she said.

"You should. It's your church. Be nice to know if it's true or not."

He sounded so satirical she almost didn't want to look at him. *I hope I don't sound too disappointed,* she thought. Julia couldn't deny he had every right to make up his own mind about things, even if his mother's family did sacrifice so much for the gospel.

"I'm still reading Parley Pratt's autobiography," he added, as if sensing the disappointment she had hoped she was disguising. He reached in his pocket again and took out a letter. "This is really for James. I'll give it to him when he's less busy." He pointed to the address. "It's a letter to him from Danila Rudiger. She's in school now."

Julia couldn't have been happier to change the subject. "The Rudigers? You stopped and saw the Rudigers?"

"Yeah. That's why I was a bit late in getting home." He held out his empty plate. "Any of the pie left?"

"Tell me first if Ursula has had her baby yet."

"Ye of little patience! She had a baby girl about a week before I knocked on their door. Pretty little thing. Everyone's fine. Karl has more orders than he can fill, and my friend who hired him is looking for another carpenter, since business is so good."

"You did a good thing," Julia said, getting him more pie.

"*We* did a good thing," he reminded her. "Ursula served me real tea with lemon in it."

"Good for her."

"I'll tell you something else too, if you won't let it go to your head."

"Speak on, sir. I'm a hard person to surprise after life on the Double Tipi."

She was wrong, almost as wrong as she had ever been in her life.

Paul took out his handkerchief. "Just to be on the safe side, mind you. Ursula named her after you."

Julia grabbed for the handkerchief.

"Of course, she pronounces it Yulia," he said, his voice soft. "And you should see that afghan your mother crocheted and the nightgowns and diapers she and probably a whole bunch of really determined ladies put together on short notice."

"The Relief Society," Julia said, when she could speak. "Joseph F. Smith—he's our prophet—once said there is no force on earth like a woman who is truly convinced. I think he was speaking of the Relief Society."

"You'd know."

Julia laughed and handed back his handkerchief. He put it back in her hand, wrapping his fingers around hers and running his thumb across her knuckles.

"Best keep it another minute or two." He had trouble speaking. "Ursula wanted to know your mother's name for a middle name, and I thought . . . well, I thought Iris might serve just as well. Welcome to the world, Julia Iris Rudiger."

She couldn't help the tears that dropped on his hand. What made the moment even more exquisite was his other hand on her head like a blessing.

Thirty-two

$\mathcal{A}$fter a lengthy conversation with his ranch hands around the kitchen table in the morning, everyone stuffed with cinnamon rolls, Paul mounted up and returned to the line shack. When he came back a week later, she heard him pacing back and forth in the parlor until late into the morning hours. The next day, he was packed and headed back to Denver. "Business," was all he would tell even Doc. All Julia got was a hand on her shoulder as she stood by the kitchen window again. She waited for him to say, "Walk with me, Darling," but he didn't.

Something had changed. There was no one to talk to about it because she knew she had no business inquiring after her employer, not then and not ever. At times during the long two weeks that took them into early March, she thought Doc was looking at her with sympathy. Perhaps she was overreacting; there was no sense in trolling for explanations when none could be offered. She kept her feelings to herself.

There was nowhere to go but to her knees. For the first few nights, Julia knelt by her bed and did nothing more than rest her head on the coverlet. This was nothing new; she prayed every night. She couldn't think of words this time because she didn't know what she wanted from the Lord except some sign that He cared about her confusion.

One night, kneeling there and saying nothing, she remembered Sister Duncan in her Salt Lake ward, a kind woman who seldom spoke. Sister Duncan's life had been one of particular hardship, filled with sorrows that Julia knew would have provoked tears and maybe anger from anyone less stoic. She never saw this in Sister Duncan. Then came the terrible week when her oldest son was killed in a mining accident on the other side of the state. Sister Duncan, already a widow and relying on that son for some of her support, was just as quiet during the funeral, eyes ahead, trained on her son's coffin.

A week later, Julia had gone with her mother to Relief Society. The meeting was nearly over, and they were bearing testimonies, when Sister Duncan stood up. She grasped the chair in front of her for support. Her face was calm but determined as she kept her eyes trained forward. "Comfort me, Jesus," she said, and sat down.

Kneeling beside her bed now, Julia remembered how embarrassed she had felt for Sister Duncan. Comfort me, Jesus? That sounded like something a backwoods person would say at a Southern camp meeting, where people rolled around and hollered.

Heavenly Father, forgive me for being so stupid, Julia thought, pressing her face against the quilt she had brought from home. "Comfort *me*, Jesus," she whispered. Her eyes filled with tears, and she stayed on her knees until she had the strength to rise.

She sat on her bed then, looking down at the floor. Two Bits scratched on the door, something he always did when Paul was gone. She opened the door, and the kitten came in, twining around her ankles and purring. Julia picked up the little morsel and got in bed, holding Two Bits close to her, touching the velvety spots at the base of his ears and then gently tickling him under his chin.

"Thanks for keeping the kitchen free from frozen snakes," she whispered. "You're a prince."

Two Bits thundered on. Julia blew out the lamp and settled herself for sleep. Two Bits curled himself into the hollow between her neck and shoulder, turning once. Julia lay there, thinking this must be precisely where the kitten slept with Paul Otto. She sniffed the kitten's fur. The scent of bay rum was faint but powerfully evident. She felt the breath go out of her in a sigh more serene than anxious.

She found herself enveloped in a cocoon of comfort that spread until she could sleep without chewing over what she had said or not said, done or not done, that had turned Paul Otto so inward, terse even. *You haven't done anything,* came to her mind. Instead of dismissing the notion, she welcomed it. When she woke, morning had come, after the first solid night's sleep she had enjoyed in the months since Iris's death.

Two Bits was sleeping against her stomach now. Julia reached down to pet him, starting up the motor again and making her smile. "Well, little buddy, maybe snake catcher is the least of your major duties." *I think I learned something,* she thought. *Heavenly Father, I intend to remember it.*

When Julia and James came down to Cheyenne the following Saturday, Paul Otto sat in the parlor, holding the youngest Gillespie and looking dubious. His eyes brightened when he saw her. He held out the baby, which she took gladly. James flashed Paul a monster smile but rushed upstairs, where muffled shouts of greeting seemed to swell out of the woodwork.

"Well, stranger," she said, keeping her voice light, "back from Denver?"

"I am, indeed, and the owner of two Hereford bulls worth more than I am, if you believe McLemore."

"Which I don't," she commented. She sat beside him,

acutely aware that she felt content for the first time since he went away.

Was that it? She felt a rosy glow start on her chest and work its way north, which gave her a sudden urge to hold the baby against her shoulder so Paul couldn't see her face. *Take another breath, Julia,* she told herself. *This happens to people every day.* No, it couldn't. It wasn't possible that anyone else in the entire universe had ever felt like this before.

He was saying something. She peeked around the baby to see his face. He looked the same: same olive complexion, same high cheekbones, same brown eyes, same mustache, same weather wrinkles around his eyes and mouth. She had regarded him for months now, enjoying his company, frustrating him with her early cooking, listening to him confide the deepest pain of his life, sharing his discoveries about James, and serving as his sole audience when he told her about Child Walking, his mother.

I love this man, she thought. Nothing she had ever felt for Ezra Quayle remotely approached the feeling inside her as she listened to him tell her about his plans to improve the stock on his ranch and then worry out loud about the scarcity of winter snow. She even loved the sound of his voice, the inflections of someone who had probably learned English second.

"Darling? Are you listening to me?"

"I-I thought I was."

"I just told you that Ursula sends her love, and Julia is sleeping through the night now."

He peered closer at her, and she felt her face flame. "That appears to be more than what you're doing lately. James keeping you up?"

She shook her head, willing herself calm. "No, but I have been a little restless lately."

Paul stood up when Sister Gillespie came into the room, took her baby back, and kissed Julia's forehead.

"I didn't even hear you, Julia!"

"I grabbed her and put her in charge of Mabel," Paul said. "Better not to send an amateur on a professional's errand. Mabel's asleep now, and I didn't do it."

So it went all weekend, Paul as affable as ever, except there was still that change she couldn't understand. *Did he touch me that much before, as offhand as it was, and now I miss it?* Julia wondered to herself as she dressed for church on Sunday. She couldn't overlook the kiss, but neither of them had commented about it. *For all that he's an experienced man, we're both so green,* she thought. He was engaging and kind but different in a way she couldn't identify. It quickly began to distress her, now that she knew Paul Otto had become the center of her universe. It was as though she had decided one thing, and he another.

❧

So began the strangest spring of her life. The day after she and Paul returned from Cheyenne, Blue Corn left. She had taken him his usual morning bowl of oatmeal, complemented by a cup of the dried apples he liked, and sausage Sister Gillespie had sent home with her. The tack shed was empty.

She brought his breakfast back to the kitchen, where Paul sat with Doc, looking at the registration papers of the two bulls he was so proud of.

"He's gone," she said.

There was no mistaking the worry line between Paul's eyes. "Spring's here. He's never left this early before. Doc, we're in trouble."

And then she might as well have not been in the room at

all as he and Doc turned their attention to drought. She put the food away, glanced at the men, and then quietly opened the kitchen door again, easing outside to walk down the slope to the distant river. She looked at the water a long time, trying to see it through a stockman's eyes—shallow. Even in Salt Lake City, she knew what happened when spring came and the snow melt swelled the rivers and streams. There was no spring rise on the river, no snow in shaded pockets of rolling land, no brisk wind suggesting winter was trying to hold on.

She perched on a branch that stretched near the deeper pool where she knew Paul like to bathe and where she had gone last summer when the men were away and James asleep. All winter, bathing and shivering in a tin bucket in her room, she had looked forward to those summer nights when the little dammed up spot in the river was hers. Now it was already shallow.

She sat there a long time, looking at the water and thinking about Sister Duncan.

The men left the next morning, riding out together. Again Paul had put his hand on her shoulder as she stood at the window. This time he gave her a little shake before going to the corral to saddle Chief.

Her mind settled a moment after breakfast when he nodded to her and said, "Walk with me, Darling."

She followed him into the yard. He put his hand on her shoulder this time as they walked slowly. He took her to the tack shed, opening the door for her.

"Blue Corn left you something. It was on the lamp shelf. I guess you missed it when you brought him his breakfast."

He held out a small decorated strip, with deerskin ties. "Hold out your wrist."

She did as he said, and he tied the bracelet around it, smiling to himself. "It's made of porcupine quills, not beads."

He still held her hand, touching the twined diamond pattern. "He uses roots and leaves for dye."

"Maybe it's for you," she said, not wanting him to ever let go of her hand.

"No, it's for a woman's wrist. A small woman. You."

She swallowed and looked up at him, irritated that her eyes seemed to be filling with tears she had promised herself, after a nearly sleepless night, that she would not shed. "It was kind of him, Mr. Otto," she managed to say.

He didn't joke this time when she called him mister. "Mr. Otto? I thought he might be back," was all he said before he took her gently by the shoulders, pulled her close, seemed to breathe deep of her fragrance, and then left her standing in the tack shed. She stayed there, hands to her ears so she could not hear him ride away.

❧

He was back in two days with his crew, augmented now by three more hands, shy men who seemed pleased to put their feet under her table and eat what one of them told her was the best chow in Wyoming. It was just steak and mashed potatoes and gravy, but she thanked him and called it good.

Even the new hands came to the Double Tipi somber men. All talk at each meal centered around little snow all winter and no rain now. The topic changed briefly when Paul and Doc brought back the two bulls from Denver. Julia had to smile when she watched the men of the Double Tipi gather around the enormous animals in their special enclosure, reminding her for all the world of the neighborhood's reaction when Papa drove up in his Pierce-Arrow. But once the bulls had been turned onto the range—as Paul put it when he thought Julia was out of earshot, "to make the girls happy"—the talk returned to drought.

One bright spot was a little note from her father for Paul, which he had slipped into a letter. She handed the folded note to him on one of the rare nights he was actually home and sitting in the parlor—or sleeping there, more often than not. No one was sleeping well, not with worries and constant flickers of heat lightning that promised nothing but spotty range fires.

"What'd he say?" he asked when she gently touched his shoulder to wake him. She was grateful that he no longer jumped slightly whenever she touched him.

"I don't read your mail, Paul Otto," she said, a little more sharply than she wanted.

He looked at her, surprised, but made no comment. He read the note and nodded. "Says it's been a bit more time-consuming to find my Hixon-Dixon-Hickman relatives than he would have thought. Maybe Mama wasn't the only secretive one." He looked at her and patted the sofa. "Sit down, Julia."

She shook her head, mumbling something about James needing her attention in the kitchen. *I can't sit with you, not when all I am craving these days is your arms around me,* she thought. *Maybe I should spend some time alone in the line shack.*

She knew she had disappointed him because the next morning, when she stood at the window and he passed by, he put his hand on her shoulder, left it there a moment, and whispered, "It's a hard time of year, Darling. That's all."

That wasn't all, but she hadn't the heart to contradict him. Not after last night in the parlor and then a hard moment in her room. After starts and stops and a lifetime of dabbling in a verse here and a thought there, she had finished the Book of Mormon, suffering with Moroni as he grieved the loss of his fair ones and wandered alone like Child Walking in a wilderness that could have turned deadly at any bend in the trail. He had kept his faith. With calmness, he was prepared to remain true to the end.

She heard Paul slap the lintel to his bedroom a little harder than usual as she softly read aloud: "And now I bid unto all, farewell. I soon go to rest in the paradise of God, until my spirit and body shall again reunite, and I am brought forth triumphant through the air, to meet you before the pleasing bar of the Great Jehovah, the Eternal Judge, both quick and dead. Amen."

She knew people, some her own relatives, who saw the dead after they had left the earth, some returning to comfort the bereaved wordlessly, others to pass on messages. She saw nothing unusual that night in her little room, but she felt Iris's presence at rest in the paradise of God, which Moroni understood. Brother Gillespie had taken her aside the last time she came to Cheyenne to tell her nothing more than his belief that the view of earth from the paradise side is a lot more peaceful than the view the other way.

"If Iris could tell you something, Sister Darling, it would be to let it go. She's fine. We won't know that until we are where she is. Until then, we have to trust and hope."

I know in whom I trust, Julia thought for the first time since her lonely trip to Utah before Christmas. *Moroni didn't go through all this for nothing. Neither did Christ.*

The thought sent her to her knees, a familiar place this spring. "Dear Father, when I asked Mr. Otto, he said he didn't need to pray to know if the Church was true. He meant it one way. I mean it another. I already know, don't I, Father? Have I always? Did I just lack confidence?"

She had always known; reading the Book of Mormon only served to firmly bind her to the Church and the gospel. Iris was out of her sight now but by no means out of her life. The temple was no pointless ritual. It led directly to the highest degree of glory. Because it did, she could no more entertain thoughts of a happy life with Paul Otto. Mortality would only be a torment when eternity without him loomed larger.

Not that anything lately pointed in that direction, she knew. He had grown more distant. It was up to her now to let him go. No matter that his mother's people had paid a huge price for the gospel. Brother Gillespie had also reminded her that everyone has his agency to choose. "We can't tamper with that right, Sister Darling," he had told her, his eyes full of sympathy. She had never said anything to him about Paul. She hadn't even thought she had been so obvious. Now that Paul was away so much, maybe she could school herself into serenity. And after September, it wouldn't matter—at least, no more than every day of her life without him.

Thirty-three

*E*asy to think of serenity; harder to live it, especially as premature summer heat turned wicked, and the land baked like a deadly Queen Atlantic. She could tell the late spring roundup must have been more harsh and brutal than any before it. The men returned dirty and grim, sunburned and silent. It was an ominously quiet group of exhausted stockmen who sat around the kitchen table a few nights after their return—powerful men, ranchers used to hard work that always brought wealth. Paul regularly shook his head over coffee; she didn't offer it anymore. When he shook his head over gooey butter cake and just rested his head in his hands as one of the other stockmen spoke of early slaughter to avoid starvation, she felt a chill go through her.

My dearest, I would comfort you if I could, Julia thought when some of the men filed off to nearby ranches while others from farther away bedded down in the parlor. She had no resource but prayer; it had already kept her on her knees until they became toughened by prayer. "Comfort me, Jesus," was no longer an afterthought when all else had failed. It was the constant in her life as she expanded it to include Paul Otto, the men of the Double Tipi, the other stockmen, and the suffering cattle. She seemed to breathe the sentence in and out. *Comfort them; comfort all of us.*

Through May and into midsummer, Paul was gone more than he was there at the Double Tipi—staying in the line shack, making trips to Denver. And when the range began to burn, he and his crew were in the center of danger. Julia could only cook when they were there and pray when they were not.

She came to dread each night, not so much anymore because she chafed that the love of her life was completely out of reach, but because of heat lightning. As tantalizing as a Lorelei luring boaters on the Rhine, the lightning promised rain and brought nothing except fire to parched ground. There was no water to put out the fast-moving range fires. The men roved in packs almost, beating out the flames with burlap sacks and quilts, trying not to get caught in the flames.

When the trouble began, they had brought one badly burned cowboy to the Double Tipi, his blackened skin falling off in sheets as he screamed and then died. Horror on his face, Paul had forced her and James into her room, begging her to cover James's ears. She did and sobbed into the pillow as the little boy shivered. "Comfort him, Jesus," she prayed for the dying cowboy and for James, who must have been reliving his own winter terror when stockmen burned down his family's homestead around them, and he alone escaped.

A month passed. She watched James grow grim around the mouth with every breath of wind that blew now, bearing smoke and ash into his life to remind and torture and leave him bereft, losing his family over and over with each whiff of burning grass. There was nothing in her mind and heart except prayer. If she ever had a doubt, it was gone now, even though the heavens seemed closed. She prayed with all her might, even when her strength was gone.

She was on her knees one night in midsummer when Paul knocked on her door and entered without her permission.

"I'm so sorry," he said and started to back away. "No.

Julia." He came to her bed and knelt beside her, burying his face in her shoulder as he sobbed. He was covered in soot and ash, and he stank, but she held him as tight as she could, splaying her fingers across his back and digging into his shirt until his sobs subsided. "There's nothing to forgive," she murmured. "I do this all day, even when I'm not on my knees."

She made him lie down on her bed and removed his boots, even when he protested and swore. She covered him with a quilt and kissed his filthy forehead and then sat on the floor for the rest of the night, dozing when she could and holding his hand when he cried.

"It was Willy Bill this time," he finally whispered, as the murky sun rose.

"Comfort Paul, Jesus," she whispered, resting her cheek against Paul's hand. "If you ever comforted anyone, comfort him."

He slept a few minutes more and then sat up, looking around as if he couldn't remember where he was. He looked at her, perfectly in control again. *Thank you,* Julia prayed.

He still held her hand. He turned it over and kissed it. "I really needed this," he told her.

"I know."

"I said some unkind things."

"Doesn't matter." She rested her cheek against his hand again. "Paul, I hate to trouble you with anything, but I have to get James out of here. He's barely hanging on with all this smoke and what must be dreams as bad as the nightmare you're living right now."

He didn't hesitate. "Take him to the Gillespies. You stay too."

"No. I'll leave him and come back."

He sighed his irritation, probably afraid of what he

would say if he spoke. She understood him completely.

"You and other crews are coming through here day and night almost. I won't have you eating out of cans, not while I can do the one thing to fight this fire that you can't." Her voice was firm, and she was struck by how much like her mother she sounded. "I'll get him down there, and I'll come back. Nothing you can do or say will stop me."

"The contract is up in two weeks."

"Forget the contract," she told him calmly.

She made James share a horse with her in the morning, when the wind was low and the ash not flying. He was too frightened to ride alone, and they couldn't spare any horses anyway. The terrain they covered was deceptively free of fire. Gun Barrel looked almost normal, except at the depot. There were two supply trucks with US Forest Service stenciled on the canvas. She had crammed James's clothes and writing tablets into her valise, along with his books. James slung his Meccano set in a canvas bag over his shoulder. He had no other treasures.

In Gun Barrel, she had the presence of mind to send a telegram to the Gillespies. His face grim, Brother Gillespie met them at the depot, gathering James in his arms and carrying him to the car when the little boy started to sob with relief.

Julia stayed overnight at the Gillespies, sleeping with James and holding him close. "You may have to do this for a while," she told Emma. Julia took a bath and washed her hair, sitting in the tub, wondering how the men of the Double Tipi were doing, until the water turned cold. She hated to put on her riding skirt again, grimy with soot, but she had nothing else.

Before Brother Gillespie took her to the depot, she asked him for a blessing. She knelt for it in the parlor, savoring the pressure of his hands on her head as he pleaded with the Lord to keep her and the men on the range safe from death. She hadn't realized how parched her soul was for a priesthood blessing until then. As the blessing calmed her heart and gave her purpose, she thought back to last fall, when her father had blessed her in their kitchen, asking the Lord to keep her safe from storm and fire, almost as if he knew.

She never felt so alone as on the train back to Gun Barrel, wearing her smoky clothes and knowing her hair was all over her head, instead of neatly wound into braided coronets or tucked in a tidy bun. *Mama, if you could see me now,* she told her reflection in the window of the railroad day car. She held her breath against a sudden urge to turn around and run back to the depot and take the next train home, where there was no smoke and no fire, and where a strong man didn't cry in her arms and a wounded boy wasn't tormented by the agent of his wounding. She thought how it could have been for Iris, growing up and marrying and taking on responsibilities on her husband's dairy farm. Iris was six years younger. "Grow up, Darling," Julia murmured. "Iris would expect it."

The air was smokier in Gun Barrel when she saddled up and rode her horse out of the livery stable. The liveryman tried to detain her, but she ignored him, digging her heels into her horse's flanks and riding toward the smoke. She turned back just outside of town to ride to the post office. A letter from her mother lay in the box, plus another letter, much thicker, for Paul.

She sucked in her breath as she idly scanned the return label: Albert Hickman, Koosharem, Utah. Hickman. "Papa, you found him!" she said, which made the postal clerk look at her and wink. She tucked the letter down her shirtwaist and opened her mother's letter, reading it as she rode out of town.

She tried to concentrate on Mama's welcome words, but her tired mind couldn't absorb a high priests social up the canyon and a baby shower for that "nice Sister Glenn in the next block." She balled up the letter and threw it to the wind. Ash blew across the high plains, and she rode steadily through it, even though her horse whinnied and tried to hang back.

She arrived at the Double Tipi in record time, giving her horse a quick curry before graining him and turning him into the pasture. Except for Two Bits, the house was empty. She picked up the young cat. "I should have taken you with me to Cheyenne," she said, breathing into his fur for the faintest odor of bay rum. All she smelled was smoke.

Within the hour, she had thrown together a stew, deckling the top of it with dumplings to make it more filling—hang the aesthetics—and a handful of this and that. "I've abandoned my standards," she told the Queen Atlantic. "Miss Farmer would frown on this stew."

It tasted wonderful. She sat by herself and ate a bowlful of the stew, meaty with venison one of the cowboys had brought to her, courtesy of a deer that could not outrun the blaze.

She popped a pan of rolls in the oven when she heard horsemen in the yard. She ran to the window, wiping her sweaty face with her ash-gray apron. Half of the men she didn't recognize or maybe they were just too soot-stained for her to make out. But there was Paul, just sitting on Chief because he looked too tired to dismount. Her heart went out to him.

They tended to their mounts first, as she knew they would. Crossing her fingers that they would not just mount up again after supper, she breathed easier when they turned their horses loose, still saddled, into the pasture to graze.

The rolls were done and nicely browned, with butter glazing their tops, by the time the men sat down at the table. Paul smiled his thanks, and everyone dug in, eating silently as though they hadn't had a meal in days. Perhaps they hadn't. They ate like starved wolves. Her heart turned over with love and admiration for all of them, thinking back to her first official dinner at the Double Tipi. How long ago that seemed now and how foolish.

She watched them eat, something Paul had laughingly accused her of doing years ago, it seemed, back when there were things to laugh about. He was right; she did do that. She watched them now, some of them Negro, some of them with at least as much Indian in them as Paul, some who couldn't read and write, and others toothless from bar fights, bad food, and poverty. She felt a pang, thinking how much she would miss them when she left.

After dinner, some of the men went to the bunkhouse. The rest just rolled up in their bedrolls in the kitchen and parlor and were soon silent in exhausted slumber. James's room was empty, so she invited them in there too. Two men were already sleeping in Paul's bed.

"Do you mind?" he said, indicating her bed.

"You know I don't. Need help with your boots?"

"Not this time." He looked at her, his expression contrite. He winced as he lay down. "I'm sorry to evict you, but I have to. I turned thirty-six yesterday, and I'm feeling every single minute of it."

"Happy birthday," she teased, wishing it sounded funny. She pulled a chair up to the bed and propped her stockinged feet on the mattress.

She remembered the letter from Albert Hickman that

she had stuck down the front of her bodice. As he watched, a little mystified, she pulled it out and handed it to him. With a grin, showing white teeth on a black face, he held the letter to his cheek. "Still warm."

"Mr. Otto!"

"I may be tired, but I'm not dead."

He looked at the return address for a long minute and set the letter on his chest. "I guess my middle name should be Hickman." He handed the letter back to her and closed his eyes. "I'm too tired to read it. Just leave it on my bed after we clear out tomorrow, and I'll get to it eventually."

"Am I heartless?" he asked a few minutes later. "I finally get some relatives, and two or three words strung together in a simple sentence just aren't registering in my head."

Julia shook her head and told him she had tried to read a letter from her mother. "It was as though everything she wrote came from another world."

No answer; Paul had fallen asleep. It touched her heart to see his fingers folded around his thumbs like a baby.

Julia woke up with the sun, the smell of smoke stronger. Wide awake, she left her bedroom quickly and tiptoed into the kitchen.

It wasn't her imagination. The smoke was thicker; she could barely see across the ranch road to the horse pasture. She turned around to go for Paul, but he was standing behind her, his hand raised to settle on her shoulder.

"It's worse, isn't it?" she asked.

No answer. Paul was already shaking the men awake in the kitchen and then heading down the hall, calling out to the other sleepers. While they whistled for their mounts, Julia made a pot of oatmeal, wished for something besides canned milk, and took out the sack of doughnuts Emma Gillespie had insisted she take along. Back inside, they practically inhaled their food, eating like men who had no idea when their next meal was coming. Most of them were on their feet and eyeing the smoke through the open door.

Paul came back for the rest of the doughnuts. "The wind is shifting. We're going to the high pasture to cut the fences and let the cattle run."

"Oh, Paul!"

"This happened once before when I was fourteen, I think. Pa was still alive. I swear we spent half the winter in Nebraska, rounding them up. But you do what you do. That's life on the range, Julia Darling. Think how much you're going to miss me."

He smiled when he said it, as though trying to calm the fear she was trying so hard to conceal so she wouldn't become one more thing he had to worry about.

If he hadn't said that, she wouldn't have reached for him. He wouldn't have opened his arms, and she wouldn't have practically leaped into them, so terrified she was. His arms were tight around her and low on her back, bending her toward him until Mama would never have approved. She didn't care. She didn't want him to ever let her go.

"Hey, now. It always seems worse than it is," he said, his hand on her hair, smoothing it down. "Smoke gets trapped in these little valleys and that is what's so scary right now. Give it an hour or two, and it will lift."

"Boss! We gotta ride!" It was Doc calling to him.

With strength from some source she must have tucked away and forgotten about, Julia freed herself from his arms. "Go do what you do," she echoed. "I'll keep a stew going because this place is busier than a train depot."

She turned toward the Queen Atlantic, forcing her

mind to a meal because she knew it would occupy her just enough to blank out most of what was happening. Paul took her hand and pulled her back. He kissed her, and it wasn't that soft kiss in the parlor of months ago. Her mind was chaotic, but he seemed to be trying to pull all the courage he could from her. She gave him all she had.

"Don't you do that to just any old stockman who wanders by," he said.

"I'll try not to," she teased, her nerves humming.

He should have left then, but he didn't. After waving to Doc and telling him that he'd catch up, he took Julia's hand again.

"Miss Darling, surely it has come to your attention that I am more than interested in you."

"What?"

She thought he was teasing, but his eyes were deadly serious. "So interested that I need to tell you I love you. Always have, always will. I'm of the opinion that you're not indifferent to me. Considering all this, and the general shortness of life—I am, after all, thirty-six now—will you marry me?"

"You're serious?" she asked.

"Never more so. I've been cleaner, and I've certainly smelled better, but I am in complete earnest."

So it came down to this. There wasn't time to let him down gently, especially when she didn't want to let him down at all, but the men were riding out of the valley and the smoke was thick.

She chose her words carefully. She only wanted this discussion once because to revisit it would cause more pain than she knew she could bear.

"Paul, I'm not even sure when it happened, but I fell in love with you too."

She thought he might smile, but his eyes were just as serious, as though she was giving him bad news.

"I love you more than words can tell, but the answer is no." She said it quietly, but the words seemed to crash into her brain like cymbals.

"Really?" he asked, his question quiet, but almost pulsing underneath the word, it sounded like relief.

How could that be? She didn't understand. "I would never tease you. I might have said yes earlier, but not now. I've been hoping you would take a greater interest in the Church, but lately, you seem to have gone the other way."

"I go to church with you," he countered.

"And I love that. But that's as far as your interest seems to stretch. Can you take me to the temple next week and marry me there?"

She tried to gauge his expression but it was beyond her.

"No, I can't," he told her slowly. "Not next week and not next month."

"We could marry, and I would hope you might decide to give my church—your mother's church!—another chance some day. It happens. Or it might not."

"Then why not take the chance? You love me."

"Probably more than you'll know, but everything changed when Iris died." She didn't care that her voice was rising. The other men were at the far end of the valley now and James was far away. "If it comes to choosing you or the Church and my family in eternity, then I can't marry you now or ever. The risk is too great. I can't gamble like that. I'd be gambling with my soul, and I won't."

React, react! she wanted to scream at him. He just stood there, his face a blank. She turned away. He never should have asked her now, not when his mind was as torn as hers was—even more, because his cattle and ranch were at stake and he had no business asking her to marry him at such a time. "Why are you doing this?" she whispered, turning back.

"I wanted to know where I stood, before the day started. It's going to be a long day, Darling."

He startled her by blowing her a kiss. "What a woman you are," he said, admiration in his voice now and not the despair she had anticipated and dreaded. She knew it should be impossible, but he almost seemed pleased about something.

I must be losing what little mind I have left, Julia thought, amazed, as he turned and walked away. Then he was in the saddle, his posture as impeccable as always. To her amazement, he started singing "Sweet Evalina" before he was out of earshot.

Her fingers to her lips, Julia watched him ride toward the smoke. If that was the last kiss she would ever enjoy from the man she loved, she would have little trouble in cementing it firmly in her mind. She had trusted the Lord enough to do the hard thing. With a clarity she had never experienced before, Julia knew the Lord was perfectly mindful of her. The knowledge put the heart back into her body. She turned to the stove and calmly reached for her cookbook.

Thirty-four

No one came for the noon meal, which frightened her more than the pervasive and growing odor of burning range grass. Paul had been right; when the sun came out, a slight breeze came with it and dispersed the smoky fog. But that was hours ago. The wind had dropped, and then stopped altogether, which gave her a cautious feeling of optimism. The sun burned hot and high overhead. Even leaving the kitchen door open gave no relief, not when it competed with the Queen Atlantic. It was as if the whole earth was waiting, wary.

She ate a bowl of stew, chafing because it was one of the best she had ever produced in the kitchen of the Double Tipi, and no one was there to appreciate it except Two Bits. She tipped a little into his dish, and she could hear him purr his way through it, even from across the room.

Beyond that small sound, ordinarily so reassuring, was the larger silence. She watched the ridge as noon came and went, her nerves on alert when the wind picked up and changed directions. Automatically, her eyes went to the horse corral. She had noticed in the past week, that when the wind changed, the horses seemed to sense trouble, whinnying and moving in tight circles.

"You're an idiot," she scolded herself. She had forgotten that the men had taken all the horses, even her own. She couldn't leave if she had to. The wind changed again, and she let out a shuddering breath.

For the next hour, she looked to the ridge over which the men had ridden early that morning. She could have fallen to her knees in gratitude when a lone horseman came riding in. She didn't think it was Chief at first because he was lathered and heaving, and Paul never overworked his mounts.

Chief it was, though, and Paul on his back. Julia hurried into the yard, and then to the wagon road as he jerked his horse to a halt and practically threw himself from the saddle.

"Darling, help me get the rest of the shovels and rakes from the horse barn."

Without a word, she ran with him into the barn, yanking the rakes from their stalls, splattering manure on them both. Most of the shovels were already in use on the fire line, but she grabbed the last two and ran with them to the wagon road, where Paul had dropped the rakes.

"May I get you anything to eat?" she asked.

He shook his head. "No time."

"It's close, isn't it?" It was the question she had been spooling through her mind all morning, the one she hated to ask.

He nodded, his eyes on hers, as if daring her to show fright. She clenched her teeth until her jaw hurt, not about to disappoint him.

"What should I do?" she asked quietly.

"Watch the ridge," he said. "Sit in the yard and watch the ridge. If you feel the wind change, watch the ridge."

If she clamped her jaw tight enough, she could control her face. There was nothing she could do about the way she started to tremble. Paul grasped her firmly by both shoulders, moving so close to her that his face was almost too close to see. He gave her a little shake.

"Listen to me. If you see billows of smoke and start

hearing something that sounds like a train, shoot the pistol that's in my bedroom. If we're close, we'll hear you."

Julia nodded.

"Then run to the river."

She couldn't help the gasp that escaped her. He leaned his forehead against hers, still speaking.

"Don't stop, don't go back for anything. Don't even look back. Run to the river."

"It's so shallow," she managed to say.

"It's all you'll have left, so you have to make it work. Mind you, all this is if the wind changes. It probably won't." He held her off again so he could see her better. "If it does, get in the pool where I bathe. The last time I was in there, I noticed more of an overhang on one side. The water's starting to undercut there. Burrow into the cutbank, if you can. I couldn't do it, but you're small."

She nodded, her breath coming faster until she felt lightheaded. He grabbed her jaw. "Slowly! That's better."

"What will happen?" *I have to know,* she thought.

"The fire will jump the river. It'll crown in the cottonwoods and jump the river. Don't even think you can outrun it. Stay in the river and get as much of yourself under the water as possible. You'll have trouble breathing because the fire sucks out all the air. Don't run when you see the flames coming at you, even when every instinct you have will tell you to run."

"I run to the river," she said as calmly as she could. He didn't need to know how her insides churned, how clammy her hands felt. He had enough to worry about.

"I love you, Darling," he was telling her when the roaring in her head quieted. "I wish we had talked sooner, but never mind."

"We'll just talk later." The same serenity that had filled

her last night as she watched him sleep filled her again. "Get on Chief, and I'll hand you the rakes and shovels."

He kissed her, said something to her in Shoshone, and mounted Chief. Lips tight together again, she handed him the tools and stepped back. Without another word or even a wave, he touched a spur to Chief and rode out of the valley.

Julia stood there until he was gone and then went into the house. She walked through all the interconnecting rooms of the small place, starting with Paul's bedroom. She opened the box that held his Bible and that terrible photograph. It was gone, which relieved her heart. There was a small deerskin bag she hadn't noticed before when she had taken that one look. She knew it was a medicine bag, maybe a treasure of Paul's father. She slipped it over her neck and tucked it down the front of her dress.

She stopped in James's little room, her hand gentle on his pillow, grateful beyond even prayer that he was safe with the Gillespies. She mourned over the parlor briefly, with its wonderful gray building paper, and her grandmother's lace curtains that Mama had given her before she left Salt Lake after Iris's death. There was her knitting by the rocking chair. She was making a sweater for Ursula's little Julia. Yarn was a dime a skein.

In her room, she held her Book of Mormon for a long while, toying with the idea of taking it into the yard and carrying it with her. She set it down. Papa had an extra book at home. If she started carrying things, she might never make the river. As an afterthought, she picked up the baby quilt that Mama had made for Iris when she was born. Julia was six at the time and had put in some of the stitches on the gold and purple irises. The quilt had been another of Mama's sad gifts to her at Christmas. She looked long and hard at Paul's gift of Shakespeare's sonnets and left it on the bedside table. Bookstores were full of copies of Shakespeare's sonnets.

In the kitchen, Julia banked the fire in the Queen Atlantic. She pumped herself a long drink of water at the sink and looked at her neat row of measuring cups and spoons and her well-used copy of the *Boston Cooking-School Cookbook*. "Miss Farmer, I came to cook, and I fell in love," she said. "Fancy that." She turned on her heel to leave but then remembered Paul's gun. She took it from the shelf over his bureau and ran out of the house before her resolve deserted her, closing the door behind her. As she did, she remembered her grandmama's story of leaving Nauvoo after sweeping the stoop and locking the door.

She sat on the folding chair in the yard, the quilt on her lap underneath the pistol. Another hour passed. She looked down at her little watch, a Christmas present from Papa, pinned to her apron bib. When she looked up, the wind changed.

She said her three-word prayer, thinking that she wanted to tell Sister Duncan someday how durable and all-purpose it was. She swallowed as smoke began to tower over the ridge, and she heard a noise unlike any other. Paul had said the fire would sound like a train, and he was right, except it was worse. The noise was all the hounds of the underworld, baying to be slipped loose.

Julia rose slowly to her feet. With calm hands, she checked the pistol's chamber, raised the gun overhead, and squeezed off two shots. She dropped the pistol, grabbed the iris quilt, and ran to the river.

The tiny ribbon of water looked so far away. She was halfway there when she stopped and turned around. The sight of the monster billows made her shriek. No wonder Paul had told her not to look back. She suddenly remembered the letter from Alfred Hickman that Paul had been too tired to read. She thought of Two Bits, somewhere in the kitchen. Maybe she had closed the door on him. She took a step toward the ranch house. It was still only smoke, even though it towered above the ridge now. She could be there in a moment.

Run to the river. Paul had said it so many times. Maybe it would be the last words she ever heard of his lovely voice. She turned and ran to the river, not stopping until, out of breath, she was waist deep in the little bathing pool.

It had never looked so small and more shallow than it did right then as the smoke finally dimmed the sun and left her in eerie shadow. She started to wade across to the opposite bank, as far as she could get away from the fire without being on dry ground on the other side. She stopped, remembering the bank's undercut on the fire side.

When she turned around, the ranch house exploded in flames. She screamed and screamed until she was gasping for air. In mere seconds since her last look, the flames, now highly visible, had consumed Paul's house and were racing toward her. She faced the flames, dragging Iris's quilt through the water and scrambling to the cutbank, a pitiful scrap of protection. She threw herself against it, digging with her fingers until she felt her nails break. Inching her way tighter and tighter into the sandy soil peppered with gravel that scraped against her bleeding fingers, she dug in relentlessly.

She made herself as small as she could, draping Iris's sodden baby quilt over her face and still exposed shoulder. The sky grew lighter and lighter as the flames raced closer. She dug her bare feet—where she had lost her shoes she had no idea—into the muddy, gravelly river bottom because she wanted so badly to run and run. She slammed her eyes shut against the brightness of the fire, the noise so close now that her ears began to ache.

She heard a crackle overhead and knew the flames were crowning in the treetops as Paul said they would. She screamed again when one of the larger branches crashed into the water, the flaming wood striking her exposed shoulder and hip. She gasped from the intense pain in her shoulder and ducked under the water, since her hair began to burn. She stayed under as long as she could. When she came up to breathe, she found she couldn't. All the air was gone.

Desperate, Julia turned her face into the muddy bank and found a tiny air hole. *I know in whom I trust. I truly do,* she thought as she struggled to breathe. Her fingers felt singed, but she grasped Iris's soaking wet quilt closer as the fire shouted its challenge at her, daring her to live.

There was nothing else she could do. She had said her last prayers. Her life was in God's hands, as it had always been. She understood that now with a clarity that sliced through her fear. Iris had never been closer, and the knowledge brought no terror. She didn't feel peaceful, but the fear was gone.

Since the fire wouldn't begrudge her more than a shallow breath, she took it. She pulled Iris's quilt over her head as the fire hunted for her, but then it gave up with an angry roar and leaped the river.

After a long, long moment, she found she could breathe again, even though every breath brought ash into her lungs. Her ears still aching, she listened as the train roared on, leaving behind only the crackle of weeds firing up and fading quickly. She began to hear the river again, just a murmur of shallow water over pebbles, the river that had saved her life. She dabbled her fingers in the water. "Thank you," she whispered.

With an effort that made her moan, Julia looked at her

shoulder, hoping not to see it black and flaking, like that poor cowboy. She looked closer, taking in the odd shape, and decided it was dislocated. There was nothing she could do about that beyond endure the pain and wait for help, if anyone was alive to render any.

She touched her neck, flinching with the pain of a burn. She fingered it gingerly and patted more mud on it. She knew her hip must be bruised, but she could move. The branch still burned, but when it finally stopped, she pushed against it with Iris's quilt until it gave way enough for her to move farther into the pool and stand up. She feared no one would find her, so she staggered to the shallower wagon crossing, sinking down several times and resting until she was able to crawl from the river and collapse on the dirt. Weeds still smoldered and stank next to the road, but the road remained unchanged. She closed her eyes, said thank you one more time, and lapsed into unconsciousness.

Doc found her when the sun was lower in the sky. He pillowed her head in his lap, his expert fingers moving over her muddy neck.

"You did that one right, sport," he told her, and she could hear the tears in his voice.

"My shoulder," she murmured. Her throat was raw.

"Your shoulder is dislocated, and I'm going to reduce it in just a moment."

"Paul."

"He's right now sitting on the ground by the ridge. Silly boy. He thought he was going to ride down here and see if you were still alive, and we thought otherwise. I don't think Matt has even thrown a better loop. Jerked him right out of the saddle. The boss fired him on the spot and then started to cry."

She tried to speak, but nothing came out.

"We didn't want him to find you burned to death," Doc said bluntly. "I'm supposed to fire two shots if you're alive, but how about I reduce that shoulder before I do? It'll hurt like the blue blazes for just a moment, but we'll spare him the sight of my foot in your armpit. You up for it? Of course you are. You just stared down a firestorm."

He worked so fast she didn't have time to brace herself as he took Iris's quilt and padded it in her armpit. He sat down next to her and put his foot against the quilt. Taking her arm in his hand, he slowly leaned back, pushing against the quilt. She closed her eyes and looked away as the pain mounted into a black void.

She felt hands on her head when she regained consciousness. She was lying on the ground, her hands folded across her stomach and Iris's baby quilt under her head. Her shoulder ached, but the sharp pain was gone. She tried to look around to see where Paul was until she realized those were his hands.

She heard his calm voice as he pressed lightly on her head. "By the power of the Melchizedek Priesthood which I hold, I give this woman a blessing of healing. I have no anointing oil. It's only me and maybe I'm not even doing this right. Father, keep her alive. She's everything to me. In the name of Jesus Christ, amen."

She must have been dreaming. What had just happened couldn't have just happened. She opened her eyes, closed them, and opened them again. She was still lying in the road, only Paul was holding her hands now.

"I don't understand," she said.

"It'll keep," he replied, his voice gentle.

"You have to give Matt back his job."

"I already rehired him. How about we get you to Cheyenne?"

Thirty-five

When Julia regained consciousness, she was wrapped in a quilt, a dry one that didn't stink of smoke. She lay in a wagon, still clutching Iris's quilt. Her head was in Paul's lap.

"We tried to take it out of your hand, but you put up quite a struggle," he told her, bending close to speak in her ear.

"It saved my life," she said, wincing because her throat was so raw. She started to cough. He put a handkerchief to her mouth, swabbing out the ash when she finished.

"Doc's worried about your lungs. Your neck has second degree burns. You're in shock, and that's why we're keeping you wrapped up, even though it's hot. We're at the Gun Barrel depot. Dr. Beck is going to give you a sedative, so we can lift you onto a door and get you on the train."

"The fire? Your cattle? You?" Julia wanted to speak in complete sentences. They sounded clear in her brain but never left her mouth that way.

"The fire? Listen."

She did, realizing first that the wagon was as close to the depot as possible under the station awning. The sound was unfamiliar at first until she realized it was rain dropping on a tin roof.

"Last time we saw the fire, it was headed toward Nebraska. Good luck to them. The cattle are scattered from Nome to Atlanta, but—but," he said, raising a finger and waving it for emphasis, "one of my beautiful Hereford bulls is not suffering any fools gladly in a corral in Wheatland, so I've heard." He shrugged. "The other's probably going to make some Nebraska rancher really happy when he finds him. Until I *refind* him."

"You?"

"Couldn't be better, Julia, because you're alive."

Even in her pain, she could hear the anguish in his voice. "Nearly turned back," she admitted. "That letter from Hickman. On the kitchen table. Two Bits."

"The letter doesn't matter. If I have to, I'll just go door-to-door in Koosharem. Can't be too big a town." He fingered her face, as though he had to touch her. "Two Bits? He worked through about eight of his nine lives this afternoon. We found him in the ice house hugged up against the only bitty sliver of ice remaining. Lost his tail, but we know he's tough. I left him with Alice Marlowe."

"Their house?" she asked, trying to sit up. "Oh, please, is it . . . ?"

He gently pushed her down. "Still standing. The fire veered again. Incidentally, our bunkhouse, barns, and corrals are a bit singed, but upright. The dirt and gravel of the road were just enough to keep the fire on one side." He kissed her forehead.

Someone cleared his throat, and she turned her head slightly to see an elderly man with a hypodermic needle.

"Never much cared for the house," she said, her eyes on the needle.

"Good thing. I'll build you a better one a whole lot closer to the river."

"For me?" She winced as the needle went in. "I thought I told you . . ." She stopped, remembering his hands on her head. "Nothing makes much sense."

"It will. Well, my dear, little Darling, good night, sleep tight."

Her lungs must not have been as bad as Doc had feared. Either that, or Paul had lobbied successfully for her release to the company of friends. When she woke up, moonlight streamed through familiar curtains. She was in Amanda Gillespie's bedroom, the one they shared whenever Julia came to church. An unfamiliar doctor was there, and so was Sister Gillespie. Someone—probably Emma—had removed her singed and ash-stained clothing, cleaned her up, and popped her into a nightgown. Her arm was in a sling, binding her shoulder just enough to keep her from moving it.

Her head felt strangely light, but her mind was clear. Cautiously, she reached up with her good hand to touch her hair as the doctor let himself out of the room.

Sister Gillespie sat on the bed, put a light hand on her face, and kissed her forehead. "You have a few bare spots, my dear, and I trimmed the rest of your hair as carefully as I could, considering that the ends of it were burned. Oh, Julia."

"Where's James?"

"He's asleep. He checked on you several times after the doctor thought you should be sedated again after Gun Barrel. We assured James you'd be awake in the morning, and he was satisfied with that. You were in some pain when we cleaned you up."

Julia took Emma's hand. "If James had been on the Double Tipi, we couldn't have both survived in that cutbank. I'm so grateful he was here. Thank you from the bottom of my heart."

"You'd have done the same for me," Sister Gillespie said simply. She stood up. "And now, if I don't let Paul Otto in here, he's going to come through the door anyway."

Julia held onto Emma's hand. "He gave me a priesthood blessing! What is going on?"

The woman smiled. "He owes you quite an explanation. Just don't be too angry with him."

"How could I be?" Julia murmured. "Let him in."

For the longest moment, Paul just stood in the doorway, taking in the sight of her. He was still dressed in the same clothes, burned in spots with ground-in ash. His face and hands were clean now, and she could see the little burn marks on them. The bald patches in his black hair stood out like dimes. She had never seen someone upright who looked so tired.

Julia held out her hand to him, and he smiled, but he turned to Sister Gillespie. "Emma, I know what I'm going to do isn't proper, but I'm going to lie down with my darling. I've never been so tired, but I won't leave her. I just can't. Please understand."

Emma touched his arm. "No one will ever hear a word about this from me or Heber." She closed the door quietly.

He came to her bed, sat down, and took off his boots with a great sigh. "I still stink, and I'm still dirty," he said, holding a boot in his hand. He dropped it as though it weighed a ton and then took off his belt. He started to lie down, but she managed to pull back the coverlet so he could lie next to her. She couldn't overlook the relief in his eyes.

He raised up on one elbow. "Can I put my arms around you without paining you?"

"Try, please."

He did, pulling her gently toward him until her back rested against his chest.

"My neck really hurts," she said.

He kissed her ear. "No wonder. That's where the burning

branch grazed you. You're going to have some criss-cross scars there." He kissed her ear again. "Just enough pattern to make you interesting."

"My neck." She felt for the deerskin cord of the medicine bag she had snatched from Paul's room. "I tried to save what I think was your father's medicine pouch," she told him. "It's not . . ."

"I'm wearing it now," he whispered in her ear. "Thanks for saving it."

She sighed with relief. "I didn't think to save those scraps of scriptures from your mother's shoes that were in the same box. I'm afraid they wouldn't have survived the river."

"Doesn't matter, as long as you survived," he told her, his arms gentle but firm around her. "Besides, I have those scriptures every time I read the Book of Mormon."

She closed her eyes with the sheer joy of hearing him say that and then smiled to herself. "You have some major explaining to do, Mr. Otto."

She waited for him to start his explanation, knowing "Mr. Otto" would get a rise out of him. Not this time; he was already asleep. She closed her eyes too, comfortable in his arms.

Julia woke before he did, content to rest in his arms until he woke up too. "All right, Paul. When did you join the Church?"

The room was midnight dark. She felt his chuckle. "The second time I went to Denver. President Herrick of the Western States Mission is a mighty persuasive man."

She took in his words, thinking back to the first time, when he came back from the Denver stock show, so restless and remote. "Maybe I should ask what happened the first time you went to Denver. You were not a happy man." She stirred in his arms, trying to see his face. He obliged by releasing her and easing her onto her back, propping himself up on one elbow.

"Happy? No, I wasn't."

"You told me you had finished reading the Book of Mormon," she said, reflecting on the conversation. "I asked you if you'd prayed to know if it was true. You said you didn't need to and clammed up."

He traced her nose and lips with his finger, as though he still couldn't believe she was there and alive. "That was no lie. I didn't need to pray about it. I knew the Church was true after I found the rest of that scripture in Mosiah on the way back from Chicago."

He laughed when she thumped his chest. "Paul! Then why . . . I'm so in the dark."

He lay down again, taking her hand in his and resting it on his chest. "You're right. It goes back to that first trip to Denver. Knowing the Church is true and doing something about it aren't the same. I don't exactly shine in this narrative, darling. Are you certain you want to hear it?"

"Positive, since you think you're going to build *me* a house on the Double Tipi. I'd like to know what inspired this burst of confidence, especially since I turned you down flat."

"Flatter than a French-made bed," he agreed. "All right, Julia. This is it. I go to Denver every year to the stock show. I check into a favorite hotel, one next door to the Cattlemen's Saloon. I go to the bar and ask the keep for his best bottle of single malt Scotch whisky. I buy the whole bottle, and he puts my name on it. Are you impressed yet?"

"Go on. I love you anyway," she grumbled.

"Well, there I am, darling," he continued, with only the hint of a quaver in his voice. "I sit in the bar with any number of well-dressed, equally successful stockmen. We drink and describe our year's progress. I know all the big ranchers in eastern Wyoming and on the Colorado and Nebraska plains. We're all drinking out of our own bottles. Typically I stop at the one-third-down spot and take it back to the keep. He puts it on the shelf until I come back, usually the next evening."

"This is what you did in January?"

"Absolutely. I might add here that before I left Cheyenne—you'll remember Brother Gillespie drove me to the depot—Heber gave me the name, address, and telephone number of President John Herrick, head of the Western States Mission. I thanked him nicely and tucked it in my pocket."

"And promptly forgot it?"

"Not quite. Julia, I *really* don't look good in this next phase of my Denver odyssey."

"Keep talking, you smooth-tongued cowboy," she said.

"If I must."

"You'd better."

"I typically stop drinking when I have a nice buzz but am still interested in the next adventure in Denver." He sighed. "I hate this."

"You'll hate it more if you don't spill the beans."

He tucked her back close to his side again. "You're a tough woman! Well, the Cattlemen's is only a block or two this side of Denver's—uh—tenderloin district. I generally visit Mattie Daw's house, and that's where I went, feeling mellow and tuned up."

He was silent a long while then. Julia knew he hadn't returned to sleep. His arms were around her again. With her good hand, she took his hand and raised it to his lips, kissing it.

There was no overlooking the tears in his voice. "I went

in there with the plan of picking out the prettiest girl and sporting with her. It's what I do in Denver. Julia, with God as my witness, I looked around that room full of lovely faces and just could not."

She tightened her grip on his hand as he struggled to compose himself.

"There I was, half drunk and in a house of considerable ill repute, with temptation less than a hand's span away, and all I wanted to do was be with you. I left."

Julia turned to look in his face, bathed in moonlight now. "What do you mean, you don't shine in this part of the narrative?" she asked him, her voice soft. "I beg to differ."

"That's a relief," he said. "Actually, President Herrick said the same thing, eventually, when I knocked on his door about midnight and insisted on talking to him. I told him all about The Cattlemen's, and Mattie Daw, and then about my mother, and my former wife, and Mosiah and you and Brother Gillespie. He just sat there in his nightshirt and robe and took in the whole jumble without a flinch. I don't think I even surprised him." He sighed. "And here I thought I was such a sinner."

"We're all sinners," Julia said. "Beggars too, my love."

"Say that again."

"What? Sinners?"

It was his turn to give her a gentle thump. "I still went to the stock show, but I spent my evenings in the mission home, getting to know some really nice missionaries." He turned contemplative. "You know, there's a bottle of single malt whisky about two-thirds full at the Cattlemen's. I should write the bartender and tell him to drink it."

She laughed and let him sleep then because he couldn't keep his eyes open. He pillowed his head this time on her good shoulder. She slept too, and when they woke, dawn was close.

"Why did you come home so unhappy?"

He put a hand over his eyes, a familiar gesture she recognized in him when he didn't want to think about something. Gently, she took his hand away.

"Julia, the last week of the stock show, President Herrick and his missionaries talked to me about Joseph Smith, and the Book of Mormon, and the Atonement. I've always believed in Jesus Christ, in case you're wondering. My father and many of the tribes in North Carolina were good Presbyterians." He thought a moment. "How to say this? When President Herrick asked if I wanted to be baptized, I turned him down, with almost the same speed you turned me down when I proposed. He asked me why, and I said I just was too big of a sinner, especially when it came to Katherine."

"Do you still love her?" She had to know.

"I never did, Julia. I know that now. But shouldn't I have figured out she was so unstable? Couldn't I have done better?"

"Paul, you were so young and trusted her parents to deal fairly with you." It was light enough now for Julia to see his wry expression.

"That's what President Herrick told me too. I assured him God couldn't possibly want me in the Church." Paul got up, finding relief in movement as he paced the floor. "You should have heard him then. Have you ever seen President Herrick?"

Julia shook her head.

"He is so elegant-looking, a really cultured gentleman. In spite of that, he gave me such a . . . a . . . *withering* look. I'll never forget what he said: 'Paul Otto, what makes you so arrogant to think that Christ's Atonement is for everyone else in the history of the world except you? You have a lot of nerve!' Oh, he thundered it out. Sister Herrick came running in from another room. I think the neighbors heard him."

Paul stopped walking and lay down again, gathering Julia close. "I stormed out of there and slammed the door so hard the glass broke. Julia, I've never been so angry. I was halfway to the railroad depot before one of the missionaries came pounding up behind me."

She saw the disbelief in his eyes, as fresh as if the incident had happened yesterday. "I think he was fresh into the mission field, a scrawny little guy from Wellington, Utah. I could have taken him with one hand, except all he did was hand me a pamphlet and back away really fast." He looked at her. "Julia, am I that intimidating?"

"Sometimes."

"Then why did you stay at the Double Tipi? And don't mention that blamed contract! Why did you *stay*?"

It was a good question. There was no hurry in her answer because she had to think through a year of life on the Double Tipi. "I think it was because you defended me when I gave that tar paper to the Rudigers and fed them. I knew then that you were a kind man, no matter what others thought." She kissed his hand again. "And after you told me about your mother, how could I leave?"

"Thank you," he said simply. The rest of his story came out easier. Julia listened as he told her about nearly using the Joseph Smith pamphlet for tinder in the camp stove at the line shack but then yanking it out at the last moment and reading it. "I stopped on that sentence: 'So it was with me. I had actually seen a light, and in the midst of that light I saw two personages.' You know how it goes. And then Joseph wrote, 'For I had seen a vision; I knew it, and I knew God knew it, and I could not deny it.' President Herrick told me it was the light of Christ testifying to me because I *knew* those were the words of an honest man. My mother and her family were right."

"I know they're true too," she told him.

He smiled at her. "I thought you did." He started to put his hand over his eyes again but took her hand instead. "Well, you know how fast I went back to Denver that second time. I went right to the mission home, apologized to President Herrick, and asked that scrawny little elder to baptize me. I've been there a time or two since for priesthood advancement."

They were both silent then. Paul spoke first. "Now you want to know why I didn't say anything."

"I do."

"I knew you were having your struggles. I didn't want my baptism to end your own search. I had a suspicion you were at least a little interested in me."

"You're a shrewd observer," she commented. "I think everyone knew that but me."

"On the off chance that you loved me, I didn't want you to borrow my light and stop looking for your own. It's that simple. Was I wrong?"

It was another good question. "Only a little," she said honestly. "By then, I had started understanding that I did have a testimony and always had. I just wasn't sure of myself, not the Lord. I wish you had said something. You were so evasive, and you broke my heart."

He groaned and reached for her.

"But then when you proposed and I told you no, you seemed almost pleased! Paul, why?"

"Because then I knew for certain you were sure enough in your own light to want nothing to do with someone who you thought couldn't take you to the temple. I couldn't have been happier."

Secure in his arms, Julia thought about what he had said. "Goodness, when I asked you if you could take me to the temple next week or in a month and you said no, it *was* true!"

"Certainly. I can't take you there until March, when I'm a member for a year."

"Oh, I could thump you again," Julia said. "*Why* did you stay away all spring? We didn't have a chance to talk! We could have settled this a month ago, or at least, before the range fires started."

"That's simple, too, Julia, if you'll pardon my blushes. It was a whole lot safer at the line shack, where I didn't have to lie in bed and think about you just a few rooms away. A couple of nights, I got as far as the kitchen. Good thing Two Bits and his midnight feedings were such a good excuse for my presence."

"Oh," was all she said.

"Forgive me?" he asked. There was no mistaking the tears in his voice then. "Darling, when I saw what had happened to the ranch house, and looked at how *shallow* that river really is . . . I could not bear to lose you."

"I forgive you," she said softly. "Over and over."

"Was the fire as scary to you as I think it must have been?"

"Words fail me. I just prayed and hung on and knew you'd come for me."

"I barely deserve that much trust," he said when he could speak. "I nearly forgot. I sent a telegram to your father before we left Gun Barrel. He sent a reply, care of Heber Gillespie. He'll be here tomorrow to take you home and . . ."

"I'm not going."

"Yes, you are, little darling Darling. I have no home here for you right now, and I'm tired of cold baths in the line shack! I'll visit you often in Salt Lake and marry you in March. And yes, this is my intimidating face."

She touched his face. "No, it isn't. You're right though. I'll go."

They kissed. "That's all a man can stand, Julia. There's one more thing your father mentioned in the telegram. My dear, he's going to be accompanied by an old gentleman from Koosharem. I'm going to meet my uncle tomorrow."

She held him as close as she could until she heard an alarm clock ring in the Gillespies' bedroom next to hers.

"Now I'm going to give you a chaste peck on the cheek and go back to sleep," Paul told her. "When the sun gets higher, James will be bounding in here to check on you. I probably should be down the hall on my own chaste cot. Or not. James is not too particular."

Paul kissed her cheek, and she settled herself into the hollow of his shoulder. He rested his arm carefully on her stomach, composing himself for sleep. "Need a lullaby?" he asked, his words slurring. "Your selections are limited to 'Sweet Evalina' or 'Redeemer.'"

"Redeemer," she told him.

He didn't make it past "our only delight" on the first line, which, all things considered, delighted her. She hoped the Lord wouldn't mind if Paul Otto was her only earthly delight, at least until children got swirled into the mix. She opened her eyes long enough to consider his face on her pillow, peaceful now in sleep.

She gave herself to slumber. In a few months, his would be the first face she would see in the morning and the last one at night. Nothing would change that ever again.

"We are all beggars," she murmured, careful not to wake Paul. *I came to cook,* she reminded herself, cherishing a little girl in the snow, whose parents had stuffed scraps of scriptures in her shoes to keep her feet from freezing. *Thanks to you, Mary Anne Hickman, I came to stay.*

About the Author

Photo by Marie Bryner-Bowles,
Bryner Photography

*A*newcomer to Cedar Fort, Inc., Carla Kelly is a veteran of the New York and international publishing world. The author of more than thirty novels and novellas for Donald I. Fine Co., Signet, and Harlequin, Carla is the recipient of two Rita Awards (think Oscars for romance writing) from Romance Writers of America and two Spur Awards (think Oscars for western fiction) from Western Writers of America.

Recently, she's been writing Regency romances (think *Pride and Prejudice*) set in the Royal Navy's Channel Fleet during the Napoleonic Wars between England and France. She comes by her love of the ocean from her childhood as a Navy brat.

Carla's history background makes her no stranger to footnote work, either. During her National Park Service days at the Fort Union Trading Post National Historic Site, Carla edited Friedrich Kurz's fur trade journal. She recently completed a short history of Fort Buford, where Sitting Bull surrendered in 1881.

Following the "dumb luck" principle that has guided their lives, the Kellys recently moved to Wellington, Utah, from North Dakota and couldn't be happier in their new location. In her spare time, Carla volunteers at the Railroad and Mining Museum in Helper, Utah. She likes to visit her five children, who live here and there around the United States. Her favorite place in Utah is Manti, located after a drive on the scenic byway through Huntington Canyon.

And why is she so happy these days? Carla looks forward to writing for an LDS audience now, where she feels most at home.